Night People

Books by Eleanor Fitzgerald:

<u>*Anthologies*</u>

Hymns for the Gallows, Volume One: The Trial

Hymns for the Gallows, Volume Two: The Last Meal

Hymns for the Gallows, Volume Three: The Hanging

Anima, Volume One: The Signal

<u>*Novels*</u>

<u>*The Ministry of Supernatural Affairs*</u>

Night People

<u>*Other Works*</u>

Oxford Junction

The Forest

This is a work of fiction. Names, characters, places, and incidents either are the product of the author's imagination or are used fictitiously. Any resemblance to actual persons, living or dead, events, or locales is entirely coincidental.

Copyright © Eleanor Fitzgerald, 2023

The moral right of Eleanor Fitzgerald to be identified as the author of this work has been asserted in accordance with the Copyright, Designs, and Patents Act of 1988.

All rights reserved. No part of this book may be reproduced in any form on by an electronic or mechanical means, including information storage and retrieval systems, without permission in writing from the publisher, except by a reviewer who may quote brief passages in a review.

Cover Art Copyright © Eleanor Fitzgerald, 2023

First paperback edition July 2023

ISBN: 9798579578136

Published Independently

Contents

Author's Note and Content Warnings.........................ix

Part One: The Creeping Fantods.................................1

Chapter One – The Gathering Dread..........................3
Chapter Two – A Glint in the Lamplight...................15
Chapter Three – The Spectre of Lye Valley...............25
Chapter Four – Breakfast with a Monster.................33
Chapter Five – Too Close For Comfort.....................43
Chapter Six – A Hell of a Memory............................53
Chapter Seven – Parlour Tricks................................61
Chapter Eight – Fear of the Dark..............................71
Chapter Nine – Outside the Law...............................79
Chapter Ten – Doing the Needful..............................89
Chapter Eleven – A Lost Legacy...............................99
Chapter Twelve – In the Hydra's Den......................109
Chapter Thirteen – Behind the Curtain....................117
Chapter Fourteen – Familiarity in the Freakish.......125
Chapter Fifteen – The Hunter, Hunted.....................135

Interlude One – Quiet as the Grave.........................143

Part Two: A Howling in the Veins............................147

Chapter Sixteen – Together at Last..........................149
Chapter Seventeen – Of a Rare Breed.....................157
Chapter Eighteen – Like a Splinter in the Mind......165
Chapter Nineteen – Paradise Risen..........................173
Chapter Twenty – Just My Type..............................183
Chapter Twenty One – A Heaven of Pain................191
Chapter Twenty Two – The Ashram of the Mind....201
Chapter Twenty Three – Intrusive Thoughts...........209

Chapter Twenty Four – Bagged Blood and Shaving Soap..217
Chapter Twenty Five – Home Sweet Home............227
Chapter Twenty Six – Dance Commander...............235
Chapter Twenty Seven – His Master's Voice...........243
Chapter Twenty Eight – Death Valley Nights..........251
Chapter Twenty Nine – The Face of Evil.................259
Chapter Thirty – Mallory Unleashed........................267

Interlude Two – With Friends Like These................273

Part Three: Our Darkling Sun...................................277

Chapter Thirty One – Dust on the Wind...................279
Chapter Thirty Two – Geometric Expansion............287
Chapter Thirty Three – Lust and Other Hungers.....295
Chapter Thirty Four – Company Enough for Grief. 303
Chapter Thirty Five – The Occultation Approaches 311
Chapter Thirty Six – Bad Medicine..........................321
Chapter Thirty Seven – The Prodigal Son................331
Chapter Thirty Eight – Do No Harm........................339
Chapter Thirty Nine – Amid Gloaming Spires........347
Chapter Forty – Beneath the House of Madness.....355
Chapter Forty One – In the Name of the Father......365

Epilogue – Regression to the Mean..........................373

Acknowledgements..377

About the Author..381

Author's Note and Content Warnings

I have drawn from my own experiences and knowledge to create this novel, and have taken some creative license with the geography of Oxford. Unfortunately, there is no Jericho Folly, much to my disappointment.

I have also taken some liberties with certain aspects of biology and medicine in service to the plot. I don't think that any of my minor changes are so large or egregious as to be plot or immersion breaking.

I hope that you will forgive me my little tweaks in light of the tense and exciting narrative that I have produced.

There are also some content warnings that I would like to point out in advance, although I will not be too specific; I do not wish to spoil the plot, after all! This will be the last mention of these warnings so that the story may unfold uninterrupted.

- **Body Horror**
- **Medical Horror/Surgery**
- **Torture**
- **Graphic Violence/Bloodshed**
- **Institutional Violence**
- **Mind Control**
- **Homophobia**
- **Religious Extremism**

Thank you for choosing this novel, dear Reader. I hope you enjoy reading it as much as I enjoyed writing it.

THE MINISTRY OF SUPERNATURAL AFFAIRS

Pugnamus In Obumbratio

For my darling Syd, who shares my love of horror,

And for my late Nana, Lorraine, who started me down this path and would've loved this book.

I think the two of you would've got on famously.

Part One: The Creeping Fantods

<u>Chapter One</u> – <u>The Gathering Dread</u>

Ivy

"Tell me about the angels, Jessica," Ivy said gently.

"You wouldn't believe me." The young woman suddenly leant forward in her chair and stared at Ivy, who fought back the urge to recoil. The deep shadows under her eyes only served to make her frenzied gaze that much more unsettling. "Nobody believes me.

"Why would they?" Jessica slumped back in her seat, muttering sullenly. "You all think I'm fucking crazy."

"I don't think that at all. People experience all sorts of strange and fantastical things, especially when they're under pressure." Ivy made a few quick scribbles in her notebook. "Do you think you're crazy, Jessica?"

"It's Jess. I'm only Jessica when I've done something wrong." She wrapped her arms around her tightly before she went on. "I honestly don't know if I'm crazy or not, Doc."

Ivy's mouth twitched reflexively. *Don't call me that.* Thankfully, Jess was not looking closely enough to notice. She took a second to gather her composure.

"Well, why don't we start with what we know for sure?"

"Okay."

"Your flatmate found you in the early hours of this morning trying to break the safety catches to fully open the kitchen window. She said that you were," Ivy glanced at her notes, "hysterical and yelling about needing to get outside. Is that correct?"

"Yes." Her voice was small, almost shameful.

"You said to my colleague earlier that you ripped several of your fingernails off trying to disengage the safety catch, and when you couldn't open it you decided to break the window instead. Also true?"

"Yes. I didn't even notice until I calmed down. I just needed to get outside; I wasn't thinking of anything else."

Ivy nodded sympathetically and glanced at Jess's hands; several of her fingers were tipped with plasters and a bandage was wound tightly over her left palm. She also noticed several scars on her forearms, stark in contrast to the her dark skin; some old, others more recent.

"We'll put a pin in the kitchen window for a moment, Jess. I want to ask you about your life more generally, if that's okay with you?"

"Sure, if you think it will help."

"You mentioned earlier that you're a student at the university, yes?"

"Yeah, I'm at Trinity College, working on my doctorate."

"What's your area of study?"

"Theology, specifically looking at the church's attitude to social issues and the rise of Methodism. It's really quite interesting; some of it isn't what you'd expect at all!" She sat up a little straighter and even gave Ivy the faintest hint of a smile. Ivy nodded warmly and gestured for her to continue as she made notes. "A lot of the more interesting intersections of clerical, legal and social norms actually revolved around death, or at least the impact of death upon the living.

"Suicide is a particularly fascinating case." She stopped dead as Ivy raised her eyebrows in interest.

"Do you think about death and suicide a lot for your work?" Ivy asked softly.

"Not as often as you might think. There's not a lot of literature on it. Besides, it's just a part of my overall research."

"I see. Is your doctorate going well?"

"It is, actually."

"Glad to hear it." Ivy closed her notebook and settled back into her chair. She and her patient regarded each other for a moment; an appraisal of trust or perhaps the wary sizing-up of an adversary. "How about the rest of your life? Are things going to plan, as it were?"

"Yes. I'm happy with my friends, I get on well with my family, and I'm in the college choir. Things are really good, Doc."

"And yet you tried to climb out of your kitchen window, which is on the third floor," Ivy said gently. "That's a fall that could easily have been fatal, Jess."

"I wasn't trying to hurt myself. I was just..." She trailed off and wrapped her arms around herself. She started to nervously chew her lip.

"Following the angels?" Ivy cocked her head to one side. "Would you say that you felt compelled to climb out of the window, Jess? Almost drawn against your will?"

She nodded. Ivy made another note in her book.

"It sounds to me, Jess, as if you've had some kind of manic episode. It's not uncommon to feel compelled or driven to do self-destructive or dangerous acts during them."

"What about the angels?"

"Whilst it's uncommon, it is possible for the mania to manifest in external audiovisual hallucinations. You mentioned being a churchgoer; perhaps an angelic choir is your mind's way of externalising the mania.

"What is important now, though, is keeping you safe going forwards. I'll arrange for a colleague at the Warneford to see you for an assessment as soon as he can and the psychiatric nurse you spoke to earlier will help you put a safety plan in place for your discharge. I'll also give you my work email, and you can let me know if you've any questions or concerns going forwards. Does that sound reasonable to you?"

"So I am crazy," Jess said sadly.

"No, you're not. You're a bright and talented young woman reacting to the stresses of the world around you in the only way your mind can manage; that doesn't make you crazy. Trust me, Jess, there are far stranger people out there than you.

"Take comfort in that, if you can."

Ivy left Jess in the care of one of the psychiatric nurses and walked up the corridor and into the waiting room. Her shift at the A&E Department of the John Radcliffe Hospital had ended a while ago but one of her colleagues had asked her to stay late to speak to the young woman who heard the angels.

I do have experience with the stranger aspects of psychology, she mused as she looked around the waiting room for Jessica's flatmate.

She saw her talking to a short man in a grey yachting cap and loden jacket, who was listening intently and nodding along to her. He had a youngish face and long hair pulled up behind the cap. Once the flatmate noticed Ivy she shook the man's hand and rose to receive news about her friend, but not before he passed something that looked like a business card to her.

"Is Jess okay?" she asked shakily.

"She's had a rough night, but I think she'll be alright in the long run. I'll arrange for a colleague of mine to see her at the Warneford as a matter of urgency. The nurse is with her now and will go over a crisis plan with the both of you. I'm sorry we can't do more tonight."

"That's fine, thank you. I'm just relieved that she's safe. Can I go and see her?"

"Of course, she's in Room Four, waiting for the nurse to speak her," Ivy said. She glanced at the curiously dressed man once more. "If you get your belongings, I'll gladly take you to her, if you'd like?"

The flatmate nodded and went to gather up her things. She gave the man a tired smile as she did so.

"Have a good evening, Mallory. It was nice talking to you."

"Likewise, Jade." He reached out and squeezed her hand once more. Ivy noticed a black leather satchel at his feet; it was full almost to bursting and leant heavily against his chair. "I hope your friend gets the help she needs. Take care."

Jade returned to Ivy's side and she led her down the corridor to the room where Jess was waiting.

"A friend of yours?" Ivy asked, trying to sound casual.

"Hmm?"

"The chap in the hat, the one you were talking to; is he a friend of yours?"

"Oh, no. We just met in the waiting room a little while ago. He's here to see a friend but they're with the doctor at the moment so we just got to talking. He's an artist."

"An artist; that's exciting. Is he local?"

"No, he's just in the city for a while for a commission. I'm an art historian, so he gave me his card."

Jade briefly showed the business card to Ivy; too quickly for her to get more than a vague impression. It was stylish with elegant curving script and a pale sunset ombre colouration to it. She saw something that looked like a website or an email address, a phone number, and a name. She could only make out the latter.

"Mallory Marsh," she said softly. Jade had already tucked the business card back into her pocket. Ivy blinked for a moment, trying to ignore the niggling worry that was forming at the back of her mind, and then walked into room four.

"Hi Jade," Jess said with a small wave. She looked at Ivy. "Can she stay here with me until the nurse comes?"

"Of course. I'm sure someone will see you soon. I've got things to attend to, so I'll say good night and good luck. You're a brave and bright young woman, Jess, and I wish you all the best. You've got my work email if you need anything. Take care, both of you."

"Thank you, Doc, for everything you said."

"You're most welcome."

Ivy smiled at the two young women and left them to it. As soon as she walked out of the room, her lips twitched and her smile faltered. The building sense of worry hit her like a breaking wave and she stopped dead in her tracks.

I've seen everyone waiting for an assessment, she thought, a*nd none of them mentioned an artist friend waiting for them.* It had been a surprisingly quiet night and there were only patients in mental health crises in this section of the department. Ivy began to walk back to the waiting room, her pace slow at first but quickening with every step.

Something feels off.

She couldn't quite put her finger on it but the strange man, Mallory, had seemed oddly intense in his interaction with Jade. She stopped one of the department nurses as he passed her.

"Isaac, I've a quick question for you. The man in the grey jacket and funny hat in the waiting room, who did he come in with?"

"He walked in and sat down with the lady whose friend is in Room Four. Jessica, I think it is. I assumed she texted a friend and he'd come in to keep her company. They've been talking for ages." He saw her frown. "Dr Livingston, is there a problem?"

"I'm not sure yet, but possibly. Could you please get someone from security to meet me in the waiting room, please? Discreetly, if they can manage it."

"Of course."

"Thank you, Isaac."

The sharp tap of her shoes rang through the corridor, a drum beat to the melodic beeping and ringing of machines and call buttons. Her mouth was set in a hard frown.

Whilst it wasn't unusual for there to be some sparse conversation between friends and family whilst their loved ones were being assessed, they would rarely sit so close together and talk in such an inquisitive manner to each other. After all, everyone in that room knew why everyone else was there, at least in the broad strokes, and the taboo around mental health problems still ran deep.

Something is very wrong.

She forced herself to slow down as she neared the waiting room and she took a measured breath. Calm and careful, she told herself; it was possible that Mallory, if that was his name, was an overly chatty person who had simply ended up in the wrong waiting room. Her instincts, however, told her that this was not the case.

Regardless, she did not want to cause a scene in front of the people in the waiting room. *They've been through enough for one night.*

She lingered around the corner for a few moments; it would take someone from the hospital's security team a couple of minutes to navigate the confusing corridors and rooms that made up the emergency department. If her instructions for discretion had been relayed they would not be hurrying and should be keeping an eye open for anyone in a grey jacket and hat acting strangely.

She hoped that her worry was for nothing, even though it would be deeply embarrassing for her.

Maybe there's another way to do this, she thought. *Perhaps I could ask Jade for the business card he gave her?*

She shook her head. That might have worked earlier when the young woman had brought it up in conversation, but to go back now would make her think that there was something wrong.

"But there *is* something wrong though," she said softly to herself. "I'm sure of it."

She glanced at a clock on the wall and decided that surely the most sedate security guard would've arrived by now. She drew herself up straight, ready to throw around her authority if necessary, and strode purposefully towards the waiting room.

As she entered, she made eye contact with the security guard talking casually to one of the nurses, and she responded with an almost imperceptible nod.

I've got your back if you need me, whispered a little voice in her head.

Ivy walked past them both and looked over the people assembled in the waiting room; faces filled with worry and exhaustion. Her face fell as she did so, and she turned back towards the security guard, muttering under her breath.

"God damn it Ivy, why did you wait so long?" she asked of herself. "Always trust your gut!"

Mallory Marsh, the mystery man in the hat, was gone.

The bus shook as it bounced over a pot hole in the road, jolting Ivy in her seat. The sudden lurch did nothing to improve her already sour mood.

The security team had searched the whole department and found no trace of the man. The receptionists had not seen or spoken to him either; if Jade hadn't shown her the business card, Ivy might've believed that she imagined him.

Maybe I should've stuck around and spoken to Jade again, she thought. Unfortunately, when the search had finished, Jade and Jess were still speaking to the crisis nurse and Ivy was dead on her feet.

Weighing up her curiosity against her exhaustion, she had decided to go home. Dawn was breaking as the bus reached her stop and she rang the bell.

The morning air was chilly as she walked the short distance to her house, her mind still in turmoil over the missing man. As she opened the gate to her front garden, she froze.

The eerie sensation of being watched crept up her spine, chilling her like ice. The hair stood up on the back of her neck and her skin turned to goose flesh. Every instinct in her screamed at her to run but she remained firmly rooted to the spot.

She felt a malevolent presence behind her, dangerous and cunning; predatory, even. She was sure she could smell its musky, animal scent on her neck and feel its hot breath stirring her hair.

I'm going to die.

A cloud shifted on the horizon as the first sliver of sun crept into the sky. A finger of golden light bathed the street, warming Ivy and breaking the fearful spell that had fallen over her. She turned around sharply, her fingernails and keys ripping through the space behind her.

Only empty air.

The entire street was deserted; abed and asleep aside from a single fox that moved from bin to bin, looking for the last easy meal of the fading night.

"Fuck," she said harshly. She bounced her keys gently, nervously, in her palm. "There's nobody there, Ivy."

It was true; there wasn't a single hiding place on the road for at least a dozen metres, at least not one big enough to obscure a person. There was a piercing yelp from a garden a not too far away; the fox had won its prize. Ivy took one final look around her before she walked up the short path to her front door.

"Get it together," she said as she unlocked the door and stepped inside. She breathed a sigh of relief once she was over the threshold and carefully locked the door behind her.

"You can't let this happen to you," she said.

Not again, a little voice added.

"It's that idiot in the hat, that's all. He's just got you spooked." She dropped her bag on the floor, feeling a little more herself. "Once you've had a cup of tea you'll feel much better."

She walked into the kitchen, flipping the small light on over the stove as she passed it, and began filling the kettle. She glanced at the whiteboard on the fridge and saw there were messages from both Edgar and Michaela.

I'll deal with those later.

As the kettle started its slow rumbling way towards boiling, her curiosity flared up once again. She fought it for a moment before finally giving in and doing the one thing she'd swore not to since leaving her shift.

She pulled her phone out of her pocket and typed 'Mallory Marsh' into a search engine. There were a few results but they weren't her man. She tried 'Mallory Marsh Art' as the kettle reached the boil and plinked off.

Nothing.

Determination gave way to panic as she continued her search, combing every social media network with his name, and description. She did not notice the ache in her legs as she leant awkwardly against the counter. The kitchen brightened with the waxing sunlight and the kettle had long since gone cold. At last, her phone ran out of battery and she let it clatter to the worktop; black, glassy, and useless.

Nothing, she thought incredulously. *Not a fucking thing.*

Mallory Marsh did not exist.

Chapter Two – A Glint in the Lamplight

Thaddeus

"Yo, what's up my Tadsters? We're here for another episode of Tad Talks and have I got a good one for you this time!" Thaddeus leant in close to his microphone and mugged for the camera, wiggling his generous eyebrows as he did so. "We're going to take another deep dive into the world of conspiracy theories; this one is centred right here, in Oxford!"

He froze for a few seconds, staring right into the lens, before relaxing and ending the recording. He watched the take back a few times, nodding as he did so. *Nice, nice; that's suitably engaging.*

Thad looked over at the untidy drift of notes that sat on his cramped desk and frowned a little. With the opening hook complete, he now had to workshop his many hours of research and delving down internet rabbit holes into something resembling a script.

"This is going to be tricky," he said to himself as he wandered through his living room turned studio, stooped and aimless. The spooky and inconvenient garret that he called home was located in Jericho, one of the trendier parts of the city, and would've been far out of his price range had he not inherited it a few years prior.

He looked at the framed photograph that held pride of place above his rickety little bed and beamed. It was of a young Thaddeus, barely a teenager, with his beloved Aunt Arabella; the two were surrounded by books on the occult and local mythology.

"I miss you, Aunty Bella," he said softly.

A few muffled buzzes snapped Thad from his reverie and he pulled his phone from his pocket and answered it; he didn't need to look who was calling.

"Hello?" he asked, already tired of the conversation.

"Eric, is that you?" a woman asked. She was shouting down the phone and Thaddeus grimaced as he held the phone a little distance from his ear.

"Mum, you don't need to shout!"

"Well, *you* don't need to sound so annoyed, Eric."

"My name is Thaddeus. You chose it, so you might as well use it."

"We named you that to please your father's side of the family, you know that! I always tried to get you to use your middle name; it's more normal."

"I'm not a normal person."

"Yes, your late aunt certainly saw to that, always encouraging you with talk of magic and monsters and-" She made an annoyed, flustered noise before continuing. "Anyway, that wasn't why I called you.

"We've not seen you in months, and your father and I were wondering if you'd like to come to dinner this evening?"

Thad paused and pinched the bridge of his nose. *Please, just leave me alone!*

"Your father can come and pick you up; no need for you to bother with the bus. It would be nice to see you."

"I'm sorry, Mum," he said evenly, "but I've got to work tonight."

"That silly video show of yours is not work, Eric!"

"It's not-" He took a deep breath. "It's not silly, and I'm not getting into that with you now, but that's not what I'm doing tonight. I'm working the lighting at the theatre tonight and I won't be done until late. Sorry."

Please don't ask what show I'm working on, he begged silently. Unfortunately, his prayer to the universe went unanswered.

"Oh, what's playing? Perhaps we can come along. It's been years since we saw a play or a musical!"

"It's a... cabaret show. Alternative stuff, a bit niche. I don't think it would be your cup of tea, Mum. Definitely not Dad's, that's for sure."

"*Cabaret?*" She asked, her tone suddenly venomous. "I do hope that you're not spending your time around cross-dressers and degenerates, Eric."

"Cross-dressers!? In the theatre?" He asked, his voice dripping with sarcasm.

"We raised you better than that. You shouldn't associate with people like that, son. People will think you're some sort of f-"

"I've got to go, Mum," he said sharply, cutting across her. "Another time, perhaps?"

"Yes. You should call more often, Eric." She made her goodbyes and hung up, leaving him staring at the empty black glass of his phone.

"It's Thaddeus," he said softly and sadly.

His parents, Barnabus and Charlotte Thane, did not approve of Thaddeus's choices in life; not his career, his friends, his hobbies, or anything else for that matter. *They especially wouldn't approve of my choice in partners,* he thought with a solemn smile. The Thanes, whilst historically an eccentric family, held very firmly with Tradition and Thad's parents had tried to instil their Traditional Values in him.

They had not been successful.

On the wall opposite Thad's bed and the portrait hung a collection of colourful flags, with the Bisexual Pride tricolour proudly displayed at their centre.

Thaddeus had almost succumbed to his parents' pressure in his early teens but his aunt, a *confirmed spinster*, had come to his rescue. His garret had been his haven long before it became his home.

She'd lived a long and storied life, full of travels and misadventure, and her theatrical style of storytelling had captivated Thad. She was confident without being arrogant and always delighted in an opportunity to make someone else the hero of the tale.

"I might've been there as the face of the whole thing," she'd say to an entranced Thaddeus, "but I never could've done it alone!"

She had encouraged Thaddeus's love of the theatre and had financed any and all training he'd needed to follow his passion. Arabella had been thrilled when he'd managed to get a job working in tech at a local theatre, the Old Fire Station. It wasn't as old or *traditionally* prestigious as some of the others in the city, but it had a focus on accessibility and diversity, which suited Thaddeus just fine.

He didn't make much but the inheritance of the garret from Arabella made a huge difference, especially in a city as expensive as Oxford. Whilst he had been saddened by her death, he had done as she'd asked of him in her last letter.

"My darling Thaddeus," he recounted to himself, "weep for me if you must, but do not be sad forever. Let what I leave behind serve not as a bitter reminder of that which is lost but instead let it be the fertile soil from which something beautiful can grow.

"Choose life, Thaddeus."

"Thaddeus, lovely, it's wonderful to see you!" The deep voice echoed through the theatre as Thad walked in. "Will you be the maestro for this evening's festivities?"

"Lovely to see you too, Poppy, and yes, you've got me tonight." He smiled at Poppy. She was a tall, energetic, flamboyant trans woman and, when in full costume, would be hosting that night's show. Poppy was her stage name; he didn't know her by anything else. "Thank you for the sound and lighting notes you sent through; thorough as always!"

"I try my best to make your life easier."

Thad was fond of Poppy and the production company that she was a part of; they always listened to the advice of the technicians and gave them quite a lot of creative license where they could. He'd asked to work that night's show especially.

"What's on the dance card for tonight, Poppy?"

"We've got some real treats in this show, Thad! I've managed to scrape the budget together for a contortionist *and* a sword swallower." She grinned at him and bounced on the balls of her feet, brimming with excitement. "I've also finally got my portable shower working, so we're going to be closing out with my much anticipated Bloodbath number!

"I'm so excited, Thad! This is gonna be wild!"

"That sounds pretty gnarly, Poppy."

"Too much, perhaps?" she asked, her enthusiasm slightly muted.

"Not at all. I'm feeling it!" He returned her grin as her energy came roaring back. "Give me ten minutes to get settled in and set up, and then we can start running through, if you want?"

"Sounds great, but take your time. I might pop out and grab a coffee first; do you want anything?"

"Thanks for the offer but I'm all good thanks."

"Sure thing, see you in a bit!" She lingered, smiling, for a few seconds before turning on her heel and strolling out of the theatre. Thad strode in the opposite direction, through the stage door and up some stairs to the tech gallery.

As he was poring over the notes for the show, he couldn't help but think about the untidy pile of notes on his desk back in the garret. Amongst them were maps of the city with important locations marked in red pen, several newspaper clippings, and his own theories about what was happening. More numerous than anything else, however, were the missing persons reports.

There were dozens of them, all in the last month.

And those are the people that have someone looking for them, he thought with a shudder. The Old Fire Station also contained a non-profit cafe that worked with Crisis, a homelessness charity. Thaddeus volunteered there once a week and was used to seeing the same people coming in regularly. In recent months, however, the city's usually large homeless population had dwindled to almost none.

It hadn't happened all at once; just one or two here and there. As the weeks wore on Crisis saw fewer and fewer of its regulars, and those that did turn up seemed terribly frightened. In the streets they only ever moved in pairs or trios; any larger groups would be broken up by the police. The most common call for assistance that Thad encountered was for relocation away from Oxford. Nobody seemed to care where they ended up as long as they got out of the city.

After six or seven weeks, the streets were empty. Every homeless person in the city had either disappeared or left.

I bet most people haven't even noticed that something's wrong, he thought bitterly. *Or if they have, they certainly don't care where they've gone.*

By his reckoning there were about seventy five people who had vanished in the city in the last seven weeks. *It must be more than that*, he thought solemnly. He thought about what Clem, one of the homeless men he'd grown friendly with, had said.

"They got the young 'uns first, Thad. They offered them a meal and a bed for the night, no questions asked. So many of them new to the street, naive and desperate." Clem had been homeless for almost three years and had experienced the entire spectrum of responses to his situation. "They didn't know any better. They never came back."

Clem was one of the people looking to relocate when he disappeared. Thaddeus had tried to file a report with the police, but they'd brushed him off. In his frustration he'd started digging and researching disappearances in the city; that was when he'd stumbled on the recent spike of missing persons cases, all of which seemed to be unsolved.

The names and pictures in the pile on Thad's desk had very little in common with each other, aside from one major factor; they had all vanished in Oxford at night. From what he could determine from social media and other sites on the net the loved ones of those missing were almost universal in their belief that the police were not doing enough.

Whilst some might call it ghoulish, he intended to make a video detailing the disappearances to raise some awareness about what was happening in the city. If enough people saw it and it got enough traction, Thaddeus hoped that it might galvanise a bit more of a response from the authorities.

Unless I disappear first.

Suddenly the tech gantry, which had always been a second home to him, seemed too dark and distant from the main theatre. Isolated, even.

Clem was streetwise and savvy, he thought with a shudder, *and they still got him.*

"Thaddeus?" asked a voice behind him.

He yelped in surprise and turned in fright to find Poppy standing there, just as shaken by his response. She blinked rapidly a few times, one hand clutched to her breast.

"Jesus, Poppy, you scared the hell out of me!" he said with a nervous chuckle.

"Sorry."

"No, it's fine, I just didn't hear you come in." He shook his head as he turned back to the computer. "I've got a bad case of the spookers today, apparently."

"You and half the city, it seems..." she said softly.

"What do you mean?"

"Ah, it's nothing, just people behaving oddly." She took a breath and was her usual self once again. "But time and stage wait for no-one! Shall we do a run through, if you're ready? I want tonight to be perfect."

Thaddeus wove his way through the streets of Jericho, a giddy smile on his face. The show had been a sell-out success and everything had gone swimmingly. Poppy had been beside herself with joy and had invited him out for a drink after the show. He'd declined, but had said that he'd gladly meet her for coffee in a few days.

Maybe Rachel, his boss, was right; perhaps Poppy was sweet on him. He was surprised to find just how much that thought pleased him. *I should give the garret a clean, who knows what might-*

He slowed slightly as his train of thought derailed. His heart beat a little faster in his chest as his conscious mind fought to keep up with the animal part of his brain, which was in a state of panic.

Thaddeus, he told himself, *whatever you do, don't run.*

His ears were the first part of him that caught up to his instincts. His footsteps had previously had a slight echo to them, at least for the last couple of streets, but with the change in his pace he realised this was not so; someone was following him. He dared not to look around, but gradually increased his pace until he was slightly swifter than whoever, or whatever, was behind him.

The pursuing footsteps quickened.

Thaddeus took a quick left down a side street, then three more after that to try to lose his follower. After rounding the final turn he realised that he was only a hundred metres or so from his front door. With a quick glance over his shoulder to confirm that his pursuer wasn't on top of him, Thad broke into a frantic sprint, yanking his keys from his pocket as he did so.

He hit the door with a thump and fumbled at the lock. Out of the corner of his eye he saw a person round the final corner in a hurried walk as the key slid home. He fell through the door as the stranger looked up the street, thankfully in the opposite direction from Thad. He shut the door quickly, only slowing at the last possible moment so that that the latch clicked shut quietly instead of slamming. He flipped the catch on the deadbolt and let out a long, low sigh of relief.

Through the spy hole he saw someone stalk

carefully up the street, inspecting each door as they went. Their eyes seemed to linger on Thad's door a touch longer than the others. Thaddeus fought the urge to back away from the door and used the time to get as good a look at the stranger as possible.

She was a woman with long dark hair, dressed entirely in completely unremarkable clothing. She had almost no distinguishing features; Thad wouldn't have been able to pick her out in a crowd if his life depended on it. Then she turned to move up the street and the strangest thing happened.

Her eyes shone with reflected light, just like a cat's would.

It was only a moment and Thad couldn't be sure that it wasn't just a chance glint on the spyhole lens, but his blood turned to ice water in his veins at the sight. He held his breath until she was long out of view. His heart thundered in his ears as he made his way carefully up the six flights of stairs, only beginning to slow when he was safely in the garret with all the lights on and the door thoroughly locked.

He glanced over at his collection of missing people, sick to his stomach.

"What the fuck is going on?"

Chapter Three – The Spectre of Lye Valley

Ivy

"Eek!"

Ivy jumped as the toaster popped and bounced a little on the kitchen worktop. The smell of almost burnt toast filled her nostrils and she placed one hand on her chest as if to still her racing heart. She felt her face flush with embarrassment and she looked sheepishly around the room to check she was alone.

"Fucking hell, Ivy," she said with an awkward chuckle. She'd been incredibly skittish in the days following the Mallory Marsh mystery at the John Radcliffe. After her distressing ordeal in the street Ivy had been unable to sleep so she had gone back to the hospital to review the security footage, just to satisfy her own morbid curiosity.

What she saw only disturbed her further.

Marsh had walked out of the waiting room, leaving the field of view of one camera, and had simply disappeared. The next camera should've caught him seconds later but there was no sign of him. There was some kind of vaguely blurred visual disturbance on the recording, but the CCTV Technician had said that it was most likely just a bit of grease.

Ivy had followed Marsh's pathway out of the waiting room and had found that she was only out of view on the cameras for three metres of otherwise empty corridor. The only exits were in the view of cameras and there were no windows. Ivy was now certain that the mysterious Mallory Marsh had somehow walked out of the John Radcliffe Hospital without being seen.

What she had envisioned as a way to ease her anxieties had done the complete opposite.

Ivy rubbed her eyes. *I can't keep obsessing over this.* She had barely slept since reviewing the footage and her mind was beginning to play tricks on her. The toast still sat in the toaster so Ivy deftly plucked it out and plopped it on to a plate.

"Overdone," she muttered. She had no memory of putting the toaster on and she certainly would've lowered the settings to her liking. *One of the others must've been hungry,* she thought.

"Once again, let's leave Ivy to clear everything up," she said bitterly. She took one bite of the toast, wrinkled her nose at the acrid taste, and spat it into the sink. She tossed the plate down on the counter top with a clatter and walked towards the staircase, enjoying the transition from cool tiles to soft carpet beneath her feet. "Just have a bath, calm down, and then head to work; that's all you have to do."

As she neared the bottom of the stairs Ivy kicked a stray hardback book that was peeking out from behind a chair. She swore loudly and angrily looked down at the book as she rubbed her throbbing toes. Only the corner was visible but she immediately recognised it as one of Michaela's esoteric mycology textbooks.

"Shelves," she muttered darkly, "we have shelves for the books."

The pain in Ivy's foot subsided quickly but it sublimated into anger as it did so; anger at the misplaced book, at the abandoned toast, at her own clumsiness. She growled through gritted teeth and tried to hold back her frustration to no avail.

"For fuck's sake," she screamed at the empty house, "stop leaving your fucking shit everywhere! How many fucking times do I need to have this conversation?"

Not for the first time, Ivy wished that she inhabited her home alone. It took every ounce of restraint in her body not to hurl the book across the room. *How the fuck am I supposed to get through to them?*

She stormed back into the kitchen and angrily rubbed off the messages on the whiteboard without even looking at them. She picked up the black dry-wipe marker, her pen, and wrote her message as large as she could.

"Keep my house tidy or fuck off," she read back to herself. She smiled. "That ought to do it."

Ivy made a second attempt at heading upstairs, but managed to kick the protruding book once again. This time the rage won out and she hurled the heavy tome across the room with a guttural scream. It landed with a heavy thud on the sofa and shortly afterwards one of the throw pillows gently fell on top of it, but by that point Ivy had already thundered upstairs.

"Please let it be a quiet night," she muttered as she started to fill the bath with near-scalding water; just how she liked it. "I've got enough going on without the patients howling at the moon."

That's a bit hypocritical of you, Ivy.

"Just let me have one moment of fucking peace, please!" Ivy's voice had lost its angry edge and she was now teetering on the edge of sobbing. "All I want is to have an hour to myself before I have to get ready for work. Is that really too much to ask?"

Ivy watched the water until the bath was suitably deep and then flicked off the tap. She dipped her fingers into the steaming water and sighed at the warmth. *Perfect, but I think we can do better.* She crossed to her bedroom and, after moment of looking for it, found her incense burner. She picked out a stick and lit it, savouring the scented smoke.

Ivy smiled, doffed her clothes, and carried the burner back to the bathroom. She placed it on the the closed toilet lid and took a step into the bath. The water was startlingly cold and she yelped as she snatched her foot out once again.

"Seriously?" she huffed as she yanked the plug out with an excessive amount of force. The water gurgled down the drain with a throaty bubbling sound that almost masked the creak of the wonky floorboard at the top of the stairs.

The unpleasant sensation that she'd experienced at her garden gate a few mornings ago returned with a vengeance; her skin immediately rose in pinpricks as the fear and adrenaline flooded her body. Unlike before, she was naked and in her own home which by all rights should've made her feel more vulnerable than ever. This time, however, Ivy's fear was rapidly replaced with another, far more useful, emotion.

Rage.

She whirled around and looked at the top of the stairs. Nobody was there, but she swore that she could feel eyes boring into her own. She straightened up and stretched one hand towards the sink. Her questing fingers found Edgar's straight razor, conveniently within reach. Ivy flicked the blade out with practised ease, her eyes never leaving the empty corridor.

"Get out of my house," she growled.

The only sound that she could hear was the steady thud of her own heart, no longer racing with terror but pounding with determined anger. Her whole body seemed to vibrate but the hand that held the razor remained steady as a rock.

Behind her, the low evening sun shone through the bathroom window and out into the corridor. The quality of the light seemed to change for just a moment as the sun finally dipped below the westward city horizon and, in the corridor before her, Ivy saw the brief glory on the wall. The rainbow rings framed a faded fuzzy shadow and she swore that, for the briefest instant, she could see a person sized glimmer in the golden light.

"Leave," she said evenly, "or I will kill you."

There was scarcely a heartbeat between her words and the sudden clatter of someone running down the stairs. This was followed by the slam of the front door as it closed behind the mystery intruder.

Ivy heard the last echoing gurgle as the bath finally emptied. With a sigh she let the tension out of her body and put the blade down. She shut the bathroom door, locked it, and started another bath. The thin smoke of the burning incense curled through the room.

Hopefully whatever that was will leave me alone now.

After towelling herself dry Ivy finally checked the time on her phone. It was a lot later than she realised, and now she ran the real risk of being late for work. *I could just call off*, she thought before bursting into nervous laughter at such a notion.

"Oh yes, what a great plan," she said to no-one in particular. "I'm sorry, I can't come into work tonight because I got hassled by a ghost in my bathroom. Yes, a ghost, or maybe the invisible man; you never can tell nowadays.

"A room, just for me *and* a comfy straightjacket too? Well, aren't I the cat that got the cream!"

She continued to chuckle as she got dressed into one of her various work outfits. She opened her laundry hamper to toss in the towel and was surprised to find it empty. *Huh, maybe one of the others did the washing for once. That, or it was the ghost.* More nervous laughter.

Ivy heard a dry rasping sound and looked down; she was scratching aggressively at her left forearm. She quickly pulled her hand away but the arm was already red and a bit raw with small beads of blood welling up where her neat nails had caught the skin.

She pulled down her sleeve, hoping that the blood would not show through the pale fabric. Nothing was immediately visible but she decided to put on a thin cardigan just in case.

Please don't give me the shift team from hell, she thought as she opened her emails to check the staffing schedule.

She smiled when she saw that she wasn't the lead that evening; Doctor Adams had that pleasure. Ivy liked Irving Adams. He was a quiet man who would always wait to be spoken to, but once coaxed out of his shell he was quite the character. He always had a kind word for Ivy and she, like the rest of the staff, trusted his judgement completely; if he ever recommended a treatment plan for a patient it was carried out without question.

I do wish he'd choose a more subtle cologne, she thought. Irving's scent of choice was Paco Rabanne Pour Homme, a classic to be sure, but it was a bit dark and mossy for Ivy's nose. *It almost reminds me of how Michaela smells after she's been in the shed.*

With perfume in mind, Ivy went over to her dresser and spritzed herself with her personal favourite, Lolita Lempicka; not an overbearing amount but enough to be noticed. She always tried to maintain a stable multisensory profile with her patients in the hope that it would help to ground them.

I swore I hung this up downstairs, she thought as she picked her jacket up off the bed. As she slipped it on she felt a weight in one of the pockets. A brief rummage turned up the razor. She held it her hand, her eyes wide with surprise.

"Now I definitely don't remember putting you in my pocket." She went to put it back in the bathroom, but hesitated. After a moment of careful consideration she slipped it into her pocket once again. "Just in case."

She slid her phone and her work pass into the other side of the coat. A glance at the clock on her bedroom wall confirmed that she would have to hustle in order to get to the Warneford before half past nine. Her stomach growled at her, perhaps in protest regarding the wasted toast.

"I'm in reserve this evening," she said as she trotted down the stairs, "I'll order something in and eat it in the office. Maybe Nepalese."

She picked up her keys with a jangle and went through the front door into the darkening evening, her mind full to bursting with thoughts of tender lamb, straight razors, and ghosts. The door locked shut behind her and the house sat silent and empty.

If Ivy had decided to take a moment to tidy the kitchen before she left, or even had decided to snack on the cold, burnt toast, she'd have seen the message

that now filled the entire white board, written in Edgar's decisive hand.
You are in danger!

Chapter Four – Breakfast with a Monster

Mallory

It was a little after nine o'clock in the morning. Mallory Marsh placed his satchel at his feet as he sat at one of the little tables by the coffee stand at the junction of Ship Street and Cornmarket, in the shadow of the nearby church. He sipped at the cup of tea he'd purchased and watched the hundreds, if not thousands, of unrecognisable faces stream past in the golden sunlight.

"Busy bees on their way to work," he muttered softly. He watched for a few more moments before he pulled a small book and a pen out of his bag. He opened up to the marked page and began to work on a crossword.

"Late, of course," he said after a quick glance at his pocket watch. "Why they saddled me with a Ghost and a Shriek on this particular venture..."

He sighed heavily and returned to his crossword. His pen hovered over the page hesitantly.

"Fantod," said a tired voice beside him. He glanced at the seat to his left, only to find it empty. "Clue number eight; nineteenth century slang, a sense of dread or uneasiness, six letters. Fantod."

"How long have you been there, Charity?" Mallory asked as he filled in the letters.

"Long enough to hear you gripe about me, Marsh." The voice belonged to Charity Walpole; a surprisingly cheerful, if slightly snide, woman in the employ of the Ministry. Mallory had never worked with her before, but someone with her particular talents was always useful.

She was a Ghost; Ministry slang for someone who could render themselves and others invisible for an amount of time. In Mallory's experience all Ghosts fell into one of three categories; psychopaths, pranksters, and perverts. Charity, however, seemed to buck this trend entirely.

"Thank you for your assistance in ensuring a swift exit from the hospital the other morning, Charity. I didn't realise that I'd attracted so much attention."

"You'd draw fewer eyes if you dressed a little less conspicuously."

"I don't know what you mean," Mallory said defensively. *Leave my hat alone,* he thought.

"I'm sure." Charity chuckled. "Where are we meeting Evans?"

"Browns Cafe, in the Covered Market. We've got a few minutes yet, and besides, I'm sure he's listening to everything we're saying." Mallory frowned at the thought of sharing breakfast with the swaggering Welshman. Whereas he could tolerate Charity's foibles in light of her usefulness, Evans was quite simply *a problem*. "Worry not, there's somewhere en route for you to get changed."

"Much appreciated, Marsh."

"Have you found anything useful in the past couple of days? Any leads?"

"Can't this wait until we've eaten?"

"I suppose, but I do find that you're a touch more forthcoming with your conclusions when it's just the two of us."

Charity said nothing in response so Mallory continued his crossword. *You're frightened of him, aren't you, Charity?*

Mallory went to ask her if she really thought they were on the right lines, but stopped himself before the words left his lips. Instead he scrawled his question regarding their path of enquiry into the margin of his crossword book and placed it on the table along with the pen.

It took only a moment for the pen to seemingly hover in mid-air pensively, before Charity wrote her reply in delicate looping script. Mallory went to read it, but was interrupted as he did so by a sharp shrill whistle.

Although it only lasted for a fraction of a second it still stung his ears and made his eyes water. Judging by the dissatisfied grunt that came from Charity, she had heard it too. Mallory drained the last of his tea in a swift gulp and gathered up his things.

"The Master beckons," Charity said grumpily and an empty chair slid away from the table with an audible screech. Mallory got to his feet also. "Lead the way, Mallory; I'm too tired to navigate this maze of a city."

He strode purposefully up Ship Street, along the Turl for a minute or so, and then on to Market Street. He gestured towards the bank of public toilets that lined the northernmost wall of the Covered Market. The accessible cubicle was locked shut, both with the usual RADAR Key and a padlock. *Accessible my arse,* Mallory thought as the padlock jiggled, seemingly of its own accord, before it unlocked and fell to the ground. The door opened shortly afterwards and closed with a sharp tap.

Mallory lingered awkwardly outside on Market Street as he waited for Charity to euphemistically 'get changed'. His guts squirmed as he heard the pained grunts and gasps through the door of the accessible toilet cubicle. He leant on it, both to muffle the sound and to block anyone else from using it. He got several dirty looks from passers-by.

Better you don't see this, he wanted to say to them. *You'll be happier not knowing.*

He wasn't entirely sure how Charity rendered herself visible once again as it was wildly different for every Ghost, but he knew that it would be unpleasant at the best. He'd worked with one some years ago who'd had to peel his skin off, inch by bloody inch, in order to shed the invisibility.

No power without pain, he thought grimly.

There was a strangled scream from the toilet cubicle. Mallory winced at the sound and his heart went out to her. *She's spent too long out of sight.* The longer a Ghost stayed invisible, the harder it was for them to turn back.

He extracted his crossword book from his jacket and flicked to the page Charity had written on. His eyebrows raised as he read her reply, but before he could do anything he was shoved in the back by the door opening behind him.

"Fucking hell, Mallory, move out of the way!" Charity's voice was tinged with pain and exhaustion. He took a few steps forward, slipping the book away as he did so. The door swung open and an impossibly pale hand reached out to shade a pair of equally pallid eyes. Even though they were in the shade, Charity rifled through her pockets to find a pair of strong sunglasses. "I always forget just how bright the world is."

"There's an eclipse soon; that'll give you about eight minutes of respite." Mallory said playfully.

"Is that so?"

"Yes, I read it in the paper yesterday. The locals are quite excited about it."

"Well, bully for them."

Mallory took a moment to look at Charity and tried hard to hold her appearance in his mind. She had pale eyes behind sunglasses, almost translucent skin, white hair, and wore a sun-faded leather jumpsuit under an equally weathered leather trench coat that held the tools of her trade; lockpicks, knives, and a wire garrotte. Ghosts were assassins as often as they were spies or detectives.

Mallory closed his eyes, and he lost the detail immediately. Upon opening them a few seconds later, Charity's face was as unfamiliar as any other stranger in the street. In fact, all he could hold on to was a single word that summed up her entire appearance.

Bleached.

The shrill sound struck their ears again, but more painful and insistent this time. Both of them flinched and Charity swore loudly.

"Fucker!" She shook her head, as if to clear the sound from her ears. "Give me a moment, will you?"

Charity turned her head and spat a bloody globule of saliva on to the pavement. She then straightened herself up and strode purposefully into the Covered Market, one hand firmly buried in a coat pocket. Mallory trotted behind her, struggling to keep up. The response she'd written in his puzzle book kept echoing in his mind.

I think you may be right.

"Are you alright?" he asked as she stumbled slightly.

"I'll live," she said wearily. "Although if this job goes on much longer the Ministry will need to sort out another round of chemo for me; too much dicking about in direct sunlight isn't good for me, you know?"

Mallory squeezed her arm gently as they reached the little cafe. She smiled back at him and walked inside. Mallory took a breath and walked in, following Charity's lead.

"Time to see the boss," he muttered.

Opinions at the Ministry were seldom aligned and almost never unanimous, but there were two things about Joseph Evans that everyone who'd ever met him would agree on. Firstly, he was one of the most capable operatives they had, and the most gifted Shriek by a country mile. Secondly, and far more importantly, he was a bully.

As Mallory and Charity sat down at the table he'd chosen he sighed dramatically and made a big gesture of checking a non-existent watch. Instead, Mallory notice, there was a faint tattoo peeking out of his shirt cuff; a stylised Victorian street lamp with a three digit code beneath it.

Lamplight, he thought. *That makes sense.*

"Well, well, well, look who finally decided to show up!" Evans frowned at them both. "Agent Marsh, I'm sure that you usual partner allows sloppy timekeeping, but I do not. As for you, Agent Walpole, you continue to be a disappointment."

In one fluid movement Charity pulled a small item from her pocket and held it close to Evan's ear. She pushed a button and it let out a sharp *click* and he snarled in pain, batting her hand away from him. Mallory couldn't help the small, satisfied smile that crept on to his face.

"You fucking bitch, Walpole!" Evans looked down at the item she held. "Is that a fucking dog clicker?"

"It sure is, and every time you act like a supercilious prick I'm going to click it right in your ear." She pulled her hand back as he made a grab for it and popped the clicker back in her pocket. "Now, now, Joseph, there's no need to snatch. Besides, if you take that I'll just get something worse."

Mallory groaned and put his head in his hands. *How on earth did I get stuck on a case with these psychopaths?*

"Something to add, Marsh?" Joseph asked testily.

"No, other than wondering why the two of you are still permitted to work together."

"We get the job done," said Charity. Mallory looked at her with surprise; he had not expected her to defend their antagonistic relationship. "We might snip at each other occasionally, but we get results quickly and quietly, which is what the Ministry values above all else.

"When you've worked as many dangerous cases as we have, you learn to let the little things go in the name of partnership."

Let things slide, more like.

"You'll realise soon enough that letting off steam and venting frustration at each other is better than letting it spill over into a mission." Evans crossed his arms resolutely as he spoke.

"That's one approach," Mallory said. "And this is not a *Mission*, it's an Investigation."

"Same difference," Evans said.

"Not if we're going by the book," Mallory retorted. "An Investigation sets out to find and resolve a problem peacefully where it can, whereas a Mission is undertaken with the explicit intention to destroy whoever or whatever is responsible. I don't know about you, but I'd rather this end without violence."

"It doesn't matter what you call it, Mallory," Charity said as she placed a sympathetic arm around his shoulders, "it'll come to bloodshed in the end."

Mallory said nothing; in his heart he agreed with her, but he still bristled at their attitude.

"Did you get any leads from the hospital girl?" Evans asked after a not inconsiderable pause. "Any new information?"

"Regrettably not but, if I may, I would like to voice my concerns as to the approach we are taking."

"Mallory, you've made your *concerns* vocal enough already. Agent Walpole and I both agree that this is a simple case of one or more Rusałki that have been preying on the city's population. Oxford's a watery place, Mallory, and what else do you make of the reports of compelling songs? It's obvious to anyone with half a brain."

"Obvious?" He scoffed. "There have been *no* reported drownings, which itself is strange at this time of year, and the witnesses said words, not songs. Besides, it just doesn't feel right."

"It doesn't *feel* right!? What, are you claiming to be a Seer now?"

"Oh yes, Evans, latch on to that part and ignore the other bits that you can't explain." Mallory tried to keep his tone in check, but his anger got the better of him. "I'm sure you've got a few potential culprits in mind too, but I doubt you'll even try to talk to them before you burst their brains like balloons!"

"I am your superior officer, Agent Marsh!"

"You are a Civil Servant, Evans, not a soldier!"

Mallory glared at him. "But then again, what else can I expect from a Lamplight Survivor?"

Charity and Joseph fell silent, stunned. *You've done it now,* Mallory thought. He braced himself against his chair, preparing for the worst, but instead of leaping at him Evans just slumped in his chair, glassy eyed.

"We follow the Rusałka line." His voice was soft, almost too quiet to hear. "We're all exhausted, so both of you get some sleep and meet me in the Cape of Good Hope after sundown."

The three of them stood up and walked out, each heading in a different direction. Nobody in the cafe paid them any mind; it was as if they'd never noticed them in the first place.

<u>Chapter Five</u> – Too Close For Comfort

Thaddeus

"So that's how that works," he marvelled.

The desk was littered with books on the biology of nocturnal animals, specifically predators. He'd carried out a bit of cursory research online but the search engine algorithms just kept throwing up misinformation or sponsored links; nothing that had been able to help him.

Fucking capitalism is ruining the world, he'd thought angrily. Instead of letting the digital dead-ends lead him to despair, he'd pulled out his trusty library card. The new library in the Westgate Centre was a favourite haunt of his, especially when drafting the early scripts for his Tad Talks. He much preferred this particular method of research; walking through shelves and shelves of books, hoping to uncover that crucial piece of the puzzle always made him a bit giddy with excitement.

Thaddeus Thane, Academic Adventurer Extraordinaire!

He smiled as he worked, noting down the ways that nocturnal creatures were adapted to their environments. Thad wasn't sure why he'd focussed so hard on predators, aside from his unusual experience the other night; something primitive told him that the mysterious woman was hunting him.

"Calm down," he told himself softly. "It might've just been a trick of the light on contacts or something."

As much as he wanted to believe the reassurances that he limply offered, the weight of the faces on his desk tipped the scales firmly in the direction of fear. Without any shadow of a doubt, something was happening in the city and the Eyeshine Lady had been part of it.

A faint shadow fell over his book as someone approached.

He glanced up from his research and looked at the pretty young woman standing over him; she had beautiful eyes and a kind smile, although it was clear at a glance that she'd not been sleeping well. He gave her a shy smile.

"I'm sorry to interrupt you, but do you mind if I sit there?" She gestured to the empty half of the table that Thaddeus was working on. "I know most of the other tables are free but I would feel better sharing. Sorry, I've only just realised how weird that sounds."

"No need to apologise, and sure thing. I always work better with someone else around, so I understand." He returned to his books as she took her seat. *Don't stare,* he told himself, although he was curious about what she was reading; most of the stack of books she had in hand had titles that mentioned faith and death.

"Sometimes I mutter as I read," she said quietly, "so if it's a problem do say so and I'll move."

"I'm a bit the same, especially when I get really focussed, so no need to worry about it."

"Thank you." Then after a momentary pause, "I'm Jess, by the way."

"Pleased to meet you. I'm Thaddeus."

They each continued to work in silence for almost an hour, with Thaddeus excitedly making notes about the sensory capabilities of owls, cats, hyenas, and a wealth of other creatures. He shivered as a chill ran down his spine and he shook his head to dissipate the sensation.

As he did so he caught sight of something that set his heart racing.

They were being watched.

He risked a sideways glance at their observer. A couple of tables over was a deathly pale woman with bleached blonde hair and faded clothes just standing there, staring at them. Her eyes unnerved him the most; the irises were almost entirely devoid of colour. He looked back down at his notes for a few seconds and then flicked his eyes back to the woman.

She still stood there. He noticed that she was taking shallow, quiet breaths. *Oh great,* he thought, *there must be some new drug flooding the streets.* Then he saw the knife strapped to her thigh and looked nervously at Jess; she seemed completely oblivious to the stranger's presence.

She took a few steps closer, walking carefully and softly so her footfalls were completely silent. Thad sat stock still, unsure of himself. He didn't think the woman would harm him, not in such a public place, but he couldn't put the creeping feeling of unease out of his mind.

His aunt had once told him that if somebody was threatening him with a knife, then it was unlikely that they would stab him. The real danger, Arabella had said knowingly, was the killer you never saw coming; the one who would say nothing, walk over, and stick you without so much as a second thought.

Courage, Thaddeus.

He turned to look at the slowly approaching woman and stared directly into her faded eyes. Her brows raised in surprise and she turned to look behind her, as if she somehow expected Thaddeus to be looking right through her. When she found no-one there and turned to face Thad once again she saw that he still held her gaze, a frown on his lips.

His frown slowly settled into a scowl and the pale woman, now seemingly in a state of panic, took several hurried steps backwards. She bumped into a bookcase and several volumes fell to the floor with a clatter and thud that resounded throughout the reading room.

The woman swore under her breath, turned on her heel, and sprinted towards the exit, dodging people whenever she encountered them; people who, strangely, did not seem to notice her. Once she was out of sight, Thaddeus replaced the books she'd knocked down.

"What the fuck was that all about?" he mumbled as he tidied the last of the volumes away. He turned to Jess, who had risen from her seat to assist him. "Did you see that?"

"Sorry, no, I wasn't paying attention. What happened?"

"Oh, just some weird woman staring at us. I stared back and it freaked her out so much that she ran away. You really didn't see her at all?"

"No. I didn't see anyone. What did she look like?"

"Pale, almost bleached. She was wearing a long faded coat and she had...," he thought better of mentioning the knife. Jess looked at him, waiting for the end of the sentence. "Really weird eyes. Super freaky looking, for sure."

"Freaky how?" Her voice was sharp, insistent.

"They were almost colourless, with massive pupils. She must have been on drugs; nobody could have pupils that big naturally."

"Was that it? Just big pupils?" Jess asked, leaning in a little closer.

"Yeah. Why?"

"I... um..." She glanced down at the books Thaddeus had been reading, her gaze settling on a picture of a cat with its eyes aglow. She tapped her finger on the image and looked back at Thad. "Was there, I mean did she... Did her eyes look like this?"

"No."

"Are you absolutely sure?" she asked, almost tearfully. The panic in her voice was plain and Thad placed a hand on her shoulder to calm her. "Maybe I'm just going crazy."

"You're not, Jess," he said gently. "Please tell me what you've seen."

Thaddeus stood back and looked at his handiwork. One entire wall of the garret was covered in a vast map of the city, with the missing persons reports surrounding it like a grim corona. Colour coded pins littered the map, charting the disappearances in chronological order.

"There are so many of them," he said sadly. He let his eyes slip out of focus and stood before the map for a few moments, his vision drifting aimlessly over the pins. Eventually he gave up and threw himself angrily on to the bed. "Nothing. Absolutely nothing!"

He'd hoped that charting everything out visually would allow him to spot something that he'd missed; maybe a pattern or series of movements. He thrashed aimlessly in frustration, scattering the pillows as he did so. The pins were arrayed randomly across the map, with no rhyme nor reason. He'd assigned each date a colour, hoping to see some sort of motion, but adjacent pins were as likely to be the same colour as not.

"It's random. Completely fucking random!" He leapt to his feet and began pacing back and forth around the garret, muttering to himself. He stepped carefully around the scattered cushions as he did so, not bothering to pick them up. There was a distant ping as an email arrived, but he ignored it.

If only you could see me now, he thought as he passed the picture of Arabella Thane for the fifteenth time. Thad glanced at the computer and saw that he'd been sent a link to the photos taken at Poppy's show.

I've not heard from her, he thought dejectedly. *Maybe she was just being nice.*

He'd expected a text from her, or at least a message on social media, but he'd received absolutely nothing. Thad had considered reaching out to a mutual friend, just to check on her, but it was the middle of show season and she was probably just taking a break from it all for a few days. Besides, he didn't want to get a reputation as one of *those* guys.

"I can take a hint," he said. He bounced on the balls of his feet, unsure of what to do. His next instalment of Tad Talks was supposed to go live in a week and he'd barely recorded anything; he'd fallen into an obsessed spiral with the Eyeshine Woman.

His conversation with Jess hadn't helped that particular fixation either. She'd told him that she'd been followed twice now by a woman with eyes that shone in the darkness. When pressed on the issue, though, she'd admitted to having a mental health crisis that had culminated with a trip to the hospital some days earlier. She was an unreliable source of information at best but something made Thad want to believe her, so they'd exchanged numbers just in case.

"Take a breather, Thaddeus. Everything will seem clearer after a nice cup of tea." He popped the kettle on and decided to review the show photos whilst the leaves steeped in the pot.

He opened the link and began to idly flick through the photos, occasionally pausing to enjoy one or two action shots. There were a few audience reactions in there too and he almost skipped past them until he saw the Eyeshine Woman in the front row.

She was looking at Poppy during the Blood Shower act, leaning forward in her seat with eager, hungry eyes. The exact same eyes that Thaddeus had seen from his front door.

Shining eyes.

What curdled his blood and sent fingers of ice up his spine, however, was not the woman's eyes. No, not hers but those of the men sat either side of her; they were exactly the same. Their skin had the same pallor and all of them held their fingers in hooked, almost predatory stances, as if they were preparing to strike.

Thaddeus flicked though the other audience photos and checked the eyes of each and every person in the theatre that night. After combing through all the photos he came to the conclusion that the Eyeshine Woman was not unique; there were six others just like her.

Seven people, all with the same unusual contact lenses? He scoffed at the unlikely scenario. *I think not.* He turned to look at the pin board, and suddenly it clicked. He'd assumed that someone was driving around the city in order to cover the distance between disappearances on the same night, but that now seemed like the wrong conclusion.

"There's more than one of them," he said softly. "This isn't a kidnapping spree; it's a hunting pattern."

Now that he could see clearly, he noticed a second, far more horrifying aspect to the pattern; the more recent the date, the more disappearances on that night. The difference was slight a few weeks ago, but the increase was creeping up until the most recent wave of disappearances was almost ten more than the previous.

This is getting worse, he realised.

He looked at the colour key for his pins and smacked his forehead in frustration; he'd been so focussed on the geographical pattern that he hadn't seen the wood for the trees. The missing persons reports were filed on different days but there were only disappearances on specific nights, no less than five days apart.

He pulled up an events calendar for the city. A quick check confirmed his hunch; the Eyeshine People were hunting at particular venues and events. He nodded to himself, pleased with his deduction. He pottered over to the kitchenette to pour his horrendously stewed tea.

"The next one is this coming Friday," he said as he scanned the calendar. "Maybe I should go along."

His computer dinged brightly once more; another email. He changed tabs and his heart beat a little faster when he saw that it was an automatic missing persons alert. The name, Abigail Richards, was not one he recognised. He excitedly clicked on the link and crossed his fingers as he hoped it would prove his hunch right.

It took a few seconds to load up the page, and when Abigail's photograph filled his screen he let out a shocked sob and dropped the cup. He didn't even notice as it shattered on the polished wooden floor; he was transfixed in horror at his computer.

Poppy never made it home.

Chapter Six – A Hell of a Memory

Mallory

Mallory pinched the bridge of his nose and tossed a handful of painkillers into his mouth before stepping into the shower. The irregular sleep schedule and Evans' demanding investigation methods were taking a toll on him.

The usual headaches are bad enough, but this might actually kill me.

The water was pleasantly cool and he took a mouthful to swallow the pills before he cranked up the heat. His hands were smeared with paint, charcoal, and ink; some of it swirled down the drain in a kaleidoscopic whirl as soon as he put his hands under the flow. The rest came off with some soap and elbow grease as he continued to cleanse the layers of sweat and grime from his body.

Good god, I hate being sweaty. He tried not to think of his surgery, some years earlier, when he couldn't wash properly for over a week. He'd despised everyone and everything during that time, but was pleased with the results.

Once clean, he shut off the shower and stepped out into the hotel bathroom; it was surprisingly spacious given its central location, but the Ministry didn't skimp when it came to travel expenses. He looked into the mirror, frowning slightly at the stranger staring back at him. Mallory stroked his chin and cheeks before tipping out the bowl of hot water that his shaving brush had been standing in.

The shaving set had been a present from his older

brother, Francis, when Mallory had first come out. He smiled as he mixed up the lather in the bowl; he didn't get to see his brother as often as he liked, but when he did it was always a raucous occasion. Both men were employed within the Ministry, but Francis was often sent overseas.

Mallory shaved with a practised hand, swift and steady, then got dressed in his usual outfit; a William Morris shirt, wool trousers, sturdy boots, and a square-ended tie. It was too warm for his usual loden jacket, but he stashed it in his satchel before popping his favourite yachting cap on his head. He left his hair hanging about his shoulders rather than tying it up, but kept a few ties on his wrist in case his particular skills were needed.

There was an unexpected knock at the door to his room. He paused, one hand on the handle. His fingers trembled slightly; his condition always made him feel slightly vulnerable in situations like this.

"Marsh, I know you're in there!" Evans' voice rang in his ears, a little louder than necessary. "Open the door, or I'll knock it down."

"We aren't supposed to be meeting for another hour and a half," Mallory grumbled as he let Joseph in. He looked the bleached blonde woman who followed up and down. "Charity?"

"Who else would it be, Marsh?" Evans said, the exasperation in his voice clear as day.

"It's me Mallory," Charity said gently. She chewed at her fingernails as she looked at Evans.

"We don't have time for this," Evans said sharply. "We've got a lead on an abduction. Marsh, bring your equipment."

Mallory's shoulders sagged and he felt more

exhausted than ever. *I'm tired of this prick ordering me around.* He let his anger linger for a moment and drew strength from it. Rallied, he picked up the satchel and slung the strap over his shoulder, before looking defiantly at Evans.

"You can't run me ragged like this, Joseph. I have to rest, recover, before I can-"

"You will use your abilities as the operation dictates, Marsh, whether it's hard for you or not. You might think that you're a special case, but you're not!"

Mallory drew himself up to his full height, which was still almost a full foot shorter than Evans. *Know your worth, Mallory.* His brother had told him that the last time they'd spoken.

"How many Shrieks are there in the Ministry, Joseph? Twenty? Twenty five? How many in the general population? Of course, your Lamplight training makes you a bit of a standout, but you are replaceable.

"But how many Artists are there? How many have there *ever* been? Hell, broaden it to Sleuths in general; how many does the Ministry have?"

Evans was silent, whilst Charity paced behind him.

"There's just one." Mallory smiled smugly. "I'm the best you've got and the only one of my kind; how about a little respect here and there?"

"You don't need to hear to draw, you jumped up little shit!" Evans growled. Charity grabbed his shoulder as he stepped towards Mallory. "Let go of me, Walpole!"

"Don't." Charity said. "Joseph, what do you think they'll do to you if you harm him?"

Evans stood trembling between Mallory and Charity, seething with rage. Mallory saw Charity's grip tighten just a little as he went to move towards the Artist.

"She's right, Joseph, and you know it." He took a step back and held his hands up in a gesture of peace. "I don't want to fight all the time, but I do need to rest or else I'm no good to you. I'm already packed up and good to go."

He tapped the satchel for emphasis and Evans seemed to relax slightly. Charity let go of his shoulder and the three of them left the hotel room. As they walked down the corridor Evans told them both where they were headed; Bulwarks Lane, in the city centre.

"How old is the site?" Mallory asked.

"A few days. Will that be a problem?"

"Not at all. At least that means it won't degrade much in the half hour it'll take to get some dinner on the way."

Charity was unusually quiet as they walked towards the abduction site. Her fingertips rarely left her mouth, and she mumbled around them as they ordered at a kebab van that was on the way. Mallory grabbed a handful of condiment packets and stuffed them into a side pocket of the satchel; ketchup, brown sauce, mustard, salt, pepper, vinegar.

"I see you're learning how to eat on the go," Evans said, not unkindly. *He's a changeable bastard, that one,* Mallory thought as he tucked into his kebab. Both men ate as they walked, vocally enjoying their food.

Charity, on the other hand, was simply picking at her small order of chips. She was nervously looking left and right, visibly shaken. Her footsteps were uneven, and she stopped more than once.

"What's wrong?" Mallory asked as he discarded his empty kebab box into a nearby bin. "Something has clearly spooked you."

Charity muttered something just as a bus rumbled past. Evans winced slightly as the driver sounded his horn. *Not that bloody invincible are you,* thought Mallory before he realised that he'd missed the answer to his question.

"What was that?" he asked. "I couldn't hear you over the bus."

"He *saw* me," she said, almost on the edge of tears. "I'm sure of it."

"When you were invisible?!" Mallory couldn't believe it. "Maybe he was looking at someone or something else, or-"

"He fucking saw me, Mallory!" Charity yelled as Evans shook his head and rolled his eyes.

"She gets like this sometimes, Marsh. You get used to it."

"Why don't you believe me?"

"How could he have seen you?" Mallory asked carefully. "I'm not saying he didn't, and I do believe you, but I just can't understand how."

"I don't know." Charity hung her head sulkily as they turned on to Bulwark Lane. "Maybe he's a Tab?"

"Fuck off, he is not a Tab!" Evans said sharply. "They're extinct, Walpole; the last one died decades ago. Don't you think the Ministry would know if there was one in Oxford?"

"Mistakes get made," Charity said.

"That they do," Evans muttered darkly, "but a Taboo going unnoticed is pretty much impossible. Maybe he heard you breathing; we find new Shrieks all the time."

"Maybe," she conceded quietly, "but I still think you're wrong."

They continued down George Street for a few minutes in silence. Evans held up a hand when they reached a narrow alleyway.

"We're here."

Mallory took a deep breath as he pulled his sketchbook and charcoal from the satchel. He rolled up his sleeves to keep them clean; once he was under he would neither care about nor notice anything but the past.

"Remember, Marsh, we want as clear a picture as possible of who or what is doing this." Evans paced to and fro, keeping an eye on either end of the narrow lane.

"Are you starting to agree with me, Joseph?" Mallory asked with a smile. "After all, this looks a bit dry for a Rusałka lair to me."

"Well, I'm sure your masterpiece will enlighten us." He looked around, realising that the two of them were alone. "And she's gone again. I hate it when she does that."

"You didn't hear her go?"

"This may surprise you, Marsh, but sometimes things do escape my attention. I'm good, but I'm not God."

Mallory paused for a moment, looking up at Evans. "Do you believe in God, Joseph?"

"I used to." His face darkened and he absent-mindedly scratched at the Lamplight tattoo on his forearm. "Enough talk, get to it."

Mallory nodded, selected a clean page, and took a piece of charcoal in hand. He closed his eyes and let his mind drift, aimlessly at first until he felt the

Tangle; the chaotic substrate of the universe and source of all things supernatural.

He found his place and time in the disorienting weblike whirl and, sure enough, there was a Knot.

"Such damage," he muttered softly as he fell into the fractal pattern of enmeshed threads. Knots only ever formed during traumatic events, as the human mind sent ripples through the Tangle; both forward and backward in time. Sleuths relied on Knots to ply their skills whereas Seers, for better or worse, could read the Tangle anywhere.

Mallory gasped as his vision snapped into focus. He was still standing on Bulwark Lane, but everything around his immediate surroundings was blurred and obscured. Sound drifted in from the shifting horizon, and he looked down the lane towards George Street. Although his hands were empty here, he knew that back in the real world they would be sketching feverishly.

Two people, a man and a woman had entered the circle of clarity. Mallory was careful to look at each face; he tried to discern the details even if he could not comprehend the whole.

The two seemed friendly, although the man's eyes glinted slightly in the pale light. *Catlike,* Mallory thought. As he positioned himself a little closer to the woman in order to catch the eyeshine once again, the man brought one hand around in a sharp, swift arc.

It flashed across her throat, almost taking her head clean off in the process. The Lane was splattered with blood and the man leapt on her, a frenzy upon him. Mallory couldn't tell if it was the blood or flesh he was most interested in, but he was feeding nonetheless.

His stomach rolled and roiled as he came crashing out of the tangle and back into the real world. He took two staggering steps away from Evans and vomited into the gutter. After a few minutes and several shuddering breaths, he felt well enough to look at what he'd drawn.

The charcoal was an accurate likeness of the woman in her moment of death. A calm look was on her face and he had used several packets of ketchup to illustrate the sheer carnage of the moment. There was no detail on the face of the man, aside from the glinting eyes.

Evans raised his eyebrows in horror as he looked at the artwork. Mallory closed his eyes to shut out the drawing, wishing that he could wipe that awful scene from his memory just as easily.

"That's Abigail Richards," Evans said. "She went missing recently."

"Well, we know what happened to her now."

"I don't understand how nobody found anything after such a grisly death!"

"I'll tell you one thing, Joseph," Mallory said, getting to his feet. "That was not a fucking Rusałka."

"What was it, then?"

"I have no idea, but whatever it was, it didn't just kill Abigail Richards." His stomach turned over again. "It devoured her."

Chapter Seven – Parlour Tricks

Ivy

"They're out in force tonight, Irving," Ivy said as she rubbed her eyes. "I've had eight reports of human bites from the John Radcliffe already."

It was her fourth night in a row as on-call doctor at the Warneford, and the second time that week working with Irving Adams. They had been sitting silently in the break room for a while, with Ivy discreetly observing her colleague out of the corner of her eye. Even the outbreak of violence that seemed to be spreading through the city did not disturb his unflappable demeanour; it was business as usual as far as he was concerned.

"Don't worry, Ivy. I'm sure it's just some new internet fad or some university prank gone awry. Things will settle down soon." His voice was firm, if quiet, and Ivy felt herself relax a little at his words. "See, you look better already."

Still, that little voice in her said, *something is going on here.*

"I suppose so, but I've got a feeling that things are going to get worse before they get better."

"Hmm, if you say so," Irving said testily, and a frown crept on to his face as he checked his watch. "I should go about my rounds. Will you be here if I need anything?"

"Yeah, I'll be here Irv. I'll try not to fall asleep." As if to emphasise her point, she stifled a yawn. "I'm glad tonight is my last one on rotation for a while."

Irving nodded and left the room. Ivy lingered for a

moment before rising from her chair and shutting the door; the razor in her pocket slapped her thigh as she walked. Although she would certainly lose her job for having a weapon on her, the presence of the blade made her feel just a little bit safer.

Edgar's message had still adorned the message board when she returned home after her first shift with Irving. In her sleep deprived state she had ignored it, but upon waking that afternoon she had sat down with both him and Michaela to talk about what had happened.

The conversation had not gone well.

Edgar had tried to mediate between Michaela and Ivy, but things soon disintegrated into a shouting match, with Michaela storming out of the Parlour to work on her next book. They hadn't spoken since, but her parting words still echoed in Ivy's head.

"I'm only trying to protect you, Ivy, just like I always have!" Michaela had yelled, spittle flying from her mouth as her glasses slipped down her nose. "Where would you be without me?"

Dead, she thought. *That's where I'd be.*

Ed had lingered after Michaela had left and he'd encouraged her to keep the razor on her person, just in case. He'd wrung his hands anxiously and shuffled his feet as he spoke; Edgar was a particularly nervous man, prone to catastrophic predictions and obsessions. She'd carried the razor to placate him, even if he was jumping at shadows.

"I can't let your conspiracies and paranoia get into my head, Edgar," she said softly as she fingered the folded blade. "I need you to be strong for all of us."

She contemplated taking her lunch break then and there but decided against it; Dr Adams might need her help with one of the patients. *Maybe we can have lunch together,* she thought. *That would be nice.*

"I don't like him."

Ivy glanced over her shoulder at the sound of Michaela's voice, but she was alone in the break room. She sighed heavily and placed her fingers on her temples.

"I am Ivy Livingston. I am in the break room at the Warneford Hospital, and it is one thirty eight on Saturday morning. I am here and I am in control." She repeated this mantra a few times and then, as much to fill the silence as anything else, flipped on the television.

She flicked through the channels, one after another, and scowled at the complete lack of watchable programming. Everything was either too stupid or a rerun or some horrible tale of murderous insanity; nothing appealed to her.

Television does not cater to the insomniacs, doctors, and other night people.

She paused and smiled when she saw the familiar face of Carl Sagan. Ivy turned up the volume and settled in to watch an episode of Cosmos. The door opened and Claire, one of the nurses, walked over to make herself a cup of coffee.

"Oh god, not more space stuff!" Claire shook her head as she stirred the liquid in her cup. "It's been all over the news, the radio, and the internet; space this, eclipse that. I'm sick of it, Ivy, I really am. Can we watch something else?"

"Sure, you can choose." Ivy handed the remote to Claire, who slumped into an armchair next to her. "I think all the space news must've passed me by; what's happening?"

"Oh, there's an eclipse coming, though I'm not exactly sure when. They say that Oxford will be slap bang in the middle of the darkest part; just what we need, more weirdness to get people worked up."

"Tell me about it," Ivy said with a conspiratorial smile. " The John Radcliffe have had eight human bites tonight!"

"It's twelve." Claire's voice was even, but the mug trembled slightly in her hand. "Twelve bites; that's unheard of, isn't it?"

"I suppose so, but Dr Adams did say-"

"My brother's housemate is missing."

"Oh, I'm sorry." The suddenness of Claire's words caught her flat-footed, but she regained herself quickly. "How long for?"

"Eighteen days. His friends say he went off with some woman he met at a club and nobody's seen him since."

"Have the police looked into it?"

"My brother filed a missing persons report, but he hasn't heard anything. Typical police, if you ask me." She took her sip of her coffee. "My neighbour mentioned that someone was knocking on her door a few days ago, right in the middle of the night.

"Something bad is going on in this city, Ivy." Her eyes lowered to her cup. "Something really bad."

"I..." Ivy hesitated, unsure of how honest she should be. "I had a case in the JR a little over a week ago that unsettled me, and I've been on edge ever since. Hell, the other evening I was certain there was someone in my house with me, but I couldn't see anyone."

That's not quite true, is it?

"What, like a ghost?"

"No. It was more human than that; a bit like the old

invisible man films, you know?"

"Damn, Ivy," Claire said with a small chuckle, "maybe you should be a patient rather than a doctor."

"I do wonder about that sometimes," she replied with a smile. "It's not happened since, though. It must've just been that case I mentioned. By the way, have you ever heard of an artist called Mal-"

She stopped short as she glanced up and saw Irving standing in the doorway, stock still and staring at her. She smiled at him.

"Dr Adams, I'm sorry, I didn't see you there. How were the rounds?"

"You shouldn't be discussing cases from the other hospital, Ivy. You know that."

"Yes, of course. My mistake." Ivy looked at Claire, who raised her eyebrows slightly before draining the last of her coffee. She quickly rinsed her cup and made her way back through the door, past Irving. "Did anyone give you any difficulty?"

"No, no problems at all. A patient was actually discharged into the housing services about half an hour ago."

"It's a bit late for that, isn't it?"

"You know how they are; it takes an age for them to sort anything out. I'm going to my office to deal with some paperwork; will you be here if I need you?"

"Of course. I'll have my lunch now, but do give me a holler if you need anything."

Irving nodded and walked off down the corridor towards his office. Ivy realised that the door was still open and, with an exasperated grunt, crossed the room to close it.

Why does he never shut the fucking door? she thought angrily.

"Because he's a creepy creep who stares at people instead of talking to them." Michaela's voice was louder than before. "Don't you roll your eyes at me, Ivy Livingston!"

"I am at work, Michaela! You know that's a boundary."

"It's an emergency, Ivy."

"It can wait."

"No, it can't!" Michaela's voice was desperate. "Edgar said something terrible is happening and I think he's right. We need to talk."

"Now?" Ivy's voice was strained; dealing with Michaela always exhausted her.

"Yes, now."

"You've got ten minutes." Ivy clicked the lock to the break room shut.

Ivy frowned at the tiled floor of the Parlour; pink and black was a touch too garish for her. Michaela and Edgar already sat around the dimly lit room's table, eyes wide and bodies still. The entire scene always reminded Ivy of a séance.

Not so far from the truth, she thought with a smile.

She mentally prepared herself before she sat at the table with the others. She shuffled until she was comfortable in her chair and took a moment to drink in their appearances.

Michaela Inglewood was Ivy's age but her hair was prematurely grey and a pair of horn rimmed spectacles made her eyes look unnaturally large. She was thin and sinewy but gave off a menacing air; not unlike a rabid dog. She wore a floral print dress and a thin white cardigan embroidered with primroses. She glared at Ivy through her glasses.

Edgar Wainwright was a twitchy, nervous mess of a man. He wore an oversized flight coat over a lurid Hawaiian shirt and bright red trousers. His eyes were mostly covered by the small round sunglasses that he always wore, no matter the time of day or, indeed, night. In the Parlour he had a neatly trimmed goatee and a fashionable faux hawk haircut, but elsewhere he was cleanly shaven. He waved awkwardly at Ivy.

"New look?" Michaela asked.

Ivy nodded. She often used the Parlour to experiment with her appearance before she made any major changes. Today she wore a fitted linen suit with sensible brown oxfords. Her hair was shorter, in a stylish pixie cut, and tinged with pink. She was shirtless, with only a decorative cream and pink coloured bra under the jacket. She glanced at the mirror and smiled approvingly.

"I might have to give this a go."

"Hmm." Michaela was less than enthusiastic. "We'll have a vote on the hair, I think."

"We could vote on the vote," Ivy said sarcastically. "What's the emergency?"

"We're in danger!" Edgar blurted out. Ivy sighed and went to reassure him, but Michaela held up a hand.

"Let him say his piece, and then you can coo over him."

"Gentle as always, Michaela." Ivy always found Michaela too brusque for her taste, but the opposite irked Michaela about Ivy. The two did not get along. "Go ahead, Edgar."

"People are going missing all over the city; there's someone I'm friends with that I'm going to meet tomorrow who has been collecting information for weeks. There's something big happening in Oxford and it's only getting worse.

"This is real, Ivy. I know you're trying to keep your head down and just carry on with your life, but you can't ignore this. The whole business with the man in the hospital was just the start; things are going to get crazy and if you keep on as you are you're going to sleepwalk us right into disaster. We'll end up missing too."

"Edgar, I know that your internet friends sometimes get a bit too excited about these things. Correlation and causation do not go hand in hand." Ivy gave Edgar's shaking shoulder a reassuring squeeze.

"Someone broke into our fucking house!" Michaela was on her feet, her eyes wild. "Are you really going to be so fucking pig headed about this?"

Before Ivy could respond, there was a gentle rumbling sound. Ivy tapped the pocket where her phone normally was and felt a phantom vibration. The others looked at her, waiting for her response.

"I think I just got a text or an email. We can continue this later." She went to stand but Michaela once again held up a commanding hand. "What? This could be important; I need to go."

"Fine, but we'll reconvene after Edgar has more information. Agreed?"

Ivy nodded and Edgar gave an eager thumbs up.

"Have a good evening, Dr Livingston," Michaela said. "And for what it's worth, I'm pleased that we're speaking again."

So am I, she thought as she opened her eyes and returned to physical world. It took her a moment to readjust to her body and surroundings. *Claire was more on the money than she'll ever know.*

She remembered why she'd abandoned the meeting

and fished her phone from her pocket. She keyed in her passcode and found an email waiting for her. Ivy saw that it was from Jessica, the young woman who'd heard the angels. She braced herself and opened the message.

"Dr Livingston," she muttered to herself, "something strange has happened. Can I meet with you tomorrow evening to show you something, please? I have proof that I'm not crazy and that I did hear something that night."

There was an address listed in the email. *This is deeply unprofessional,* she thought as she agreed to meet Jessica, *but then again, so is bringing a weapon to work.*

As much as she wished it to be otherwise, Ivy found herself starting to accept that there was something terrible unfolding in Oxford. *What's the harm in looking into it just a little closer?*

Little did she know just how dangerous things would turn out to be.

Chapter Eight – Fear of the Dark

Thaddeus

Thaddeus hurried up the Cowley Road, glancing at his phone as he did so.

Shit, I'm late! Why did I have to pick somewhere so far away? Thad had published his video on the rash of disappearances two days earlier and the response was, at best, lukewarm. He'd received dozens of comments calling him all manner of names for 'making sport' of the chaos unfolding in the city, but amongst the detractors there were several who'd taken his call to action seriously.

So seriously, in fact, that they'd agreed to meet him in person to help with the investigation. He recognised several of the users as loyal fans of his Tad Talks channel; he hoped that they were genuinely there to help and not just chasing the clout of meeting a minor internet personality.

His bag was chafing his shoulder as he trotted along. He'd made printed copies of his maps, notes, and missing persons dossier for the meeting but it was mostly laden with new purchases that he intended to discuss with his team.

My team, he thought with a slightly winded chuckle. *This is getting out of hand.*

He neared his destination and slowed a little to catch his breath and to wipe the sweat from his brow. He straightened up, checked his appearance in a shop window, and nodded.

"You've got this, Thaddeus."

His quintet of intrepid internet investigators were already clustered around a table when he entered the coffee shop. He would never have admitted it to anyone but a small part of him had hoped for an almost reverential gasp from his team; instead he was greeted with a curt nod from an individual with round sunglasses and a flamingo print shirt. He strolled over and took a seat.

"Hi, everyone, nice to meet you and thank you for coming. I guess I've already missed introductions, but can I just get everyone's names and pronouns, please? Obviously, I'm Thaddeus, and he/him will do just fine."

"I'm Edgar, and he/him also," said the man in the flamingo shirt, "although I'd rather you didn't refer to or perceive me at all, if that's cool."

Fuck me, Thaddeus thought with an inward groan.

"Kaylee, she/they," said a smiling person in a battered band t-shirt.

"Mikey, but you can call me Triple B; my username is BigBadBaddy92. Trip is cool also." Trip reached out for a fist bump. "Yeah, man, whatever pronouns you want, it's all just window dressing to me."

"Harlan, they/them," said a much older American. "For what it's worth, I've looked at the map on your video and I've got a fair idea of what's happening here."

"Do tell," said the fifth person. "Honey, she/her."

"Well, Honey," Harlan said, "what we've got here is a classic case of alien abduction. Bona fide UFOs, without a shadow of a doubt."

This was a mistake.

"I was abducted myself back in 1987," Harlan continued, "so I've got some idea of what we're up against."

This was a huge mistake, Thad realised as Harlan slammed a folder filled to bursting down on the table. He decided to order a pot of tea whilst the supposed abductee outlined the difference between Greys and Reptoids. Thad sighed wearily as he approached the counter.

"Hi, can I get a pot of breakfast tea for table six, please?"

"Of course," the cheery man behind the counter said. "You want any milk or sugar with that?"

"Plenty of both, please."

"Sure thing, boss. If you could give your card a tap, that'll be great, thank you." As Thad paid for his tea, the man looked over his shoulder at the assembled internet team. "Are you some sort of gaming group or something?"

"More something, I think," he looked at the man's name tag, "Ray."

"Ah, like a secret society?"

"I guess. We're looking into the disappearances happening in the city," Thad said, tiredly. "Harlan thinks we've got a bad case of alien abduction going on."

"Nah, it's not aliens man."

"No, it's not." Thad smiled as Ray handed him the tray with his tea. "Thank you."

"I don't know what they are," he said as Thad turned away, "but the Nightwalkers sure as fuck ain't aliens. My guess would be lycanthropes, given the eyeshine."

There was a crash as Thaddeus dropped his tray and whirled around.

"Shit, man, are you okay?" Ray asked. The group at the table was staring at him; Edgar and Trip were paying particular attention.

"Sorry, I'll pay for the breakage, I-" Thad paused to compose himself. "Ray, have you seen one of these things?"

"Don't worry about it, and do you mean a Nightwalker?"

"Yeah, the Nightwalkers. What do they look like?"

"Ordinary people, for the most part, but their eyes shine like a cat's when the light catches them just right. I've seen more than one."

"Where?"

"Right here in Cowley, man. They tend to move in groups, unless they're hunting; then they go alone."

"How could you possibly have seen that?" asked Harlan.

"I live upstairs. I've seen them, both through the window and on the security cameras. They always head up Cowley Road an hour or so before dawn; that's why I call 'em Nightwalkers." Ray leant forward on the counter. "I've never seen one in the daylight, not once."

"That is highly improbable," Harlan said haughtily. "Given the behaviour of the Greys, I'd suggest-"

"Shut the fuck up, Harlan," said Edgar. He turned to Ray. "Have you ever seen a kind of shimmering distortion on your cameras? It would look like tape damage or electrical interference, but it would move across the screen."

"I have, once or twice, but only in the last week or so." Ray waved Edgar over. "Would you both want to take a look at the footage?"

"This is preposterous!" Harlan said, huffing slightly. "I am an expert in my field and will not be ignored like this."

They grabbed their bag and folder before striding through the door and into the daylight. *That's a relief,* Thaddeus thought. Trip came over to join them but Honey and Kaylee remained in their seats.

"I'm gonna be honest," Honey said, "I thought this was gonna be a bit less intense. I'm gonna go. Sorry."

"Me too," said Kaylee. "I thought this was some kind of deep lore augmented reality game or something, but you're actually serious about this. Maybe speak to a doctor, Thaddeus?"

They both gathered their belongings and followed Harlan. Edgar and Trip grabbed their bags and trailed after Ray as he went into a back room. After feeling dejected for a moment, Thaddeus joined them to review the footage.

"This is pretty bad, isn't it?" Trip said quietly.

The four of them had spent almost three hours in the cramped backroom poring over weeks of security footage. Ray had actually closed up the coffee shop to focus on helping them search the grainy images for the Nightwalkers.

After printing out all the frames, including the distortions Edgar had mentioned, they had decamped upstairs to Ray's flat. Trip ordered pizza whilst the others compared the Nightwalkers to each other in an attempt to figure out how many they were dealing with.

"Here," Thad said to Ray as he handed him a bundle of his findings, "this is everything I've got so far."

"Thanks, man. I'm glad someone else is paying attention to this. I've been closing before sunset for a few weeks just to make sure everything is locked up and secure."

"That's smart," Thaddeus said. "One followed me home after a show I was working; she was really fast, but I managed to lose her. At least I think I did, but I could swear she was looking right at me through the peephole in my front door, but that's impossible."

"There's a lot about this that's impossible, Thaddeus." Edgar looked at the distorted frames. Thaddeus tried not to stare at the obvious burn scar on the man's left arm, and focussed on his words instead. "We saw something like this on the security cameras in the John Radcliffe Hospital a while ago. Specifically after a patient described an experience that just struck us, me, as a little bit off and literally moments after that a strange man disappeared from the waiting room."

"Disappeared?" Thad asked. "As in slipped away?"

"Nope, no way for him to do that. He straight up vanished in a windowless corridor." Edgar tapped the table and seemed to ponder something for a moment. "I know how this is going to sound, but I'm certain that there's someone in this city who is, or at least can, turn invisible."

"These?" Ray said, gesturing to the Nightwalkers.

"No. These things are different. I think our invisible man is linked to these things; maybe studying them?"

"Right, so we've got the Nightwalkers and now there's an invisible man too?" Trip asked through a mouthful of pepperoni pizza. "Sensational."

"It's a woman," Thaddeus said softly.

"What makes you say that?" Edgar asked

"I think I've seen her."

"Hold up, hold up," Ray said. "So, even assuming that there is an invisible woman out there, which is hard to believe in the first place, how the fuck did you see her?"

"I honestly can't tell you," Thad said, "but she seemed genuinely startled that I could see her. Nobody else seemed to notice her; just the aftermath in her wake. This was somewhere public, too, with lots of people around.

"There's no way that I'm the only one who noticed her."

"Was she armed?" Edgar asked.

"That's a weird fucking question, Ed." Trip had started on a second slice. "Lads, pizza's getting cold."

"She had a knife, but that's all I noticed in the few moments I saw her. She had a long coat that could've hidden a lot of weapons."

"Wait, wait, was this woman blonde? Long coat, some kind of overalls, all faded black; really unhealthy looking kind of constitution?" Ray asked. Thad nodded. "She came in here earlier yesterday with two guys. They just sat in silence at the table. Wait a moment, I'll get you the footage."

A few minutes later Ray returned with a pen drive and played the security tape for them on his laptop. He sped through a few seconds and then pointed out the mystery trio. The woman seemed to shimmer and distort a little on the tape.

"Yeah, that's her," Thad said eagerly. "Their mouths are moving, but you said they were silent; maybe one of them can mess with sound?"

"I guess, if invisible people exist!"

"That man," Edgar said sharply, "the one in the hat; we've seen him before. He's the one that disappeared from the John Radcliffe. His name is Mallory Marsh."

"Okay, we've got a name; that's a start," Thad said. He was positively bouncing with excitement. "We should start searching-"

"Already tried, I'm afraid. He doesn't exist; he's a ghost."

"Not a ghost," Trip said excitedly, "but a spook, maybe? Like a spy?"

"Could be, Trip. The important thing is that he was interested in a case that involved these Nightwalkers." Edgar briefly relayed the details of Ivy's conversation with Jessica, careful to omit any identifying information.

"That doesn't sound like lycanthropes to me," Trip said with a frown once Edgar had finished speaking. "Not at all."

"What do you think it is?" Thad asked. "And, for the love of god, please don't say aliens."

"If you put it all together, it's obvious." Edgar said, nodding. "Nocturnal activity, human appearance with a few telltale signs, compelling voices, and a reluctance to cross thresholds can only mean one thing."

"Oh my god," Thad said, as the penny dropped. "Vampires."

"Then what does that make us?" Ray said.

"The Oxford Vampire Hunters," Edgar said with a smile.

Chapter Nine – Outside the Law

Mallory

The cafe on the high street was bustling. Mallory sat quietly in a cramped corner and sipped a strong cup of Turkish coffee. The cafe purported to be the oldest in the country, as did a similar establishment across the street, but this was Joseph's choice of venue.

I'm amazed that he handles crowds as well as he does, Mallory thought. Shrieks tended to shun the hubbub of civilisation for the much quieter environments that came with rural isolation; at least until they got their abilities under control. Of course, by that point they were on the Ministry radar and were offered the standard ultimatum.

"Either work for us or be policed by us," Mallory recalled. He'd seen the latter happen to his brother; surprise inspections in the middle of the night by Sleuths, monitoring by Shrieks and Ghosts, and other things that Francis swore never to mention. Eventually they wore him down and he signed on to torment others in exchange for his own freedom.

When they came for Mallory, he'd signed up immediately.

He'd been taken under the wing of his mentor, Elspeth Whist, who'd been his investigation partner for eighteen months until she'd been killed on assignment in North Wales; torn apart by feral werewolves. Mallory had seen it happen and was put on two months of administrative leave, meanwhile the Ministry moved forward with its mandatory registration of all semi-human and non-human persons residing in the Commonwealth.

These individuals, along with humans with supernatural abilities, were collectively known as Exceptions, or Ceps for short. Whist had often railed against this title; she felt demeaned and othered by it. Mallory had tried to stay neutral on the issue, but every time he saw some atrocity committed by an 'ordinary' or 'normal' person Whist's voice would echo in his head.

Why do these people get to be the default?
Who are they to make us police our own?
Look what they do to us and each other! How dare they call us monsters?

When he returned he was promoted and assigned his permanent partner; a Tracer by the name of Teaser Malarkey. The two hit it off immediately and became thick as thieves. They never met a case that they couldn't solve and, much to his relief, she shared his policy on violence only as a last resort.

Mallory pulled out his phone and shot her a quick text to see how she was recovering. *Heal up soon, Teaser,* he thought. *I miss you.*

She was currently still in St Thomas's Hospital in London after getting hit by a car. She wasn't even working a case; she'd been going about her day to day when an idiot blew through a red and ploughed into her.

"Evans not here yet?" asked a woman with blonde hair and faded clothes as she pulled up a seat. She reached out and gave Mallory a complicated secret handshake, confirming his initial assessment; it was indeed Charity Walpole.

"Good to see you, Charity," Mallory said with a smile, "or should it be Agent Walpole?"

"Give it a rest, Mallory. Evans has always been a stickler for ranks and titles, even when we were kids. I guess that's what happens when they rank all one hundred and sixty four of you on a public leader board. He always wanted to be the best." She perused the menu and went up to order.

"Charity," he said tentatively when she returned, " were you also-"

"A Lamplight brat?" Her interruption startled him, but he managed a nod. "Sure was; Subject Number Zero Eight One, Codename Hillgreen."

"Hillgreen?"

"Yup. It's a nod to Cuesta Verde, the neighbourhood from Poltergeist; some of the admin staff were part of a cinema club. A whole bunch of us got film themed codenames." She grinned at Mallory. "If it had been a few years later, I'm sure Joseph would've been Codename Ghostface."

They both laughed, although Mallory's mirth was tinged with worry.

"Talking of Evans, where is he? Is this typical for him?" Mallory asked, looking around. "I'm half expecting a shrill whistle in my ears for going to the wrong 'oldest' coffee house."

"Same here. Oh, marvellous, thank you." A waitress delivered their food to the table, along with a pot of tea for Charity. "I never had you figured for an omelette man, Marsh."

"I like them from time to time, and this place has an excellent selection. Besides, I can't usually have them when I'm on a case with Teaser; she can't bear the smell." He tucked into his eggs with great enjoyment. "You, on the other hand, are absolutely a fry up kind of gal, through and through."

"Guilty as charged," she said happily. "You know, Marsh, you're alright. I know it's Ministry policy to work in pairs, but it's not unknown for a trio to come together naturally. Have you ever thought about that?"

"I couldn't do that to Teaser, the same way I'm sure you'd never split with Joseph." Mallory frowned and picked a speck of eggshell from his mouth. *There's always one, isn't there?* "Have you not heard from him at all?"

"Not a peep."

"No texts or voicemails?"

"I actually hadn't even thought of that, to tell the truth." She rummaged in her jacket before producing the most ancient mobile phone Mallory had ever seen.

"Good grief, Charity, you need to carry something a little more modern."

"Modern tech is too delicate; it doesn't withstand the invisibility."

"Ah. Fair enough. I guess working with a Shriek makes phone calls a bit redundant, doesn't it?"

Charity didn't respond. She was staring at her phone with a look of disbelief. She held it up for Mallory to see; three missed calls from Joseph and a thirteen second voicemail.

"Son of a bitch," Charity said softly. She held the phone up to her ear after keying in the passcode to her mailbox. There was a lot of static, along with a few words that Mallory couldn't quite make out. The screaming that followed, however, was audible even from his side of the table. What little colour there was in Charity's face drained away to leave her looking an even more sickly grey. She hung up the phone and pushed her plate away, appetite gone.

"So," she said with a sigh, "he's dead."

"What do we do now?" Mallory asked as the eggs in his stomach seemed to sour. "Do we go back to London and get reinforcements?"

"No. There were background sounds in that call, and he said he'd found something important before they jumped him. We need someone familiar with the city to help us track him down or we need to catch one of these fuckers and squeeze them until they squeal."

"I'm not sure I'm entirely comfortable with torture, Charity." He looked at her decisively and took her hands in his. "I mean it; no torture."

"Fine." She stood up and tossed enough money to cover their breakfast and then some on to the table. "But if tracking him comes up cold, we do it my way, okay?"

"Sure, but I don't think it'll come to that." He grabbed his satchel before following her out on to the High Street and down Queens Lane. "Where are we going now?"

"To get some local knowledge," she said as he hurried to keep up with her determined stride.

"A tour guide?"

"Nope. We're going to the pub."

Oxford was a city riddled with vaults, tunnels, and underground rooms, with some being so old and cleverly hidden that their location had been lost to the ages. Several of these subterranean locations housed some of the city's more sinister secret societies whilst others were little more than storage.

Deep beneath Broad Street, nestled between the bowels of the Bodleian Library and the cavernous Norrington Room of Blackwell's book shop, was Oxford's best kept secret; the Ichor Merchant. It was

Oxford's only drinking establishment exclusively for Ceps and, by uneasy agreement, a sanctuary for those who the Ministry viewed in a less favourable light.

Charity kept her eyes low as she led Mallory through the back roads towards Broad Street, scanning the meeting point of pavement and building.

"What are you looking for?" he asked as she suddenly slowed. She stooped and pointed to a tiny fairy door set into the sandstone wall. "Isn't that just decorative?"

"Technically it is, but for those in the know it's also a signifier." She crossed the road and gestured to a walled up archway, just big enough for a single person. Mallory approached it and realised that some of the bricks were slightly blue in colour, and some of them matched up with the pattern on the fairy door. Charity clapped him on the back. "Now you're learning to see rather than just look!"

She ran her fingers around the inside of the archway until she found a nook barely bigger than her finger. She glanced up and down the street once more to ensure they were alone and then flicked a concealed switch. The wall slid away, revealing a stone staircase lit by dim electric lights. She quickly trotted down the steps.

Mallory hesitated for a moment and then followed her. He jumped slightly as the wall slid shut behind him. The two of them went down and north, roughly in the direction of Broad Street by Mallory's reckoning. After a minute or two of walking down the cobwebbed tunnel they arrived at a confluence of four other passages.

There was a heavy wooden door before them adorned with a sign that simply read 'The Ichor

Merchant'. Beside the door was a list of house rules that Mallory read aloud.

"No Guns, No Ministry, No Gambling, No Killing, and..." he squinted to read the last one, as it was partly scratched out, "Arabella Thane Is Banned."

"You got all that, Mallory?" Charity asked, more serious than before. "As long as we're in here, we're not on official business; we're just looking for a missing friend."

"I understand." He felt his heart race a little. He'd been to Cep Exclusive venues in London before, but this was the first one he'd seen that was openly operating outside the law. "Are they going to check my bag?"

The door opened and a stern older woman with a shaved head, cat eyes, and hands that looked more like paws stood in their way. She looked them both up and down, shaking her head disapprovingly. She wore a leather jacket that was heavily scuffed and scarred, and clusters of sharp metal points protruded from the shoulders.

"Depends on what's in the bag, don't it?" She stared at Mallory. "Well then, sunshine, I ain't got all day."

"It's just full of art supplies. Paper, charcoal, watercolours; that kind of thing." His voice shook as he realised that this woman was a Sphinx. *She could kill me in an instant,* he thought with a gulp. "Is that okay?"

"Yeah," she said as her face broke into a beaming grin. "No need to look so frightened, lad. I'm just the bouncer. You ain't carrying, are you, Chaz?"

"Just sharps, Spike, same as always." Charity smiled at the Sphinx, who was still grinning. "Spike, this is Mallory Marsh, a friend of mine."

"Pleased to meet you, Marsh, and sharps are fine, Chaz, as long as you don't use 'em." Spike winked at Mallory. "Of course, there is the customary fee to pass; you must answer a riddle."

"And if we get it wrong?" *This is insane.*

"I guess you'll find out, won't you?"

We're going to die here, he thought as his omelette threatened to make a reappearance.

"Lay it on us, Spike," Charity said. The Sphinx took a deep, serious breath before she spoke.

"What looks like a pig and squeals like a pig, but walks on two legs?" She clapped Mallory on the shoulder as he started laughing. "You got an answer, Marsh?"

"A Cop," he said with a chuckle.

"Too fucking right," Spike said as she stepped aside. "Have a nice time, both of you."

Charity led Mallory into the surprisingly large underground room that comprised the main bar of the Ichor Merchant. The patrons were mainly gathered in twos or threes in booths that lined the wall, enjoying both their drinks and their privacy.

Charity waved to the barman who gave her a winning smile and immediately placed two rocks glasses on the counter. He filled them with a lurid purple liquid and handed them to Charity and Mallory as they approached.

"Miss Walpole," he said, "always a pleasure. I don't believe I've met your companion before?"

"This is Mallory, a colleague of mine." She placed the glass back on the bar. "We're not here to drink, Ross. I need to see Lola. Is she here?"

"Your people really don't talk to each other, do they?" He knocked back the purple drink that Charity had refused and looked her squarely in the eye; Mallory was struck by just how vividly green Ross's eyes were. "Lola's away for work; apparently there's a big operation going down overseas and they've called in all available agents."

"Fuck!" Charity swore angrily. "In that case, Ross, I need your help."

"Your friend still owes me for the last time I helped you both. Where is Joseph, anyway?"

"That's the problem, Ross," she said quietly. "He's dead; someone or something murdered him."

"I think we'd better have a more private talk, don't you?"

Ross led them both to a quiet back room. It was plushly decorated and, most importantly, soundproofed. Once Mallory and Charity were settled in, their host sat opposite them, his poison-green eyes alert and focussed.

"Start at the beginning. Tell me everything."

Chapter Ten – Doing the Needful

Ivy

The sun hung low and golden on the horizon as Ivy disembarked the bus. The streets of north Oxford were lined with old trees and their leaves stirred and rustled gently in the evening breeze. Edgar's sunglasses protected her eyes from the creeping finger of glare that filtered between the large, expensive houses that lined Woodstock Road.

I wonder how much these cost, she thought as she walked towards the corner of Staverton Road, where Jessica's flat was located. *More than I'll ever be able to afford, that's for sure.*

Although the leafy streets and shady roads of the city's affluent north were out of her reach, she felt no envy. Her little house in Lye Valley suited her just fine and her neighbours were pleasant, if unobtrusive, which was ideal given her *situation* with Edgar and Michaela.

"Speaking of which," she said to the empty air, "you could've at least gone home and got changed, Edgar."

She still wore Edgar's ridiculous flamingo patterned shirt and maroon board shorts, but at least he'd worn their communal black trainers instead of his usual mismatched high-tops. Suddenly finding herself in unexpected clothing was one of the more amusing aspects of her condition.

Look in the bag, said Edgar's quiet voice. Ivy paused and realised that she was, indeed, wearing Edgar's army surplus backpack. She slipped it from one shoulder and peered inside.

As well as her handbag and one of her summer outfits there was a small perfume sample that served as her travel bottle. She smiled and hoped that Jessica would have somewhere for her to get changed.

She quickly spritzed herself and was enveloped in the familiar scent; the reassuring notes of violet, iris, licorice, and ivy always made her feel much more herself. Both Edgar and Michaela had their own signature scents, but Edgar's aesthetic was so visually stark from either of the women's that he rarely had to rely on it in the same way.

Switching was always tiring for them, but Ivy certainly felt it more when she stepped out after Edgar had been at the front; his nervous nature meant that he was constantly tense and ready for action. Ivy's whole body ached from the stress and strain of being on alert for hours on end.

As she put the perfume back in the bag she found one item that she was not familiar with. It was a plastic tube, about five inches long, with a switch on one end and a cluster of LEDs at the other. She pushed the power button and was immediately dazzled by a rapid strobe light.

"Argh, fuck!" She fumbled for a few seconds then managed to turn it off. The after images lingered in her vision; dark spots burned on to her retina. She blinked quickly and repeatedly, hoping to clear her eyes. "Why the fuck do we have a strobe light?"

For the Vampires, Edgar whispered conspiratorially.

"Vampires!?" she asked with a snort. "Are you fucking kidding me?"

Not kidding, he replied sulkily. She felt him shuffle off deeper into her head, to hide somewhere in the Parlour. Ivy's eyes started to clear a little and she inspected the strobe light once more, albeit with a great deal more care. It had an adjustable focus and there was a wheel that controlled the frequency of the light.

"This is heavy," she said weighing it in her palm, "so it's probably expensive. Where did you get this?"

Silence.

"Was it from one of your friends?" Ivy asked, her voice soft and almost cooing. Edgar was prone to hiding away when he was upset. Michaela would just leave him to it, but Ivy much preferred to coax him back into being sociable.

On this particular occasion, however, he did not want to listen.

She shrugged and popped it back into the backpack. She let the bag dangle loosely from one hand as she walked through the balmy evening towards Jessica's flat. Ivy felt strangely calm about it all, especially given that visiting a former patient at their home could absolutely cause a huge mess for her at work, assuming that it didn't cost Ivy her job outright.

Even in the face of all that, Ivy felt that this was where she was supposed to be tonight. She hadn't trusted her instincts with Mallory Marsh and he'd disappeared. A small part of her was worried about being out after dark but she quickly reasoned that vampires wouldn't need to feed every night.

She stopped dead in her tracks.

She felt around her head for Edgar to see if he was hiding near the front but came up empty handed. *No*, she thought, *those words were all mine.* She started to walk again, her pace quicker than before. Her skin prickled into goose flesh even though the air was still warm.

"Come on, Ivy, nearly there," she muttered. She looked up and down Woodstock Road; aside from the occasional passing car or odd cyclist, the whole area seemed deserted. Given that it was still term time and the weather was fine, it should've been full of people going about their business. "Where is everyone?"

Now that she thought about it, Ivy had noticed the evenings and early mornings gradually get quieter and quieter over the past month or so. She'd heard fewer and fewer people out and about at night too; whilst Lye Valley wasn't as busy as the bustling centre or vibrant Cowley Road, it wasn't a graveyard either.

The pubs and clubs had started closing earlier too, much to Michaela's annoyance and frustration. Her usual circle of drinking acquaintances had transitioned to having invitation only parties at their homes instead of venturing out into the dark. Some of the more reliable club nights and cabaret shows were still going on, although Ivy wondered if the audience had thinned out somewhat.

It's been a while since you've seen anyone homeless, hasn't it? Michaela's voice was not sharp or snide, but genuinely worried. *Something awful is happening here.*

"It really is, isn't it?" Ivy said as she reached Staverton Road. The more she thought about it the less certain she was in her disbelief; Edgar was weird, but he was logical. *Things don't exist,* Ivy thought, *until someone discovers the first one.*

She reached Jessica's block of flats; it was four stories tall and, if memory served, she lived on the top floor. Ivy rang the bell and stood sheepishly on the doorstep in Edgar's slightly surreal, incredibly flamboyant clothing. There was a click and the door opened.

"Dr Livingston?" Jess asked. Her eyes were red and puffy; she'd clearly been crying. They both lingered for a moment before Jess threw herself into Ivy's arms and began sobbing. "I'm so glad you came."

"I said I would, didn't I?" she said softly. She stroked the girl's hair and made soothing noises. "Jess, talk to me. What's wrong?"

"My friend, Jade, who came to hospital with me," she said with a sniffle, "she went out last night and didn't come home. I messaged all her other friends; she's not with them either, and apparently several of them are missing too.

"What the fuck is happening, Doc?"

Vampires, Edgar said softly, and Ivy realised that she agreed with him.

Ivy sat Jessica down in the kitchen of the flat and busied herself making the young woman a cup of tea. She was impressed at how logically the kitchen was laid out and was about to comment on it when the spider plant swaying gently in the breeze on the window ledge caught her eye.

It wasn't a particularly unusual plant and at first she couldn't quite fathom why she was so transfixed by it until she looked past the leaves and cheerily decorated pot, and gasped. The window had been nailed shut, but something or someone had tried to shove it open.

The force had cracked the frame and was letting a gentle, although not inconsiderable, flow of air into the flat.

"Jessica," Ivy asked, kettle still in hand, "who nailed the window shut?"

"I did."

"What happened? Did one of them try to get in?"

"Not exactly," she said. Her voice was quiet and slightly shaky. "I got rid of anything I could use to pry the nails out. I'm glad I did."

"Did you do this to the window?" Ivy asked, shocked. Jess nodded. "Why?"

"The angels came back. I heard them whispering and calling to me. I couldn't do anything to stop myself until they finally went away. That's when I emailed you."

"They didn't break through the window?"

"No. The window in Jade's room was open, yet they didn't come in." She looked awkwardly at the floor. "I know this is going to sound crazy, but I don't think they can enter a building without being invited. Just like-"

"A vampire," Ivy said softly. "Is this what you wanted to show me?"

"No. Follow me."

Jess rose from her chair and led Ivy into her bedroom. The window was nailed shut, much as the kitchen frame had been, although there was no damage to this one. Ivy followed Jessica's gaze through the pane and saw the wall around the sealed kitchen window.

"This is what I wanted you to see."

The wall was covered in deep scratches, as if some awful creature had scrambled its way up the wall to lurk outside the window. Some of the damage was old but several sets of deep, jagged furrows looked fresh.

Ivy felt a bead of cold sweat run down her face. She shivered despite the warmth of the room and realised that Jess was looking at her expectantly.

"Do you believe me now, Doc?"

"Oh, I absolutely do." She thought for a moment before continuing. "I think we should formulate a plan. First things first; do you have somewhere I can get changed, please?"

"Sure, you can stay in here and I'll finish making the tea. That's a snazzy shirt, by the way. Not what I expected you to wear out of office hours, but who am I to judge?"

"It's..." Ivy hesitated. "It's complicated, but I'll explain over tea."

Once she was dressed in her own clothes and Edgar's were safely stashed away in the backpack, Ivy rejoined Jessica in the kitchen. The young woman was still trembling slightly, but she gave Ivy a weak smile.

"Now you look more like I imagined. Your tea's on the worktop, by the way. Sugar is in the caddy if you want any." She waited for Ivy to get her tea and take a seat. "Whilst you were getting changed I messaged a friend to see if I could stay with him for a few nights; he knows what's going on, so I figured that it would be safer with him than here."

"That's very sensible." Ivy was impressed with her pragmatism in the face of the strange events that were unfolding. "I believe I promised you an explanation for the clothes, didn't I?"

"You don't have to tell me if you don't want to."

"No, it's alright. I have a condition that means I have alternate personalities that I share my body with. Their names are Edgar and Michaela; they're nice enough, even if we do have our disagreements at times. I was wearing Edgar's clothing earlier as he had some business to take care of in town.

"The media, movies and television shows in particular, have made a lot of hay about people like me, us, being dangerous. I don't have an evil alter, nor do I switch a hundred times a day; most of the time it's me, and the others are just ordinary people too. Granted, Ed's a little bit weird and Michaela can be a bit rash at times, but they're not monsters. Does that make any kind of sense to you?"

"That sounds completely sane to me." She laughed a little at Ivy's reaction. "I mean it. I'm not unaware of things like DID and related conditions, and I've spent years working on medieval theology, after all."

"Why would that be relevant?"

"It's one of the theories proposed to explain both possession and hauntings."

"Oh. Yeah, I can see that, for sure." Ivy took a sip of her tea and allowed herself to relax. She gave Jess a warm smile. "It's refreshing to meet someone so matter-of-fact about the whole thing. A lot of my colleagues don't know; hell, most of my friends don't know either."

What friends? Michaela said softly.

"Thank you for trusting me." She leant towards Ivy, her face suddenly serious. "Do you have any ideas as to what you'll do next?"

"Regarding the whole vampire thing?"

"Yes."

"I've got an inkling. The night we met there was a man that spoke to Jade in the waiting room before he disappeared into thin air; I think he knows something about what was going on. He gave her a business card; I don't suppose you've seen it?"

Jess got to her feet and nipped out of the room. She returned less than a minute later with the sunset coloured card in her hand. She gave it to Ivy who inspected it carefully. *Now I can finally get some answers,* she thought.

"My friend will be here soon, Ivy," Jessica said, "so I should probably get my things together. Thank you for coming to see me."

"You're welcome. Thank you for being so open with me, and especially for giving me this." She gestured with the business card. "I'll be in touch when I know more. Will you be staying in the city?"

"Yes, only over in Jericho. It isn't far, but it's probably a lot safer than being here." As she was about to leave the room, Jessica turned to face Ivy. "No matter what comes next, promise me you'll stay safe? All of you."

"I promise," Ivy said. Jessica winked at her and then went to pack her clothes. Ivy pulled her phone out of her backpack and began to key in a phone number. "I think I'm long overdue for a little chat with Mallory Marsh."

<u>Chapter Eleven</u> – A Lost Legacy

Thaddeus

Thaddeus kept his strobe light handy as he walked through the rapidly darkening streets. He glanced over his shoulder every dozen paces or so, convinced that he could hear echoing footsteps pursuing him.
I wish I had some kind of weapon, he thought.
It had taken him far longer to walk to Summertown's tree-lined avenues than he'd expected; too many streets had darkened lamps and narrow choke points. *This city is a massacre waiting to happen.* He felt his phone vibrate in his pocket, but resisted the urge to check it until he was safely at Jessica's flat.
It would be all too easy for someone to sneak up on him whilst he was distracted and dazzled by the bright screen. Thaddeus gripped the slim plastic cylinder of the strobe as tight as he dared, drawing almost spiritual comfort from it.
"I hope I'm right," he muttered as he neared the bright lights of Woodstock Road. He'd not had to use the light yet and its effectiveness, whilst based on fairly solid reasoning, was a guess at best. He heard a creaking sound behind him and spun around, his heart in his mouth.
It took a moment for his eyes to adjust and a few more seconds to realise that it was simply a cyclist. He breathed a heavy sigh of relief and let out a nervous laugh. *I'm going to end up in the fucking Warneford before the end of this,* he thought, only half joking.
He made it to Jess's block of flats without incident, although he did stop in his tracks when he caught sight

of a woman walking back towards the city centre; she looked remarkably like Edgar. Something made him want to call out to her, or to see where she went, but he thought better of it. *No need to hassle the poor woman.* He shrugged it off as a weird coincidence and rang the bell.

Jess appeared at the door shortly afterwards and greeted Thaddeus with a quick hug. He was surprised, but not unpleasantly so. The two had been messaging back and forth since they'd met and Thaddeus had genuinely enjoyed their conversation. Upon seeing her in person once again, he realised just how appealing he found her.

Focus, Thaddeus!

"Thank you for inviting me to stay," she said quietly. "I would say that you have no idea how frightened I've been, but I must've told you fifty times by now. It's good to see you."

"You mentioned that you had a friend over; are they coming too?"

"No, she left not long ago; she had other business to take care of in the city. She's meeting someone who might have more information. She'll text me when she knows more." Jess paused for a moment, as if to weigh her thoughts. "I think you'd like her. She's *unusual*, to say the least, but so are we."

"I look forward to meeting her," Thaddeus said. He was distracted and trying his best not to jump at shadows; every passing car and rustling leaf could spell their doom. "We're exposed here; we should go."

"Definitely. How far is it to your place?"

"Maybe a mile, but not much more. I live in a little garret just off Canal Street, not far from the Community Centre. The houses around are squat little things, but my home is at the top of The Jericho Folly; the teetering structure that towers over pretty much everything else for a fair few streets. You know the one I mean?"

"Yeah," Jessica said with a smile. "I know exactly which building you mean. I've often wondered why it was built or who lived there."

"Well, now you know *and* you'll get to see inside." Thaddeus started walking and Jess quickly fell into step. "You'll only see the staircase and my particular little corner of it, but it's still quite impressive."

"I'm looking forward to it."

"Oh yes, I'm sure you're all aquiver with excitement," he said.

"I'm being serious, Thaddeus. It'll be nice to be around someone who doesn't think I'm crazy or paranoid or desperate for attention."

"I don't think that a healthy dose of paranoia is all that bad right now." He glanced down a side street and was sure that he saw someone duck out of sight behind a wall. *Maybe it's just my mind playing tricks on me,* he thought. "You can call me Thad, if you want; most other people do."

"Well, *Thad*, I think that sticking to the main road for now is definitely the best move; I think I saw something in the shadows back there." Jess quickened her pace and move closer to him. She slipped a hand into his. "Do the windows of your flat lock?"

"Yes, but given that we're on the top floor-"

"I had to nail the ones in my flat shut," she said quietly, "and that barely held when they came for me last night."

"They tried to break in?"

"No. I tried to force my way out. They had climbed

up the building and were calling to me. I felt powerless to resist." She slowed for a moment, deep in thought. "No, that's not quite right. I didn't want to fight; it just seemed like the right thing to do. It's like they got into my head and knew exactly what to say."

"The windows have strong locks and sturdy frames; Aunty Bella was incredibly security minded and had a bunch of renovations done. I'm sure we'll be fine. Safe as houses, I promise." He gave her hand an affectionate squeeze. "Besides, if things get a bit hairy, there are metal shutters inside that we can close to go full lockdown."

"Why would she install shutters? Isn't that a bit excessive?"

"I'm not sure," Thaddeus said quietly, his eyes roving back and forth. "I guess I've never thought about it before but now you mention it, it is a really weird thing to do."

"Weird or not, I'm grateful." Jess squeezed his hand this time, and inched a little closer. "I'm pleased I met you, Thaddeus Thane."

"Likewise," he said, although he was still thinking about the heavy metal shutters and the other strange security measures the garret was kitted out with. He glanced down Plantation Road and caught the telltale glint of eyeshine before it vanished. "We should hurry."

They broke into a gentle jog as Thaddeus ensured the strobe light was ready to go. His mind lingered over just how defensible his home was and he wished his Aunt Arabella was still alive; he had so many questions for her, but one in particular stuck in his brain.

Did you see this coming?

The deadbolt slid into place with a satisfying thud as Thaddeus closed the final set of shutters. Jessica was sitting at his desk, reading one of the dossiers that he'd prepared for that afternoon's meeting. She was muttering softly to herself as she went through the comprehensive stack of paper.

Thad stepped away from the window and turned to look around the garret. It wasn't a large space, but it could house the two of them comfortably for a while. He'd stocked the cupboards that morning, and had grabbed a case of bottled water, just in case. *We could wait out a siege if we had to,* he thought with a wry smile.

His looked up at the portrait of his late aunt and beamed, certain in the knowledge that she'd be proud of him for taking someone in during their hour of need. Thaddeus had tried to do right by his conscience for as long as he could remember and could say, with reasonable confidence, that he'd done his best.

I'm no saint, he thought, *but I think a case could be made for me being a decent person.*

"What're you looking at, Thad?" Jess asked playfully. "Is the bed really so interesting?"

"Oh, I'm just..." His words petered out as he realised that there was nowhere comfortable for Jess to sleep, other than in his bed. *There's the box room, but that's always been a bit claustrophobic, and it's safer to be together.* "I'm just, ah, working out the best way to make sleeping on the floor comfortable."

"Is that so?" she asked coyly. She rose from the desk and plopped herself on the bed. She let herself fall backwards, her hair fanned out around her head like a halo. "There's room enough for two, you know."

"I know that. I'm just trying to make sure that you're comfortable and be gentlemanly and whatnot." He bounced a little on the balls of his feet as he felt his face flush. "I should probably stay up and keep watch, just in case."

"This place is a fortress, Thad, and you look dead on your feet." She smiled at the ceiling. "I'm not going to kick you out of your own bed."

"I won't let you sleep on the floor! I'm not that bad a host, you know."

"I never said I'd be doing that. We're both adults, aren't we?"

Thaddeus noticed that her fingers were delicately tracing their way over the covers; back and forth, back and forth. Her touch was so light that the fabric was completely undisturbed. He realised that he was staring but was transfixed.

"Thaddeus?" she asked softly.

"Uh, yes?" he said, blinking rapidly as he tried to regain his focus. "Sorry, I got a bit distracted for a moment."

"I noticed."

"Oh. Sorry."

"I don't mind." Her voice was playful. "In fact, I quite like it."

"I'm not really sure this is the time for that, Jess."

"Why not?" She propped herself up on one elbow and her hair fell in a lazy haze around her face. "We're safe, we're alone, and it would do us some good to... decompress a little, wouldn't it?"

"I guess it couldn't hurt," he said gently as he walked towards her. "I want you to know that this isn't why I invited you here, though. I do want you to be safe, Jess."

"I know, Thaddeus. I didn't expect this evening to end like this either, although a small part of me did hope it would."

She reached out and took his hand in hers. As she did so, the window key slipped from his grasp and clattered to the floor. It bounced loudly once before falling through a crack in the floorboards.

"Fuck, I'm sorry, Thad." Jess joined him on the floor as he bent down to peer into the crack. She grabbed her phone and turned on the torch, illuminating the space beneath the floor. The key glinted in the light, far closer than either of them expected; it rested on a dusty leather surface.

"I think there's something down there," he said. "These boards aren't firmly attached, we can definitely pry them loose."

"Good idea. I'll help you move the bed." She looked at him and grinned. "We're still gonna shag, though, right?"

"I'm up for it if you are," he said with a chuckle, "but I really want to know what that is first."

"Me too, on both counts."

"Great."

It took them a few minutes to move enough furniture to expose the necessary boards and a while longer for Thaddeus to dig out his tool box, but they had the floorboards up quicker than he had expected. When he saw what was down there, he let out a low whistle.

The window key was resting on a huge black trunk, at least five and a half feet long. He grabbed the key and stuffed it in his pocket before the two of them hauled the mystery box out of the floor. Once they had it positioned on the floor he realised that it was a Mayfair Steamer Trunk Secretary.

"Jesus, Thad, this thing alone must be worth thousands!" Jess blew some of the dust off and read the gold lettering that adorned the worn black leather. "Arabella Thane; is that your aunt?"

"Yeah," he replied, still looking down into the space beneath the floor. "I think there's another box down here."

He grunted and strained as he pulled a long narrow chest out by its worn rope handle. It was made of dark green wood and had the words *Ministry of Supernatural Affairs* stencilled on it in white paint. It was padlocked shut. A final cursory glance showed that there was nothing else hiding under the floor, so he enlisted Jess to help replace the boards.

Once the room was roughly straightened out, he inspected the secretary steamer. It was locked shut, but Thaddeus pulled out the ring of keys that had come with the garret and, sure enough, one of them fit.

The chest opened with a creak. There were several leather-bound notebooks stashed in it, along with a collection of knives, leather armour, and an unusual assortment of medical equipment. In one of the drawers he found the key to the green chest. He set about opening it as Jess flicked through one of the notebooks.

"Thaddeus," she said excitedly, "I think your aunt was some kind of vampire hunter!"

The padlock opened with a heavy clunk, and the lid of the box creaked as he lifted it. Inside, padded with straw, were several guns and boxes of ammunition. The weapons looked well-maintained, if a bit old, and there was a yellowing letter stapled to the inside of the lid. The envelope was addressed to Thaddeus; he gasped when he recognised his aunt's handwriting.

He tore it open and joined Jess on the bed, each of them lost in their reading. Outside, the night grew ever darker, and soon the two were nestled against each other, just sitting wordlessly. Thaddeus continued to stare at the two chests with utter disbelief.

Aunty Bella, he thought, *just who the hell were you?*

<u>Chapter Twelve</u> – In the Hydra's Den

Mallory

"This is bad, guys," said Ross once Charity had finished explaining the situation. "This sounds really bad."

"So you'll help us?" Mallory asked eagerly. Charity did not seem to share his enthusiasm.

"In whatever way I can," Ross replied, "as long as it doesn't tread on too many toes or violate my arrangement with the Ministry."

"What, exactly, is your arrangement?" Mallory said carefully. "Just so we're all clear on what kind of help you're willing to give."

"Whatever happens in these walls is my purview, *Agent* Marsh, but everything outside is your jurisdiction. Any organisation of Ceps or mobilisation of force will be seen as terrorism; you know that.

"I'll give you what weapons I can spare, what information I know, and I'll point you in the direction of Evans' killer *if* I can. Anything more than that will bring the righteous hand of the government down on me, and I would prefer to face whatever the fuck is out there a hundred times over than tangle with the Tiger or that lunatic he calls a bodyguard." Ross paused as a thought struck him. "Say, Charity, are you one hundred percent certain that what you're hunting got Evans?"

"You know Joseph," Charity said, "and you know that there isn't much out there that would get the drop on him, so what are you getting at?"

"Joseph always had a complicated relationship with

authority and pissed off more than his fair share of Ministry suits; hell, he was a prick but I respect him to hell and back for that. Maybe he became too much of liability for those upstairs and they decided to deal with him once and for all?

"It wouldn't be the first time they'd set the Dingo loose on one of their own, would it?"

"As much as I hate to admit it, Charity, he's got a good point." Mallory said. "There's certainly a precedent for eliminating agents who... *acted out*, so to speak. Do you think it could be an inside job?"

"No." Her tone was firm and her face set in a hard frown. "Absolutely not. Joseph walked right up to the line at times, but he never did anything to warrant a hit like that. Besides, they'd have told me by now; they won't leave us chasing our tails when people are still going missing.

"So, Mallory, I do not think it was a Ministry sanctioned killing." She picked her glass up and downed the brandy Ross had poured for her. "Whatever killed that girl on Bulwark Lane killed Evans."

"Okay." Mallory took a sip of his own drink, a sour cherry liqueur, and nodded. "We need to be a united front on this, so I'm with you. Ross, do any of the sounds in the voicemail spark any connections?"

"There's no traffic noise nor the chatter of people; that suggests it's somewhere away from the main roads and clubs. What was the time on the recording again?"

"A little after four in the morning. Why?" Charity asked. She tapped her glass.

"There's birdsong." Ross poured her more brandy as he replied.

"And?" She drained the glass in one swallow. "It's called the dawn chorus for a reason."

"There's no need to be churlish, Charity," he said. "I was just pointing out details. It could be relevant, although I'm not necessarily sure how."

Mallory felt the wheels in his brain turning as pieces of the puzzle began to fall into place. He tapped his glass in a gentle rhythm as he went over the timeline in his head.

Evans finds a creature, somehow.

He tracks it for a while.

It becomes aware of him, leads him into an ambush?
He shook his head, suddenly certain that particular series of events was incorrect. He had no proof, but it didn't feel right to him. Mallory realised that the others were staring at him.

"Care to share, Marsh?" Charity said as she sipped from yet another glass of brandy. "Come on, spit it out, Sleuth."

"Okay," Mallory said, more to himself, than anyone else, "Evans picks up the trail of one of these things just before dawn; likely from afar and he homes in on it. He's overconfident and gets too close. It notices him, he tries to flee, and is cornered.

"He realises that there's no way out and calls you, but is killed on the phone. He knows that the message is enough for us to work out where he is."

"What good does that do?" Charity hissed. "You already know what they look like, so that gets us a big fat nothing. Why do I even bother?"

Mallory sat back in his chair and massaged his temples. *I'm missing something; I need to think like Evans. What would he pay attention to?* He sat up sharply.

"The birds are important!" He grinned at Charity. "If we could hear the birds over the phone there must've been hundreds of them!"

"So what? It was before sunrise, that just means that they're..." Her voice trailed off as she finally caught up with Mallory. "They're nesting!"

"I feel I've missed something," said Ross.

"The creatures are nocturnal," Mallory said, "so if they attacked Evans minutes before dawn it was because he found their nest."

"Mallory Marsh, you're brilliant!" Charity leant over and planted a tipsy kiss on his cheek. "Ross, where do birds nest in such large numbers?"

"In this city there are dozens of places. Port Meadow, any of the parks, Magdalen College; too many to list."

"We better start searching." Mallory reached over and shook Ross's hand. "Thank you for all your help, Ross. You'll let us know if you hear anything?"

"Of course, and you're welcome." He noticed Mallory reaching for his wallet. "No, drinks are on the house today. You can repay me plenty by stopping whatever is running rampant in this city."

"Will do." Mallory stood up to leave and was about to open the door when he realised Charity had drawn a handful of throwing knives from the sheath on her arm. "Charity, what are you doing!?"

"Relax, Mallory." She handed the blades to Ross. "Our attentive host is a Hydra and I need a little venom for my throwing knives. Something that paralyses rather than kills, please."

"For you, Charity, of course." Ross's eyes glinted evilly and he swished and swirled the saliva in his mouth before he licked each of the blades. Once they were coated in the viscous venom he handed them back to Charity. She sheathed each of them carefully. "That should be stable for ten days or so. You know where I am if you need more."

"Much appreciated, Ross." She stood up to leave. "When Lola finally gets back from wherever the fuck she is now, can you tell her to get in touch with me? She'll want to pour one out for Joseph and, if she's back soon enough, we could use her help.

"Take care. Come on, Marsh, we're burning daylight."

With a tip of his hat Mallory wished their jovial host a good day before following Charity as she staggered out of the subterranean bar, pausing only to bid Spike farewell. Once they reached street level, the pair realised just how late in the day it was; the golden sun hung low above the horizon and the clouds were little more than pink streaks across the evening sky.

"We should head back to my hotel room," Mallory said.

"Why?"

"We need to formulate a plan before we go after these things, and I would prefer to survive the encounter. Sound reasonable to you?"

"Sure. Rest, reload, and rearm. Lead the way!" She swept her arm in a wide arc, slightly wobbling as she did so.

We also need you to sober up, he thought, although he decided to leave that particular comment unsaid.

"So," Mallory said as he handed Charity a glass of water and some painkillers, "who's Lola? A friend of yours?"

Charity popped the pills into her mouth and washed them down with the water. She'd quickly transitioned from enthusiastically tipsy to a slightly hungover puddle on Mallory's bed. She looked at him with a mixture of discomfort and confusion; it was obvious enough that even he was able to pick up on it.

"What's that face for?" he asked. "Have I suddenly grown an extra head?"

"Do you somehow go through life without paying any attention to the internal workings and politics of the Ministry, or were you just born without a sense of curiosity?"

"That's uncalled for."

"Come on, Mallory, everyone knows who Lola is, and I mean that literally!" She shook her head in disbelief and immediately regretted it. She placed one pale hand against her temple and groaned.

"Clearly not everyone." He dropped into an armchair and looked at her as she struggled to stay upright. *You're as much of a liability as Evans,* he thought.

"Fine," she said, her voice strained. "For the blissfully unaware, uninformed, or uninitiated, Lola is another one of the Lamplight survivors; Subject Number Zero Zero Three, Codename Lolita. She didn't have a birth name, at least as far as she knew, so she took that as her given name."

"Wait," Mallory said as a shiver went up his spine, "are you talking about Lolita Oriole?"

"See, I told you that you knew her!" Charity smiled in mock triumph. "Look at you, paying attention in class!"

"Why are you on first name terms with her?" he asked coldly.

"What's the matter, Marsh? Got something against Lamplighters?" Charity got awkwardly to her feet and walked over to him with an unsteady gait. "If you've got a problem with me you'd better say it."

"Not against your cohort, no."

"Good, because we only had two options; we either complied or died. Not that it mattered much in the end, though." She half sat, half fell into the chair opposite him. "You have no fucking idea what we went through, Mallory, and I hope to God that you never find out."

"So do I, although I'm here to talk if you need to." He gave her a wan smile. "I just didn't think you'd continue to associate with someone like that."

"A Juliet?"

"No," he said, "a Ravenblade. I thought you wouldn't be on board with anything related to deniable ops, given Lamplight and all. It's not a judgement on you or her, though."

"You sound pretty fucking judgemental."

"I know," he said with a sigh, "but it's aimed at the system and those running it, rather than those produced by it."

"We all have to exist within the Ministry rules, Mallory, including people like Ross who pretend that they don't. As long as we play the game we're complicit in the outcomes, good or bad."

"We don't have a choice!"

"Sure we do," she said, "but you want to pretend that you haven't made it. It's the same as it's always been; comply or die. You're a collaborator by choice, so don't act all holier than thou when it comes to Lola, or Wags, or me, or even Joseph for that matter.

"Every drop of blood spilled in the name of the

Ministry stains all our hands, no matter how far removed we are from the actual act." She closed her eyes and settled back in her chair. "Just make your peace with it. Trust me, it makes the job easier."

Mallory was about to respond when his phone rang. The caller was unknown, which puzzled him. *Who even has this number?* He thought about letting it go to voicemail, but realised that it was an easy way out of the spiralling conversation with Charity.

"Hello?" he said.

"Is that Mallory Marsh?" said a stern woman's voice.

"Yes, it is. Who are you and how did you get this number?"

"My name is Ivy Livingston and we need to talk."

Chapter Thirteen – Behind the Curtain

Ivy

Ivy knocked sharply on the hotel room door. The sound of someone getting to their feet filtered through the wood and she smiled; she had arrived almost an hour early to deliberately catch Marsh on the back foot. She could feel Michaela nodding in approval and she tightened her grip on the straight razor hidden in her pocket.

At last, the door opened. Mallory Marsh looked like he hadn't slept in days as he peered through the small gap; he'd kept the security chain latched shut. He raised his eyebrows in surprise.

"Yes?" he asked.

"I'm here, just like you asked." Ivy said. *Why does he look so confused?* "Are you going to let me in or am I just going to stand in the corridor all day?"

"I'm sorry, I'm not expecting anyone. Perhaps you've got the wrong room?"

"For fuck's sake, Marsh, stop acting like you don't recognise me!"

"What's your name?" he asked after a moment of hesitation.

"Are you kidding?" Ivy groaned in exasperation. *This is not what I had in mind!* "I'm Ivy Livingston; we spoke on the phone last night. You asked me to be here."

"You're early," he said, "how was I supposed to know it was you?"

He closed the door momentarily before opening it again, this time without the security chain. He gestured for her to come in. She walked slowly, carefully making note of as many details as she could. She stopped short when she saw the collected artwork on the dresser.

The assorted sketches, drawings, and paintings all depicted scenes of graphic violence. Most of them where in black and white with red detailing to highlight the blood; so much blood. Ivy quickly regained her faculties as her initial surprise turned to fury.

"What the fuck is this!?" She wheeled around and flicked the razor open. "Are you some kind of serial killer?"

"No, of course not!" He seemed unsure of what to say next. He kicked the door shut behind him and reached for his leather satchel. Ivy went to lunge at him but was brought up short by the sharp edge of a blade held against her neck. Marsh saw her freeze and immediately looked at the empty air over her shoulder. "Charity, don't hurt her!"

"I won't," said a disembodied voice from somewhere behind Ivy, "as long as she doesn't do anything stupid. Dr Livingston, would you be so kind as to drop that razor of yours, please?"

When Ivy gripped the blade even tighter she felt the edge of the knife break her skin ever so slightly. Her heart was thundering in her ears and her hands were shaking. The blade of the razor shone in the light, casting a glinting reflection on the nearby wall. A few beads of bright blood trickled down the invisible blade.

"Charity, just let her go."

"Only if she drops the weapon," she said as the knife was pushed in with a fraction more force. Ivy was trying to work out where her unseen assailant's body was. "Listen to me very carefully, Doc. I've been in this situation before and I know that you're trying to figure out where I am. I'll make this easy for you; I am faster and better trained that you can imagine. If you attempt to fight, I will not hesitate to kill you."

"Try it, you invisible bitch!" Ivy hissed as she threw herself backwards, bringing the razor around to where she assumed her assailant was standing. Unluckily for her, she hit empty air and lost her balance. She took a staggering step until something caught her by the neck.

Ivy felt a strong arm lock around her and after only a few seconds of pressure her vision darkened. She tried to curse Mallory Marsh and his invisible bodyguard, but instead the razor slipped from her grasp as she lost consciousness.

Ivy's vision came flooding back moments later as she was being hefted into a chair. She was thrown back with a thud and she realised that her hands were bound behind her back; the bindings felt makeshift, more like a cable tie than a set of handcuffs.

"Please," Marsh said from across the room, "just sit and listen for a few minutes. We don't want to hurt you."

"So why the fuck am I tied up?" She strained and struggled to get her hands free. "What do you think will happen when I get loose, Marsh?"

Marsh groaned and rubbed his eyes for a moment. The door to the bathroom slammed shut, seemingly of its own accord. He walked towards her and sat in the opposite chair. Ivy flailed at him with one of her feet, but only succeeded in slipping in the chair slightly.

Ivy was about to speak when she heard moans of pain coming from the bathroom.

"My colleague is just taking a moment to render herself visible," Marsh said softly, "and as you can hear it is a rather painful process."

"Why throw away your advantage?" Ivy asked.

"Because this isn't a fight, Dr Livingston. I mean it when I said that all we want to do is talk."

"What about your little collection of psycho bastard artwork over there? Are those your day job as a murderer or just a hobby?"

"The day job, actually." He gave her a smile. "I work for the government as a crime scene sketch artist, although that is a bit of an oversimplification. Those drawings are part of our investigation into the rash of disappearances sweeping the city."

"You're with the police?"

"No, not exactly." Marsh was about to continue when the door to the bathroom opened and an impossibly pale woman staggered out. She took a few faltering steps across the room before perching on the bed and smiling smugly at Ivy. "We work for a government agency that is tasked with overseeing anything that falls beyond the bounds of what you might consider normal; the Ministry of Supernatural Affairs."

Ivy let out a snort. Marsh did not seem amused, but the pale woman chuckled playfully.

"Yeah, it's a bit silly, isn't it?" she asked. Ivy nodded. "Why, who could expect you to believe anything we say to you?"

"I don't," Ivy said, but in her heart she was less certain.

"Is an encounter with an invisible woman not

enough?" Marsh asked. "Those paintings and sketches are recreations of the past; I can sense traumatic events through the scars they leave on the fabric of the world. Is all this still not enough proof for you?"

"So you're in the city investigating a couple of disappearances?" she asked. "Is that worth sending in the Magic Squad?"

"To date," the pale woman said, "we have a grand total of three hundred and seven people, missing or dead, one of whom is a close friend of mine. His name is Joseph Evans and he was investigating these disappearances when whatever the fuck is doing this killed him.

"So maybe you should try to take this a bit more seriously, Dr Livingston."

"Did you follow me home the morning I first saw Mallory?"

"Yes, and before you ask, it was also me that was inside your house." She paused, her sunglasses casting dark reflections of Ivy. "We were looking into you because Joseph had a hunch that you were involved somehow; he was wrong and that mistake seems to have rather soured things here."

"You don't say..." Ivy turned her gaze towards Marsh as she tried to wriggle out of her restraints. "Why did you pretend not to recognise me when I showed up here?"

"You were an hour early; you could've been anyone. Why did you arrive when you did? You set the time, after all."

"I wanted to catch you off-guard," Ivy said. "That way you were less likely to have hidden any evidence or got into a head space to lie to me. I wasn't expecting you to fake me out like that; assuming I was a stranger really threw me off kilter."

"Oh my god," the woman said with a laugh, "you stupid bitch, you played yourself? Oh, that's fucking priceless, absolute gold. Just so you know, our dear Mallory's ability to recreate the past through art comes with a little downside; it makes him completely face-blind. He didn't recognise you because he can't recognise anyone!"

Once my hands are free I'm going to smack that smirk off your face, Ivy thought. The woman wiggled her eyebrows defiantly, as if she knew what Ivy was thinking.

"I'm a spy, Livingston, among other things; I can read faces plenty well and I know that particular look. I'll make a deal with you." She pulled out one of the knives that were strapped to her thigh. "I'll cut you loose and you can take a swing at me, hard as you like. I won't move, I'll just take it. In return, I get to hit you. I won't do any lasting damage nor hit you in the face. Once we've got that out of our systems, we make our peace and get on with things.

"Have we got ourselves a deal?"

"Sure, why the hell not?" Ivy leant forward so that the blonde woman could remove her restraints, which she did with one practised flick of the blade. Ivy got up and rubbed her wrists; they were sore but not bloodied. The blonde woman sheathed the knife and stood still, waiting for Ivy to take her shot.

She put her entire weight behind the punch, a mean left hook that sent the blonde woman staggering a step or two after it landed on her jaw. She nodded at Ivy as she spat a little blood into a cup. Ivy smiled in satisfaction despite the throbbing pain in her hand.

"Not bad, Doc, not bad indeed." She straightened

out and squared up to Ivy once again. "I personally favour an open-handed technique; it's less risky than a closed fist."

She suddenly slammed her palm into the soft tissue just below Ivy's ribcage, driving all the breath from her body. She crumpled around the blow and fell to the floor, curled up and wheezing. She flinched when the blonde woman extended a hand towards her, fearing another blow, but was surprised when she was helped to her feet.

"You took that one well, Doc. I know grown men who would've spewed their guts out after a hit like that; you can take a licking, that's for sure." She smiled at Ivy, warm and genuine. "My name is Charity Walpole, by the way. Are we good?"

"Yeah," said Ivy breathlessly, "we're good."

"So, to recap now that you two have sorted that out," Mallory said, "there's a mystery creature or creatures stalking the city at night killing or kidnapping people. The nights are clearly specific, but we can't seem to work out why; there's no rhyme or reason to it at all. Did I miss anything, Charity?"

"Not that I can think of. All our suspects have been dead ends, as have our leads, and we're a man down. Hell, we still don't even know what we're dealing with!"

"Vampires," Ivy said. "You're dealing with vampires."

"See, I told you!" Mallory said excitedly before Charity held up one bleached hand.

"That's all very well and good, you two, but unfortunately vampires don't exist."

"But you work for the Ministry of Monsters or whatever-"

"Exactly. In the hundreds of years that the Ministry has been around, we've seen pretty much everything from werewolves to golems to the Loch Ness Monster. Do you want to know what we haven't seen?

"Vampires. Not a single fucking one. They're a myth, Doc. A fucking children's story."

"For what it's worth, Ivy," Mallory said as he handed the razor back to her, "I believe you."

"Thank you." She paused for a moment. "I'm sorry I called you a serial killer."

"Instead of all this talk," Charity said, "why don't we just find out for certain?"

She gestured to the window. As they had been talking and bickering, the bright day had deepened into soft evening twilight. Ivy tightened her grip on the razor and on her sanity as she looked at her strange new allies. *She might be a bitch,* she thought, *but Charity is right.*

"Sure," Ivy said as she slipped the blade back into her pocket. "Let's go hunting."

Chapter Fourteen – Familiarity in the Freakish

Thaddeus

Thaddeus yawned as he rose from the bed a little after nine o'clock in the morning and crossed the room to open the heavy metal shutters. Even though they hadn't been attacked during the night, both of them had gotten very little sleep. *A quiet night, perhaps,* thought Thaddeus with a grin, *but not an uneventful one.*

The discovery of Arabella's hidden supernatural paraphernalia had not fully distracted them from the building tension and after a brief examination of the contents of both trunks they had fallen into bed together. It had been past dawn when they'd finally glanced upwards at the clock, sweaty and exhausted, but sated.

Jess groaned a little as the light streamed in through the window, and covered her face with the duvet. Thaddeus chuckled softly to himself as he pulled on his pyjama bottoms and a scruffy old t-shirt. He took a moment to check his emails, daring to hope that the evening's performance at the Old Fire Station had been cancelled.

The universe dashed his hopes, as it often did.

"Ah, shit," he hissed quietly. He opened up a blank email to his boss and one of his fellow technicians to ask to swap shifts for the next few evenings, citing a close friend having an emergency. *I'm always super flexible and help out where I can,* he thought, *so hopefully they'll cut me some slack.*

He read through his message once more before sending it, and then sat back in his chair and sighed heavily. He caught movement out of the corner of his eye; Jess was watching him from a little gap in the covers. He winked at her and then set about making a pot of tea.

By the time he was finished pouring for them both she was up and about, safe and snug in his dressing gown. She took the cup with a grateful smile and perched on the window seat, looking out over the surrounding streets.

"I wonder if they took anyone else tonight?" she asked quietly.

"I've got an email alert set up in case anyone mentions a missing person, and the rest of my guys are combing socials looking for anyone that I've missed. They've already turned up a dozen or so disappearances that flew under my radar."

"Your guys?" Jess asked. "You've been putting a team together?"

"Only in the last day or so. There are four of us; me, Trip, Ray, and Ed."

"Five if you count me," she said with a smile. "Do you have a name?"

"For the group?"

"Yeah."

"The Oxford Vampire Hunters."

"To the point, I guess, but I was hoping for something a little bit more fun, like Thad's Lads or something." She took a long sip of tea and grinned. "Last night was a lot of fun; we should definitely do it again some time."

"Whenever you want," he said. "You are very

talented."

"Thank you. You fuck like a girl," she said with an even broader smile. Thad blinked, confused for a moment. "That's a compliment, Thaddeus, from one queer to another."

"I had my suspicions."

"How rich an existence might pass me by if I never wondered or questioned why," she said dreamily. "Or, to paraphrase, being straight looks awfully dull. You never asked if I was seeing anyone before we shagged, by the way."

"That doesn't matter to me," he said, "as long as you're being open and honest with whoever else you're with."

"Ah, an enlightened man," she laughed. "I am of the same mind; love is infinite and I find social norms a bit restrictive."

"You've piqued my curiosity though; are you seeing anyone?"

"No. Not everyone else shares our view of the world, Mister Thane."

"What a shame, Miss-" Thaddeus faltered, realising that he only knew her first name.

"Holloway," she said. "Jessica Evangeline Holloway, if you were interested."

"Evangeline is a hell of a middle name; mine's Eric."

"Thaddeus *Eric* Thane? Good god, what a shame that is."

"My Aunt pushed for Thaddeus, and I'm glad she did." He looked up at the portrait and smiled. "She was more a parent to me than my mum and dad ever were."

"That alone would make me like her, but being a vampire hunter definitely adds something extra, doesn't it?" Jessica stood on the bed to examine the photograph. "Oh my god!"

"What?"

"Thaddeus, where was this photo taken?"

"In here, by the bookcase." He joined her on the bed and peered at the picture. "Why do you ask?"

"Were these her books?"

"Yes. She was a fan of the occult and mysticism in general." He smiled at the thought. "I used to love sitting up here, going through them with her. I was mostly interested in the symbols and illustrations, rather than any of the actual contents; all the same, it used to drive my parents mad."

"Some of these aren't occult, Thad." She gestured at a particular shelf in the photograph. "From what I can see of the titles, these are religious texts."

"You were reading books on faith in the library, weren't you?"

"Uh huh. I'm a theology student."

"You didn't mention that before."

"I didn't want you to get the wrong idea about me. People think that we're all uptight bible bashers, but that isn't all of us. Anyway, to get back to the point I was trying to make; some of these books are exceptionally rare, several out of print for decades. I would've loved to get my hands on them for my doctoral research."

"Oh, they're in that cupboard over there," Thad said casually as he pointed it out. "Help yourself."

He returned to Arabella's copious notes as Jessica pored over the collection of books; both were largely silent as they did so, with the occasional gasp from Jess when she found a particularly intriguing book.

"Apparently," Thaddeus said to her after a while,

"around one in every thousand people has some sort of supernatural gift but the Ministry of Supernatural Affairs only contacts the ones with significant abilities; about ten percent of those with a gift."

"That's a lot more common than I would've thought," Jess said, "although if they only publish the one in ten thousand that would make sense. It's easier to keep people down if they feel isolated. It certainly sounds like your aunt wasn't exactly- Holy shit!"

"What?" Thad rushed over to her. "What's wrong?"

Jessica held up a worn book in her hand. It was a hardback with faded gold lettering spelling out the title; The Final Temptation, by Reverend Edwin Finnster. *That's just one of Aunty Bella's books,* he thought with relief. He put a hand on her shoulder and gave it a gentle squeeze.

"Thaddeus, look at this." Her voice was barely audible and the book trembled in her hands. "Do you have any idea how rare this book is?"

"Not really, no. I assumed that some of her books were valuable, but she rarely spoke of that one; what's it about?"

"Edwin Finnster was the head of a nineteenth century breakaway sect of Methodist Christianity called The Brotherhood of the Light of Jesus."

"Catchy," Thad said softly.

"Yeah, it's a bit of a mouthful. They believed that humanity had a dual nature and the sinful part of us only appeared when the sun went down; as such they did most of their mission work after dark, earning them the name 'Night People'. This," she said as she held up the book for emphasis, "was the work that finally caused mainstream Methodism to sever all ties with him and his Night People."

"What's it about?" He looked at her as she answered, smiling. *Good god,* he thought, *it's really hot when she talks about this.*

"*If* I'm right, and I think I am, this book details Finnster's personal struggle with suicidality; he was a deeply unhappy man whose life was littered with tragedy. He found meaning in faith in his late twenties before skyrocketing to prominence as head of the Night People. Once he had the backing of his followers, who were rumoured to do absolutely anything he asked, he set about searching for the answer to what he referred to as 'The Final Temptation'."

"Death?" Thaddeus asked. Jess nodded. "So this book is his search for eternal life?"

"It's a big part of the draw, isn't it?" She asked absent mindedly. "I've read several sources that all claimed that a single conversation with Finnster could convert even the most stubborn non-believer to his cause."

"This must be a convincing book," he said with a laugh. "You've still not answered my question; how rare is this thing?"

"There were only thirty copies ever printed, and they are all accounted for save one; twenty two were destroyed, three are in the Vatican Vaults, and the final four are in the hands of private collectors. If this is genuine, Thaddeus, this is the last and most important copy of this work."

"Why?" he asked as she carefully opened the cover. He found the answer scrawled in cramped cursive on the first page. "Property of Reverend Edwin Finnster; is this his actual copy?"

"It seems that way." She was already leafing through

it. The margins were filled with more ink in the same hand as before. "It even has his handwritten notes!"

"How much do you think it's worth, Jess?" He paused for a second. "Not that I'm going to sell it, but I should probably keep it somewhere a little bit safer."

"I'm not sure anyone could put a price on it, Thaddeus." She looked at him, her eyes wild with excitement. "This book is absolutely priceless."

Thaddeus brought the blade of the kukri round in a sharp arc at neck height, careful to let the shape of the weapon dictate his blow. He smiled as it hissed through the empty air; another imaginary foe slain.

Jess chuckled softly as she watched from the bed and muttered something that Thaddeus couldn't hear. She winked at him as he practised a few more swings. He smiled in response, both at her amusement and at just how easy handling a weapon was for him. *It's like I've done this before,* he thought, *maybe in an earlier life.*

"So," he said as he tried a more complicated move, "aside from decapitation, what else does Aunty Bella's diary say about hurting or killing these things?"

"Burning, especially with phosphorus or sulphur based incendiaries. Any of the weapons in here," she said gesturing at the secretary steamer, "will give 'a most grievous wound' to our vampires, apparently, because they are coated in-"

"Silver," Thad said with a smile.

"A copper and nickel alloy, actually."

"What?" Thad stopped short and joined her on the bed after sheathing the blade. "Are you sure?"

"Yes, she's quite plain about that. Are you thinking of werewolves, because I saw those mentioned in one of her books."

"I always thought silver killed vampires," he said, "so what about the rest; garlic, crosses, stakes to the heart?"

"Garlic is mentioned as a repellent to bites, if applied strongly enough to the skin. The same goes for horseradish and wasabi, as well as mustard. No mention of stakes or crosses, but she writes extensively on the subject of sunlight."

"Go on," he said as he lay back on the bed. Jess settled in next to him; book in one hand as the other lazily played with Thad's hair. "Oh, that's nice, you can do that whenever you like."

"You're like a giant cat," she said playfully. "So, regarding sunlight, Arabella's notes say that it will destroy a thrall outright, but it only hurts the higher vampires. In fact, she seems to believe that the Master isn't harmed by sunlight at all."

"The Master?" Thad scoffed. "I'm not completely certain that she wasn't mental, you know."

"We both know what we've seen, Thaddeus." She looked at him sternly. "We were fumbling in the dark before, but now we actually have something."

"Your point is well seen, Jess. Please, go on."

"The Master, whoever or whatever that is, is the source of the vampires. If it is killed, she thinks the rest will either die or turn feral. Those that are turned are either higher vampires, with intelligence and greater freedom, or thralls, which operate entirely on instinct when not under direct control of one of the full vamps or the Master himself."

"Makes sense, I guess. Does the blood drinking still apply?"

"Very much so," she said gleefully.

"You're a ghoul," he said with mock disdain. "How is this thing spread? Bites?"

"It actually doesn't specify, but that's what all the mythology says, right? I know some accounts differ but-" She was cut off by a rumble and ping from her phone that was charging across the room. "That's an email. It might be my friend, I should check it."

Thad took the book from her and flicked through it lazily whilst Jessica checked her phone. *Vampires, Seers, Ghosts, Shrieks, Juliets, Hydras, and even the Ministry of Supernatural Affairs,* he thought as his head span a little. *A whole world I never even knew existed was right here all along.*

That thought brought his mind to a screeching halt as it seemed to echo back through time. When he was younger Thad's parents had worked hard to shelter him from anything and anyone that did not fit their narrow world view. He knew that they were just trying to do their best, albeit in a very misguided way.

Then his aunt had burst into his life like a firework and soon he was immersed in a life much richer and more colourful than he'd ever thought possible. He'd met people that his parents would never have let him within a mile of; gay men, lesbians, bisexual transwomen, and so many more. His vocabulary had exploded with new words and wonderful terms and, in the midst of that unchecked expansion, he'd found himself.

Thaddeus felt that same sensation of unfolding and growth now, admittedly into a darker and far more dangerous place. He was equally exhilarated and terrified at the vastness of it all, at just how much of everyday society was riddled with monsters and mystic powers. It was a brave new world and at the centre of it all, in that moment, he understood his place.

Thaddeus Thane, amongst the horrors and wonders of the demi-monde, finally felt at home.

Chapter Fifteen – The Hunter, Hunted

Mallory

Mallory Marsh, Charity Walpole, and Ivy Livingston walked through the streets of Jericho as the sun slipped beneath the westward horizon. His satchel was slung over one shoulder and weighed heavily on the straps; he'd stashed his Ministry issue sidearm in there, just in case.

Charity was still covered in her usual array of blades and she had, much to Mallory's surprise, given her service weapon to Ivy. Her light jacket did a bad job of concealing the holster and he was more worried about running into a police officer than one of the mysterious creatures they were hunting.

"The standard service weapon given to field agents," Charity had gleefully told Ivy, "is the double barrelled Taylor & Bullock Mark Three .357 Giantslayer Revolver, or the 'Jack' in Ministry slang. It's an over-under affair with seven shots in each barrel for a total of fourteen. It kicks like a motherfucker but it will stop a rabid werewolf dead in its tracks."

Charity had demonstrated how to reload the Jack as well as how to hold and aim it properly. Mallory was still thinking about it as they made their meandering way through Jericho. Ivy was looking about nervously and it seemed to him that she jumped at every single noise or shadow.

"Take it easy, Doc," Charity said, as if she'd read his mind. "Just breathe and let your senses filter out anything that isn't a threat."

"That's simple enough for you," she said, "but I'm

not a trained killer like you."

"You'll get there sooner than you think," Charity replied cryptically.

"If you say so. Thank you for showing me how to use your gun."

"You're welcome. It was a selfish endeavour, though; I fight up close and I'd rather you hit the enemy instead of me."

"If you're invisible-" Ivy started.

"If I'm out of sight then it's my job to stay out of your line of fire, Doc. Like you said, I'm a professional; you just point it at the monster and trust me to stay out of the way."

"Maybe we should be quiet?" Mallory hissed.

"These things attack in the open, Marsh," Charity said. "We want them to come to us. Besides, you'll never be as quiet as Evans could be and they still killed him, didn't they?"

Whilst she tried to act aloof and detached, Mallory could hear the pain in his colleague's voice, so he simply shrugged in response. He slowed his pace a little and dropped back behind the two women; although she claimed to be on board with the plan, he still suspected that Ivy would do something rash.

Or we'll encounter one of these vampires, he thought, *and she'll freeze up or go to pieces.*

He'd been on too many investigations with both Whist and Teaser to know all too well that normal people did not handle the truth about the world well. Admittedly, Ivy Livingston was doing better than most, but deep in his heart Mallory knew that when faced with the reality of the situation, she would fold. He didn't judge her for it.

In fact, the first time he'd come face to face with the

real danger of being a Ministry field agent, he had frozen too. If it hadn't have been for Whist's quick reflexes and total mastery of her gift, he would've been torn to pieces by a Flickerfox.

It wasn't even that dangerous an assignment, he thought angrily, *and I still fell to fucking pieces!*

"Mallory, what's wrong?" Ivy asked. He hadn't realised that he'd completely stopped moving and was now almost ten metres behind them. "We have to stay together."

"Unless you want to be bait in a little vampire trap!" Charity asked mockingly. She laughed and it echoed around the buildings on Walton Street. "Fucking vampires, Mallory, are you kidding me?"

"We'll know soon enough," he said testily. "If we see one, don't let it get away; we need information and we need it tonight."

He walked briskly to catch up with the two women and did not slow as he passed them. *Let them come,* he thought. *By dawn tomorrow there will be one less vampire to worry about.*

The three of them rounded the corner on to Little Clarendon Street. They walked a short way up towards the main road before Mallory spotted a skulking figure as it darted down a passageway to their right.

"Come on!" He said as he ran after his quarry.

"Mallory, wait!" Charity yelled, but he ignored her cry. Ivy went after him and Charity roared in frustration. "Why does no one ever listen to me!?"

Mallory turned the corner and saw the creature hop the fence into the common at the centre of Wellington Square. He barely broke his stride as he gave chase and sprinted at the street sign in front of the railings.

He jumped, using the sign as a stepping stone and cleared the wrought iron spikes without incident. He landed on the sun-hardened grass with a thud.

"I'm right behind you," Ivy called to him from behind the fence. "I'm going to find a gate, just wait for me."

Mallory saw her rush past as he drew his service weapon. He dropped into a crouch, one knee on the ground, and peered through the gloom.

He saw a lone figure standing in the centre of the green, pale and motionless. *I've got you now, you son of a bitch,* he thought as grim determination filled his heart. He took careful aim at the creature's leg and squeezed the trigger.

At that moment Ivy kicked in the gate to the green, shattering the fragile locking mechanism, and ran headlong at the creature. Marsh's gun kicked heavily in his hand and the bullet whistled through the air and struck the creature, clipping its left knee.

Ivy collided with their target, knocking it to the ground. Mallory grinned at their success but his glee was short lived.

Several more creatures appeared in the green, stepping out of the shadows of trees and leaping over the fence; Mallory counted at least eight of them. On the ground in the centre of all this, Ivy was wrestling with the wounded creature as it hissed in pain and snapped its jaws at her.

He levelled his weapon again, but in the darkness he could not make out enough detail to tell Ivy and the monster apart.

"Mallory," she yelled, "shoot it!"

He saw one of the figures get knocked back as the other one rose above it, one arm raised up high. The hand moved into the dim lamplight and the jagged claws glinted; it wasn't much, but it was enough.

Mallory fired.

He anticipated the recoil this time and his aim was true. The round caught the creature squarely in the forehead, killing it instantly. It crumpled backwards away from Ivy, who had drawn her own weapon.

He leapt into motion shooting as he ran to drive the encircling monsters away from her as she got to her feet. The flashes from both guns lit up the small park, and the features of the approaching creatures were suddenly visible.

Cat-like reflections in the pupils.

A mouth full of dark, sharp teeth.

Deathly pale skin.

Razor edged claws.

Hungry eyes brimming with malice.

Vampires, Mallory thought as any lingering doubts were banished.

One of the monsters leapt at Ivy as she fired, knocking her to the ground once again. He saw her franticly mash the trigger, but her Jack was empty and she was helpless.

He squeezed the trigger, again and again, completely disregarding his training and firing wildly at the vampires as they came closer and closer. His ears were ringing as he reached the centre of the park.

He stood above the prone Ivy and reached down to roughly haul her to her feet. The closest vampire tensed, its claws quivering as it prepared to leap at them. Mallory aimed the gun squarely at the creature and pulled the trigger.

Click.

He groaned. The weapon was empty and there was no time to reload. He pulled Ivy upright and behind him as he stepped forward into the vampire's path.

The creature grinned, bearing its jagged black teeth, and leapt at him. It was faster than he could believe and closed the distance in what seemed like an instant. He braced for the impact and tried to drive the image he'd seen on Bulwark Lane from his mind.

Courage, Mallory.

The vampire caught on something mid-leap and its neck hooked awkwardly around it. The momentum carried its body forward, almost taking its head clean off.

All this happened in an instant, and in the next another vampire was downed as an invisible blade slashed its throat. Mallory whooped when he realised what was happening.

There was a burst of gunfire from behind him; Ivy had reloaded her weapon. *We might actually get out of this alive,* he thought hopefully. He broke open his weapon and emptied the spent cartridges on to the ground.

He looked down to fish a speed loader from his satchel. Once he had it, he slotted the fresh rounds into the gun and snapped it shut. He looked up, weapon reloaded and ready to fight.

A vampire was less than a metre in front of him.

He brought the weapon up as the vampire slashed at him. Mallory was fast, but the vampire was faster.

Its claws ripped through his shirt and into his flesh. He screamed in pain and fired. He squeezed the trigger again and again and again as the vampire tore into him.

The creature staggered back and thick glistening fluid dribbled from the corner of its mouth. It twitched and convulsed for a second, and then spewed a stream of viscous slime all over Mallory.

He was still gasping from the pain. The noxious liquid got in his mouth, his eyes, and poured all over his injuries. The vampire collapsed backwards, dead, as Mallory spat the gunk out and wiped his eyes to clear his vision.

The slime thickened and hardened at an alarming pace, stifling his movement but also sealing his wounds and preventing him from bleeding out. He backed up and leant against a tree, shooting from the hip at the vampires that closed in around him.

Ivy was losing ground as more and more of the creatures entered the green, surrounding them. *They're herding us together,* he realised. He tried to call out to Charity but all he could manage was a wet wheeze as blood and slime bubbled from his mouth.

I hope she makes it out alive. His vision was beginning to darken and his Jack was empty once again. *Someone has to go for help.*

Then Ivy was next to him, her weapon also empty. She was saying something to him, but all he could make out was a mess of distorted sound. He smiled at her weakly as if to apologise for dragging her into all this.

He was about to pass out completely when a blinding light filled the green of Wellington Square. Many of the vampires were ablaze and some simply disintegrated on the spot. Two others hissed and retreated back into the shadows further up the street.

Mallory smiled as he slid down to the ground and sprawled on the dry grass. Two people, a dark haired man and a determined looking woman, were brandishing blueish white flares and yelling at the blazing creatures.

His heartbeat slowed as the man ran over to where he and Ivy had made their stand. The man was bristling with weapons and still carrying the burning flare. Mallory's eyes widened in shock as he realised something incredible.

I can see your face!

"My name is Thaddeus Thane," the man said as Mallory blacked out. "We've come to save you."

Interlude One – Quiet as the Grave

The night air in Kidlington was warm and still as the man made his slow, meandering way through the streets. It had not been dark long, but the clocks had already chimed eleven and the respectable folks were either indoors or already sweating in their beds, unable to sleep.

His world had always been one brimming with sound, but with the Master's gift spreading through his body like a divine light, he found that all of his senses were supernaturally sharp. He could smell the salty tang of sweat as far away as he could hear the beating of a nervous heart. He smiled as he drank in the night, almost tipsy on the fear that saturated the air.

The Master had chosen him for a very special task.

Even though he had not been a part of the Congregation very long, he felt the inspiring spirit of the Master coursing through him in much the same way as the physical gifts took hold. *Revival,* he thought, *in every sense of the word.*

The Master had not given him explicit directions, but it was easy enough for the man to home in on his prey. The foul stink of middle class desperation covered the city like a fog but this particular family had a scent all of their own; shame, tradition, and hatred all added razor edged notes to an already sharp perfume.

The man had initially thought that he would find it unpleasant and was surprised by just how appealing fear could be. He'd already cultivated a taste for killing and had developed a fixation on the final sounds of the dying, but the true thrill of the hunt had eluded him until now.

Street by street and house by house he grew ever closer to the intended targets of the night's bloodshed. The rest of the Congregation would be gathered around the Master that night, still sated by the orgy of violence from which the man had been born again.

God is with the Master, he thought, *and the Master is with me.*

I will not fail.

There was a commotion nearby; two drunken men were having a shouting match across the street. The man could hear their hearts pounding and their blood rushing through their arteries. A desire stirred in him, something base and animal yet altogether alien. He took two staggering steps towards the drunkards, intoxicated himself on the lure of blood.

Thankfully the Master was with him and the Master's will was absolute.

He turned his back on the now brawling men and continued to stalk up the street until he arrived at a modest house. The garden was exceptionally well maintained, almost to the point of being sterile, and not a single thing about the house was out of place.

Yes, he thought gleefully, *these are the ones.*

He walked up to the front door and rang the bell. It took a few moments but the door was eventually opened by a red-faced man in his late fifties. The man smiled warmly at this flustered resident, his new teeth sharp and his eyes glinting in the light that spilled from the doorway.

"What do you want?"

"Are you Barnabus Thane?" the man asked, leaning as close to the threshold as he dared. "Brother of Arabella Thane?"

"Yes, I am." Barnabus's voice was uneven, almost dreamlike in quality.

"Magnificent," said the man with a grin. "My name is Joseph Evans. May I come in?"

Part Two: A Howling in the Veins

Chapter Sixteen – Together at Last

Ivy

Ivy was hot on Mallory's heels when she saw him use the street sign to hop the spiked railings. She briefly considered following him but after a rapid assessment of her own athletic abilities she decided to bank sharply left towards the gate to the green.

Marsh might be more nimble, she thought, *but this is my city and I know it well.*

The gate to the Wellington Square green was always locked after dark, but Ivy had enough momentum to break the ageing mechanism. She jumped at the last moment and brought her legs up to deliver a forceful kick.

The gate burst open just as Mallory fired a shot at the vampire and Ivy staggered out of the kick, barely keeping her feet. She still had most of her momentum and picked up enough speed to carry the unbalanced vamp off its feet and to the ground.

"Mallory, shoot it!" she yelled as the creature rolled atop her.

The vampire was snarling and snapping at her face with glistening black teeth that looked more like the jagged fringe of some awful beak. A thick gelatinous slime fell in rancid globules from its lips with each frenzied bite. She turned her face away, trying to keep the foul substance out of her eyes.

Ivy felt the creature shift its weight forwards as its teeth came ever closer to her exposed neck. *Do or die,* she thought, and wrapped her legs around the vampire's body. With a groan of exertion she threw their combined mass to one side and positioned herself atop the vampire. She let out a chuckle of of triumph and looked down at her thrashing enemy, determined to finish the fight.

Then, at the fringes of her vision, she saw movement.

Ivy, stop! Michaela's voice rang in her ears as she tried to pin the squirming creature. *This is a fucking trap!*

She froze in horrified realisation, just for a heartbeat, and the vampire knocked her backwards. She hit the dry ground with a thud that knocked all the breath from her lungs. She struggled to get the revolver free from its holster as the horrifying creature loomed above her, its claws and teeth glinting black in the lamplight.

"Just give in, Ivy." The vampire's eyes glinted evilly as it spoke softly. She felt the words worm their way inside her, tugging at the very core of her. She wanted so much to obey, to lie down and accept her fate; to give in and die.

Whilst the command had ensnared Ivy, Edgar and Michaela had escaped its grasp.

I don't think so, Michaela hissed and Ivy felt a sudden strength flowing through her; a torrent of rage and determination.

"No." She spoke through gritted teeth as she heard a gunshot and the vampire was thrown to one side by the force of the impact. As it died, the insidious compulsion faded and Ivy drew her weapon.

"Choirs of angels indeed," she muttered as she climbed to her feet and looked around her at the vampires that were closing in.

She held the weapon shakily in one hand and fired a shot; it went wide and her wrist flared in pain from the recoil. Her heart raced and her breathing came in short sharp bursts as panic flooded through her. She was dimly aware of Marsh slowly approaching from her right, shooting as he went.

"We're going to die," Ivy whimpered as she almost let the weapon fall from her grasp.

No, we are not! Michaela's voice was firm and authoritative; it snapped Ivy out of her fear and into action. *Legs apart, shoulders square, two hands on the gun, and squeeze the trigger.*

Ivy moved as if she were a marionette pulled by invisible strings as her body reacted to Michaela's commands. She sighted one of the vampires down the barrel of the weapon and fired. The bullet struck it in the chest, sending it reeling but Ivy barely noticed; she was already lining up her next target.

Shot after shot, flash after flash; it didn't seem to make any difference. Their enemy was just too numerous. She turned on her heel as she heard a screech from beside her and saw a vamp leaping through the air at her. She fired her gun, the blast angled upwards to tear through its head. Its lifeless form smashed into her, sending her sprawling.

More vampires were closing in, and she brought the weapon round to defend herself. A pull of the trigger and one heart stopping *click* sent fingers of ice through her veins. She was out of ammunition and unable to run. Ivy opened her mouth to scream in defiance at her enemy one last time.

Gunshots tore through the little park as Mallory charged headlong towards her. Ivy looked around in panic, desperately trying to find an escape route.

Instead, she saw the gate clang open by itself and the dry grass rustled as their invisible ally made her way into the fray.

Mallory's bullets definitely crossed Charity's path, but none seemed to hit her. Even in the face of imminent death, Ivy was impressed.

Don't just sit there, Michaela roared in her head, *reload the fucking gun!*

Mallory reached her side and pulled her upright in one swift movement. Ivy was startled at just how strong he was. She looked down as her fingers fumbled over the weapon to find the break latch.

She heard Mallory's weapon click empty as she finally broke hers. Her fingers danced back and forth as she picked all of the empty bullet casings from the gun before putting fresh ones in. *Thank god Charity made me practice!* She snapped the revolver shut as Mallory let out a loud whoop.

Ivy looked up and saw the devastation the invisible woman was wreaking on the vampires. She smiled and took aim once again, more carefully selecting her targets this time. She slowly started backing away from the fight towards the gate and, hopefully, escape.

She turned to call to Mallory and saw one of the vampires tearing into him.

"Mallory, no!" she screamed. Marsh fired his weapon into the creature's chest and staggered backwards, glistening with the vile slime. Her hands trembled and her shots started to go wild as the vampires closed in.

At least somebody will know what happened to me, she thought as her revolver clicked empty once again; she'd emailed Jessica earlier in the evening to tell her of their plan and instructed her to get out of the city. *At least she'll be safe.*

Then, as if the universe wanted to mock her one last time, she heard Jess's voice.

"Ivy!" The shout echoed around the square.

Mallory collapsed to the ground as he reached her. Ivy knelt down beside him and took his hand in hers.

"I'm here, Mallory. You're not alone." Her voice was soft and he smiled weakly as blinding light filled the park. She turned, shielding her eyes against the glare and saw Jessica holding a burning flare and a sword. Behind her was another man with a flare and blade, and two more men with long guns.

The light cleared the park in seconds and Ivy heard Charity scream in agony. She got to her feet as the man carrying the flare tended to Mallory, and staggered a few steps before throwing herself into Jessica's arms.

"We came to save you," Jess said through barely constrained tears. "We couldn't leave you to die."

"Who are these people?" Ivy asked.

"The Oxford Vampire Hunters," she replied. Ivy noticed one of the men with rifles looking at her with an expression of confusion.

"Edgar?" Trip asked.

"I'll explain later," Ivy said. "We need to get out of here, all of us. You need to find Charity, she's somewhere over there."

She gestured to the clump of shrubs at the side of the park where she thought the invisible agent had been last. As if on cue, the now visible Charity Walpole emerged from the bushes, blood streaked and weary. Her pale skin was burned and blistered from her exposure to the flares.

"Charity, are you alright?" Ivy yelled.

The blonde woman gave her a shaky thumbs up and then promptly collapsed.

As they made their way back through the streets of Jericho, Ivy brought those unaware of her condition up to speed. Trip nodded knowingly, although Ray and Thaddeus looked a bit startled by the whole thing.

Jessica and Ivy had Charity propped up between them whilst Trip and Ray carried Mallory on a collapsible stretcher the Vampire Hunters had brought with them. Ivy could hear the pain in Charity's breath every time she knocked or chafed one of her burned areas.

"Were those ultraviolet flares?" Charity asked.

"Yes, we mixed them up ourselves using the last of the photography chemicals Thaddeus had leftover from a previous project." Jess beamed at Thaddeus, who winked back at her. "We didn't know if they would work, but I'm glad they did!"

"I'd rather not go toe to toe with a street full of vamps," Ray said.

"How many do you have left?" Ivy asked Jess.

"Just two more. We didn't have a lot to work with."

"Damn. They really seem to do the trick."

"They only kill the thralls outright," said Thaddeus, who was leading the way, "but it hurts the higher vamps enough to spook them. We don't know if it will have any effect on the Master, though."

"The Master!?" Charity said with a pained laugh. "It's bad enough that we were rescued by children, but now they're also on board with this vampire bullshit?"

"The words you're looking for, Charity, are *thank you*," Ivy said sharply.

"Oh, yes, for sure. Thank you for burning me to a fucking cinder, I really appreciate it." She chuckled darkly before turning to Thaddeus. "Hey, kid, can you see me?"

"We all can," Ray said.

"No, no, this was back in-"

"The library?" Thaddeus asked. Charity nodded. "Yeah, I could see you. I just thought you were on drugs or something."

"Ha! Do you hear that, Marsh?" she asked Mallory's unconscious form. "He can see me! I'm not crazy!"

"Well, not about that at least," Jessica said quietly.

"True enough," Charity replied as the rest of the group fell silent. Up ahead a strange towering structure loomed up over the surrounding houses. It took Ivy a moment to recognise it; the Jericho Folly.

Thaddeus led them through the dark streets with swift ease. Ivy was troubled by how many of the street lights were out. *I'm sure Jericho wasn't this dark earlier tonight.* Soon they were at the base of the folly and Thaddeus unlocked the door as Mallory groaned weakly on the stretcher. Ivy saw Charity reach out one burned hand to give his arm a reassuring squeeze.

"You're gonna be fine, Marsh," she said softly, "the good doctor here is gonna patch you up so you're right as rain."

"Right," Thaddeus said, "we're on the top floor and it's a narrow staircase; Trip, Ray, be careful not to tip Mallory out of the stretcher. I'll go first to unlock the door and Jess will bring up the rear."

They all murmured in agreement and followed him up the rickety staircase to the safety of the garret. The stretcher proved tricky at some points, but they managed to get everyone inside without incident. Trip and Ray placed Mallory on the bed as Ivy deposited Charity in a nearby chair.

Thaddeus and Jessica bustled around the small flat, bringing Ivy a comprehensive first aid kit and a bowl of clean water. Ivy snapped on a pair of surgical gloves and took a moment to look at Mallory's injuries. She frowned as she gently probed the hardened ooze.

"There's no way to tell how deep his wounds are without removing this," she said, "and there's a good chance that whatever the fuck this is has stopped him bleeding out. I'm going to leave this in place, for now, and when it gets light we can take him to the hospital-"

"No," Charity said softly. "you're a doctor; get the supplies you need and help him here. He's too vulnerable in the hospital, but this place is set up like a fortress."

Ivy opened her mouth to argue, but thought better of it. *What we need is a unified front,* Michaela said, *and deep down you know she's right.* Instead of dissenting, Ivy simply nodded as she removed the gloves.

Charity dragged her chair over to the bed and slumped in it once again, exhausted.

"Don't you dare die on me, Marsh," she said softly as she held his hand. "If you do, I'll fucking kill you."

Chapter Seventeen – Of a Rare Breed

Thaddeus

"This is technically the first party I've had here," Thad joked to Jess as they busied themselves making several pots of tea. "The atmosphere is a bit more serious than I hoped for but the company is as weird as I'd imagined."

She chuckled and gave him a tired smile. He planted a small kiss on her forehead and he carried the teapots through to the main room of the garret where the cups were already waiting. Jess followed with the milk and sugar.

"All I've got for now is standard breakfast tea, but a couple of us can do a supply run when it gets light." He gestured to a door through the kitchen. "There's a little bedroom in the box room back there, along with the bathroom. I've got an airbed that I can pump up along with a camping mat, so we can get some sleep if we take it in turns. The main bed comfortably fits two, so we can use that when Mallory is back on his feet."

"I think we should get plenty of non-perishable food," Ivy said, "as this is likely going to get worse before it gets better. I'll get what medical supplies I can from the hospital."

"Now that we know the flares work we could bulk buy some of the chemicals-" he started.

"And blow us all to kingdom come?" Charity interrupted snarkily. "No, kid, don't stockpile more of that than we need, or at least don't store it here. One small fire and we're fucking toast."

Thaddeus rankled at being called 'kid', but he didn't

snap at Charity. For all her snideness and snark, she was right. He gestured for her to go on.

"We've got arms and ammunition stored at several drop points throughout the city," she said as she looked at both of Arabella's hidden trunks, "but it looks like you're doing pretty well on that front. Are you using silver blades and bullets?"

"No," Jess said. "The blades are coated in a mixture of copper and nickel, and the bullets are standard lead with a copper jacket."

"Well, that's fucking weird." Charity leant back against the headboard of the bed; she'd not left Mallory's side. "Doesn't anyone else think that's weird?"

"I know in the lore that vampires were harmed by silver, but maybe that's just a myth," Trip said. He looked at Thaddeus. "Say, Thad, doesn't your aunt's diary mention silver bullets?"

"There was a box of silver ones, but she expressly said that vampires are harmed by the copper jacketed ones more."

"Yes, and that is *weird,* isn't it?" Charity looked down at Mallory and smoothed the hair from his face. "If Marsh was awake, he'd agree with me because he knows that silver fucks up pretty much anything supernatural. In fact, everyone at the Ministry knows that, so why doesn't it hurt your vampires, kid?"

"Stop calling me that!" His voice was hard; the events of the night had worn his nerves raw. "My name is Thaddeus, or Mister Thane if you want to be formal."

"Thane?" Charity's eyes widened and she peered at the secretary steamer. "You're related to Arabella Thane?"

"Yes."

"By blood?"

"She's my aunt; my father's sister."

"Ah, now this is starting to make sense." Charity gentled nudged Mallory. "Do you hear that, Marsh? He's Bella Thane's nephew!"

"Did you know my aunt?" Thaddeus asked gently. He leant forward, his eyes reflected in her dark glasses.

"Not personally, no, but amongst the Ministry field agents she's a bit of a legend." She smiled and settled back. "She was a Taboo, as are you. Normally the Ministry keeps an eye on the blood relatives of Ceps like us, but Tabs are always infertile so they assumed she was just an odd mutation.

"Seeing you, though, I think they might be wrong about that; perhaps it's a recessive or epigenetic trait. Anyway, it's nowhere near as well documented as the Janus gene, so-"

"Excuse me," Trip said as he raised his hand. "Just a quick question; what the fuck are you talking about?"

"Right, here's the speed run version," Charity said. "Supernatural creatures and whatnot are regulated by the Ministry of Supernatural Affairs. People with supernatural gifts, good or bad, are known as Exceptions, shortened to Ceps, due to their comparative rarity in the population of ordinary humans.

"Your boy Thaddeus, here, is a Taboo; a rare breed of Cep whose supernatural gift is the negation of other supernatural gifts. I can turn invisible, but he can see me. Preachers, for example, can mess with your mind but Thaddeus would be immune to that. He also wouldn't turn if bitten by a werewolf. You get the idea?"

"Yeah, thank you."

"No problem."

"What's the Janus gene?" Thaddeus asked.

"It's the particular mutation that gives Seers their power. It's called the Janus gene because they can either look forwards through visions or back through psychometry. The two are mutually exclusive, except in very rare cases where a set of twins fuses in utero; those particular Seers tend to be completely insane though, so they're not much use.

"May I continue with what I was saying, now?" Charity asked of the room. Everyone nodded and she continued; it seemed she enjoyed holding court. "Good. So, Bella Thane was a damn good field agent because she was largely immune to all the bullshit the rogue Ceps could throw at her."

"That sounds like her," Thaddeus said and smiled with pride. "She had so many adventures that she used to tell me about."

"However," Charity said, "back in eighty six Bella Thane suddenly went off the rails. Her partner got killed on an investigation and she would not stop ranting and raving about how the killer was a vampire.

"Unfortunately for her, vampires do not exist. The Ministry has never encountered one in the entire time it has been operating, and we're talking back to the days of the Empire so that spans most of the bloody globe. Still, she would not stop going on about it.

"She was obsessed, Thaddeus."

"But she was right! What happened tonight proves it!"

"We fought something tonight, but I'm still not convinced either way." Charity sighed heavily. "But that's by the by. Bella Thane's obsession meant that she wasn't focussed on her work and people died; innocent people. The Ministry tried to have her evaluated, citing concerns for her mental well-being, but she refused."

"And they fired her?" Thad asked sadly.

"No. She quit before they could do so; it was said that she always did things on her own terms, and I respect the hell out of her for that." Charity peered up at the clock and got to her feet. "I didn't tell you that to dishearten you, Thaddeus; you're a plenty capable young man.

"I just want you to take what you read in those journals with a pinch of salt; don't throw your life away chasing a dead woman's obsession."

"I won't," Thaddeus said tearfully, "but I still believe her."

"And that is your choice to make." Charity walked towards the staircase door. "I'll see you soon."

"Where are you going?" Ivy asked, seemingly waking from a deep reverie. "It's not safe."

"The sun rose about fifteen minutes ago, so those things will be all holed up by now. I'm heading back to Wellington Square; there's something I need to do there, but it won't take long."

"I'll come with you," she said, rising from her seat.

"No, you stay here and watch Marsh, keep him alive. Work out what we need from the hospital and when I'm back we'll go together. I won't be long."

"Be careful." Ivy said softly.

Charity opened the door and looked back at Trip, Ray, Jess, and Thad.

"The proud part of me wants to say that we had it under control last night, but I know for a fact we didn't." She smiled sheepishly at them. "Thanks for the rescue; I'm glad you found us when you did."

Without waiting for a response she opened the door and left them in the garret. On the bed, Mallory Marsh remained unconscious, with only the gentle rise and fall of his chest to show he was still alive.

Thaddeus and Jess retired to the small bed in the cramped back room. The morning sun filtered through the tiny gaps in the shutters, casting them in a soft twilight. They nestled close to each other both out of necessity and a desire for intimacy in the wake of the night's violence. Thad had his back to Jess, who was wrapped around him; one hand gently running through his hair.

"Does it bother you?" he asked after a while.

"Does what bother me, Thad?" she said softly.

"What Charity said about my aunt," he sighed, "and about me; that I'm not exactly human."

"She didn't say that you weren't human, Thaddeus. She said that you were different."

"An *Exception*," he said sharply. "She said it in the same tone that my mother says *Queer*."

"Like it's something shameful?"

"Exactly."

"Are you ashamed of being queer, Thaddeus?" She kissed him softly on the back of his head.

"No."

"Then why be ashamed of this?"

"I'm not." He wriggled in bed and turned to face her. He lowered his voice, so they could not be overheard. "Ever since this all started, I've felt like I'm on the right path in life. Then I met you and we found the trunks beneath the floor and suddenly the world makes so much more sense."

"There you go then," she said happily. "As long as you're happy with it, it doesn't bother me in the slightest."

"Thank you."

"Any time." She fingered the cross that hung around her neck by a delicate chain. "Is it weird that finding all this out has only firmed up my belief in some kind of God?"

"I don't think so. If vampires and invisible people are real, then why not a creator?" He paused, then went on. "I personally don't believe, but I'm the sort of person who will always want proof; I've got too many doubts."

"Belief without doubt is certainty and I don't think that's what I want." She gave him a small kiss. "I can't speak for the rest of humanity, but for me faith has to exist alongside doubt; it's a choice you make, not an inherent characteristic."

"That makes sense," he said. "I can't see it myself, but I can at least understand where you're coming from. Is that enough for you?"

"Of course. It's my personal belief and I'm not one for evangelising. Hell, I only attend a church at Trinity for the choir, not the service."

Thaddeus was about to respond when he heard a sharp knocking on the door of the garret. A small commotion followed in the main room and there was the sound of the door opening. He pulled on his trousers and Jess wrapped herself in his robe before they left the back room.

Charity had arrived back, waking several of the others who'd nodded off in the interim. Someone had opened the shutters to let the light into the kitchen, but the main room remained dark. Even in the gloom Thad winced at the sight of Charity's skin; the burns looked particularly bad and blisters were forming on almost all of her exposed skin.

"Did you go back to find any leads?" he asked her.

"No, I went back for this." She held up a grey yachting cap. "Mallory would never forgive me if I let him lose it. Hear that Marsh? I rescued your hat!"

She walked over to put the cap next to him on the bed. As she did so, he stirred and there was a sharp cracking sound as the solidified slime shattered; the shards fell into the bed and Charity let out a shocked gasp. Ivy was beside them both in seconds and held Charity's hands away from Mallory's body.

"No, Charity, don't touch him!" Her tone was deadly serious. "Is this normal for him?"

"Not by a fucking long shot."

Thaddeus walked over to the bed and froze when he saw Mallory's skin beneath his shredded clothes. His wounds were little more than shining pink scar tissue; such healing should've taken days, if not weeks.

"What does this mean, Doc?" Charity asked. Ivy didn't answer, but Mallory stirred on the bed and spoke weakly instead.

"I'm infected, aren't I?"

<u>Chapter Eighteen</u> – <u>Like a Splinter in the Mind</u>

Mallory

"Well, am I?" Mallory asked as he propped himself up against the headboard. The sea of unknowable faces swam before him, but he recognised the faded leather coat of Charity Walpole and the face of Thaddeus Thane, his unexpected saviour, was as clear as day. He frowned and shook his head slightly; his ears were still ringing from the gunfire.

"It's hard to say," said a sympathetic voice that he recognised as Ivy Livingston's, "but whatever attacked you has certainly manifested certain changes in you. These wounds should've killed you, Mallory, but instead you're almost completely healed. How do you feel?"

Mallory.

"I actually feel pretty good, at least physically speaking. My ears are ringing though, must've been all the shooting." He tried to smile, but one of the faceless strangers moved and the glaring light from the kitchen made him flinch. "Fuck! Can someone please turn out that light? It's blinding!"

"Well, that's not good at all," said Charity as she walked into the kitchen. There was a clunk and the light was switched off. "Better?"

"Yes, thank you. What was that, your interrogation light?" he joked.

"That was the sun, Mallory." Ivy sat next to him on the bed. "May I examine you more thoroughly? I'd rather clip away your shirt than have you take it off; in fact, stay as still as you can until we know what we're dealing with."

"Of course; you know more than we do." As she began to gently clip away the tattered remains of his stylish William Morris shirt he sighed heavily. "This was my only Strawberry Thief; I'll have to get a replacement. At least the tie is salvageable."

"I went back for your hat," Charity said gently. Her eyes looked a little tearful. She placed it gently on his head. "You look much more like yourself now."

"Charity, is this the man who saw you?" he asked, pointing at Thaddeus Thane.

"Sure is." She cocked her head to one side, suddenly curious. "Can you see his face, Marsh?"

"I can." Then, to Thaddeus, "I've never been able to see a face properly before; it's the price I pay for my particular gift."

"I'm sorry it's not a more handsome face," Thaddeus said with a nervous chuckle.

It's plenty handsome enough, Mallory thought.

"There's more to life than looks you kn-" Mallory stopped abruptly as Ivy shone a light in his eyes and hissed in pain. "Fucking hell, Livingston, give me some warning next time!"

"You're having an abnormal reaction to light, Mallory, and the accelerated rate of healing bothers me greatly. Can I see your fingers, please?"

He held his hands out before him and Ivy bent in close to inspect them. She went over them carefully, feeling up and down each of his fingers; he couldn't help but notice that she'd doubled up her gloves.

"There are some strange ridges forming underneath your skin, especially around your fingertips. Are you in any pain?" He shook his head. "They're too soft to be bone, but to rigid to be anything less structural.

"This is absolutely fascinating, and all in the span of several hours! Whatever attacked you must be highly mutagenic or..." She trailed off, but he noticed a difference in her voice and general body language. "May I see your teeth, please?"

"As you wish. Charity, why don't you introduce these people to me?" He opened his mouth wide and Ivy peered in, using the torch on her phone to illuminate his throat and soft palate.

"Well, you've met the good doctor," she began, "although something tells me that we're currently in the presence of one of her... housemates, for want of a better word."

"You're correct." Ivy's voice was strangely flat yet incredibly intense. Mallory's mind conjured images of coiled snakes or scorpions poised to strike. "I'll hand back to Ivy once I'm done here; she isn't much of a medical doctor."

"But you are?" Thaddeus asked.

"I'm a biologist," she answered nebulously. "Please continue with your introductions."

"Right, so we have Ivy's imaginary friend, and Thaddeus Thane, our gracious host. These two," she said gesturing to an older man and a young woman, "are Ray, who owns a local cafe, and Jessica, who seems to be involved with our host."

That's a shame, he thought.

"I'm the one who went to the hospital after hearing the angels at my window," Jessica said. "You spent some time talking to my friend in the waiting room. Do you remember her?"

Mallory went to respond but Ivy shushed him as she

continued her examination, so he gave her a thumbs up instead. She smiled sadly at him.

"She spoke kindly of you. Her name was Jade." Her smile faltered a little. "She's missing now; either dead or one of those things."

"The final member of our ragtag little group is the fellow over by the steamer case; his name is Trip, who is some sort of competitive video gamer or something." Charity gave Mallory a grin. "With such an expert team how can we possibly fail?"

Mallory Marsh.

He shook his head as the ringing in his ears sharpened for a moment, sending a spike of pain through his left eye and all the way back through his brain. Ivy sighed in exasperation and pulled her hands away from his mouth as he fell back on the bed clutching his head. He groaned, but as suddenly as it came on, the pain passed.

"If you're not going to stay still, I won't be able to examine you," said Ivy, her hands on her hips.

"I'm sorry." He thought for a moment. "It was like a migraine, but it only lasted a few seconds. It was awful. You can carry on if you want."

"There's no need. You're developing more ridges inside your mouth and your salivary production has increased. Coupled with the other symptoms, I'd say that you are most definitely infected." She removed the gloves in a nonchalant manner before swiftly drawing her weapon. "It's only a matter of time before you turn into one of those things and attack us."

"And what are you going to do with that, Doc?" Jessica said as she positioned herself between Mallory and Ivy.

"He's infected. The only decent thing to do is

euthanise him."

"Hey, Not-Ivy, why don't you go and get some sleep?" Charity suggested. "It's been a long night for all of us and I think we're all a bit tired to be making big medical decisions, aren't we?"

"And if I don't want to?" She tightened her grip on the gun.

"Let's not get to that point." Jessica moved closer as she spoke. "It's Michaela, right?"

"Yes."

"Well, Michaela, we can just restrain him for now; see how things play out. Wouldn't it be beneficial to learn how the infection progresses?" Her voice was calm and soothing.

"You make a good point," Michaela said. She placed the gun on the bedside table. "But if anything goes wrong we deal with him swiftly and decisively."

"Of course," Mallory said.

"Very good. I think I'll go and have a little lie down." She walked towards the bedroom, but turned to face Charity as she went. "And don't think I didn't notice the blade in your hand, Walpole."

Everyone left in the room let out a collective sigh of relief when the door to the back bedroom closed. Jessica turned to face Mallory and leant in to reassure him. As she did so, the cross at her neck slipped out of the robe and dangled before his eyes.

Mallory let out a snarl and scrambled backwards, recoiling from the religious symbol. Behind her dark glasses, Charity's eyes were wide with surprise.

"Weird," she said emphatically. "Very fucking weird."

Can you hear me, Mallory Marsh?

Mallory sat up in the bed with a yelp, drenched in sweat and breathing heavily. He glanced at the clock; it was late in the afternoon and the garret was empty aside from him. Charity and Ivy, who was now fully Ivy once again, had headed to the hospital for medical supplies. Thaddeus and Jessica were out buying food while Trip and Ray each got a change of clothes and whatever else they would need to wait out a siege in the garret.

"Which leaves me all alone," Mallory said to the empty air.

You're not alone, Mister Marsh.

He looked wildly around, straining against his bonds as he did so. Jessica had tied them so they were comfortable yet tight, and whilst he had some movement he could not leave the bed. She'd smiled knowingly when Charity had asked where she'd learned her rope skills and left it at that.

He fanned his face with his hands as best he could. It was unbearably hot in the garret and the bed was already moist with perspiration. He craned his neck to reach the straw poking out of the glass of ice water that was just within reach.

The cold drink was soothing, but his mouth and throat felt as if they were being torn apart by razor blades. He groaned in pain as he drained the glass and the ice clacked around in the empty tumbler. He looked at the frozen cubes, still mostly intact and his brain began to slowly process what was happening.

"It's not that hot in here."

Oh?

"The issue is me," he said triumphantly to the mystery voice. "I have a fever because I'm fighting whatever is inside me."

That sounds like a tremendous effort, the voice said sympathetically. *Perhaps too much effort?*

"I can't just give up."

It's not giving up, Mallory Marsh. It's simply choosing a new path.

"No," he panted as he blinked the sweat from his eyes. The ridges in his fingers were larger now, more prominent, and he looked desperately at the ice; he had a thirst that seemed unquenchable.

A better path.

He shook his head, both in defiance and to clear the insidious voice from his mind. He could almost feel it taking root in his head like some awful creeping plant. Inch by inch, moment by moment, he felt it colonising his thoughts, trying to change him.

Your life has been a difficult one, Mister Marsh.

"Get out of my head!" he roared, spittle flicking across the room. His heart thundered in his ears as he yelled and thrashed on the bed. "You don't know anything about me."

I can show you a new world, Mallory. A world where you will belong.

"I already belong here, you bastard." He growled and snapped at the air, no longer caring how animalistic he appeared. "I am going to beat this thing."

I doubt that, Mister Marsh. Everyone understands in the end.

Everyone comes around.

Every single one.

"Not me, and when I find you I am going to kill you. Consider that payment in kind for what you did to Joseph Evans."

My dear Mallory, Joseph Evans is not dead. In fact,

he has joined our noble cause, just as you will.

"Fine," he said through the burning pain that was spreading throughout his body, "I'll kill you just because you've pissed me off!"

Fight all you want, Mallory Marsh. You'll beg for mercy soon enough.

You will cry out for me to save you, and I will.

"Just who the fuck do you think you are?"

I am the Master, Mallory, and I hold the key to Paradise on Earth.

"Then I'll see you in hell!" Marsh yelled. His mind was suddenly filled with nightmarish images and unspeakable agony, the likes of which he had never experienced before. He screamed and screamed, but still the voice of the Master cut through all else.

As you wish, Mallory Marsh. As you wish.

Chapter Nineteen – Paradise Risen

Ivy

"Do you have a list of what we need?" Charity asked as they approached the Warneford Hospital.

"Yes, but getting it is going to be a bit more complicated. There's a general storeroom, but medicines like antibiotics and sedatives are locked in the pharmacy."

"Not a problem, Doc," Charity said with glee. She waved a small black pouch and grinned. "I've been picking locks since I was a child."

"There's an electronic card reader as well as a standard lock; they'll know it was me when I buzz us in." Ivy was looking around nervously, afraid of bumping into a colleague on her day off. "I'm worried someone will recognise me and ask to know what I'm doing."

"Just tell them you're saving the world, Doc."

"This isn't the time to be flippant!" Ivy stopped and began wringing her hands nervously. "It's taken most of my life to reach this point and I will definitely lose my job if I'm caught."

"Ivy," Charity said as she placed her hands on Ivy's shoulders, "look at me and take a deep breath."

"Okay."

"Right." Charity smiled at her. "There are two nuns driving down a country road late at night-"

"Are you fucking kidding me, Charity? This is not the time."

"Shut up and listen, Doc." She continued. "Late at night, when suddenly a vampire leaps on to the bonnet of their vehicle. One nun turns to the other and says, 'Quick, show him your cross'. So the other nun leans out of the window and yells-"

"Get the fuck off my car!" Ivy said with a giggle. "Thanks, Charity, I do feel a bit better."

"If you're serious about not wanting to be seen, then you're with the right woman for the job. The chances of anyone catching me are," she lowered her dark glasses and winked at Ivy, "vanishingly small."

"Are you always like this?"

"Only with you, Doc." She gently bumped her shoulder into Ivy and smiled. "Just relax and we'll get through this. Marsh and the others are counting on us, after all."

Ivy took a moment to gather herself and nodded in determination. Charity gestured for her to continue and the two women walked towards the main entrance of the Warneford.

"So, should we disappear now?" Ivy said as they drew closer to the front door. Charity didn't respond and when Ivy looked to her side there was only empty air. "Charity?"

"I'm here, Doc," she whispered. "Try not to talk to thin air so obviously though, unless you want to end up a patient instead of a doctor."

The two reached the front door and Ivy opened it; as she did so she felt a sudden breeze as her invisible companion slipped past her.

What if I bump into her? Her mind suddenly filled with scenarios of getting tangled in the flapping coat of an invisible woman. *Oh god, this is going to end so badly!*

Ivy! Michaela snapped at her. *Just focus on yourself and trust Charity to stay out of your way.*

I will.

And move; you're standing here gawking like an idiot!

"Dr Livingston, are you alright?" asked the receptionist; a pretty man with dark hair and icy grey eyes, whose name Ivy could never recall. "I assume you're here for the meeting?"

"I... I'm fine, thank you." She smiled, suddenly tired. "I've just had a long night, is all."

"Of course, Dr Livingston. The meeting starts in a few minutes, although I don't think anyone would blame you if you didn't show up today." He smiled at her sympathetically. "I know you worked closely with Dr Adams."

"I did," she said, her mind reeling. "Can you remind me which room the meeting is in, please? I've suddenly drawn a blank."

"Completely understandable given the circumstances, Dr Livingston." The receptionist gave her the time and location of the meeting; just five minutes hence. She thanked him and made her way through the maze of corridors and locked wards that made up the Warneford Hospital.

She felt Charity flit past her as she buzzed through each set of electronic locks and secure doors as they went deeper into the bowels of the building. As they neared the meeting room Ivy felt breath by her ear and heard her co-conspirator's hushed voice.

"Where is the pharmacy, Doc?"

"Down that hall, on the right," Ivy said softly as she tried not to point or speak too obviously. "I've got the list in my pocket. The general storeroom isn't far from here either, just through that door and round the first left."

"Great. I'll take the list and your key card." Ivy felt hands brush over her briefly and gasped as the plastic ID card and crumpled paper vanished before her. "Pretty neat, isn't it?"

"It's one hell of a party trick. Do you want me to come with you?"

"No. Attend the meeting, get yourself a credible alibi, and I'll meet you back here." Ivy could hear discomfort in Charity's voice, but decided that it was not the time for an interrogation. "I hope the meeting is informative, Doc."

"Good luck, Charity."

Ivy got no response, but the slight ripple of movement in the papers pinned to the wall as Charity Walpole made her way down the corridor was reply enough. *She doesn't need luck,* Ivy thought. *She has skill.*

Ivy suppressed a small smile. In spite of her abrasiveness, a part of her was starting to like Charity. Admittedly that part was Michaela, who, historically, had shown terrible judgement in people. *I hope you're right this time,* Ivy thought.

I'm always right, Michaela replied.

Ivy chuckled and shook her head; not for the first time she marvelled that somehow she wasn't one of the patients in the hospital. She took a moment to straighten her clothes out and arrange her hair to cover the worst of the night's injuries; after a quick glance in her pocket mirror she felt suitably prepared.

"Let's get this over with," she whispered to herself as she walked into the meeting.

"I'm sorry to call some of you into work on your day off," Pamela Jennings, Director of the Warneford, said as she addressed the assembled doctors, nurses, and support staff, "but I'm sure that you are all aware that there is something happening in the city.

"For those who aren't aware, there has been a sudden up-tick in number of violent incidents in Oxford, especially ones where the assailants appeared under to be under the influence of some sort of psychoactive substance. We've been seeing a dramatic rise in the number of human inflicted bites across the entire trust.

"What is less well known, however, is that there has been a spate of disappearances throughout the past few weeks. Several members of our own staff have reported strangers stalking the grounds at night, with multiple accounts of people being followed home."

Pamela stopped abruptly as if she'd lost her train of thought. Ivy had always felt sorry for her; she was a small woman with a nervous disposition, and was not who she'd have picked to run the county's largest psychiatric hospital. The Director fiddled with her badger streaked hair, as she glanced over her notes, frantically searching for her place.

She's been followed, Edgar said softly. *Look at her; she's absolutely terrified.*

"I... um... What I mean to say," she said, regaining a little of her earlier composure, "is that these reports were largely unsubstantiated and whilst the police have been looking into the disappearances, it does appear that most of these are related to Paradise, a new street drug.

"However, as of last night three members of staff have been reported missing; Nurse Ella Peake, Christina Ruiz, one of the maintenance team, and Dr Irving Adams. All three never made it home after their shift last night, although they were all seen leaving the hospital.

"Whilst I understand that this is a distressing time, we can't let our own feelings impact the care of our patients; if you feel the need to take leave please discuss it with me first so I can assure that we have sufficient cover.

"In light of this particular spate of, um, absent persons, we are instituting both a buddy system within the hospital and shuttle buses to and from work for those who need transport. We're hoping that this will help ease the anxieties of people working on night shifts and reduce what little risk there is to our staff."

Good luck with that, Ivy thought incredulously as she remembered the savageness of the attack in Wellington Square.

"Please rest assured that the police are looking into this with all urgency. I would now like to take a moment to discuss the signs of drug use that have characterised these attacks. Firstly..."

Ivy let her mind wander as Pamela Jennings elaborated on the fictional drug epidemic that was gripping the city. She weighed up the pros and cons of standing up and declaring the truth; that vampires were tearing through the city and hunting anyone out at night. She decided against it, though, as it would most likely do nothing but destroy her credibility with her peers.

All this misinformation is going to get more people killed, Edgar admonished.

As much as it pained her, Ivy could not disagree with him.

Ivy waited for the majority of the people in the meeting room to filter out through the door before she approached Pamela Jennings. She did her best to look forlorn and stressed which, given the situation, was not a hardship at all.

"Dr Livingston," Jennings said as she approached, "thank you for taking the time to come in on your day off; I appreciate that this meeting can't have been easy for you."

"I was shocked to hear that three people had gone missing on one night," she said. "Irving and I worked together regularly and he was always a source of comfort and wisdom during difficult shifts."

"I am sorry, Ivy," Jennings said as she patted her gently on the shoulder. "I can completely understand if you want to take a day or two to process everything."

"Actually, Director Jennings, I have quite a lot of leave banked from overtime and covering others. I was wondering if I could take a few weeks to both use the excess leave and to work through everything that's happened." She sniffled, fighting back tears that were all too real as the stresses of barely escaping the battle in Wellington Square finally hit her. "I would really appreciate it if you would sign off on that."

"Three weeks is a long time, Ivy, and you're one of our best members of staff-"

"I've seen one," she said suddenly. "It followed me home after a shift in the John Radcliffe, and I saw another one last night."

"But you made it home safely, though."

"Only just," Ivy said as she swept her hair aside to reveal the bruises and scrapes from her tussle with the vampire. "Please, Pamela, I'm frightened. I just want to get out of Oxford for a while until this all blows over."

"Alright then, Ivy. We'll see you back here in a few weeks. Please look after yourself." Pamela gave her a quick hug.

"You too. Stay inside at night, if you can help it, and don't go out until dawn." Ivy gave her one last squeeze. "Stay safe."

"Excuse me, Dr Livingston?" Ivy turned at the sound of a stern man's voice. It was one of the security personnel. "I'm sorry to bother you, but the system registered your key card unlocking the pharmacy a few minutes ago."

Ivy began to speak but Director Jennings cut across her immediately.

"Dr Livingston has been in this meeting for the past twenty minutes; I saw her come in."

"Of course, Director." He turned to Ivy. "Is it possible someone else could've had access to your card? Did you lend it out to a colleague or perhaps leave it in the break room?"

"I didn't lend it out. It's," she said as she reached to her belt lanyard where she normally kept it, "right here."

She tried to keep the surprise out of her voice as her fingers closed around the plastic rectangle. She showed it to the concerned security guard, and smiled.

"Huh. That's really odd." He was puzzled but not openly suspicious of her.

"The card readers do throw out glitches from time to time," Jennings said. "I know our IT team is working on fixing it. Is that all?"

"Yes, that's everything. Thank you for your time, Dr Livingston. Have a good day."

He walked away, perplexed. Ivy thanked the Director for being so understanding and made her way out of the building. As she walked she became aware of a slight echo to her footsteps. A smile crossed her lips. *How long have you been there?*

They made it to the main entrance without interruption, and the receptionist wished her a good day.

"You too, Wesley," she said, suddenly remembering his name. He smiled broadly at her and she winked back before walking through the front door into the warm afternoon sunshine. Once Ivy was sufficiently clear of the building, she heard Charity's voice coming from the air beside her.

"I got everything you wanted, Doc."

"Brilliant. Nice work with the key card, by the way." Ivy grinned at the invisible woman. "I didn't even notice you putting it back."

"I'm the best Ghost the Ministry has, bar none." Ivy could hear the smug grin on her face. "Was your meeting interesting?"

"Yes. Several of my colleagues have gone missing. This is worsening with each passing day, isn't it?"

"Sure is."

"The police are finally getting involved, but they seem to be working with some bad information; they seem convinced that this is all due to some new street drug called P-"

"Paradise?" Charity asked sharply. Ivy nodded in affirmation. "Fuck!"

There was a clang as Charity kicked a nearby bin, sending it toppling over. *She is surprisingly strong,* Ivy thought with not a little fear. Charity continued to spew a string of obscenities into the air.

"What's wrong, Charity?" Ivy asked when she finally calmed down.

"Paradise was one of the false leads we were going to feed to the local filth to cover up what happened here; it was Joseph Evans's idea."

"It certainly seems plausible to them."

"But that's the problem, Doc! We never gave them that info; it all got out of hand too fast. Evans was still planning on it when he disappeared, but Marsh and I haven't had a chance to speak to anyone in authority."

"But couldn't someone else in the Ministry have sent it to them?" Ivy asked as fingers of ice made their way down her spine.

"Nobody else knew. For better or worse, we were a minimal contact team; we'd just check in when the job was done."

"So that means Evans is alive!"

"Yes, Doc, it does." Ivy could hear the rage in Charity's voice. "He's alive and working for the Master."

<u>Chapter Twenty</u> – Just My Type

Thaddeus

Thaddeus groaned as Charity tossed him to the floor once again. He glowered at her as he got to his feet and brushed the grass stains from his trousers. Charity grinned at him and lunged once again, knocking him to the ground and winding him.

"You could have let me get up!" He gasped out his words as he rolled on to his back.

"The Master and his cronies won't let you get up, Thane!" She reached down to haul him to his feet. Exhausted, Thaddeus took her hand and she pulled him up into her next blow. He slammed backwards into the ground, tasting blood. "If you fall, Thaddeus, you will die."

There are worse things than death, he thought as she leant in for another strike. He waited until she pulled back her fist before he kicked her legs out from under her. She fell sideways as he staggered upright, his arms already in a guarding stance.

"Good, Thane, very good." She smiled at him from the dusty ground. Her glasses glinted in the golden sunlight; it would be dusk soon enough and their corner of Port Meadow was almost deserted. "Seize any advantage that you can. Fighting fair will only get you killed."

"You didn't have to hit me so hard," he said as he helped her to her feet.

"Did it hurt?" she asked. He nodded and she chuckled slightly. "That blow would've cracked the ribs of an ordinary person, Thane."

"But not mine?"

"No. You're an Exception, Thaddeus. You're naturally stronger, faster, and more agile than ordinary humans; not much, mind, but enough to give you a slight edge. If you train you can hone it into a razor sharp advantage that will keep you alive. Trust your body, kid." She clapped him on the back. "We're the next stage of human evolution."

"Then why do we hide?"

"Most people aren't ready to see behind the curtain, Thane. You've seen how this city has let the Master and his progeny take hold and fester, like a cancer." Her tone was one of bitterness and resentment. "So it's up to us to save them, and when we're done they'll sleep soundly in their beds, none the wiser. It's always been this way; Ceps holding back the terrors of the night because the majority refuse to acknowledge the reality of the world."

"You don't think very highly of them, do you?" Thaddeus asked as he stepped between Charity and the late afternoon sun.

"No, I don't." She swung at him, but he was ready for her. He sidestepped her blow and snatched the glasses from her face. She shrieked and covered her eyes, blinded by the sun. She hissed and snarled as she flailed at him, but he was already several paces away.

"Any advantage," he repeated. "Here, take them."

"Nicely done," she said as she donned her spectacles with a sigh of relief. "Although I'd appreciate it if you didn't do that again; blinding me doesn't exactly shift the scales in our favour."

"It's that bad?"

"You have no idea. When I'm invisible the world is so much darker, so my body has adapted. It makes the real world harder to live in, though."

"That's a considerable downside," he said sadly.

"That's not the worst of it, but I'll take all the pains of being a Ghost over yours every time I'm asked." She raised her eyebrows as he looked at her, puzzled. "What, do you think being a Tab has no downsides?"

"None that I can see."

"That's because you're new to this world, Thane." She gestured for him to sit. "First off, you're never going to be as welcome amongst Ceps as you should be; we don't like it when someone messes with our gifts. You'll be an outcast amongst the regular humans too."

"Why?" he asked, already knowing the answer.

"You belong in this world, Thane, and they don't. They'll never understand what you are and the more you see, the more it will change you. The life of a Tab is a lonely one."

"But if I had children-"

"You won't." She held up her hand to silence his protests. "I already told you that Tabs are infertile; it's best to just make your peace with that now."

"Easier said than done," he said quietly. "But that still doesn't sound as bad as yours."

"It affects all gifts all the time, Thaddeus, both good and bad. I can't shroud you the same way I could with Ivy or Mallory. If you get hurt in the line of duty you can't rely on a Libra to heal you; you'll have to recover the old fashioned way."

"I see your point," he said. "Will you teach me to shoot tomorrow?"

"I know the basics, but I'm a terrible shot," Charity said with a laugh. She pulled a blade out of its sheath and began twirling it in her fingers. "I'll gladly show you some knife tricks, though. These don't run out of bullets and a little bit of nifty knife work can save your life in a tight spot."

"Thank you."

"If you want some instruction when it comes to guns," she said with a stretch, "you should ask the Doc."

"Ivy!?" Thaddeus asked in surprise.

"Yeah. I know a lot about guns and their manufacture, but during the whole mess in Wellington Square she fired twenty eight shots and missed *once*. Every hit was a killing blow." She shook her head in disbelief. "That was her first time using any kind of firearm, to hear her tell it. Either way, she's got some freakish skills."

"I'll ask her tomorrow." Thaddeus looked west, towards the rapidly setting sun. "We should get going."

When they returned to the garret they found Mallory writhing on the bed, gasping and panting as a gloved Ivy felt his pulse. Thaddeus went to her side as Charity busied herself in the kitchen.

"Shall I make some tea?" she called through to them. Thad gave her a thumbs up and she nodded enthusiastically.

"I don't particularly want tea," Ivy muttered quietly.

"Nor do I," he said softly, "but what's happening to Mallory is tearing her apart. I'm sure she's holding herself responsible."

"No doubt there," Ivy said quietly. "His pulse is weak and he's dehydrated. I've seen him drink eleven glasses of water this afternoon, and it hasn't helped in the slightest. I don't understand the biology of these things one bit. I don't know how to help him, Thaddeus."

"It's a shame the ones in Wellington Square burned up. We could dissect them to work out what is happening to him; it might not tell us everything, but it would be a start."

"I would normally agree with you, but this," she said gesturing to Marsh, "is what happened last time we tried to hunt these things."

Before Thaddeus could respond, Mallory screamed in pain and thrashed his head from side to side. The tortured artist was muttering something under his breath, over and over. Someone had tied his hair into a messy bun to keep it out of his eyes. Thaddeus looked at his glistening brow and pained grimace with pity.

"I'll be right back," he said, as he rose from the bedside and walked into the kitchen. He fished around in the cupboard for a metal bowl and a tea towel before filling the former with cold water. He dunked the towel in several times before wringing the excess from it.

He returned to the bedside and began to wipe the sweat from Mallory's skin with the cold cloth. Thaddeus whispered to him as he did so, trying to soothe and comfort the infected man.

"Come on, Mallory, you can beat this thing. We're all here with you. We'll keep you safe."

"Thaddeus, you should be wearing gloves!" The panic in Ivy's remark was matched only by the concern on her face. "We don't know how the infection spreads!"

"I won't get it," Thaddeus said as he left the cold compress on Mallory's brow. He gently stroked the youthful artist's cheek with one finger. "I'm safe from infection."

"He could still hurt you!"

"He won't." Thaddeus took Mallory's hand in his and squeezed it gently. Marsh's olive skin was clammy and the ridges on his fingers were starting to poke through under the fingernails; they were dark and shiny, almost like a beetle's carapace.

"Are you alright to watch him for now?" Ivy asked. Thaddeus nodded. "Thank you. I think I need to eat something or have a nap or both. If you need me, or his condition changes, just yell."

Thaddeus watched her walk into the kitchen before he looked back at Mallory. He tilted his head to one side as he looked at Marsh more carefully. The man had a soft face, with a small nose and gentle mouth; a five o'clock shadow had formed.

Thad tried to imagine Mallory with a full beard, but just couldn't do it. *No,* he thought, *he wouldn't be half as beautiful with a beard.* He smiled as he suddenly realised, much as he had with Jess, just how attracted to the wounded artist he was.

"You're a handsome gentleman, Mallory Marsh." Thaddeus's voice was quiet, even though the living room in the garret was empty aside from the two of them. "A part of me hopes that you think I'm just as dashing."

Mallory was no longer squirming in pain; in fact he looked comparatively serene. Thaddeus brought Mallory's hand to his lips and softly kissed it. *Please let him recover from this,* he thought. He felt Marsh limply squeeze his hand in return.

"You think I'm handsome?" he asked weakly, his eyes still closed.

"I do," Thaddeus replied as he refreshed the cold

towel. "Is that a problem?"

"Not at all, Thaddeus; you're quite the dish yourself. I thought I heard Charity say you were with Jessica."

"I am, I think, but we're not exclusive."

"How very modern," Mallory said with a pained laugh. "Tell me, Thaddeus, as you are clearly a man who can accurately appraise aesthetics and beauty-"

"That's a self-serving compliment if I've ever heard one."

"Well, quite, but I do trust your opinions. As I was saying, will you describe our comrades to me?"

"I'll try. Who should I start with."

"Thank you. I already know enough about Charity, so we can skip her. What about the good doctor?"

"Ivy is..." Thaddeus paused as he searched for the right words. "She's kind of weird looking, in a not unattractive way. I wouldn't call her pretty or beautiful, but she has a sort of ambiguity that is intriguing. Her hair is a mousy brown, almost nondescript in the way she wears it. Her face is fairly round and her eyes are alert and intelligent. She's pale; not like Charity, but still enough to stand out.

"Weird, intense, but interesting," he summarised.

"Now tell me about Ray."

"Ray is tall, muscular, with a goatee and short black hair. His family is originally from Turkey, if my memory is correct-"

"I don't need a family history, Thaddeus." Mallory's voice was strained and a little exasperated. "You don't need to describe skin colour or height; I know that you're tall and that Jessica is black. I can see the individual features perfectly well but I can't compose them into an overall impression.

"That's what I want. You did it well with Ivy."

"Oh. That's easy, then. Ray is handsome in a way that's both easy and intimidating. He's confident, but playful with it. Is that more like it?"

"Perfect. I think it's safe to assume that you think Jessica is beautiful and enticing, isn't it?"

"That would be fair." Thaddeus felt his cheeks flush a little. "Trip is energetic and fun, but there's a lot of intensity behind his carefree attitude. The way he dresses is eccentric, in a mismatched way. I would go as far as to describe him as a colourful goblin of a person."

"Terrific!" Mallory said with a laugh. He squeezed Thad's hand tightly and an intense look settled on his face. "Now, Thaddeus, this one is important; what do I look like?"

Thaddeus took a moment to drink in Mallory's appearance before answering. He looked past the restraints, the sweat, and the vampiric infection ravaging his body to see a confident man with a defined sense of style and an unmistakable swagger. His voice caught in his throat.

"Well?" Mallory asked. "How do I look to you?"

"Mallory Marsh, you are breathtaking."

Chapter Twenty One – A Heaven of Pain

Mallory

Mallory looked at Thaddeus's sleeping form. His dark hair was tousled and messy as it rested on the sweat drenched sheets; even as he slept, Thad continued to hold Mallory's hand. The two had spoken long into the night, even as the room had filled with people once again.

Charity sat on the other side of the bed, her blades within easy reach.

"Why don't you get some sleep?" Mallory asked her.

"I don't need it." She gestured to the shuttered windows. "Besides, if something comes through the window I want the first crack at it."

"Make sure you give it a good stab for me," Mallory said with a dark smile. He gasped as a pang of ravenous hunger shot through him. Whilst he could feel the infection colonising his body and changing him from the inside, the voice of the Master was strangely silent.

He was about to mention that particular aspect of his experience to Charity, but he noticed that she had a pair of noise cancelling headphones handy. *Interesting choice,* he thought.

"What are those for?" he asked.

"Dealing with the vam... no, I'm not going to call them that. I refuse." Charity was adamant in her disbelief in their enemy's true nature. "The *creatures* have some sort of enthralling call, so I'm hoping this will protect me enough to get a few good hits in. Both Jess and Ivy mentioned experiencing it, but it affected them differently."

"That's really strange. Was it worse for one of them?"

"Jess couldn't control herself at all; she tried to force her kitchen window out of its frame."

"Fucking hell!"

"And Ivy shrugged it off." Charity looked over at Dr Livingston, who was snoring softly in an armchair. "There's something about her that bothers me, Marsh, but I can't put my finger on what exactly. Part of me wants to just cut her throat and be rid of her."

"Charity..."

"I'm not going to! She just gives me the heebie-jeebies is all, and last I checked that's not a capital offence." She looked at the solid metal of the shutters. "I would give anything to know what's happening out there tonight."

"Have you tried looking up traffic cameras or other public webcams?"

"No, but that's a really good idea." Charity smiled. "You're not bad at this, Marsh."

"It's not my idea." He sat back, sullenly. "Teaser would set up a little digital command post whenever we were on a case; it was one of her standard sources of information."

"Is she good with computers in general?" Mallory nodded and Charity chuckled. "I'm fucking hopeless. In all seriousness, she sounds like a great partner."

"I wish she was here now."

"I know, but focus on the fact that's she's in London and safe from all this."

"For now, sure, but what if we can't contain this? What if it spreads?"

"It won't." She pulled down her glasses and looked

him dead in the eye. "As long as I still have strength in me, I will not let this nightmare leave Oxford. That's a fucking promise."

"And if I turn into one of those things?"

"You won't." Her voice was stern and forceful. "Don't you dare give up, Marsh."

"I'm just being pragmatic."

"Fatalistic, more like."

"Charity, don't let me hurt anyone." He looked at her beseechingly. "Please."

"I won't," she said softly. "If you turn into one of those things or the Master takes you, I'll put a blade in your brainstem. You won't feel a thing."

"Thank you." He chuckled slightly and Thaddeus stirred a little in his sleep. "You know, Walpole, you're incredibly comforting, albeit in a very disturbing way."

"Always glad to help." She pushed her glasses back up and settled back in her chair. She let the silence sit for a while, but Mallory could tell that she wasn't done talking just yet.

"What's wrong?"

"The cops are following the Paradise line."

"How do you know?"

"Livingston found out when we did the smash and grab at the hospital. Her boss was holding a meeting and it came up."

"But we never-"

"No, we did not." Her voice was filled with fury and she held one of her blades in a white knuckled hand. "Which means that Joseph is still alive."

"That's good news."

"No, it isn't. He hasn't tried to contact us in days; we have to assume that he's defected."

"The Master might have him under the kind of control that bewitched Jessica." Mallory sighed. "I can hear his voice in my head sometimes, like an irresistible compulsion."

"Do you hear him now?" Charity asked, leaning forwards.

"I don't think so."

"No good, Mallory. I need a more definite answer than that." Charity's glasses were only a few inches from his face; he could see his own confused expression reflected in them.

"No," he said after a moment. "I don't hear him at all."

"Interesting." She sat back in her chair, suddenly pensive. "Evans wouldn't be under the Master's spell for long, if it hit him in the first place."

"You think so?"

"I know so; it was part of our training in Lamplight. They had us throw off everything from Sirens to Fae. The only thing that could hit him with enough force to get through all that would be some kind of telepath, but even then it wouldn't hold him forever.

"No, Joseph has thrown his lot in with the Master of his own free will."

"Why would he do that?"

"Because he enjoys hurting people. He gets off on it."

"So not only do we have a cadre of vampires with a powerful leader against us, but we also get to deal with a sadistic Ministry agent with a lifetime of military training?"

"Pretty much."

"The odds aren't exactly in our favour, are they?"

"Not in the slightest." She grinned at him and

gestured with the knife. "Want me to do you now, and save you the hassle of it all?"

"No thanks." Mallory leant back against the pillow as the spreading infection sent another wave of nauseous agony through his nerves. His stomach ached and his throat felt sandpaper dry, no matter how much he drank. "I'm enjoying your distrust of Ivy far too much to duck out now."

"Suit yourself," she said as she got to her feet.

"Where are you off to?" he asked.

"I'm going to make myself some supper," she said, "and to look up a few things. Are you hungry?"

"Ravenous."

"I'll make you a sandwich." She smiled at his forlorn appearance. "Don't look so disappointed, Marsh; I make a mean Reuben."

"I was hoping for something a little more filling."

"Watch yourself, Mallory!" Charity chuckled as she walked away. "If I make you anything else you'll be begging for that blade to the brain."

"I believe it," he said as she slipped out of sight. He shifted in his seat and Thaddeus's hand slipped from his.

Mallory.

The Master pushed deeper and deeper into Mallory's mind.

The further he went, the more he forced Marsh to reveal his memories to him. He felt the information being plucked from him as one might pull weeds from a garden. One by one he was forced to give up his secrets.

Where are you, Mallory Marsh?

"I won't tell you!" he hissed through gritted teeth.

That is the wrong answer, Mallory.

He grimaced as his body was flooded with agony, firing along each and every nerve. It was more pain than he had ever endured, but still he resisted. He focussed on the ropes that strapped him to the bed and pulled against them until he felt the knots scraping into his flesh.

"You will get nothing from me."

You will relent, child.

The pain came again, somehow more intense than before, and Mallory was taken almost to the edge of unconsciousness. The Master stopped before he could pass out, and as the agony ebbed away, Mallory realised that it took a familiar pathway between him and the Master.

"The Tangle," he said softly, and mentally reached out along the trembling strings of reality. Suddenly immersed, he was not only immune to the ravages of the Master but could sense each and every one of the vampires as they spread out through the city.

"You're looking for me, aren't you?" he asked.

Beside him, Thaddeus stirred in his sleep.

I will break you.

More pain followed, but Marsh simply let it slip into the Tangle, to be dissipated throughout the network. He let out a small laugh.

"I'll never tell you," he said defiantly, "so torture me all you want!"

"Mallory, who are you talking to?" Thaddeus muttered softly as he began to wake up.

I have other tools at my disposal.

Mallory braced for the pain but it never came. In its place was a flood of blinding light, love, and spiritual ecstasy; it caught him completely unawares and he came tumbling back to reality as his defences crumbled. He could only let out a strangled gasp as the Master ploughed deeper and deeper into his mind, plunging into the very depths of his soul.

Soon you will be mine. Soon I will know all abo-

The flood of light vanished along with the voice of the Master as Thaddeus took his hand and held it tight. Mallory gasped with relief and looked at his saviour with grateful eyes.

"You rescued me," he said, "again."

"I'm not keeping score." Thaddeus looked down at Mallory's hand, which was clasped in his. "I guess my touch is enough to keep the Master out of your head."

"It seems that way," Mallory said with a smile. His happiness was short lived, however, as the infection sent a pang of desperate hunger through him which was accompanied by an ache that went all the way down to his bones.

"But it doesn't seem to halt the infection, does it?" Charity said as she walked back into the room with a plate of sandwiches. She offered one to Thad, who took it gratefully. "So, Mister Thane, what does that mean?"

"I have no idea," he said thickly around a mouthful of food.

Charity sighed heavily and rolled her eyes. In the corner, Ivy was muttering and moving in her sleep. *She's chasing rabbits,* Thad thought absent-mindedly.

Mallory eyed the sandwiches greedily. They were piled high with corned beef, cheese, pickled gherkins, and mustard; his stomach growled hungrily, but Charity held the plate out of reach. She looked pointedly at Thaddeus through her glasses.

"Come on, kid, this is your gift. You know how it

works, so draw some inferences from it." She looked at Mallory. "Don't help him, Marsh; he needs to learn to do this on his own."

"I can't," Thaddeus said sadly. "I'm not clever like that."

"Bullshit," Mallory said as he gestured to the map on the wall and the dossier on the desk. "You spotted this before anyone else, and you were better informed than we were. You're a Cep, Thaddeus; you're sharper than most people, even if you don't realise it."

"He's right, Thane." Charity dropped the plate enough for Mallory to snatch a sandwich from it. "So what does it mean?"

"This is really good, Charity," Mallory said with a smile as he swallowed his first bite. "Although it makes my mouth feel a bit funny."

"The Master is a supernatural being," Thad said slowly as his mind whirred, "because my powers affect him. The infection, however, isn't; he's just using it to spread his power."

"Correct," Charity said. "We're dealing with a double threat; something that's both supernatural and mundane at the same time."

"How does that help us?" Thad asked.

"Charity, I'm not feeling too well," Mallory muttered.

"It gives us a starting point to start ruling things out. Most importantly-"

She was cut off as Mallory began to twitch and convulse in the bed, his mouth foaming and his veins standing out darkly beneath his flesh. The hideous black ridges under his fingernails and above his teeth were seizing along with the rest of him. Thaddeus kept hold of his hand as Charity tried to keep him on the bed.

"Ivy!" she yelled. "Doc, we need you!"

Ivy Livingston sat bolt upright in her chair and screamed.

Chapter Twenty Two – The Ashram of the Mind

Ivy

"We're all set, Doc," the man at the controls said.

"Good. Very good." The Doctor's voice was almost without accent; the faintest trace lingered but Ivy couldn't place it. There was a clatter as the Doctor rolled her lollipop around her mouth, the sound muted by her closed lips. Her lipstick was a violent shade of pink, almost neon, .

The Doctor's mouth curled into a smile.

I hate her, Ivy thought.

"Are you ready, little bird?" The Doctor's question was rhetorical and Ivy knew it; they would start whether she said yes or no. Ivy nodded gently as the machine whirred and buzzed into life. The contact gel holding the electrodes at her temples was sticky and slimy; it made her stomach turn.

A light on the wall switched from red to green and the Doctor leant in, her eyes almost luminous in the stark fluorescent lights. Ivy stared at her, frowning as she strained against the straps holding her down.

"Now, little bird, I need you to tell me what you see."

There was a click as an old fashioned stopwatch was started. The rapid ticking made Ivy's heart race, breaking her concentration. In her mind's eye she could see the second hand of the watch sweeping round; the thought of failing the test filled her with dread.

"Talk to me," the Doctor said, her breath unbearably sweet. "Tell me what you see."

Ivy tried to clear her mind. She sat back in the chair and opened her thoughts as she'd been taught. She counted the steps up to her little mountaintop, away from the ticking of the stopwatch and the horrible sensation of the gel.

Nobody can touch me on my mountain.

The flapping of the canvas walls of the tent.

Just follow the path.

The smell of a hot cup of tea in her hands.

Don't stop walking.

The gentle jingle of the bells as they swayed in the wind.

Take all the time you need.

The chill of the Himalayan air.

Learn how to partition yourself.

The coarse hair of the hide blanket.

Build an ashram in your mind.

Ivy opened her eyes and saw both the Doctor with her pink lips and the dimly lit interior of her mountaintop retreat. She smiled and sighed with relief. The man at the controls said something, but she chose not to hear it.

I am safe.

"The next room," said the Doctor. "Tell me all about it."

"Yes, Doc," Ivy said. From her ashram she peered through the clouds and looked down into the adjacent room. "There's a man. He's bald, fat, and he has an envelope in his hands. He's waiting to open it."

Out of Ivy's sight, the Doctor pressed a button.

"A light has gone on in the room. He's opening the envelope." Ivy's gaze narrowed. "He's looking at a picture. It's a photograph; he likes it."

"Tell me how much he likes it, little bird." The Doctor's eyes were gleaming with excitement. "Tell me how he feels."

"He feels funny," she said. "He's short of breath and he's squirming in his seat. He feels-"

Ivy suddenly came crashing from her mountaintop, instead trapped between the Doctor and the strange man in the next room. No matter how she tried, she could not tear her mind's eye away.

"I don't like it! I don't like it, I want it to stop!" Ivy thrashed and screamed in her chair. "Make it stop! Make it stop! Now!"

The man by the controls wavered for a moment, suddenly faint. He was pale and unsteady; he looked about ready to collapse. The Doctor looked unwell too, and after a few seconds she snapped a sharp order.

"Stop her!"

The man hit a big red button on the control board and hundreds of volts zapped through the electrodes on Ivy's head. She twitched and bucked in the chair, screaming at the top of her lungs as her vision dissolved before her. In the next room, the man with the photograph dropped dead, blood streaming from his eyes.

"Make a note," the Doctor said over the screams, "the test was a failure."

Still strapped to the chair, Ivy felt the world dissolve away around her as the electricity burned through her brain. Her little limbs strained against the straps but she was too weak to escape; too small, too frail.

Just a child.

In the main room of the garret, Ivy Livingston snapped awake from the nightmare with a piercing scream.

"Doc, get it together!" Charity yelled from across the room.

The dream immediately faded from memory as Ivy looked across the room and saw Mallory Marsh trembling in some sort of seizure. His veins were dark beneath his skin, but more disturbing was the black webbing that seethed and pulsated just beneath the surface.

That does not look good, said Michaela. *Don't let him bleed on you.*

Ivy snatched up the box of surgical gloves and snapped two pairs on with practised ease. She got to Mallory's side and used a piece of tissue to wipe the spittle from his mouth; a cursory glance showed that his airway was clear.

"Help me lower him down," she said to Charity and Thaddeus.

"Don't let go of him, Thane!" Charity's voice was assertive and he nodded at her instructions. Between the three of them they managed to lay Mallory flat and held him still until the seizure passed. He slipped into an uneasy rest, still turning and moaning slightly.

Ivy leant in close to examine him. The webbing beneath his skin was less visible now, but the area surrounding it seemed inflamed and irritated. She checked his gums and the same was true of the black material that was protruding over his teeth, glistening like wet leather. She looked at it with fascination and at last the word came to her.

"Chitin!" Ivy exclaimed excitedly. "This looks like chitin."

"Isn't that what bugs have?" Charity asked. "Are you

telling me that the Master is some kind of giant gnat?"

"Maybe a mosquito or something similar," Ivy said as she continued her examination, "but chitin is found throughout the entire animal and plant kingdom, so it doesn't exactly narrow it down. Besides, the way this is spreading doesn't exactly scream insect to me."

"Maybe he'll cocoon and turn into one of those things?" Thaddeus said with concern. "What do we do if that happens?"

"I doubt he'll end up like that, but we'll cross that bridge when we come to it." She stood back up and looked directly at Charity. "I've two questions for you."

"Fire away."

"Why does Thaddeus have to keep hold of him?"

"My ability, my gift, it keeps the Master out of Mallory's head, but only so long as I touch him."

"Okay, that makes sense, even if it isn't sustainable in the long term."

"The other?" Charity asked.

"Before his seizure, did anything unusual happen? Was he slurring his speech or suddenly dizzy?"

"No," she replied, "but he did feel a bit funny after eating something."

"What did he eat?"

"This," Charity said as she handed Ivy the plate of sandwiches.

This is very weird, Ivy thought as she carefully examined the food. *It doesn't look like there's anything strange in here, so maybe it's one of the ingredients?*

"Mustard." Ivy turned to look at Jess who was standing in the doorway. "Thad, didn't your aunt's book mention mustard as some sort of repellent to the vampires?"

"Must we keep calling them that?" Charity said with an exasperated groan.

"Ray called them Nightwalkers." Thaddeus looked at Charity in frustration. "Does that meet your exacting standards?"

"It'll do. So, Jess, what's so special about mustard? Isn't it usually garlic in the lore?"

"We could try him with garlic to see if we get a reaction," Thaddeus suggested.

"No!" Ivy and Charity both said in unison. Ivy went on. "Thaddeus, he's already under a tremendous amount of stress and I don't want to risk another seizure; messing around with this in a slapdash manner could kill him."

"Is he stable?" Charity asked Ivy.

"I think so, for now."

"Good. Get your coat on. You too, Jess, and we'll need the remaining UV flares."

"Where are we going?" Jess asked. "It's still dark!"

"Hunting."

"Because that worked so well last time!" Ivy said sarcastically.

"We need to get the Master before he completely takes over Mallory!" Charity stood over the bed and yelled at Ivy. "Do you have a better idea?"

"If you stop yelling and let me think, then yes, I'm sure I will come up with something." Ivy pinched the bridge of her nose and closed her eyes. *Breathe, Ivy. Just take a moment to centre yourself and you'll find all the answers you need.*

Think it through, Livingston. Approach from all angles.

"I need to go to my house," she said after a few

minutes. "We'll go tomorrow evening."

"Why not go as soon as it's light?" Charity demanded.

"You need to sleep, Charity. How long have you been awake?"

"That's unimportant."

"Is it?" Ivy asked as Charity drew a blade from her belt and took a single menacing step towards her. In that moment, Mallory stirred from his stupor and groaned as he struggled to sit back up.

"Go to sleep Walpole," Mallory said, only half opening his eyes. "You're getting paranoid and twitchy. Thank you for checking me over, Doc."

"Think nothing of it." Ivy looked at Charity. The dark circles beneath her eyes were apparent, even with the dark glasses. "Please try to get some rest, Charity. You're no good to Mallory if you wind up dead."

"Going out tomorrow night will be suicide. What if there are Nightwalkers roaming the streets?"

"Oh, I'm certain they will be, but not on that side of the city." Ivy walked over to the desk and picked up Thad's dossier. She flicked through it and nodded to herself as she did so. "Tomorrow night is one of the scheduled events that our Nightwalkers show up to; they'll be otherwise occupied and we can cross the city without incident."

"We could go to the event," Jess said. "Trip, Ray, and I could study them, learn more about their behaviour."

"It's too risky without Thaddeus," Charity said. "He's the only one who we know for sure is immune to the Master's bewitchments, but unfortunately Mallory needs him for exactly the same reason."

"It's a shame I can't be in two places at once."

Thaddeus said sadly. Ivy grinned at him. "What?"

"But what if you could be, or at least functionally be in both places at the same time? Would that work?" Ivy laughed in triumph as Thaddeus nodded. She crossed the room and carried the backpack full of medical supplies over to the bedside.

"Livingston, what are you planning?" Charity asked as Ivy began pulling bags and tubing from their assorted hospital loot.

"Thaddeus Thane," she said gleefully, "have you ever given blood?"

<u>Chapter Twenty Three</u> – Intrusive Thoughts

Thaddeus

"Sharp scratch," Ivy said.

Thaddeus winced as she inserted the needle into a vein on his arm. She filled a small vial before swapping to the empty collection bag. He looked away as she busied herself with setting up the necessary tubes and blood bags for the full donation. He clenched and relaxed his right hand to keep the blood flowing whilst he held Mallory in his left.

"How will we know how much to give him?" Thaddeus asked as Ivy drew up the vial of blood into a clean syringe.

"I'm not sure; this isn't an exact science, you know."

"Why are you so sure that blood is the right thing to give him?" Charity asked moodily. She still hadn't slept but had at least consigned herself to the armchair where she scowled like a cranky toddler.

It's all going to kick off between them, Thaddeus thought. Jessica was in the bedroom getting some rest, and Trip and Ray had headed out to prepare for the evening's hunting; that left Thaddeus alone with the two volatile women and the barely lucid Mallory Marsh. *Between a powder keg and a vampire-to-be.*

"It's always blood in the lore, Charity, and Arabella's diary seems to confirm our assumptions." Ivy gave Thaddeus a reassuring wink. "Thad's late aunt has been right about everything else so far."

"But that all works on the assumption that the

Nightwalkers are vampires, which they aren't!" Charity practically growled the last word in frustration.

"The Nightwalkers occupy the same ecological niche as vampires do in folklore." Ivy said. Thaddeus agreed with her thoughts, but not the slightly smug tone she had taken.

"Livingston," Charity began, "I need you to know that I really, *emphatically,* dislike you."

"It's mutual, Walpole." She leant down beside Mallory. "Sharp scratch, Marsh."

"How much are you giving him?" Thaddeus asked.

"Just a few millilitres; I just want to see if there's any reaction." She carefully injected the blood into a vein on Mallory's arm. Thaddeus felt the young artist squeeze his hand even tighter.

"Are you sure this is safe, Ivy?" Mallory asked breathlessly. "People have been receiving blood transfusions for hundreds of years, right?"

"Of course, and we've perfected the art," Ivy said with a smile. "It's perfectly safe unless..."

Her voice trailed off when Marsh began to stare at his arm as the injection site broke out in hives. Thaddeus saw the colour drain from her face as she looked at him in panic.

"Thaddeus, please tell me that your blood type is O negative!"

"I'm pretty sure I'm A positive, Doc." Mallory gripped his hand so hard that it hurt. "Is that bad?"

"Ivy, my arm hurts and it itches so much!" Marsh hissed and thrashed on the bed. "What's happening to me?"

"Ivy, you stupid bitch!" She admonished herself as she scrambled in the medical bag. "Marsh, what blood type are you?"

"I don't know! Who fucking knows that!?"

"He's almost certainly B neg," Charity said as she rose from the chair.

"That's an incredibly rare blood type, Charity. Are you absolutely sure?" Ivy asked as she filled another syringe. "Hold still Mallory!"

"What is that?" Charity roared as she crossed the room. She grabbed Ivy's wrist in one hand, keeping the glinting hypodermic needle away from Marsh's arm. "Tell me what that is or I'll snap your wrist, Livingston."

"Charity, I- Owww!" Ivy screeched in pain as Charity squeezed her arm.

"I'm not fucking around, Doc. Tell me what that is."

"An immunosuppressant; it'll stop the reaction to Thaddeus's blood antibodies."

"Will that much blood kill him?" Thaddeus asked.

"No, but it's not going to be pleasant." Ivy looked at Charity. "Will you let me go now?"

"Fine, but you aren't giving that to him." She released the doctor's wrist but still stood menacingly close to her.

"It could ease his symptoms."

"He's fighting the vampire infection, Ivy." Thaddeus spoke softly as he tried to defuse the tension in the room. "If you give him that, we could lose him."

"Oh. I didn't think-"

"No, Doc, of course you didn't!" Charity put her face up in Ivy's as she spoke; their noses were almost touching. "Too busy being smug to check something crucial like blood type compatibility, and then almost handing him over to the fucking Master as you rushed to fix your mistake. You're a disgrace, Livingston!"

"If you're so clever, why didn't you say something?" Ivy retorted sharply. "Huh?"

"I'm not a fucking doctor! I kill people for a living!" Charity had a mad grin on her face. "Your days are fucking numbered, Doc, especially if you do something stupid like that again."

"You want to fight, Walpole?" Ivy tossed the syringe on to the bed. "Fine, let's fucking do this!"

"SIT DOWN, BOTH OF YOU!" Charity and Ivy both jumped at the ferocity of Jessica's voice as she stormed into the room.

"She-" Charity began.

"I don't care who started it!" Jessica shoved Charity roughly into the armchair. "Yes, Ivy fucked up, but you will not threaten to kill anyone, understood?"

"I..." Charity opened her mouth to argue but thought better of it. "Sure thing, you're the boss."

"Good." She turned to face Ivy. "As for you, Ivy, you do not make any more unilateral medical decisions, alright? If you think we should do something, you explain it to all of us and we'll make sure that you have all the information."

"I'm assuming that doesn't include emergency first aid?" Ivy asked quietly.

"First aid in an emergency is fine, but no more experimental blood transfusions or other procedures based on guesswork. Agreed?" Ivy nodded. "Good. Lastly, the two of you need to stop fighting; whatever issues you have can wait until Mallory is safe and we've defeated the Master."

Both women gave each other one final dirty look. Thaddeus watched Ivy stalk away into the kitchen as Charity curled up in the chair once again. Thad ran his hands through his hair and breathed a tremendous sigh of relief.

"Thaddeus!" Jessica was looking at him with her eyes wide. "When did you let go of Mallory?"

"Oh shit," he said as he turned to look at the infected artist. *Please let the blood transfusion have worked!*

"I'm fine," Mallory said quietly. "I can't hear the Master at all."

"Thank god for that!" Jessica said with relief.

"Why do you look so frightened, Marsh?" Charity asked from the armchair.

"I can see your faces." He looked at Thaddeus, his eyes wide. "All your faces."

"There's just one problem," Thaddeus said, "I only have a limited supply of blood. What happens when we run out?"

The evening air was cool as Thaddeus and Jessica walked towards the centre of town. They were wearing all black with dramatic makeup. Thad had chosen to go down a more New Romantic avenue and had adopted a style based loosely on Robert Smith in his heyday. Jessica was dressed as a gender-bent *Tom of Finland*, complete with a leather cap and spiked collar.

They got several odd looks as they went; how many were for their unusual outfits and how many were for being out so close to nightfall was a mystery. Thaddeus felt a little self-conscious at the stares but Jessica seemed to take them all in her stride.

"You look absolutely amazing," he said. He leant in and gave her a small kiss on her cheek, leaving a faint mark from his lipstick. "I'm proud to be seen with you."

"And I you, Thad." She grinned at him. "Are we

meeting Trip and Ray there?"

"Yeah; they went back to Trip's place to get ready; they'll be a bit late." He shuddered as the evening turned strangely cold. "I hope we don't have to fend off the Nightwalkers without them."

"We're capable enough," she said in response, and slipped an arm around him. "I'll look after you, Thaddeus."

"Thank you. At least we're armed." He could feel the cupro-nickel knife strapped to his leg and the rustle of plastic in his pocket as he walked. "Last time I went there wasn't a metal detector or anything, so we should be able to get in without getting arrested."

"Yeah, tangling with the cops would definitely put a downer on things. It's a shame we couldn't bring any firepower with us."

"I know The Coven pretty well; I helped install the new lighting rig a few years back. We'll be able to get out easily enough if we need to." He smiled at her. "Have you been to many goth themed club nights before?"

"No, but I'm looking forward to it. Even if we don't find any Nightwalkers it should still be fun."

"I'm hoping to see a few friends there," Thaddeus said quietly. "It'll be enough just to know they're okay."

They continued walking as the sun slipped below the horizon. The street lights were burning bright as they turned on to Oxpens Road, where they saw several other people dressed similarly to them heading towards The Coven like moths to a flame.

As they drew closer they could hear the dull thudding of music from the club. Jess had a small bounce in her step and Thaddeus felt a little giddy, both from excitement and blood loss. *This feels right,* he thought, *this is exactly where we're supposed to be.*

They made their way to the entrance of the nightclub and Thaddeus paid their entry fee. They got their stamps and entered The Coven. The bar level was still sparsely populated but down below on the dance floor the event was in full swing.

Jess and Thaddeus made their way to the bar and tried to get the bartender's attention. He was leaning on the bar talking to one of the other patrons, seemingly oblivious to all the other customers. Thaddeus felt the hair on his arms stand on end as the music blared and the lights pulsed.

He went to say something to Jess when he saw the telltale eyeshine flash of a Nightwalker; it was the woman talking to the bartender. *They're already here!* He whirled around, reaching for his blade but a strong arm slammed him into the bar.

A clawed hand held his shoulder and forced him to the ground. He looked around frantically for Jessica but his panicked yell was drowned out by the music. The lights flared once more and he saw her, expression glazed, as one of the Nightwalkers led her down to the dance floor; it was her room mate, Jade.

"Say goodbye to your pretty friend, Thane," growled one of the Nightwalkers. Thaddeus looked around and saw that most, if not all, of the other patrons had the shine in their eyes. *This entire club is full of Nightwalkers,* he realised in horror. He slipped his hand into his pocket, fingers scrabbling for one of the packets he'd stashed there.

"The Master sends his regards." The Nightwalker holding him opened its mouth wide, revealing slimy chitinous teeth capable of tearing through Thaddeus in a single bite. It lunged downwards, aiming for his throat.

Any advantage, he thought as he tore open the mustard packet, covering the creature's mouth in yellow gloop. It screamed in agony, and loosened its grip enough for him to slip free. As he did so he pulled out the blade and drove it into the base of the creature's skull, just like Charity had showed him that afternoon.

"Nifty knife work, indeed," he said softly. He noticed that his little trick with the mustard has disoriented all the nearby Nightwalkers. *Very interesting,* he thought as he dashed towards the dance floor in pursuit of Jess and her captor.

Chapter Twenty Four – Bagged Blood and Shaving Soap

Mallory

I can see their faces, Mallory thought once again as Ivy and Charity geared up to leave the garret. Dr Livingston was still quite subdued after the transfusion mishap, but perhaps that was for the best; they could do without the headbutting on their mission across the city.

"How are you feeling, Marsh? Still not a slave to the Master?" Charity asked. She was more cheerful and upbeat after almost ten hours of sleep. Mallory gave her a thumbs up. "Good. Whilst I hate to say it, Doc, using Thaddeus's blood was a stroke of genius."

"Thank you," Ivy said with a quiet smile. "Are you sure you're doing well enough to be left alone, Mallory?"

"I'm sure, Doc. Besides, Jess and Thaddeus will be here for a little while longer." He settled back in the bed, his arms still restrained. He frowned as he felt the now familiar pangs of hunger shoot through his body. Even though the Master's voice was out of his head, the Nightwalker sickness was still changing him from the inside.

He flexed his hands and the chitin claws extended out a few inches; they were tapering to jagged edges. *I could really do some damage with these.* He craned his neck and bared his teeth, trying to catch a glimpse of the painful growths in his mouth.

"Can one of you please get me a mirror?" Mallory

asked.

"I'm not so sure that's a good idea." Ivy hovered nervously in the doorway. "Wouldn't you agree, Charity?"

"Yeah, Marsh, I wouldn't if I were you. You don't look so hot."

"I've never been able to see my face properly before, and this might be my only chance. Please, I only want to have a quick look."

"Alright then," Ivy said as she fished a small compact mirror from her bag. "In fact, you can use it as a quick test to see if you are still protected from the Master's influence."

"That's a clever idea, Doc," he said. He took the mirror in one bound hand and flipped it open, angled away from him. *Remember, Mallory, the Nightwalker sickness is going to make you look monstrous; it's not how you usually are.* He brought the mirror up to catch his reflection and gasped at what he saw.

His eyes were bloodshot and rimmed with dark circles. He blinked and a milky tear trickled down his face. *I look exhausted,* he thought. His usually full cheeks were gaunt and his olive skin was tinged with jaundice. His veins were dark and the unsettling black webbing spread over his face, just beneath the surface; he swore that he could see it moving.

The glistening black growths that comprised his Nightwalker teeth deformed his mouth and jutted out from behind his lips. He opened his mouth and thick slimy strings of saliva dangled from the insect-like protrusions.

Mallory strained slightly, tensing the muscles in his face. The black teeth trembled and retracted into his gums. He smiled at his reflection; he looked more human now, albeit a bit sickly. *I have a face,* he thought, *a real face!*

"Are you alright there, Mallory?" Ivy asked gently.

"I'm okay thanks, Doc. Just stunned at how good I look, all things considered." He gave her a tired wink.

"What do we do if the effects of Thaddeus's blood wear off?" Charity asked. "We can't hook him up to an intravenous drip, can we, Doc?"

"Hmmm," Ivy mused. "It seems a small amount of the blood lasts a very long time. It's unlikely that it'll just stop working all of a sudden; biology doesn't really work like that."

"So it could be permanent?" Mallory asked. "I don't want to fall back under the Master's control, but I also don't want to lose my gift, Doc."

"I don't think it will be permanent, although when we understand more about what's happening to you we should have a better idea of how to proceed." She looked at him, thoughtful for a moment. "I think that the effects of our current treatment will wear off gradually, so you'll have some warning before the Master can exert any control over you."

"What do we do, Ivy?" Charity asked. "We're burning daylight."

"I'm going to rig you up a saline drip, with the bag of Thaddeus's blood attached by a little valve; if you feel yourself starting to slip, you can switch yourself over from the saline until you start to feel more in control."

"It's that simple?" he asked, sceptical.

"Yes, in theory." Ivy looked nervously at Charity.

"Go ahead, Doc, you've got my vote on this."

"Alright. The most important thing, Mallory, is that you *must* switch back to the saline as soon as you can;

the immune response will get more severe each time. It will kill you eventually." She looked at him, suddenly deadly serious. "This is not a permanent solution, so anything you can tell us about the Master is vital."

"I'll have a think and write down as much as I can."

Ivy nodded and proceeded to set up the saline and blood bags, along with the valve assembly. As she did so, he watched Charity show Thaddeus several methods to quickly dispatch an enemy. Mallory watched him practice the motions over and over, and realised that the movements of Thad's muscles were getting him a little hot under the collar.

"Are you alright, Mallory?" Ivy asked as she inserted a cannula into his arm. "You've gone very red."

"I'm fine, Doc, or at least as well as can be expected." He gave her a quick smile, and she turned her head slightly to look at Thaddeus.

"Ah, I see," she said softly. "Good for you, Marsh."

"Before you go, can you put my satchel within reach, please? It would be nice to pass the time painting or drawing."

"Of course." She placed the bag on the bed beside him. "I'll also get you the dossier that Thaddeus compiled of all the missing persons."

"Are we all set, Doc?" Charity asked. Ivy nodded as she handed the folder to Mallory. "Excellent. Good work, Thane; you'll be a top agent in the Ministry in no time. Try not to get killed tonight."

"I'll do my best," he said breathlessly. His shirt was drenched in sweat, so he pulled it over his head. "I should have a shower before I get dressed up."

"As for you, Marsh," Charity said with a grin, "have

fun with your blood and crayons."

Mallory waved them off. Ivy took a quick glance at Thaddeus before shooting the artist a passing wink. The door swung shut behind them.

"Here," Thaddeus said as he walked over, shirtless, "you should take a look through these."

"Oh, yes," Mallory said as he was handed two books, "good thinking."

He looked down at them; they were Arabella's field notebook and diary. *I'm sure I can find something useful in here,* he thought, *if I can focus.* Thaddeus glistened slightly in the dim light of the garret and smiled at Mallory.

He leant in and gently kissed him. Mallory kissed back with a little more force and urgency, but pulled back sharply as the door to the stairway opened. Ivy breezed in, trying and failing to avert her gaze from the two men.

"Sorry, sorry, I don't mean to interrupt. I just forgot something very important."

"Don't worry, Ivy, it's fine!" Mallory said with a laugh. "We're all adults here."

"This is true," she said, "but I am sorry about this."

Before he could ask her what she meant, she reached out with a pair of pliers held in one gloved hand and ripped one of the chitinous claws from his fingers.

Mallory massaged his aching hand as Thaddeus and Jessica got ready for the event at The Coven. *I can't believe she did that so casually!* He was still reeling from Ivy tearing out the unsettling growth almost an hour ago; she had clearly expected it to break easily and was shocked when she ripped out almost six inches of fibrous material.

She had stood there for a moment, transfixed by the dangling threads that sprouted from the torn edge of the claw, but hastily transferred it to a specimen jar when those same tendrils began to move in an insidious, questing manner.

"How's your hand?" Jessica asked softly as she came to sit with him. "Thad told me what Ivy did and I can't say that I'm too impressed at her medical ethics."

"I'll live," he said with a grim chuckle, "but I don't think she takes the 'do no harm' part of her oath very seriously."

"You can say that again." She traced a finger down his cheek. "You've got some serious stubble going on, Mal."

"I'm not exactly in a position to shave." He held up his hands and strained at his restraints to prove his point. "It does itch something awful though."

"I can do it for you, if you'd like?" She asked him, with a slightly sultry smile.

"Aren't you worried I'll get loose and hurt you?"

"You'd need to cut your way out of those, Mallory. I'm good with knots. I'm sure that when this is all over I can find some time to teach you." She winked at him.

I can see why Thad likes her, he thought. He noticed that Thane was watching the two of them with a knowing look on his face. Mallory had to fight back a giggle; Thaddeus was halfway through wrangling his hair into an artfully tousled mess and it looked ridiculous.

"You can borrow my shaving set, Mallory," he said, "but only if I'm allowed to watch."

"Pervert," he replied jokingly. "In all seriousness, though, I would kill for a shave."

"No bloodshed needed, but I will bank a favour with you, Mallory." Jess grinned and headed for the bathroom. *I wonder what kind of favour she wants?* He let his mind run to the best and worst places all at once as he settled back more comfortably on the bed.

"Now that's one hell of an expression!" Thaddeus said.

"It matches your one half of a hairdo, Thad."

"Play nicely, lads," Jessica said as she walked back in with Thaddeus's razor, bowl, and brush. "I'll get some hot water and a shaving soap. Any preferences?"

"I don't know what's on offer."

"Let me pick one for you," Thaddeus said. He trailed one hand over Jess's waist as he passed her.

"This, um, this..." Mallory paused as he searched for the right words, but came up short. "This feels like a *thing*, you know?"

"What kind of thing, Mallory?" Jess asked with mock innocence.

"Something sex adjacent, at the very least," he said after a moment's hesitation.

"Is that a problem?" Thaddeus asked as he entered with a small wooden pot.

"Not for me," Mallory said. "I assume you're both agreeable to this?"

Thaddeus and Jessica both nodded in affirmation. Mallory, delighted to be receiving such close attention from two beautiful people, squirmed ever deeper into the bed. Thaddeus let Mallory sniff the soap; it was heady with lavender and bergamot. He went to fetch the rest of the items as Jessica began soaking the brush.

He groaned in pleasure as Thaddeus applied a hot towel to his face; a glorious contrast to the cold compress of the previous night. He heard, rather than saw, Jess mix up the soap into a rich, foamy lather. As soon as Thaddeus removed the towel, she set about him with the brush.

The bristles were softened slightly from the hot water, but still pleasingly stiff. The soap was thick and unctuously perfumed; he felt his toes quiver as she lathered his face in easy practised strokes. *Oh, this is heaven,* he thought.

Beside him Thaddeus stropped his blade on a leather and the rough sound was the perfect accompaniment to the gentle sensation of the soap bubbles slowly collapsing. Then Jess was before him, razor in hand as Thaddeus sat in his armchair to watch.

"Stay still now," she told him softly as she placed her empty hand on his thigh. With deliberate care she slid the blade down his face, audibly cutting the hair with a faint rasp. She rinsed the blade and repeated; again and again until Mallory was as closely shaven as he'd ever been. Thaddeus wiped his face clean with a fresh towel and spritzed him with a fern scented aftershave.

"Good boy," Jess said. She planted a kiss on his left cheek as Thaddeus gave him one on his right. "Now you get to watch us get ready, which I'm sure will be a treat for you."

"When you're free of the Master fully," Thaddeus said, "the three of us are going to have so much fun."

"That's as good a reason to fight this as there ever could be," Mallory said with a beaming, satisfied grin. "I'm looking forward to it already."

He was still smiling when they headed out to The Coven, leaving him alone with his books, art supplies, and a bag of Thaddeus's blood. He stretched and settled down to try and get some rest, despite the urgent growling of his stomach. He'd just closed his eyes and was gently dropping off to sleep when he was jolted awake.

Mallory.

Chapter Twenty Five – Home Sweet Home

Ivy

"I can't believe that you ripped that out of his hand, Ivy!"

"I need a sample." Ivy blushed as she spoke. "I thought a bit would break off. I didn't expect the whole thing to come away completely and-"

She stopped in the street as a sudden flash of realisation hit her. *Why didn't I see this before?* She resumed walking, much faster than before with a determined look on her face. Charity trotted along, keeping pace and looking equal parts concerned and confused.

"Everything alright in there, Doc?"

"Yes, it's fine; I just had a thought about Mallory's condition."

"Care to share with the rest of the class?"

"I pulled that thing out of his finger in its entirety, yet it had no blood vessels or connective tissue save those creepy little tendrils. You know what that means?" Ivy asked excitedly. Charity shook her head blankly. "The claws and the teeth and the webbing aren't Mallory's at all!"

"What, they're some sort of *thing* growing inside him?"

"Yes."

"Like a parasite?"

"Exactly!" Ivy jumped and made an excited little squeak as she walked. "If the Nightwalker infection is just a parasite that the Master is using to spread his influence, then it should be possible to cure it."

"So that horrible slime that the Nightwalker puked all over Mallory was some sort of reproductive material?"

"Most likely, yes."

"That's fucking rank." Charity grimaced and shook her head. "Nah, I don't like that one bit. That is absolutely rancid."

"We can definitely agree on that." Ivy's mind was abuzz with questions and ideas as the two women strode purposefully towards the High Street; so much so, in fact, that she didn't notice Charity talking at first. "I'm sorry, my mind was elsewhere; what did you say?"

"I asked if you planned on walking or if you wanted to get the number ten bus up to your place?"

"We'll get the fifteen; it's quicker and usually less busy, especially at this time of day." They'd lost track of time in the sunless main room of the garret and evening was fast approaching. The streets were thronging with people hurrying to get home before nightfall. *They know something is wrong,* Ivy thought, *but I wonder how many of them would be willing to do something about it?*

"The fifteen goes past the Warneford and the Churchill hospitals, doesn't it?" Charity asked.

"It does, but I'm not worried about being seen."

"That's not why I mentioned it." Charity pushed her glasses further up her nose, hiding her eyes completely. "I'd just really rather get the ten, if it's all the same to you."

"If I agree to get the bus you want, will you tell me what's bothering you?" Ivy asked. When Charity groaned in response, she sighed and continued. "I am a licensed therapist, Charity; I might actually be able to help you, at least a little bit."

"Fine," Charity said, "but it goes no further."

"Of course not."

"And I'm not paying you!" Ivy chuckled at how insistent the pale woman was. "The Ministry doesn't pay particularly well, even with all my training."

"I'll waive my usual fee on one condition; you have to stop calling me 'Doc'."

"Is that it?"

"Yes." Ivy sighed as the echoes of her dream came flooding back to her. "I fucking hate it when people call me that. If you must shorten 'Dr Livingston', please just call me Liv."

"Sure thing, D- I mean, Liv."

They walked in silence for a few minutes, filtering through the crowd. Fortune smiled on them as they reached the top of Cornmarket Street; a number ten bus stood ready and waiting at the stop. Ivy scanned her bus pass and took a seat. She watched in amusement as Charity pulled a handful of change out of her pocket and counted out the fare.

"You can pay by card, you know."

"I don't carry one," she replied. "Being invisible fucks with all kinds of technology, bank cards included."

"Huh. I'd never have expected that." She grinned at Charity as the bus's engine rumbled and they pulled away. "Every day's a school day, it seems. So, Charity Walpole, why this bus instead of the fifteen?"

"I want to avoid the hospitals if I can help it," she said quietly as she drew her arms tight around her. "I fucking hate hospitals."

"You don't strike me as someone who gets sick a lot, or at least admits they're sick enough to get medical attention." Ivy moved to sit next to Charity and took one of her hands in hers. "So what's the story?"

"It's nothing special," Charity said offhandedly. When Ivy continued to sit in receptive silence, she went on. "I've got cancer; I can't tell you what kind because I really don't know, nor do I want to find out."

"I'm so sorry."

"It comes with the territory. When you're invisible, most of the light passes through you without interaction. Some of it does, though, especially the UV rays; you spend long enough out of sight and it will absolutely wreck your genetic material." She frowned sadly. "I've been in and out of hospital my whole life and I'm fucking sick of it."

"Can't they cure you?"

"They can kick it back into remission for a while, but it'll always come back. The Ministry has some pretty decent doctors and the chemotherapy works well, even if the side effects are a bitch to deal with."

"I'm surprised that there aren't people with healing gifts who can make you better."

"There are," Charity said bitterly, "but their abilities are limited. The problem with a Libra healing you is that they take on your illness, and they have to recover before they can heal again; it's either that or take on so much damage that they die."

"That doesn't sound like much of a gift to me."

"We're all cursed, Ivy. The rest is just window dressing." She shook her head angrily. "And even if I was the sort of person comfortable with offloading my cancer on some poor Libra, I wouldn't be able to; the Ministry tightly controls who they're allowed to treat.

"Do you think the Royals live so long by virtue of good genetics?" she asked with a dark laugh. "The Queen got through three or four of the best healers out there before she finally died. So much to keep one useless person alive."

"That's awful!"

"That's the worst of the Ministry for you, Liv; comply or die." Ivy squeezed Charity's hand gently. "So that's my problem with hospitals. Are you satisfied?"

"Thank you for opening up to me." She gave the pale woman a smile. "I won't tell anyone, Charity."

They rode the rest of the way in silence and as the bus neared their destination the last slivers of sunlight faded into darkness.

It's only been a few days, Ivy thought as she walked up the garden path to her front door, *and yet it feels like this is no longer my home.*

"Joseph wanted me to kill you," Charity said softly. "When I followed you home from the hospital the night you met Mallory; I was supposed to then, but I couldn't. I just thought I should tell you."

"Thank you. I'd already come to that conclusion, but it's good of you to tell me." She fumbled in her coat pocket for her door keys, but Charity leant past her and pushed the door open. The handle wobbled loosely as the door moved, and the frame was damaged and splintered around the latch plate. "Has someone broken into my house?"

"That's Joseph's handiwork; I'd recognise it anywhere."

"But that's impossible, isn't it?" Ivy asked as the other woman drew a blade. "They can't enter where they aren't invited; that's one of the rules!"

"It's possible that the rules don't quite work like that, or that they're bunk altogether." She bent down to examine the damage more carefully. "This isn't that recent; this might've happened last night or the one before."

"How could he enter my house?" Ivy's voice was panicked, almost shrill. "Vampires don't work like that!"

"The Nightwalkers, as we agreed to call them, seem to be bound by some extremely strange conventions and compulsions, but I can take a guess why Evans could enter here so freely." She smiled sheepishly at Ivy. "The evening you threatened me with the razor, he made me bring him here and I let him in. It was the only way to get him off your case."

"Does that mean he can go anywhere he's previously had access?"

"Sure looks that way, and I'd be willing to bet that it lets the rest of them in too. We should hurry, Ivy."

She nodded and breezed past Charity and into the living room. She stopped on her way to the kitchen to retrieve Michaela's textbook from the sofa; it was still where she had left it. With the book safely under one arm, she rummaged in a cupboard for a large wooden box with a handle atop it.

"Is that a fucking microscope?" Charity asked as Ivy unclipped the box and pulled the heavy instrument out of it.

"Yes, it is. Can you plug it in and switch it on, please? The bulb will need to warm up a little before we use it. I need to get some slides and Michaela's chemistry kit."

"Sure thing." Charity peered at the cover of the

book. "Diagnostic Mycology, by Michaela Inglewood. Wait a second!"

Ivy smiled as she heard Charity gasp. When she walked back into the kitchen, she found the pale woman tapping Michaela's author portrait with her finger.

"This is you!"

"Nope, that's Michaela. I don't need glasses." Ivy grinned at her. "And before you say it, yes, it is tremendously weird but it's also my life."

"Michaela is respected in her field enough to publish textbooks?"

"Uh huh. If you're going to be technical about it, we've got something like six degrees between us, ranging from a BA in Contemporary Cinema through my Medical Degree, to Michaela's Doctorate in Medical Mycology. I lose track, truth be told."

"How old are you?" Charity said, peering over her glasses.

"Thirty eight." She gave the stunned pale woman a wink. "I know, I look good for my age."

"That's still a lot of education, Ivy."

"I was a precocious child. I had my A-Levels firmly under my belt when I was thirteen, although I switched into medicine from chemistry, and became a psychiatrist after that." Ivy looked up from the chemistry kit as Charity just gawped at her. "What's the matter, Walpole?"

"I'm thirty seven," she muttered.

"It's not a competition," Ivy responded with a little too much glee. "Could you pass me that chopping board, please?"

Charity wordlessly handed her the chopping board, but as Ivy reached out to take it the pale woman grabbed her by the wrists and pulled up her sleeve. Ivy squirmed, but Charity's grip was too strong.

"Let me go!" Ivy yelled in protest as Charity peered at her forearms. "What are you looking for? I'm not infected, if that's what you're thinking."

"What is this?" Charity demanded as she shook Ivy's left arm. Ivy tried not to look at the deformed red patch on the inside of her forearm; it always made her feel dreadfully self-conscious. "Answer me, Livingston!"

"It's a burn. I was in a fire when I was younger; you saw me naked the day you broke in here. I'm covered in them." She yanked herself free of Charity's grasp. "What's your fucking problem?"

Charity opened her mouth to answer, but instead of speaking she pointed to the kitchen window. Ivy turned and saw three Nightwalkers staring in at them. Charity drew a knife in each hand as there was a deafening crash as the front door was smashed in. Ivy was speechless but Charity's eyes flared with the thrill of the fight.

"Here we go again!"

Chapter Twenty Six – Dance Commander

Thaddeus

Thaddeus's heart thundered in his ears as he slashed at the Nightwalkers in his path as he gave chase through the Coven. *Thank fuck they're all a bit messed up by the mustard,* he thought with relief.

He brought his blade round in a broad arc from his left shoulder all the way round to his right flank, and grimaced as he was splattered with gore and slime from the injured creatures. They staggered slightly and he was able to barge past them. One of the Nightwalkers tumbled over the railing and landed on a raised part of the dance floor below with a crack that was audible over the pounding of the music.

Thad glanced down and saw Jess being led towards the private rooms near the back of the club. He briefly considered throwing his blade at her former room mate, but he wasn't confident enough in his aim and it would leave him completely unarmed.

Charity would go through these like a hot knife through butter, he thought angrily. *I wish I had a gun or at least my kukri.*

The Nightwalkers were beginning to recover from their confusion and were closing in fast. Thad had only seconds to make a decision; either fight his way down the stairs to rescue Jess or break for the street in an attempt to escape. He looked frantically around him and chose a third option.

Thaddeus rolled under a sweeping blow from one of the creatures and dashed to the left, away from the stairs. The Nightwalkers followed him in one lurching mass with a single goal; to kill him and drink him dry.

He led them back towards the bar. Several of the creatures leapt on to the counter, slipping on bar mats as they gained their feet. Thad dropped down and slid towards the hard wood of the bar; wood decorated with inverted crosses.

He hit the bar with a thud and hooked his fingers under the decorative metal and pulled. His hands bled and his muscles screamed in agony; a normal human would never be able to pry one of the crosses loose, but Thaddeus wasn't normal.

I am stronger and faster, he thought as the Nightwalkers surrounded him.

With a cracking sound he pulled the cross from the wall and flipped it the right way up. The creatures immediately shrieked and recoiled from it and he screamed out in triumph.

"Back!" he cried as he got to his feet. He thrust the cross forwards, driving the creatures towards the dance floor. "Back, I say!"

He lashed out and kicked another cringing Nightwalker over the railings and slashed the throat of another. As he gained ground he noticed that some of the creatures were growing bolder and they lashed out with their ragged claws as he passed them. His circle of safety was rapidly shrinking and his time was running out.

Now or never.

He swung the cross like an axe, cutting down the Nightwalker closest to the stairs. He dropped down and sheathed his blade. He ducked back, dodging a swipe that would've taken his head clean off, then lurched towards the stairs. He scrambled upright, desperate to keep as much of his momentum as possible, and took the stairs two at a time. He nearly lost his balance and saw movement in the corner of his eye; more Nightwalkers were coming up from the dance floor.

The fear rose in his heart and something inside him screamed at him to stop; to turn tail and run. He ignored it and barrelled down the stairs towards the hairpin turn that would take him fully on to the dance floor. He'd slipped on these stairs on a previous visit and had crashed into the railings, breaking a rib. Memories of that pain made his feet leaden, but he pushed through them.

"Trust your body, kid," he whispered to himself.

He leapt when he was still six steps from the turn, his left leg leading through the air. His foot landed atop the railing and he used the solid metal to hop forwards, towards the dance floor. As he sailed through the air, he brought the metal cross up high above his head with one of the sharp edges pointing forwards.

He landed on a Nightwalker. As he knocked it to the ground he whipped the cross sharply downward, like a pickaxe. The metal spike drove through the creature's skull and into the floor. Thaddeus had to lean to one side to avoid being skewered on the other end of the metal cruciform.

He rolled once again, his chest burning from the exertion. There were too many Nightwalkers between him and Jess, so he changed his plan once again and sped towards the DJ platform. He grunted as a set of claws raked down his back, but kept going; the damage was superficial.

He crashed into the platform and scrambled on to it as the Nightwalkers caught up to him. They were pouring in, now; all the ones from the bar upstairs were heading towards him, desperate for a kill, and the creature holding Jess lingered to watch his bloody end.

The track changed over as Thaddeus staggered to the lighting deck and smiled.

"Fire in the disco!" the lead singer yelled through the speakers. "Fire in the Taco Bell!"

Go to hell, all of you, he thought as his fingers danced over the switches and dials.

"Fire in the disco!" he sang along as he flicked on The Coven's Ultraviolet Strobe. "Fire in the Gates of Hell!"

The lights flashed an eerie blueish purple and the Nightwalkers began to scream as they fought their way towards the stairs, but it was too late. Thaddeus let out a triumphant war cry as the club full of creatures howled and thrashed their way to a horrid, blazing death.

It took a few moments for the Nightwalker spell to release Jess. When she came back to herself, surfacing as if from a deep dream, she heard a saxophone solo as Thaddeus danced in celebration above a room of smouldering remains.

"Thaddeus," she called out, "what the fuck happened here?"

The two of them staggered out of The Coven as the fire alarm blared. Thaddeus had pulled it after some of the burning debris from the dance floor had started several small fires; he was fairly certain that they were the only ones alive in the nightclub, but he wanted to be sure.

Smoke began to pour from the doorway and Thad, suddenly exhausted, collapsed in a heap on the pavement. Jess sat next to him and put one arm tenderly around his shoulders. He winced slightly; the wounds in his back weren't deep, but they were painful.

"Thank you for rescuing me," she said softly. "I can't explain how it feels when they get their words in your head, Thaddeus; it's awful and wonderful all at once. It's like I forgot that we were meant to be fighting them."

"That sounds horrifying. I'm sorry I let them separate us; it won't happen again." He looked down Oxpens Road and saw two figures hurrying towards them. He was about to pull his blade from his boot when he realised that it was Trip and Ray. Thaddeus sighed with relief and slumped into Jess's arms.

"Hey," Trip yelled when they were close enough to be heard, "are you two okay?"

"Thad's hurt." Jess helped Thaddeus to his feet as their friends reached them. Ray pulled off a long scarf and used it as a makeshift bandage to wrap Thaddeus's torso with.

"Jesus Christ," Ray said as a tongue of flame spurted out from the nightclub door, "what happened here?"

"It was a fucking trap. They knew we were coming." Thaddeus groaned with exertion as he took a few unsteady steps up the road in the direction of Jericho. "I don't know how they got the drop on us, but we need to get back to the safety of the garret."

"I took the time to make these," Trip said as he handed Thad and Jess two long tubes; each comprised one of the strobe lights with a cylinder of liquid attached to it. "They can strobe or they can be on constantly, only the latter drains the batteries faster. Give them a go."

Jess flicked hers on and the tube lit up with an intense glow. She waved it back and forth, amazed at how bright it was, before switching it off.

"Is that UV?" Thaddeus asked, clearly impressed.

"Yeah, and the chemicals in the liquid only make it more intense."

"How did you come up with this?" Jess asked.

"Internet," Trip said casually, with a shrug. "I can make more later, but we should get moving."

The four of them hurried as fast as they could through the deserted city streets. *It isn't yet eleven o'clock,* Thaddeus thought, *and it's fucking deserted here.* He glanced down every side street as they went, and they crossed the Hythe Bridge into the city proper. There was slightly more life here, but still far less than Thaddeus would have expected for that time on a Tuesday night, especially given the balmy weather.

They swung on to Worcester street as they left the bridge, and hurried the short distance to reach Walton Street. The closer they got to Jericho the better Thaddeus started to feel. *When we're home we can work out our next steps.*

His calm was shattered as they turned down Richmond Road. A single man was stood in the centre of the street some thirty metres away. He had short sandy hair and wore a long black leather coat, much like Charity's, albeit far less bleached.

"Thaddeus Thane!" The man called as he walked slowly towards them. His Welsh accent was unmistakable and Thad saw the other three wince a little at the sound. "Oh, Thaddeus Thane!"

Thad saw him take a deep breath in. He immediately grabbed hold of Jess and pulled her in close to him. He turned his back to the man, shielding her, as he slipped his hands over her ears. He closed his eyes tight as Joseph Evans screamed.

The deadly wave of sound moved down the road, shattering windows and shaking cars as it went. It broke harmlessly over Thaddeus and Jessica as his Taboo gift nullified the Shriek's supernatural voice. Trip and Ray, unfortunately, took the full force of it.

They let out strangled cries as their veins ruptured and their lungs collapsed under the sheer force of the noise. Evans changed his pitch slightly and Trip dropped dead as his heart burst. Ray managed a few seconds longer, but succumbed as the blood vessels in his brain popped.

Thaddeus heard the dying gasps of his fallen comrades and his heart filled with rage. He waited until the scream was over and rounded on Evans as Jess retreated, careful to keep Thad between her and the psychopathic Shriek.

"You'll have to go through me to get her!" Thaddeus roared.

"She can go; in fact I couldn't care less about her, Mister Thane." Evans strolled up the road towards him, smiling as he went. "She's only human, after all; just a provincial. When the Master is done with this city we can easily hunt her down like the bitch she is."

"What do you want from me?" He asked warily. *Come a little bit closer, you bastard.*

"I want nothing from you, Thaddeus, but the Master wants you on side. He can't persuade you like he can with others, so you will need to submit willingly."

"And if I refuse?"

"I get to kill you, just like I killed your parents." Evans chuckled to himself. "Feel free to thank me for that whenever you want; good god they must've been insufferable!"

"I'm not taking the bait, Evans. I'm going to walk away and there's not a thing you can do to stop me."

"Perhaps not, but I can still enjoy the fact that I killed two of your little friends, not to mention that Charity and her pet human are being torn to pieces in Lye Valley as we speak." He was close enough for Thaddeus to see the webbing beneath his skin. "But most of all, I am shocked that you thought a few drops of your blood could possibly hold the will of the Master at bay.

"You've been played, Thaddeus, and your girlfriend is going to be torn to pieces the second she sets foot in that miserable little flat of-"

Evans screamed as Thaddeus lit up the UV lamp, and he recoiled down the street at phenomenal speed, disappearing down an alley. At that point, Thad was already sprinting back to the garret, hoping that, against all odds, he wasn't too late.

Chapter Twenty Seven – His Master's Voice

Mallory

I can see you, Mallory Marsh.

Mallory reached for the blood bag valve as he looked at his reflection in the small mirror Ivy had given him. What he saw gave him pause.

"I can still see my face." His mouth set in a defiant snarl. "How can you be here if I can still see my face?"

A few drops of accursed blood might lessen your gifts and alleviate your curse, but nothing can hold me back, Mallory. Nothing at all.

"And yet you aren't flooding me with pain or your divine inspiration," he said as he puzzled through the situation. "Perhaps a few drops isn't enough to cut you off entirely, but it's sufficient to keep the worst of you walled off."

If I took a bigger dose would it sever the link completely? Mallory waited for the Master to respond to his thoughts, but nothing happened. *Aha.*

"You can only see what I want to share, can't you?" He smiled and pulled some of his art materials close. "How does it feel to not have complete control for once?"

You will address me by my title!

"Why?"

I am the Master! I am God's instrument on earth, the saviour of humanity; you cannot resist my divine mandate.

"I like to think of myself as more of a humanist agnostic, so I don't really gel with your plan." Mallory laughed as he felt the Master's frustration. "How about you just tell me your name?"

I have taken many names over the years, and worn many faces, Mallory Marsh. Knowledge of any of them would do you no good.

"Call it idle curiosity then." He picked up a piece of the charcoal as his eyes hovered halfway closed. Mallory's mind reached out probing for the tangle, hoping that his gift wasn't completely washed away by Thaddeus's blood.

It was there, but the connection was weak and unstable. *There isn't enough of a Knot here,* he thought angrily. *I can't force him out if I can't get enough of a link!*

Mallory's cheeks flushed with frustration and he was on the verge of hurling his charcoal across the room when he had a sudden flash of inspiration.

"You want me to let you in?" he asked.

Yes, Mallory Marsh. Open yourself to me.

"As you wish," he said, closing his eyes entirely.

The rain hammered on the glass of the conservatory as the thunder rumbled darkly in the sky. A young girl, barely eight years old, sat on the floor amongst a landslide of paper and crayons. She wore a pretty black frock and a glazed expression. Atop her head perched an oversized black yachting cap festooned with badges.

Her tongue poked out of the corner of her mouth as she tried to sketch face after face, but all the features were dead looking and generic. She grunted in exasperation and flung the papers against the glass.

Unseen in the corner of the room, Mallory stood and watched the girl sadly. Beside him was a formless mass of questing darkness; the Master. *He'll take shape soon enough,* Mallory thought with a smile.

"Why are we here, Mallory Marsh?" asked the Master. His voice was twisted and echoing, like a chorus of the damned.

"We're here because you want to know me. I'm simply doing as you asked."

"Who is this child?"

"That's me," Mallory said. "This is the day of my father's funeral. He was a good man."

"I can understand grief on such a day, but why such anger at your drawings?" The Master's voice was getting clearer with every passing moment. Mallory did not answer, instead choosing to walk to the centre of the room. He crouched down beside the little girl and smiled sadly.

"I'm sorry this was such a difficult day for you," he said softly to his younger self, "but it gets better. I promise."

"There you are!" All three of them turned as a young man, probably sixteen or seventeen years of age, strode into the room. He bore a striking resemblance to Mallory, both past and present. He joined the young Mallory on the floor. "We were worried that you'd run off into the storm."

"I can't remember him, Francis!" she said as the tears came fast and hot. "I keep trying to draw him but I don't remember what he looks like!"

Francis Marsh took the young Mallory in his arms and held her tight, stroking her hair and making soothing noises. After a few moments he reached into his black suit jacket and pulled out a pocket watch.

"Here. You can have this, if you like." Francis popped the watch open to reveal a small photograph of the Marsh family. "You can look at it whenever you need to."

"Thank you, Francis," both versions of Mallory said in unison.

"Keep it safe, little one." He kissed her on top of her head.

"I promise I will," said the child as the memory began to dissolve.

"I've still got the watch," Mallory said as he rose and turned towards the Master. "I keep my word and I pay my debts."

He smiled as he saw the Master had taken on a physical form. His face was still blank, but he wore the black suit and clerical collar of a holy man; Mallory was not surprised at this in the slightest, but it confirmed his hunch.

"Why show me this?" The Master's voice was deep and sonorous, without a readily discernible accent.

"I want you to know me," he said. "I want you to truly, deeply, know me and to realise just how fucked you are."

The pounding of the rain on the conservatory glass morphed into the rapid staccato beat of a snare drum. Mallory and the Master once again lurked in the sidelines of the room, now the grand hall of the Ministry of Supernatural Affairs.

On the stage stood the Director of the Ministry, Mohinder Desai, and his bodyguard, Kimberly Daniels; amongst Exceptions they were known as the Tiger and Dingo, respectively. Waiting in the wings was the latest crop of field operatives, in full dress uniforms.

Suddenly, the drums stopped. One of the various administrative clerks who worked in the Ministry walked on to the stage with a microphone.

"What is happening here?"

"You'll see." Mallory said quietly.

Names were called in alphabetical order, but the younger Mallory Marsh did not hear his name read out. He looked back and forth, confused and panicked. When the rest of the newly qualified Ministry agents were seated, Director Desai stepped up to the microphone. He smiled at the audience, revealing a row of razor sharp teeth.

"We are gathered here today to mark the graduation of this fine group of cadets into fully qualified field operatives. I couldn't be more proud of you all." He turned and smiled at the increasingly confused cadet Mallory. "You might have noticed that I didn't read the name of one of our cadets in the general ceremony; I wanted to call him on to the stage myself.

"Mallory Marsh, please join me." As Mallory made his uncertain way to the microphone, Desai continued to speak. "Mister Marsh has proven himself to be one of the most capable cadets we've ever seen. Not only did he conduct himself with poise and grace during his training, he showed courage and valour in the face of adversity during his final assessment.

"After his mentor and assessor was slain in the field, Mallory Marsh not only kept his head in the heat of the moment but dispatched a pack of feral werewolves single-handedly; a feat of peerless skill."

He gestured for Kimberly Daniels to come forwards as Mallory arrived at the microphone. She carried a large wooden box with a smaller purple box balanced atop it. Desai opened the smaller box, revealing a medal in the shape of an eye.

"For the completion of duties against tremendous odds and adversity, I award you, Mallory Marsh, with the Eye of Empire, the highest honour that the Ministry can bestow. As you may know, this award is rarely given to those with non-combat gifts; as such, you are also inducted into the Order of the Third Eye.

"To recognise this incredible feat, I present you with these to better serve the Ministry." Desai handed Mallory the other box. "I shall watch your career with great interest, Agent Marsh."

There was a round of thunderous applause. Mallory and the Master stood in the corner, watching the entire scene unfold. Mallory glanced at the Master, who now had a mop of black hair atop his featureless head.

Not far to go now.

"What is in the box, Mallory Marsh?" the Master asked. "Guns, or maybe knives?"

"No," Mallory said with a chuckle. "Paintbrushes. An antique set with hawthorn handles, to be exact. I still have them; I take them with me everywhere."

"An odd gift."

"I don't think so. I always paint better when I use them." He smiled at the Master. "I make my own paint and pigments too, you know; there are some you can't buy anywhere and comparable colours are never quite right."

"And you decided to show me this because it proves that you are going to defeat me?"

"Perhaps," Mallory said softly, "or maybe I just wanted to show you something I'm proud of."

"Where next?" The Master's voice was impatient. "Another memory to waste my time?"

"No," Mallory said as the scene around them dissolved once again, "this will be a little different."

It took a moment for the next vision to swirl into focus, but when it did, Mallory Marsh smiled.

Gotcha.

They were stood outside, in one of the city's many parks. The grass was thronging with people, all staring up at the sky; they were wearing strange glasses and gasps of amazement filled the air. Mallory let his gaze drift upwards as the day grew dimmer and darker.

The birds, previously noisy, were quiet in the trees. He shielded his eyes as the last fingers of sunlight were blocked by the moon. His breath caught in his chest at the majesty of the eclipse.

A steady wind blew in from the east, rustling the trees and sending ripples through the grass. A few moments after the complete occultation of the sun, Mallory noticed fluffy white motes drifting through the air.

Of course, he thought as he turned to face the Master.

His appearance was completely clear; his dark hair framed a middle aged face with a thin nose, a nasty slash of a mouth, and bloodshot, watery eyes. Back in the real world, Mallory's hands drew a perfect likeness of the man.

"You tricked me!" the Master yelled. "How dare you?"

"You wanted me to open up, and I did," Mallory said with a smirk. "Turns out this is a two way street."

"Your friends are going to die, Marsh!" the Master roared as he lunged at Mallory.

"I'm hanging up now." Back in the garret, he pushed the artwork aside, protecting it, and seized the bag full of Thaddeus's blood. "Permanently."

"I will see you soon, Marsh."

"I'm counting on it."

Mallory opened his eyes in the garret just as the Master threw everything he had at his defences. He could feel the tide of power rushing in, but he wasn't afraid; he'd done everything he could and now it was time to sever the connection forever.

Mallory Marsh ripped open the bag of blood and poured it down his throat.

All of it.

Every last drop.

Chapter Twenty Eight – Death Valley Nights

Ivy

"Get ready to run, Ivy!" Charity yelled as the Nightwalkers funnelled into the living room. "Grab what you need and let's go!"

"Fucking hell!" Ivy screamed in frustration as she unplugged the microscope and crammed it back into its box. Charity stood menacingly between her and the creatures, blades glinting in the electric light. She reached under the counter and pulled out a heavy duty bag that she usually used for her grocery shopping. *Fuck it, it'll do.*

"What are you waiting for?" Charity goaded as she twirled her knives. She glanced past the Nightwalkers and saw a fourth clawing at the fuse box in the hallway. The creatures outside the kitchen window began to bang and pound on the glass, shrieking with excitement. "Come on, Ivy, we don't have all day."

"Right, ready!" she said triumphantly and hoisted the overly full bag off the counter just as the lights went out. "Charity, do something!"

Charity Walpole did not respond. Instead there was the wet sound of something sharp slicing through flesh; Ivy could not tell if it was Charity's knife or the claws of a Nightwalker. She backed up towards the glass doors to the garden, but the sound of chitinous tapping stopped her in her tracks.

There were more moist noises and Ivy heard her comrade groan in pain. She dithered for a moment, temporarily overcome with fear. Inside her head, both Michaela and Edgar were screaming at her to move, but she was frozen.

There was a sharp cracking sound, followed by a chemical whoosh as the room was bathed in brilliant blue-white light. Charity brandished the UV flare as the Nightwalkers attacking her either disintegrated or recoiled from the deadly rays.

Ivy's paralysis ended and she hauled the pale woman to her feet. A quick glance confirmed that she was unharmed; winded perhaps, but not hurt. The Nightwalkers outside still scrambled at the glass of the windows and doors.

"Come on, let's go," Charity said as she dragged Ivy towards the door. "Hurry up, Ivy!"

"We don't have enough flares to get to safety. We need to defend ourselves here." She turned at the bottom of the hallway and started upstairs. "Come on, up here!"

"You better be right about this," Charity grumbled as she lit the way with her flare. "Why isn't this destroying the ones outside?"

"Glass filters out most of the UV, and the intensity diminishes rapidly with distance." Ivy went into her bedroom. "In here, and block the door as best you can."

Charity placed the flare in a vase where it continued to burn with a low hiss. She dragged a dresser in front of the door and wedged it with a chair. Out of the corner of her eye she saw Ivy unlocking a chest that she'd dragged from the wardrobe. There was a commotion in the hallway as the Nightwalkers flooded the house.

"This should do the trick," Ivy said as she pulled a

pair of Japanese swords from the chest and tied them to her with a sash. Charity looked on with disbelief. "What?"

"We're about to die and you decide that this is the time to play weeb games?"

"They're Michaela's," Ivy said defensively.

"Oh, even better, they belong to your imaginary friend!" Charity yelled.

"Walpole," Ivy shouted as the flare began to burn out and sounds of banging filled the room, "brace the door. I have an idea."

"What are you going to do?" the pale woman asked as she leant on the dresser.

There was no reply.

"Ivy?" Charity asked as she spun around to face Ivy. A look of horror filled her face when she saw Ivy's gun only inches from her face. "Doc?"

"Trust me."

Charity screamed as Ivy pulled the trigger.

Ivy fired twice; once close to Charity's ears and the other close to her own. In the confined space the shots were deafening, which was exactly what Ivy hoped for. *With any luck someone else on the street heard the gunshots and called the police.*

Tangling with law enforcement was not high on Ivy's priority list, but she hoped that the sound of approaching police cars would scare off some of the Nightwalkers, or at least distract them enough for the two women to escape.

She saw Charity shake her head to try and clear the ringing from her ears, and she tapped her on the shoulder after holstering the weapon. Walpole looked up at her in confused fury and yelled something incomprehensible.

"So they can't mind control us!" Ivy said at the top of her lungs. She hoped that her words were obvious enough to lip read.

Either they were or Charity arrived at the same conclusion independently and grinned at her, giving her a thumbs up. She drew another knife as the dresser shook and the door frame splintered. Ivy reached down and flipped on a small battery powered lamp; it wasn't much, but combined with the street lights a few houses away it gave them enough to see by.

The flare sputtered out as Ivy drew the shorter of the two swords, a wakizashi, which was much better suited to using indoors. The folded steel glinted in the dim light as she adopted a waki-gamae stance, holding the blade behind her.

"Death before dishonour," she said softly as the door finally gave way.

The dresser tumbled down as the Nightwalkers forced their way into the room. Charity stepped back, throwing her knives to slay the first two through the doorway. Another pursued her, but Ivy brought the blade forwards in an upward strike, almost cutting the monster clean in two. She shifted her feet as two more burst through the doorway and delivered a fatal downward slice, adding to the bodies on the floor.

Ivy overbalanced slightly with the force of her swing, and was left bent over in a half crouch with no time to recover as yet more Nightwalkers bore down on her. Charity Walpole, however, had rearmed herself and was ready to fight.

She lurched forwards and rolled over Ivy's back, landing between the doctor and her assailants. Charity let the angular momentum from her artful manoeuvre transfer into her knives as they slashed through the Nightwalkers.

As she finished her blow, Ivy thrust forward with her sword to skewer another creature. It fell backward, dead, and no more Nightwalkers followed. For the moment, they were safe.

Charity clapped Ivy on the back and gave her an impressed nod. The ringing in their ears still made speech impossible but the two exchanged a knowing look that acknowledged the surprising truth.

We make a hell of a team.

Ivy moved to the window as Charity continued to guard the door. She peeked around the edge of the curtain and her stomach churned in horror; there were dozens of Nightwalkers in the street. *Is everybody dead?*

Her expression alone was enough to convey their dire situation to Charity. The pale assassin looked like she was about to start speaking, but they both stopped as the unmistakable smell of smoke drifted from downstairs.

This is a trap, Ivy realised far too late. *Perhaps the Master could hear us through Mallory after all.*

Charity sheathed her blades and yanked the two she'd thrown from the dead Nightwalkers. She twirled them to remove the excess slime and wiped them on Ivy's bedclothes to clean them properly.

"Charity, what the fuck?" Ivy yelled angrily. Charity just shrugged and tapped one blade against her ear with a look of performative confusion. She stowed her knives as Ivy glared at her.

Ivy sheathed her wakizashi and picked up the bag containing the microscope and other diagnostic supplies. She hesitated for a few seconds before grabbing a backpack from the wardrobe. She tossed a hodgepodge of clothes in it, as well as her more expensive perfumes. *This is all going to go up in flames soon enough.*

She slipped on the bag with her clothes, handing the other to Charity, and the two made a speedy exit from the bedroom. As they descended the stairs the smoke grew thicker and the heat more intense. Charity made for the front door but Ivy yanked her towards the kitchen.

They passed through the living room, where the bookcase was ablaze, and through into the kitchen. The windows and garden door were clear of Nightwalkers and Ivy pushed Charity towards them as she turned on the gas hob, leaving it unlit. As soon as she realised what was happening, Charity dashed into the garden with Ivy hot on her heels.

There was a crash behind them as more Nightwalkers spilled into the house and through the side alley into the garden. Ivy and Charity kept running towards the flimsy wooden fence that separated Ivy's garden from that of her neighbours.

Charity tried to mantle over the fence but it gave way as Ivy ploughed right into it, one shoulder driving through the rotten wood. Both women hit the ground with a muted thud just as the house behind them exploded.

"Get up, Charity!" Ivy yelled.

Charity groaned as she lifted herself off the ground and out of the scattered debris. Ivy looked back at the burning wreck of her home and saw the silhouettes of Nightwalkers through the flames. *That's not going to hold them back for long.*

She drew the longer of her two swords, her katana, and led Charity through her neighbour's garden. The gate at the side of the house was bolted shut, but luckily there was no padlock. The wooden door swung inwards with a creak and Ivy braced herself for an attack.

Nothing lunged at her from the darkness; the street appeared to be empty. Ivy moved forwards on to the pavement and swiftly crossed the road to a little footpath that led down into Lye Valley Nature Reserve.

The going was steep and she stumbled more than once, but never lost her footing. As they reached the bottom of the hill the path was hemmed in by two trees; it was only wide enough for one to pass through at a time.

"We can cut through there," Ivy said as she pointed to the path leading south, "which will take us on to the golf course. We can lose them there, then head on to Cowley Road from the nearby bridleway. Charity, are you listening?"

"Just about, Ivy," Charity said as she tied an end of her garotte wire to one of the trees crowding the path. "Sounds like a plan to me."

"Then let's go!"

"In a second; I just want to finish this first." There was a screech from the top of the path; the Nightwalkers had found them. Charity stretched the wire over to the other tree and wrapped it so it was taut and secure. "Okay, let's split."

The sound of pounding footsteps echoed around the trees as the first Nightwalker came charging down the footpath towards them. Charity snatched up the bag and followed Ivy south as the creature reached the bottom of the slope.

There was a wet slicing sound and a reverberating metal twang as the creature's momentum carried it into the wire, decapitating it. Charity let out a loud whoop and Ivy couldn't help but smile. More shrieks and screeches filled the woods as the Nightwalkers pursued them.

"Keep that last flare handy, Charity," Ivy said as they rushed along the path. "I've got a feeling that we're going to need it."

Chapter Twenty Nine – The Face of Evil

Thaddeus

"Please," Thaddeus begged as he raced towards the garret, "please let them be safe."

It seemed impossibly far to Canal Street and his lungs were burning with exertion as the improbable silhouette of the Jericho Folly loomed into sight. He brandished the ultraviolet baton as he ran, no longer caring about being spotted by the Nightwalkers.

It was a trap, he thought angrily. *The Master fucking played us!*

He caught sight of movement down an alley and waved the UV baton in that direction; there was a hiss and a screech as a cat darted away from the light. He saw a faint glow emanating from just around the corner; the source was just outside the Folly!

Thad lost his footing as he rounded the corner; the baton went clattering across the ground and blinked twice before going out. He tried to roll out of the fall but ended up flat on his back looking up at the garret.

"Thaddeus, are you alright?" Jess asked as she brandished her own baton. There was a howl from further up the street and they both turned to look at the source of the sound.

His shirt was open and his hair was tangled about his head. The tattered remains of the rope restraints hung limply from his wrists. The street lamps illuminated the jagged black teeth and chitinous claws, and as he moved his head the light landed at the right angle to highlight the telltale eyeshine.

Worst of all, he was drenched in blood.

"Mallory?" Thaddeus asked quietly.

Marsh let out a blood curdling shriek and raced off into the night.

"We need to get inside," Jess said as she helped him to his feet. "Come on."

They made their way inside the Folly and up the winding stairs to the garret. As they approached the open door, Thad couldn't believe what he saw.

The bed was covered in blood and the sheets were absolutely sodden with it. All around the room were horrifying drawings, mostly with faceless people in them. On the floor was Mallory's hat, discarded.

On the map that Thaddeus had used to track the Nightwalker attacks there were two additions. The first was an eerily realistic portrait of a man with a thin nose and watery eyes surrounded by some sort of jagged halo. The second was the word *JAZZ*, scrawled in blood in a space largely devoid of pins. Jess looked on in horror as Thaddeus walked around the room ensuring that the shutters were safely locked.

"That's it, isn't it?" he said angrily. "The Master has taken Mallory. Trip and Ray are dead, and Evans is still at large. We're no closer to solving this thing.

"Let's face it, Jess; we've lost."

"We can't give up, Thaddeus!" She gestured to the photograph that hung above the bed. "What would Arabella do? Would she want you to just throw everything away?"

"Then what do you propose we do?"

"Maybe Charity and Ivy learned something important when they were in Lye Valley. We need to wait for them to get back here."

"They aren't coming back, Jess! It's just us now; even my parents are dead." His eyes filled with tears as he fell to the floor. "You're the only one left that I care about, Jess; the Master has taken everyone else."

"What shall we do?"

"We need to get out of the city. You saw how many Nightwalkers there were in The Coven; god only knows how many more are out there now."

"We should wait for morning, though," she said. "It'll be safer then, and there's always a chance that the others will come back alive."

"Evans knew where they were; it was a trap." Thaddeus looked up at her, his eyes red rimmed and filled with tears. He could barely speak through the sobbing. "Charity and Ivy-"

"Live to fight another day," said Charity wearily as she staggered into the garret. Ivy was hot on her heels. The pale Ministry operative looked down at Thaddeus and hauled him upright. "On your feet, kid; the war ain't over til it's over."

Thaddeus sniffled and wiped his eyes. He nodded at Charity who squeezed his shoulder. *How do I explain what happened to Mallory?*

"What's all this for?" Jess asked as she looked through the heavy bag that Charity had deposited on the floor before adopting her usual spot in the armchair. "Charity?"

"Don't look at me, I'm just the courier." She gestured to Ivy who was busy locking and bolting the door. "Ask Ivy-san, it's her stuff."

"I heard that." Ivy scowled at Charity as she untied a sash and leant her blades against a wall.

"Bully for you, Livingston. Here's hoping that I get my hearing back properly or you'll-"

"Enough!" roared Thaddeus. "I am sick of your constant bickering! Either you learn to get along or you get the fuck out of my home!"

"And go where, Thaddeus?" Ivy said as she perched on the desk. "My house was blown to pieces this evening, so I'd appreciate a little breathing room."

"I'm sorry you had a tough night, Ivy," Thaddeus said bitterly, "but you're not the only one to have lost something tonight."

"Is that so?" said Charity as she peered over the top of her glasses. "I take it you're about to apologise for *misplacing* Mallory?"

"No, I'm not, Walpole. Your friend Evans attacked us this evening."

"He did?" Charity said, suddenly cowed. "I'm amazed you got away alive."

"Ray and Trip didn't," Jess said sadly. "Thad saved me. He held off Evans long enough for me to escape."

"Fucking hell." Charity was shocked. "I'm sorry that you had to see that, both of you. Joseph's method of killing is... messy. I'll make sure that he pays for it."

"He killed my parents too."

"Holy shit." Charity got to her feet and headed into the kitchen. She called out to Thaddeus as she rummaged through the cupboards. "I'll concede that you had a worse time than we did. Do you have any booze?"

"Top cupboard, over the sink," he said. "The nightclub was a trap; it was full of Nightwalkers."

"And you fought your way out?" Ivy asked, clearly impressed.

"There were UV lights above the dance floor. I fought my way down to the DJ deck and lit the place up."

"Nicely done, Thane." Charity called out as she poured them each a measure of bourbon. "You too Jess; I'm sure there will be a place at the Ministry for you if we survive this."

Thaddeus took a glass from her as she walked past. She distributed drinks to the other two and raised her glass.

"For Ray, for Trip, and for Mallory; we shall avenge you!" She downed her glass and then gestured to Jessica.

"For Jade."

"For my parents," Thaddeus said. He looked at Ivy, expecting her to go next, but she was staring at the wall in a state of shock. "Doc, what's wrong?"

"Who drew this?"

"That's Mallory's handiwork," Charity said. "I'd wager that he got a good look at the Master before he lost the fight, so he wanted to leave us one last clue. No idea what he means with 'jazz', though."

There was a smash as Ivy dropped her glass, and Thaddeus's brain finally figured out the last piece of the puzzle. The two of them stood up at the same time and walked over to the map.

"Jazz," he said as he examined the map, "is as much about the notes you don't play as the ones you do; this map has a glaring great gap in it."

"You don't hunt where you nest," Ivy said as she removed the portrait. "It draws too much attention. Charity, are you sure that this is the Master?"

"As sure as I can be. Why?"

"You know him, don't you?" Thaddeus asked. "And I'll be willing to bet that he works here."

Thaddeus jabbed his finger at the very centre of the empty patch on the map; the Warneford Hospital.

Charity let out a low whistle and raised her empty glass to Thaddeus.

"Is he right, Livingston?"

"Yes," Ivy said as the portrait trembled in her hands. "I've worked with this man for years. His name is Irving Adams."

They all sat around Thad's cramped desk as Ivy set up the microscope and chemistry kit. Thaddeus looked through the chemicals and was pleased to find enough material for two more ultraviolet flares.

"That'll give us four in total, counting the two we've already got." Jess said. "That's one each for our attack on the Master."

"Sorry to disappoint you, Jess," Charity said, "but we used two to fight back the Nightwalkers at Ivy's place; one in the house and another to get us to Cowley Road. Thank fuck the buses were still running, right, Liv?"

"Mhmm." Ivy was focused on cutting a fine slice of the claw she'd extracted from Mallory.

"What are you looking for?" Thaddeus asked as she placed a tiny part of it on a microscope slide.

"I think what we have here," Ivy said as she put the slide under the scope and adjusted the focus, "is some kind of parasite."

"Like an insect?"

"Not quite." She opened a heavy textbook and flicked through it. The three of them watched in silence as Ivy's eyes moved from the eyepiece to the book and back. A smile slowly started to form on her face. "What we have here, is a fungus."

"The Nightwalkers are mushroom monsters?" Charity said gleefully.

"Sort of. Mushrooms as we commonly know them are the fruiting bodies of large fungal networks." Ivy leant back in her chair and smiled. "Mycelial networks can span for hundreds of metres, sometimes over a kilometre. The structure of this particular fungus is unlike anything I've ever seen; it's almost reminiscent of human neural tissue."

"That's gross, Ivy." Charity was staring at the images in the textbook. "These aren't supernatural, though?"

"Not at all."

"Then how does the Master communicate with his minions?" Thaddeus asked.

"Clearly this parasitic fungus has formed some sort of symbiotic relationship with a supernatural being, with the combination being more powerful than the sum of the parts." Ivy looked under the microscope once again. "Some of these structures look like blood cells, albeit very weird ones; maybe that's why the Nightwalkers crave blood so much?"

"It helps them to grow in the bodies of infected people?" Jess asked.

"Grow and maintain themselves." Ivy looked over at Thaddeus. "We've encountered far more of these things than your numbers would suggest. Either the number of missing people has been obscured in a dramatic fashion or many of the Nightwalkers were already in the city, most likely in a dormant state."

"That explains how this got so bad so quickly." Thaddeus said. "And now the Master has two Exceptions under his spell."

"I'm not so sure about that, kid."

"What do you mean?" Thaddeus felt hope flutter in his heart.

"From what we know about this fungus and the way

Mallory and Jess have described their experiences, I can make an educated guess about what we're up against." Charity turned to Ivy. "There's one way to tell for certain, though; Ivy, in the whole time you worked with Irving Adams, did he ever speak to you first?"

"You mean starting a conversation?"

"Anything. Did he *ever* initiate a dialogue, even once?"

Ivy thought for a moment, and then shook her head. Charity let out a little cheer and slapped her knee in glee.

"What?" Thaddeus asked. "What's got you so excited?"

"I know what we're dealing with; this is a Preacher." Charity grinned. "They can mess with your mind and make you do anything they want, but you have to talk to them first; they can't strike up a conversation with someone who doesn't want to listen."

"You have to invite them in!" Ivy said as the gears started to turn. "Do you think that by drinking such a large amount of Thaddeus's blood at once it could sever the connection permanently?"

"That's exactly what I think."

"Does that mean we can still save him?" Jess asked quietly.

"Yes, I think so." Ivy tapped the book excitedly. "I'm sure that Michaela and I can come up with a treatment if we put our heads together. Leave no man behind, right?"

"Damn right, Ivy." Charity said. "There's one problem though."

"We have to find Mallory first," Thaddeus said, "and then we need to catch him."

Chapter Thirty – Mallory Unleashed

Mallory

Mallory stood panting on the street as Jessica rounded the corner. He looked at her with crazed bloodshot eyes as milky tears streamed down his face.

The entity inside him, the awful parasite, twitched and shuddered at the sight of an uninfected human brimming with fresh, hot blood. He took one faltering, unsteady step towards her.

Jess activated some sort of high intensity light; the colour made Mallory recoil in pain as the mycelium fought against his will. He began to drool uncontrollably as the hideous black fangs sprouted from his gums and his remaining claws extended from his fingertips.

He growled; a long low predatory sound that emanated from deep within his chest. The thing within him had finally tasted blood and it demanded more.

Feed.

No, he thought sharply. *I will not hurt my friends.*

Feed!

I did not give in to the Master and I will not give in to you.

FEED!

A sharp pang of hunger stabbed through his stomach and he twitched in agony, but still he held his ground. *I am accustomed to pain.*

Jess looked at him with a mixture of horror and pity, and suddenly Mallory realised the inadvertent virtue of his curse.

I've never seen someone look at me like that before, he thought. He wanted to break down and burst into shameful tears, but he couldn't; keeping any kind of control over the twisting invader took all of his concentration.

Mallory forced his body to remain still as the parasite flooded his brain and nervous system with chemicals that made him ache with hunger and his world bend and distort. He was on the cusp of giving in when Thaddeus Thane, beautiful naïve Thaddeus, lurched on to the street and fell to the ground not twenty metres from him.

HUNT.
KILL.
FEED.

I will not! Mallory threw his head back and let out an unearthly shriek. He knew that he could not hold off the unrelenting will of the fungus forever, but in his addled mind a plan was forming. *This is either brilliant or completely insane*, he thought.

HUNT KILL FEED!
HUNT KILL FEED!
HUNT KILL FEED!
HUNT KILL FEED!
HUNT KILL FEED!
HUNT KILL FEED!

Over and over, the same message was driven into his brain like an ice pick; each repetition a hammer blow against his iron will. He saw Thaddeus looking at him in terror and he could bear the struggle no longer.

With one final howl he tore off into the night, running as far away from his friends as he could. Where he was headed he did not know, but he accepted that when the sun crept over the eastern horizon it would mean the end for him.

   The streets were blessedly empty, much to Mallory's relief. The predatory desires of the parasite only seemed to activate when his prey was directly in his line of sight. As long as he did not think too closely about the countless people curled up in their beds they would be safe from him.

He marvelled at how bright the night could be as the fungus modified his eyes and gave him the telltale eyeshine that marked the Nightwalkers. *Am I one of them or something else?*

Something different?

He could feel the psychic web that spread throughout the city, linking the thralls to their Master. Even though their connection was forever severed Mallory could still feel him through the Tangle and the mycelial mind network; crouched in the Warneford he shone like a beacon of tremendous power.

I hope they understand my messages, he thought, *especially regarding the eclipse. They don't have a lot of time.* Mallory was worried about the state of the city and about what would become of the world if the Master's plan succeeded, but most of all he was concerned for the safety of his friends. He wished that there was some way to help them.

"Perhaps the best thing I can do for them now is die," he said sadly as he wandered through the dark and leafy streets of North Oxford. "Somewhere public, so they don't waste time looking for me."

He continued walking, sinking further and further into melancholy with every step. He growled at his own incompetence, at his continual failings; a member of the Order of the Third Eye, and what did he have to show for it?

"A death sentence due to a fungal infection." He stopped in the middle of the street and laughed darkly at his situation. "Slain by athlete's foot, brought low by fucking ringworm."

HUNT KILL FEED!

"Yeah, yeah, whatever." He looked down the road and saw a figure approaching him with fast jerky motions. "Oh look, a Nightwalker; just what I need right now!"

For all his bravado and bluster, Mallory was genuinely afraid of encountering the Master's congregation; he had no idea if it would be enough to re-establish a connection between the two of them and he had absolutely no desire to find out.

I guess I'll get an answer to that particular question sooner than I'd hoped.

The Nightwalker thrall rushed up to Mallory, its teeth bared and claws extended, but instead of attacking him, it simply stopped and regarded him with curiosity. Marsh braced himself for the inevitable onslaught of the Master's power, but it never came.

The Nightwalker just stood there, cooing softly as it looked at him with baffled eyes. Mallory's own claws were extended and he watched his adversary look left and right, feeling the rhythm of the movement and biding his time for the perfect moment to strike.

He brought his claws in a savage arc through the air and ripped out the throat of the Nightwalker. He was careful not to get any of the slime on him; he was certain that was a one way ticket back to the Master's mind. The mortally wounded creature gargled its last breath as Mallory stood above it, watching with fascination.

He reached out into the mind network and saw that the Master did not control his thralls directly. Mallory smiled as he saw swarms of thralls connected and controlled by nodes in the system; the Higher Vampires that Arabella Thane had written about.

Suddenly his plan was no longer quite so insane.

"I can really do some damage here." He wasn't sure if destroying the Nightwalkers controlling the thralls would force the Master to expend more energy on them or if it would sever the link entirely, but he didn't care; any disruption would help his allies in their fight.

HUNT!

"No!" Mallory said loudly. A pang of pain and hunger shot through him. "Oh, you want to play games? I can play fucking games, you stupid parasite. I can play games all night long."

He reached inside his pocket and pulled out one of several plastic packets he'd taken from Thaddeus's kitchen. He tore the corner open and squeezed a tiny amount into his mouth. As soon as the wasabi hit the chitinous growths they shivered and retracted. His vision flashed white and he grew unsteady, but he gritted his teeth and held on.

POISON.

"You want more of it, huh?"

BAD. POISON. NO.

"I think we're getting somewhere." Mallory smiled and put another blob of the green paste into his mouth. It made his eyes water and his nose sting, but he could feel the parasite squirming beneath his skin and could almost hear it screaming. "What's wrong?"

STOP.

"Ask me nicely, or I'll eat more of it." Mallory laughed at the absurdity of his situation. *I'm threatening an evil mushroom with a sushi condiment.* "I wonder how much it would take to kill you?"

Stop. Don't.

"What did I say?" Mallory raised the wasabi to his mouth again.

Please.

"That's more like it." Mallory put the wasabi away but took care to keep it handy, just in case. "Now we're going to have to work together for a little while. Do you think you can manage that?"

If you do not feed we will die.

"Not my problem."

If I cannot consume blood I will consume yours. You will die first.

"Ah. That is a problem, but I think I can solve it. No more ordering me about, though, or else I will fill my mouth with wasabi, horseradish, and mustard; enough to obliterate you a thousand times over. Understand?"

Understood. We must have sustenance, though.

"We will."

From hunting?

"No. I remember where the blood bank is at the hospital; that will serve for the time being."

Agreed. Then what?

"I'll tell you when we've eaten," Mallory said as he began to jog in the direction of the John Radcliffe Hospital. "Trust me, it's going to satisfy your desire to hunt, that's for sure."

I might be able to make this work, after all, Mallory thought with glee. *I hope the Master is ready for a little payback.*

Interlude Two – With Friends Like These

It's too quiet, she thought to herself. *I know it's a Wednesday night, but where is everyone?*

Cowley Road was somewhere that you could always find life, good and bad, at any time of the day. If the nebulous sprawl of the university was the brain of the city, Cowley Road was its beating heart; its very soul.

Yet, at just after eleven o'clock on this warm Wednesday night in term time, it was deserted. Charity wrapped her coat tightly about herself as the fear jangling along her nerves sent shivers down her spine. All the usual establishments were closed; pubs, cocktail bars, and even the indefatigable chicken shops were locked up and shuttered.

This is hopeless, she thought. *Mallory could be anywhere in this silent city!*

It was as if the whole of Oxford had fallen prey to the creeping dread that now sent Charity peeling off down Leopold Street, away from the emptiness of the main road. The street lamps here were older, burning a warm sodium orange instead of the usual harsh white. She risked a half smile and removed her sunglasses.

A fox yowled down a side close and an owl hooted, seemingly in response. She saw the quick flit of bats around the lampposts as they feasted on the gathered moths.

"Some life after all," she whispered to herself. "The night creatures are abroad-"

Charity's instincts had been sharpened to a razor edge during her horrifying ordeal as a Lamplight Subject. Whilst that edge had been knocked off balance by all that had happened, it was still sharp enough to throw her out of harm's way when Joseph Evans attacked her.

The shrill whistle would've burst her eardrums and ruptured the blood vessels in her eyes had she not dropped to the ground. Instead, it shattered the glass in the car behind her. There was not enough time for her to vanish, however, before the next wave of sound hit her like a freight train; broader and less focused, but much louder.

She clapped her hands over her ears and curled up to protect her soft organs from the sonic onslaught. Joseph's voice could easily kill regular humans and Ceps alike; she had witnessed it far too many times before.

Seen and done nothing, she thought as her anger cut through the pain.

The sound faded but her ears still rang, causing agony with every sound. Her eyes were reddened with scleral bleeding and her nose was bloodied too. Bruises covered her body, but the damage was superficial. She was still alive, for now.

She faintly heard Joseph walking towards her. He sang a jaunty little song as he closed in on her; his killing motif, she realised with horror.

I've only got one chance at this.

As Lamplight Subjects, Charity and Joseph had been trained on how to maximise the effect of their abilities in combat. For Joseph that simply meant learning what frequencies and harmonies were best at harming humans. Charity's education, however, had emphasised cunning and initiative; they couldn't make her any more invisible but they could teach her how to capitalise on any advantage she could get.

In a fair fight, Joseph would slaughter Charity every single time.

Charity did not fight fairly.

As soon as he stopped singing she knew he was close enough to deliver the finishing blow. He could've killed her there and then, but he had to have the last word.

"Charity, I-" was all he had time to say before she pushed the button on the deafening personal alarm hidden in her sleeve. The piercing ringing deafened Joseph, who screamed in pain and rage.

As she did this, Charity strained and forced her body to let the light through each and every part of her. Her skin shimmered sickly and she looked faded, like poorly developed film, before she vanished. Joseph leapt at where she had been, but deafened by the alarm he could not find her.

They had worked together long enough for Joseph to anticipate her next move and he quickly leant backwards and to the left. An invisible blade hissed through the empty air where his neck had been seconds before.

He was not fast enough, however, and the leading edge of the knife sliced upwards across his face, cutting his lips and blinding him in one eye. The alarm rang again, blurring what vision he had left and miring him in pain.

He lashed out around him with his deadly voice and chitinous claws, all to no avail. Another knife flashed into visibility as it flew through the air towards him. He ducked awkwardly and it struck him deep in his shoulder instead of landing a killing blow.

The poison on the blade took effect quickly, relaxing Joseph's muscles and causing him to slump to the ground. The invisible Charity smiled in triumph, but still turned and fled when yet more thralls rounded the corner.

Better to live and fight another day, she thought. Before she completely lost sight of him, Charity took a long look at Joseph Evans. Here was the man who'd stuck by her side since childhood, who had bullied her relentlessly and saved her life more times than she could count.

"I'll kill you next time, Joe," she said solemnly, before she ran off into the night. "That's a promise."

Part Three: Our Darkling Sun

Chapter Thirty One – Dust on the Wind

Ivy

"Jesus Christ, Charity, it's a wonder that you're still alive," Ivy said as she checked over the pale woman after her near-fatal encounter with Joseph Evans. "You really should've let one of us come with you."

"I can take Evans one on one," she said sulkily. "It's just a shame that he had reinforcements; I'd have ended him, otherwise. I did leave him with some pretty facial decoration and a lack of depth perception, so that's something."

"Remind me not to piss you off," Ivy muttered as she worked.

"But what would you do with all the free time you'd gain?"

"Charity," Jess said threateningly, "give it a fucking rest, yeah?"

"Yes, boss. Ouch!" She winced as Ivy felt around her ribs; there was already substantial bruising. "There's no need to push so hard, Livingston!"

"Did you find any leads on Mallory?" Thaddeus asked from across the room. He had spent the past twenty four hours obsessively combing through Arabella's writings to find any information that could give them even the slightest advantage.

"Neither hide nor hair," Charity said sadly, "but I did find several knackered Nightwalkers; they'd had their throats ripped out. Every single one of them was in a hell of a state."

"Do you think there's another group out there?" Jess asked as she sipped her tea. "Maybe we should try and reach out to them and pool our resources?"

"I think it's infighting, personally." Charity winced again as Ivy dabbed iodine on some of her cuts and scrapes. She glared at the doctor who smiled sarcastically back at her. "They are human at heart, after all."

"What makes you say that?"

"All the mutilated Nightwalkers were surrounded by thralls. I couldn't get a good look, but it seemed like they were all 'higher vampires', as Arabella's book calls them."

"Some sort of worker's revolt?" Ivy scoffed as she finished up with Charity. "Maybe next they'll present the Master with written demands or call a wildcat strike."

"Well, *Doc*," Charity said with considerable venom, "what brilliant theory do you have? Or do you need five minutes to have a little team huddle with your alter egos; maybe you can find an Apache tracker in there for us?"

"If you don't stop this I'm going to shoot both of you," Jess muttered.

"It could be Mallory," Thaddeus said softly. "He was keyed into the Master's network for long enough to understand how it works; maybe he's killing strategic targets to weaken the Master in some way."

"That would account for why the Nightwalkers let a threat get so close." Charity pulled her shirt back on as she spoke. "Maybe his condition grants him some kind of camouflage."

"That's a good word," Jess said.

"What is?" Ivy asked.

"Camouflage. It's fun to say."

"Thank you for your input," Thaddeus said testily.

He threw Arabella's diary on to the desk and moaned in frustration. "This is fucking hopeless! So much of what she recorded was irrelevant bullshit. Who cares what the weather and wind direction were in March of nineteen eighty six?"

"Day or night?" Jess asked.

"Night," Thaddeus said, "not that it makes a lick of difference."

"I'm not sure why the wind conditions matter, but if it was a clear night you'd be able to see Halley's Comet." She smiled at Ivy, whose mouth was agape. "What, you think I don't know anything outside of my subject area?"

"No, that's not it," Ivy said as the horror of their situation dawned on her. She got to her feet and looked at the picture of Irving Adams once again. "This isn't a halo."

"He's a Preacher, Liv. That's what Mallory was trying to say. Don't go all conspiracy theorist on us."

"Thaddeus," Ivy asked, "did your aunt mention areas where people gathered outside to watch the comet?"

"Yes, she does. University and South parks are both mentioned."

"What was the wind direction?"

"South Westerly, for the whole month. Why?"

"This thing is a fungus which spreads by infecting you with the slime if you come into contact with it, but that's just those who get with an arm's reach of the Nightwalkers; that's not an efficient way to spread." Ivy paced excitedly, both horrified and intrigued by the Master's plan. "Fungus does not only spread through contact.

"In fact, they most commonly propagate through wind blown spores."

"And if people are going to be outside looking at the comet, they'll get infected." Thaddeus looked at the diary. "But she doesn't mention a massive outbreak, so maybe it didn't happen."

"The wind was in the wrong direction. A south westerly blowing across the Warneford doesn't hit any of the viewing locations." She looked at the map. "An easterly wind would carry the spores from the Warneford across both parks; the Master could infect thousands."

"Then why not wait for a day where an easterly wind is blowing and do it then?" Thaddeus asked.

"The sunlight!" Jess sat bolt upright in her chair. "It would destroy the spores. The Master wouldn't need long in a strong wind; they'd cover the city in a little under fifteen minutes in the right conditions."

"Well, Halley's Comet isn't due back for another forty years, so that's a relief." Charity walked towards the bedroom. "Seeing as we've got so much time, I'm going to get some sleep."

"We don't have forty years, Charity," Ivy said darkly. "We've got three days."

Please let me be wrong, Ivy thought as she scrolled through her phone, searching for her weather app. She finally found it and opened it up; her blood ran cold when she saw the forecast.

"Fuck," she swore quietly. "In three days the city will have clear skies and a strong easterly wind; we're fucked."

"What happens in three days, Ivy?" Charity asked. Ivy pointed at the jagged ring around Irving Adams's head. "Yeah, the halo, what of it?"

"It's not a halo, Walpole. It's a corona," Ivy said. "Mallory is warning us about the eclipse."

"I need someone to help me," Ivy said as she looked around the room. "Just one of you will be enough."

"What do you need?" Charity asked, getting to her feet.

"You should rest, Charity. One of the others can help me."

"No way, Ivy. You and I can both hold our own against the Master and his minions; no need to put the kids in harm's way." She held up her hand to silence Thaddeus and Jess's protests at being treated like children. "No disrespect to either of you, but we need fresh eyes and young minds working on our plan of attack. I can look after the good doctor whilst you come up with our next move."

"We'll be back before dark." Ivy said.

"You're going armed, though, right?" Jess said and Ivy looked sheepishly at her swords.

"They're a bit conspicuous to carry in broad daylight. We should be fine though; this is a supply run, not an offensive strike."

"Besides, I've got more than enough knives for the both of us," Charity said as she strapped her blade bandolier to her chest. "You two hold the fort, and if we're not back by dark, assume we've been killed."

"I... Okay." Thaddeus seemed worried by Charity's cavalier attitude to death.

"Thaddeus, give me your phone number," Ivy said, "and if we get held up we'll text you to let you know we're alright."

Charity looked on as the two exchanged numbers, a bemused smile on her face. Ivy raised an eyebrow at her. *What's so funny, Walpole?* she wanted to ask, but thought better of it. Instead she gave Thaddeus and

Jess each a quick hug before she grabbed her bag and headed out of the garret.

The afternoon sun was warm on her skin and she took a moment to bask in it as her pale bespectacled assistant trotted down the stairs behind her. She heard Charity grunt as she stepped into the bright summer sunlight.

Ivy flexed her fingers; a strange tingle had set in when she'd hugged Thad and Jess goodbye, but it was quickly fading. She shook her left hand a little and the sensation disappeared entirely.

Weird.

"What's wrong, Livingston? You're not having a stroke or something, are you?"

"Just a weird tingle, that's all; nothing to worry about."

"Alright then," Charity said, but her tone implied that it was anything but. "Good idea with the phone, by the way; I'd never have thought of something so simple."

"Really?" Ivy asked as they walked through Jericho. The bustle of day-to-day life was reassuring and she drew strength from it. "Or are you just trying to toss me a cheap compliment?"

"I mean it. When you're in the Ministry so many things rely on the supernatural that you forget the mundane way of living can sometimes be better." She nudged Ivy's shoulder as they walked and lowered her voice. "Look at all these people; completely unaware that world is so much stranger than they could possibly imagine."

"I miss being one of them," Ivy said, not entirely truthfully.

"You weren't, though, were you?"

"What do you mean?" Ivy asked. Charity just smiled at her as they walked. "I don't know what you're insinuating, but my *condition* doesn't make me one of you."

"That's not what I'm saying, Ivy." Her smile faltered as Ivy groaned in frustration.

"Keep your games to yourself, Walpole." She shook her head in annoyance. "This is not the time."

"Fine." The two walked in silence until they reached the end of Little Clarendon Street. Charity went to peel off right, down St Giles and towards the city centre, but Ivy went to cross the street. "Where are we going?"

"We're cutting across to Parks Road. We can either take Keble Road or the Lamb and Flag Passage, although I'd prefer the former as it's more likely to be in direct sunlight."

"What's there that's so important? Not another hospital, I hope."

"From there we can head down South Parks Road to the Chemistry Department. I've a lab tech friend that owes me a favour," she said with a grin. "He's agreed to *lose* some chemicals that we might find useful. Most are just standard laboratory reagents, but there's one specialist reagent that our entire plan hinges on and it just so happens that he can get us almost two kilos of it."

"Go on then," Charity said as they strolled down Keble Road. The day was warm and the leaves rustled in the breeze; a gentle easterly that was sure to pick up strength as the weekend bore down on them. "I'm waiting for the big reveal; what is this magical chemical?"

"Allyl Isothiocyanate," she said happily. "It's in a

stabiliser, so it'll keep for when we need it."

"Right," said Charity who had no idea what Ivy was talking about. "Why do we need this and how can you be sure it'll work?"

"We need it as part of the cure for Mallory." *And everyone else that gets infected three days from now.* "We're going in a bit uninformed, but this is a good place to start."

"More information from Michaela?"

"From you, actually." Ivy smiled at Charity's surprise. "Allyl Isothiocyanate is the active ingredient in mustard."

"Huh. That actually makes sense. How long do you think it'll take to make the cure?"

"No idea," Ivy said as a cloud passed in front of the sun, "but I've only got three days."

"You'll pull it off." Charity gave Ivy's hand a quick squeeze. "I believe in you."

I'm glad one of us does.

Chapter Thirty Two – Geometric Expansion

Thaddeus

"Why here?"

"What?" Jess looked up from her book, suddenly aware of the world around her.

"Why here?" Thad asked again.

"Are you talking about me or the Master or-"

"The Master," Thaddeus said. "Why not London? Hell, he could even pick Liverpool, Glasgow, or Newcastle; all of them have far more underground infrastructure than Oxford. What is so special about this city?"

"It's the birthplace of Methodism?" Jess said with a smile.

"You know the age old adage about hammers, right?"

"That's a fair point," she said, "but I was serious. So many big movements start in this city; I'm sure part of it is the University but sometimes I feel there's something more at work here. Something-"

"Supernatural?" Thaddeus asked. Jess nodded. "I've always got an uncanny vibe from Oxford, even in the areas that are more residential than academic."

"I completely get that. If you told me Jesus was living above a chicken shop on Cowley Road I'd probably believe you." Jess looked at him with a silly grin. "You've not seen him, have you?"

"Oh, yeah, for sure, but it was an off-license, not a chicken shop. He does a roaring trade, what with the whole water to wine thing." He chuckled at his own joke.

"You're a daft git," Jess said through her giggles.

"You started it!" he said playfully. "I was being serious though; do you think the Master has a plan that's specific to the city?"

"Aside from Oxford being a nexus of the weird and eerie?"

"Yes."

"I guess it's geographically small, which will help the Master conquer the city. A lot of the population in the area he'll be targeting are students, though, and they have..." Jess trailed off as her eyes widened. "Oh no, that's not good at all."

"Tell me."

"I was going to say that the students have limited power, but that's only true whilst they're at the University itself. If the Master can seed his influence amongst the majority of students at the University, it won't be long until they end up in the governments and companies that run the world."

"You really think that's his end game?"

"I do. How many of our Prime Ministers were educated in this city? How many influential figures have moved through here?" She drew her knees up to her chest. "Think about it, Thaddeus; he only needs one Nightwalker in a city to start an outbreak there."

"One intern in Parliament dosing the tea with the noxious slime that got Mallory and the whole country is his." Thaddeus ran his fingers through his hair and grimaced. *I'm missing something crucial, I know I am!* "This still feels like the mechanism; I can't help but think there's something obvious that explains why he wants to spread his influence throughout the world."

"Delusions of grandeur?" Jess suggested.

"Perhaps. Charity called him a Preacher; maybe that's a part of it? Are they compelled to spread their message?"

"It could very well be true, but how does that help us?"

"It doesn't."

"Honestly, I'm kind of amazed that your aunt didn't figure out who he was. She was in the city for decades; did she just give up or assumed that he moved on?"

"I don't know." Thaddeus picked up Arabella's journal and began to look through it for the tenth time. He flicked through to a passage about the Master that had confused him every single time he'd read it. "What do you make of this, Jess?

"The Master, if, returns to birthplace under a sky of Holy Fire," Thaddeus read aloud before handing the book to Jessica. "The holy fire must be Halley's Comet, right?"

"Mhmm." She peered closely at the page, squinting as she did so. "How sure are you that 'if' isn't the letters I and F? They're both upper case, so they could be initials."

"The Master's initials? I thought about that, but I can't find any other references to an I.F. anywhere else in her writings. Why couldn't she have just given us a name?"

"She clearly expected you to work it out. She probably wrote cryptically in case one of the Master's minions found it." She smiled at Thaddeus. "Why don't we give this a rest and get some sleep?"

"I don't think I can, especially not when I feel that I'm so close to understanding what she means." He rubbed his eyes and groaned. "Why can't anything ever be easy?"

"Thaddeus," Jess said softly as she examined the other pages of the journal, "your aunt had really bad handwriting."

"I know, and yet she insisted on cursive; maybe just to make it super difficult to read when we needed to."

"Is there any chance that this 'I' could be an 'E'?"

"Possibly." He raised an eyebrow, curious all of a sudden. "Does that make a difference?"

"If it is a code of some sort, it might reference another book she had." Jess stood up and went to fetch The Final Temptation. "The initials could stand for Edwin Finnster! This book is absolutely full of notes; it would be really easy to hide something in here, and Oxford is the birthplace of Methodism."

"You make a compelling argument. Let me google this Finnster guy to see whether he has any link to Halley's comet."

They did their work in silence; Jess poring over the priceless tome while Thaddeus rattled away at the computer. After a few minutes of intense searching, Thaddeus let out a gasp.

"Did you find something?" she asked. He nodded and beckoned her to come to the computer. She crossed the room, but stopped dead in her tracks when the computer screen was in sight. "Is that him?"

"Yes," Thaddeus said quietly. "That's Reverend Edwin Finnster, born in the year eighteen thirty five under Halley's Comet. His mother was Margaret Finnster, a patient in the Oxford Lunatic Asylum, and he was taken in by a local Methodist Presbyter."

"Well, now we know why the Master chose Oxford." Jess said as she looked from the portrait on the screen to Mallory's drawing of the Master; they were almost identical.

"Irving Adams is actually Edwin Finnster," Thaddeus said, "which means that he's almost two hundred years old."

"He actually did it," Jessica said with awe. "He conquered death."

They were going through Finnster's notes with a fine tooth comb when Ivy and Charity returned, their bags laden with clinking bottles and heavy plastic pots. Thaddeus got up to put the kettle on, unsure of where to start explaining their revelations.

It's getting dark, he thought as he filled the kettle. *I should lock down the shutters soon.*

"What are you reading?" asked Ivy as she set her backpack down with a thud. "Anything useful?"

"I certainly hope so," she said as she lifted the cover for them to see.

"Oh shit," said Charity with a smile, "that's Finnster's book! I've always wanted to read it; word around the Ministry is that he was absolutely mental."

"You know about him?" Thaddeus asked.

"Sure. He's the original Preacher; hell, that's why that whole species got the name. He kicked around with the Ministry for a few years before he went off on his little cult building journey to South America." She grinned at them. "He did the whole Jonestown thing before it was cool."

"His followers died?" Ivy asked.

"Probably. They weren't ever heard from again, that's for sure." Charity peered at the book. "That looks like an original; where did you get it?"

"My aunt had it-" Thaddeus began, but he shook his

head to clear out any distraction. "The how isn't important Charity! You knew about Edwin Finnster and didn't tell us?"

"I'm sorry, Thad; everyone knows about him in the Ministry so I just assumed that you would too. It's not important, though." She grinned sheepishly. "I mean, what, the guy must've been dead for over a hundred years."

"He's the Master!" Jess said sharply.

"What? I thought that he," she said as she pointed at Mallory's drawing, "was the Master; Irving Adams."

"They're the same person, Charity. Look." Thaddeus walked her over to the computer and showed her the painting and the description. "It's really him."

"I can't believe you didn't tell us!" Jess said angrily. "It's vital information!"

"I'm sorry, I didn't know it was important."

"Please don't be too harsh on her, Jess," Thaddeus said. "Aunty Bella didn't mention it either; I guess she assumed that I'd be trained by the Ministry by the time I found all of this and that I'd pick up on the clues immediately. Everything is obvious when you already know the answers.

"Did you two get what you need?" he asked. Ivy nodded whilst Charity just stared into space.

"How did you get that book?" she asked again, more softly this time.

"It was in my Aunt's collection."

"The only one not accounted for is Finnster's personal copy." Charity looked at the handwritten notes. "I'm judging that's what it is, given the annotations."

"It certainly looks that way," Jess said, "although it doesn't help us much."

"But it does!" Charity took the book from her hands and began to flick through it rapidly.

"Be careful with that, it's priceless!" said Jess.

"This really is Finnster's copy, isn't it?"

"Why does that matter?" Thad asked. "What does it have to do with the Nightwalkers?"

"He took this book with him to South America; it was rumoured to have been lost along with him." She stopped leafing through the pages and turned to show them an illustration of a plant in the margin. "This is Maya Blue; it's indigo dye mixed with palygorskite clay, which is only found in Central and South America."

"So what?" Ivy asked as she unpacked the bottles from her bag. "It's just a drawing of a plant."

"He wrote in that book when he was in South America," Jess said, her eyes wide with excitement, "so he might chronicle the origins of the fungus, and if we know where it came from we can find a cure!"

"I'll do you one better," Charity said as she skimmed a few pages ahead. "Not only does our man Edwin list where he contracted his nasty fungal infection, but he also talks about the treatment one of the local tribes had for such a disease.

"Dr Livingston," she said as she handed the book to Ivy, "I give you your cure."

"Yes," Ivy nodded as she spoke. "This looks promising; it's definitely the right place to start."

"That's the best news I've heard all day," said a pained voice from the shadows around the door to the garret. The figure stepped into the light and Thaddeus gasped at how much blood covered his body. A handful of blood bags dangled from his clawed hand and the tattered William Morris shirt clung to his torso by a thread.

"Mallory?" he asked.

"Yes, it's me."

"You came back!" Thad said, tears in his eyes.

"Of course I did," he said with a wheezing laugh, "I left my hat behind."

Chapter Thirty Three – Lust and Other Hungers

Mallory

"God damn you, Marsh!" Charity said as she embraced him. "I nearly got killed by Joseph Evans looking for you. Where the fuck have you been?"

He felt her heartbeat, strong and vital, and felt the sprawling fungus in him stir. His fingertips trembled and his gums ached, but he fought hard and kept the bloodthirsty compulsion at bay. He quickly stepped back from her, and the static crackle in his head faded.

"Maybe let's not get too close for the moment," he said to her.

"I take it the fungus is still proving to be a problem?" Ivy said as she pored through bottles of chemicals. She'd set up what seemed to be some kind of miniature laboratory in the corner of the garret, with reagent bottles, a hotplate, glassware, and even a microscope. "Give me a couple of hours to put a few chemicals together and I should hopefully have a little something to take the edge off."

"When I heard you mention a cure, I have to say that I imagined something a little bit more permanent."

"It will be, but I need to reverse engineer it from some poorly transcribed folklore." She smiled at him. "I'm glad you're back with us; it's been a bit of a wild ride the past few days."

"It's not over yet," he said. "I'm not sure if you deciphered my drawing, but the important part is that the Master is a Preacher and he plans to spread his spores during the eclipse on Sunday."

"We know, Mallory," Jess said as she walked over to give his shoulder an affectionate squeeze, "your artwork helped us to figure it all out, and we've got a positive identification on the Master."

"You have?" he asked. "Did someone recognise him?"

"I did," Ivy said. "He works at the Warneford. He went 'missing' a few days ago, but he's clearly withdrawn to control things from the shadows."

"That would explain the shining light at the hospital, then."

"Shining light?" Charity asked.

"I can tap into some sort of psychic fungal network," he said, "and the more powerful a given individual is, the brighter they are. It also showed me how the Nightwalkers are organised. The weaker ones, the thralls, they need to be directly controlled by the Master or commanded by one of his more powerful underlings."

"The Higher Vampires," Thaddeus said.

"Can we not call them that," Charity said in an exasperated tone, "please?"

"She's right," Ivy said, "we need to be realistic about what we're up against and ditch any preconceived notions that are going to get us killed."

"And I take it we're no longer talking to Ivy," Charity said.

"What gave it away?" Michaela asked.

"You agreed with me."

"She really can be quite petty at times, can't she?" Michaela asked. She held up her hand when Charity opened her mouth to reply. "That was rhetorical, by the way."

Feed.
Not now, you can wait a while.
Feed. Now.

Mallory felt the weight of the blood bags in his hand as the gnawing hunger crept into the pit of his stomach once again. His fingers trembled as the fungal claws strained against his flesh, desperate to spring forth and rend through friend or foe alike.

"I think I should be alone for a little while," Mallory said awkwardly. "I need to feed the monster, as it were."

"How does it work?" Jess said as she leant forwards. "You obviously don't have to answer, of course, but I would love to know."

"I, on the other hand," said Michaela as she set a small flask on the hotplate, "would rather not. If you can hold out for a few hours, Mallory, I think the suppressant will be in good working order. Hopefully from there we can begin developing a more permanent solution.

"For now, though, I am heading to bed."

"Goodnight," Thaddeus said. Mallory found himself strangely drawn to the Taboo once again; *his face is the only constant in my world at the moment.* He flushed as a tide of lewd thoughts filled his mind. *I want to pull his hair,* he thought with a sigh.

"I'm also in dire need of some sleep," Charity said. "The last time I didn't get enough rack time I pulled a knife on Ivy; best to avoid that now that she's actually proving useful. Goodnight, Mallory. Try not to kill us all before dawn, okay?"

The door to the cramped back bedroom clicked shut.

"Well," Thaddeus said softly as he rose from his chair, "it's just the three of us now."

"Are you going to tie me up and shave me again?" Mallory asked. "Or was that just an isolated incident?"

"You look smooth enough to me, Marsh." Jess traced a finger down his face as Thaddeus slipped his arms around Mallory's waist.

"You really shouldn't be touching me," Mallory protested, albeit weakly. He felt the predatory urge rising as the fungus twisted his thoughts and scrambled his brain. "Please, I don't want to hurt you."

Feed.

"You won't hurt us, Mallory." Thaddeus's voice was gentle, yet confident. "Besides, you've got your blood bags, haven't you?"

FEED.

"We could help you, Mallory," Jess said as she walked into the kitchen, only to return with a knife and a large wine glass. "Thad, will you take those bags for Mallory, please?"

Thaddeus took the blood bags from Mallory's clawed hands and carried all but one through to the kitchen. When he returned he slipped his shirt over his head and stood shirtless before them both. He took the knife from Jessica and twirled it playfully in his fingers.

"Tell me, Mallory, can you see Jess's face?" Mallory shook his head. Thad trailed the tip of the blade over his own stomach, smiling as he did so. "Would you like to?"

"Yes." His breath came in short gasps. "I would."

"Very well," he said as he pressed the blade into the skin of his abdomen. The cut was not deep, but tiny beads of blood welled up like a trail of glistening rubies. Mallory walked slowly over to Thaddeus, his mind in a daze of desire.

"Thank you." He dropped to his knees and traced his tongue along the knife wound, savouring every salty metallic drop. He felt the creature within him twitch and shudder as it thirsted for more; always more, never enough.

Mallory's vision swam before his eyes for a few seconds. He blinked rapidly to clear the shadows away and Jessica's beautiful face came crashing into focus. *They're both so gorgeous.* He smile at them both as Thaddeus ran his fingers through Mallory's hair.

Jess picked up the one blood bag that Thaddeus had left behind and placed the wine glass on the table. She took the blade from Thad and nicked open the bottom of the bag to let the blood fill the glass.

Mallory twitched and trembled with anticipation as the crimson liquid slowly glugged into the glass. When it was half full, Jessica inverted the blood bag and dangled it above Mallory's head, smiling as she did so.

"Am I supposed to beg for it?" he asked, squirming in desperation. His heartbeat thundered in his ears, drowning out the insidious whispers of the parasite.

"No. Thaddeus, would you be so kind as to get a second glass for us, please?" She continued to dangle the blood bag as Thad walked into the kitchen with agonisingly sluggish steps. "I'm just dangling this here to keep you keen, Mallory."

"Why two glasses?" he asked.

"You already know the answer to that. Thank you, Thaddeus."

"I do," Mallory said, "but I want to hear you say it."

"One is for you, Mallory dearest, and the other is for me." She smiled and looked at Thaddeus. "I guess you can share some of mine if you want."

"I think I'll just watch," Thad said, "but I might join in for the next round."

"Can I have it now?" Mallory asked, almost pleading. Jess shook her head and chuckled slightly. "Why not?"

"Take your clothes off first, and get on to the bed," she said as she slipped out of her own comfortable dress. Mallory and Thaddeus both watched as she shed her bra and knickers, leaving them in a little pile on the floor.

Thad was quick to follow suit, and then they were both looking at Mallory, who hesitated for a moment. He was about to voice his concerns when Jessica leant in and kissed him. He reached out and ran his hands greedily over her skin.

"We know that you're trans, Mallory," said Thaddeus softly. "It doesn't change how we feel about you or how much we want you. Now get undressed and come to bed."

Mallory slipped off his trousers, shirt, and underwear, but kept his yachting cap perched jauntily on his head.

"The hat stays on," he said defiantly.

"Fine by me," Jessica said as she knelt amongst the ruffled covers. She raised one of the glasses to her lips and took a delicate sip. She ran her tongue over her bloodstained teeth and smiled. "That is far better than I was expecting."

"You develop a taste for it pretty quickly," Mallory said as he reached out for the glass. She pulled it away from his questing hands with a laugh. He was about to protest when she held it close to her and poured a small amount of blood over her breasts.

The crimson liquid trickled down the graceful curve

of her chest and she gasped at the sensation when a little of it coated her nipples. Mallory, unable to help himself any longer, leapt at her. He ran his ravenous tongue over her skin, lapping up the blood in long messy licks.

She grabbed him by his hair and forced his face between her breasts, his head tilted upwards; their eyes met as Thaddeus began to kiss Mallory's back, slowly working down from the nape of his neck.

This is absolute bliss, he thought as Jess began to pour the blood down her skin once again. It collected in a confluence at his mouth and he reached his hands up to squeeze her impossibly soft thighs.

Thaddeus's teeth grazed his skin and he gasped in delight. Jess continued the crimson deluge until the glass was completely empty. She ran her fingers around the inside of it and licked them clean.

"Waste not," she said with a smile as Mallory licked the last few drops from her velvety skin. She placed the empty vessel next to the full one on the bedside table and fell back into the pillows, laughing as she did so.

"Had enough, Mallory?"

"I've had enough blood to quiet the monster for now," he said with a smile, "but not enough of you two."

Mallory tossed Thaddeus into bed with a laugh and nestled in between the two of them, losing himself in an endless sea of touches, kisses, and reckless affection.

It's good to be alive.

Chapter Thirty Four – Company Enough for Grief

Ivy

Ivy woke up with a start as the early morning sunlight streamed through the narrow space around the shutters and into the small bedroom. It took her a moment to work out where she was; the last thing she remembered was greeting Mallory when he returned.

Michaela! Ivy thought angrily. *We've spoken about you taking over suddenly!*

There was no response. Ivy tried to move a little in the bed, and she realised that she wasn't alone; pinning her against the wall was the slumbering Charity Walpole. They had been in the bed for some time if the wet patch on the pillow by Charity's mouth was anything to go by.

Who dribbles that much in their sleep!?

Charity had one arm draped over Ivy, holding her firmly in place. Ivy tried to gently lift the arm so she could get up, but Charity pushed it down harder and made a noise like a disgruntled guinea pig.

"Vrrrrt," she hissed, still sound asleep. Ivy was painfully aware of how full her bladder was and tried to move the arm again. "VRRRRT!"

"Oh, for fuck's sake!" Ivy whispered and shoved Charity with her shoulder. Charity withdrew her arm and Ivy seized the moment to sit up and shuffle off the end of the bed. Not a moment too soon either, as Charity dragged a blade from her vest and drove it into the bed where Ivy had been only seconds before.

"Jesus Christ, Charity!" she yelled. Charity's eyes snapped open and she twirled the knife in her hand, ready to throw it at Ivy. "Stop! It's me, you fucking psycho bitch!"

"Ivy?" she said thickly, squinting in the dim light. She slipped the blade back into its sheath and popped her glasses on. "It's not cool to yell at people first thing in the morning, Ivy. Not very cool at all."

"You nearly stabbed me!" Ivy said as her heartbeat gradually slowed.

"Don't sneak up on me when I'm asleep, idiot. The fuck did you think would happen?"

"You," Ivy said, still on the verge of hysterics, "were sleeping on top of me. All I tried to do was move your arm."

"Really?"

"Yes!" Ivy said, her voice shrill. "You nearly killed me."

"Oops." Charity scratched her head, disturbing the messy halo of white blonde hair that framed her in the dim light. "Sorry about that. Don't do it again though, okay?"

"Don't... Fuck it, whatever." Ivy took a deep breath and counted to ten. "I am going to make a pot of tea. Would you like some?"

"Yes," she said as she fell back into the pillow, sprawling out on the small bed.

"Manners go a long way, Charity."

"Kitchen ain't that far," she mumbled. "I need my beauty sleep."

"Being pretty doesn't mean anything if you're an asshole."

"At least I'm pretty, Ivy. It's more than you."

"I'm gonna scald you with that fucking tea if you

keep this up."

Charity didn't say anything, but lazily raised a middle finger in response. Ivy muttered angrily to herself as she left the cramped bedroom. In the main room of the garret, lit by the dim glow around the edges of the secured windows, Mallory, Jessica, and Thaddeus lay on the bed in a tangled heap.

I'm not even going to ask, she thought as she saw two wine glasses and an empty blood bag on the table. Suddenly the garret felt claustrophobic and cramped, and she could bear it no longer. *I'll head outside, have a day in the sun just to think.*

She walked past the naked trio, doing her best to not look too closely at them, and she filled two syringes from the flask on the hotplate and put them on the desk with a note. *That should clear up my whereabouts to them,* she thought, *and give me some much needed breathing space.*

She considered making a pot of tea before she left, but decided that Charity could go without. She laced up her boots as quietly as she could and, after slinging a long bag containing her swords over her shoulder, slipped out of the garret. She trotted down the stairs and emerged in the golden sunshine. She took a deep breath and sighed with relief.

"What a glorious morning!" she said cheerfully as she strolled down the street in search of breakfast. In the back of her mind, however, was the lingering anxiety surrounding the upcoming eclipse, dug into her brain like a splinter. No matter how chirpy she felt, Ivy couldn't quite drive the thought from her mind.

In two and a half days, all this ends.

Ivy Livingston wandered throughout the city,

aimlessly exploring in a way that she hadn't done for years; not since she'd first arrived in Oxford and was finding her bearings. She stopped to smell the roses in a window box in Jericho before idly strolling up Little Clarendon Street; she'd been in such a rush the day before that she hadn't even thought of looking at the little green in Wellington Square.

Curious, she cast a weather eye in the direction of the wrought iron railings as she walked slowly towards St Giles. Ivy half expected the entire space to be under some sort of police cordon, but it was as empty as she'd ever seen it; untouched, even.

It's mad to think that just over a week ago I was living an ordinary life. Ivy tried to smile at the absurdity of it all, but she was startled to find herself blinking back tears. She noticed the stares of others as they went about their business, and she tried to hide her face.

"Yes, let's all stare at the mad woman," she muttered to herself. She didn't notice someone approaching to her left and was startled when they spoke.

"Excuse me, miss, are you alright?" The young man had a kind smile and warm eyes.

"Just struggling with the inevitable, I'm afraid. Thank you for asking, though." She looked at him, her eyes wide. *He's too young to die.* "Get out of the city, kid."

"What?"

"I mean it," she said sharply, "get away from this place as fast as you can or you'll never make it out alive!"

"Is there someone I can call?" he asked as he took a measured step backwards. "A friend or family member, maybe?"

"I'm not crazy!" Ivy shouted. "I'm a fucking doctor; don't you think I'd know if I was crazy?"

"Jesus, lady, I don't want any trouble." The man backed away quickly as even more people started staring at Ivy. "I hope you get the help you need."

She looked around at everyone in the street as she felt dozens of eyes boring into her soul. A part of her wanted to sink to the floor and burst into terrified sobs, but she refused to show such weakness.

Get a grip, Ivy, Michaela said sharply. *You're going to end up arrested and in the Warneford if you're not careful!*

"The Warneford," she said softly. "I know every inch of that building and I can't think of a single place the Master could possibly hide, let alone with his entire horde of Nightwalkers."

Maybe you don't know as much as you think.

"What should I do about it, oh genius one?" she asked sarcastically. She was walking towards St Giles and her one-sided conversation was still drawing confused glances.

Why not go and see for yourself?

You could always check the security footage, Edgar added helpfully. *Maybe you'll see where they're nesting.*

"That's not a bad idea, Ed. Not a bad idea at all." She shrugged the bag on her shoulder, feeling the weight of her weapons. "It's not like I'm defenceless either."

You never have been.

Ivy let Michaela's last comment slide as she crossed the road and waited for a bus that would take her to the very mouth of the Master's lair.

The reception was unmanned as Ivy stepped through

the door. The lights were on and everything seemed to be normal, except for the lack of people. *I've never noticed how few windows this place has.* She walked slowly and carefully down the corridor, trying to be as quiet as possible.

"Where are you?" she muttered gently to herself as she inspected the map on the wall by reception. "Aha! Security Office, that way."

She half crept, half ran down the seemingly abandoned corridor in a way that made her feel entirely too much like a rat in a maze. The frantic beating of her heart was the only sound that she could hear, but she held firm and refused to give in to panic.

As she approached the door to the Security Office, she could see that it stood ajar and was lit by the flickering of television screens. The salty metallic tang of blood filled her nostrils and she brought one hand up to cover her mouth, suddenly nauseous.

This is a bad idea, Ivy, Michaela said in a fearful tone. *Get out now.*

"Ivy..." She spun around at the sound of someone whispering her name.

Run!

Ivy tried to move towards the exit and the safety of the sunlight, but another whisper came from that very direction. Instead she bolted inside the security office and slammed the heavy door shut. She pulled her phone out of her bag, but it had no signal. Mobile service was always spotty in the older areas of the city, especially with so much thick stone getting in the way.

She rattled out a text to Thaddeus detailing her location, and hit send.

There was a quiet ding as the message failed to send.

"Fuck, fuck, fuck!" She copied the text and put it

into an email; that would send even if the signal drifted in later on, after she was-

Don't think about that!

"I don't know what to do!" Ivy said tearfully. "Help me!"

You are armed, so draw a fucking sword. Ivy nodded at Michaela's words. In fact, she had been so preoccupied with sending the messages that she had completely failed to notice the two security officers that still sat in their chairs, throats torn out.

She began to hyperventilate and a high pitched keening noise escaped her lips.

Get it together!

Ivy tried to respond, but it was no use; her voice was gone entirely. The sword bag rattled uncontrollably in her shaking hands. She managed to tie the sash around her waist and drew the wakizashi. She was trembling too much to hold any kind of stance so she simply brandished the blade in front of her.

"Ivy!" The voice was louder now and it filled the room, echoing around the walls. She looked at the security cameras, but they all showed nothing but static. She took a deep breath and squared up to the door.

"Out the door, and break hard to the left." She bounced on the balls of her feet, ready to make the dash of her life. "Keep going straight and don't stop until you hit sunlight."

Go!

Ivy ripped open the security room door and banked out of the room, heading towards the exit. Unfortunately, there was someone in her way. She went to swing her sword, but Joseph Evans was faster; he put a plastic mask over her face and a sickly sweet scent filled her nostrils.

Don't breathe... Michaela tried to warn her, but Ivy was unconscious before she knew what was happening.

Chapter Thirty Five – The Occultation Approaches

Mallory

"Good morning!" Charity Walpole yelled with unnecessary glee. Thaddeus, Jess, and Mallory all sat up in the bed with a start as the pale Ghost chuckled to herself.

Fucking hell, it's bright in here, thought Mallory.

"Did we have a good night?" she asked, grinning like a lunatic.

"You could say that," Thad said as he pulled on a pair of pyjama bottoms. "Where's Ivy?"

"Oh, the Doc and I had a little bit of a disagreement this morning. I think she's gone out for the day to cool down; I'm sure that she's working on that cure in the back of her mind, so we don't need to worry about that.

"What we do need to do is come up with a plan of attack for when we face the Master in his lair."

"What time is it?" Jessica asked. "It's got to still be early, right?"

"It's a little after four in the afternoon. You lot clearly had a big night." Charity brandished a syringe filled with a pale straw coloured fluid. "Ivy left a note telling you to take this; apparently it will suppress the parasite enough for you to be your usual self."

"Intravenous or intramuscular?" he asked.

"Into the parasite itself, if at all possible," Charity said as she referenced the note. Mallory grimaced as he saw the horrific growths moving under his skin like a mesh of worms. "Do you want me to do it?"

"Please." He looked away as Charity studied at the pulsating mass beneath his skin. After a few seconds, he couldn't help but glance at her. She had a look of concentration on her face as the tip of the hypodermic hovered mere millimetres above his skin. "What's the matter?"

"I'm not sure I can get it." She frowned in annoyance, and Mallory could feel the heat of her blood radiating through his skin. Unbidden, the claws extended and the fangs descended as the buzzing static in his brain kicked into an impossibly high gear.

FEED.
KILL.
FEED.
KILL.

He growled as he fought the urges, baring his awful chitinous maw at Charity. She muttered an apology and jabbed the needle into one of the parasite's teeth. She injected the fluid in one smooth motion and Mallory recoiled in agony.

I'm going to die, he thought as he kicked and screamed in pain. He writhed on the floor for a few seconds, but then the agony and the hunger disappeared entirely; even the whisper of the parasite was a distant dull murmur rather than an all encompassing roar.

"How do you feel?" asked Jess.

"I actually feel really good; better than I've felt since the fight in Wellington Square, truth be told." He looked down at his claws as they receded into his fingertips; they seemed to be turning white around the edges. "Do my teeth look different to you?"

"Yeah, they've got this feathery white substance

starting to grow out of them," Thaddeus said. "I think you're starting to fruit, Mallory."

"What does that mean?"

"You're getting ready to release spores during the eclipse." Charity said. She tapped the handle of one of her blades. "Don't worry, Mallory. If it gets to that point and you're still not cured I'll make good on my promise."

"I know you will."

"The important thing," Jess said, "is getting to the Master before the eclipse can occur. If he gets the chance to infect the whole city we're completely done for."

"We still don't know where he's hiding, do we?" asked Thaddeus. "We know it's around the Warneford, but we can't be sure where."

"I know where he is," Charity said with a knowing smile.

"Where?" asked Mallory. "I can see his light centred on the Warneford, but it must be all muddled up because it looks as if he's underground."

"That's exactly where he is!" She brandished a printout of an early building plan of the Oxford Lunatic Asylum. "When the old nuthouse was designed and built it had an entire subsurface structure, but that's all been lost to time.

"All I had to do was dig through the council planning records and I eventually found this vast catacomb system right underneath the hospital's main buildings."

"Nicely done, Charity." Thaddeus said. "Now all we need is a plan of attack and then we can head in."

"We'll attack in daylight on the morning of the eclipse; it gives us a couple of days to rest up and gather our strength. We can arm ourselves with the most devastating weapons we can find and we hit them hard with everything we've got."

"Normally I would counsel against a full frontal assault," Mallory said as he looked carefully at the map and frowned, "and it seems that there is only one way in and out, so why not wait for the Master here and pick them off at range?"

"If even one of the Nightwalkers make it outside during the eclipse we've lost." Thaddeus said. "It's a much riskier play, even if it is safer for us. They might also have tunnels that aren't on this map; we have to take the fight to them when they're hemmed in by the daylight."

"There will be hundreds of them in a very small space," Mallory said with considerable frustration. "You are going to get massacred!"

"We'll use the various UV sources to drive them back, outright killing some of the thralls." Jess leant forward and looked at Mallory. "When the Master tried to trap us in the nightclub, the close proximity worked against the Nightwalkers, not for them; whenever Thaddeus harmed one it disoriented the others.

"A complete frontal assault might throw the Master off balance enough to give us an opening. You said that Evans was the only Higher Nightwalker left, didn't you?"

"I did." Mallory nodded slightly as he got to his feet. "Okay, this might actually work. Most importantly, though, I'm going to put the kettle on."

They sat quietly while Mallory bustled around the kitchen and waited for the kettle to boil. In the main room Thaddeus's computer dinged softly as an email arrived, but was ignored.

I'm sure there's something here that I've missed, Mallory thought. As the kettle clicked and he filled the teapot, the obvious hit him.

"The issue with this plan," Mallory said as he walked back into the living space, "is that if we go in daylight, I won't be able to help you."

"I know." Charity's words were like a slap.

"But I can help you! I tore through those Higher Vampires like they were made of fucking tissue paper!"

"You did and it has been a tremendous help," Charity said in a measured voice, "but we need to focus on getting you cured; it's likely that the procedure is going to put you out of action for a little while."

"I don't care, the fucking cure can wait! I will not be benched during the most important fight of my life!" Mallory's voice was loud enough to rattle the walls of the garret. "He was in my fucking head, Charity!

"This ends with me killing him; that's not optional."

"Mallory," she said softly, "look at this logically-"

"No, Charity, I will not be logical or impartial or unemotional," he yelled, the anger burning in his chest, "the Master fucking tortured me and I want to look in his watery cowardly eyes as he dies. I want him to know that I killed him, just like I said I would."

"And if we lose?" Thaddeus said sharply. "What happens then, Mallory?"

"The Ministry will send more people if we all die."

"And the city will be full of Nightwalkers," Jess said. "Anyone they send will get massacred."

"Look at all the information we have, Mallory," Charity said, "and even with a weakened Master we're cowering behind metal shutters every night and hoping that they won't attack directly.

"We know who the Master is, what he is, where he is, and what he's planning yet we're most definitely on the back foot here. Let's be honest with ourselves for a moment, shall we?

"We are almost certainly going to die beneath the Warneford, even if we do beat the Master. We are going to get shredded and there will still be Nightwalkers roaming the city; someone needs to stay behind to let the Ministry know what happened here, especially if it all goes wrong!"

"But why me?" Mallory whined. "Why not one of the others? Why not you?"

"You and I are the only ones with Ministry credentials, Mallory, and I'm a Lamplight Subject; that diminishes my credibility massively." She took him by the shoulder and looked into his eyes. "You are a member of the Order of the Third Eye and one of the most decorated Sleuths in Ministry history! You have a personal relationship with the Director, Mallory.

"It has to be you."

Mallory was looking over the map of the catacombs when the doorbell rang. Charity trotted downstairs and returned a few minutes later with a large carrier bag filled with metal takeaway containers. She winked at Mallory as she spread the food out over the table and nipped to the kitchen to get cutlery and plates.

"What's all this for?" Thaddeus asked as he joined them. Jess was just behind him, drying her hair after a long shower. "If it's some kind of last supper, I think you're a day early."

"This smells amazing," Mallory said sadly. "Does

everything have-"

"These," Charity said as she passed Mallory several dishes, "do not have appreciable amounts of anything that can hurt you, at least according to the restaurant's allergen guidelines."

"Thank you," he said, genuinely touched. *You tip your hand sometimes, Walpole,* he thought with a smile. *You aren't as heartless as you pretend to be.*

"I'm amazed anyone is still delivering, given everything that's going on." Jess smiled at Charity. "I'm glad they are, though, as this looks incredible. I hope the driver gets home safe."

"I think he will, it's not quite dark yet." Charity began spooning keema rice and lamb Rogan Josh on to her plate, smiling hungrily as she did so. "As for your question, Thaddeus, I just fancied it and I have barely used my meal stipend for this trip so I thought I'd splash out and treat us."

Mallory moaned softly as he took a bite of a peshwari naan. *Has bread always tasted this good?*

"Enjoying being back on solid food once again?" Thaddeus asked playfully.

"Uh huh," Mallory nodded around a mouthful of sweet bread.

"Is Ivy in the bedroom?" Jess asked. "I've not seen her all day."

"She must be," Charity said. "She probably slipped in earlier when I wasn't looking and is sitting in there in a sulk. Mallory, you've seen her, right?"

"Nope." Mallory shook his head, far too focused on the food to care about Ivy's temper tantrum. "Let her have her little strop if that's what she needs."

"She should get some of this," Charity said, standing up. "I ordered the Maruti Lamb because it's her favourite."

"Why do you know what her favourite food is?" asked Mallory with a laugh. "Are you two suddenly best friends?"

"I know what everyone's favourite is." Her voice was quiet, almost embarrassed. "I do pay attention to the people I'm around, you know."

"I wasn't making fun," Mallory said, "I was just surprised, that's all. You and Ivy have a rather antagonistic relationship; I didn't figure you'd discussed favourite foods."

"I don't make friends very easily," she said with a sniffle as she wrapped her arms around herself tightly. "For fuck's sake, can you all please stop staring at me!"

"Charity, I-"

"No, just fucking leave it, Mallory," she said as she stalked towards the bedroom. "I'll get Ivy and we can eat in peace."

"I haven't seen her either." Thaddeus went to his desk to check his phone as Charity rushed back into the room.

"She's not there!" She immediately started putting on her boots and blades. "She never came back and it's getting dark."

"Oh my god," Thaddeus said quietly, "she emailed me hours ago; she was at the Warneford scoping things out. Charity, we have to help her!"

"Get your boots on, Thane, and bring whatever weapons you'll need for a stand-up fight."

"We'll come too," Mallory said but Charity shook her head.

"No. The same rules still apply. If we're not back by dawn, the two of you get out of the city however you can. Head to London and tell the Ministry what's happening here."

"We will," Mallory said as he gave Charity a tight hug. "Bring her back alive, Charity."

"I intend to, Marsh," she said through gritted teeth, "or at least die trying."

Chapter Thirty Six – Bad Medicine

Ivy

"Ivy Livingston?" said a soft voice. Ivy's eyelids fluttered as she slowly regained consciousness. "Wake up, Dr Livingston."

Ivy suddenly bolted awake, recognising the voice of Joseph Evans. She tried to throw herself in the direction of his voice, but something held her down. She finally forced her eyes open and she could see the room she was held in; it was a sterile medical setting, possibly a surgical theatre.

She was sat in a large chair, with straps restraining her wrists, legs, waist, and head; she squeezed and wriggled, but she couldn't get free. *Why hasn't he just killed me already?* Ivy looked frantically around, wild eyed as a cornered rabbit, but she couldn't see the rogue Ministry agent.

"Where are you?" she said angrily. "If you're going to kill me you should at least look me in the eye as you do it!"

She heard Evans chuckle at her frustration. It was a gentle musical laugh that would've been attractive in any other circumstance, but now it just made Ivy's blood run cold. There was the familiar snapping sound of someone putting on surgical gloves which sent a shudder down Ivy's spine.

"I'm not here to kill you, Ivy." She jumped as he leant into view, almost intimately close to her face; there was a pink line where Charity had slashed him, but otherwise he had completely recovered. "In fact, I've got express orders not to kill you, although that doesn't mean I can't have a little fun with you first."

"Fuck you!" she yelled as she strained against the straps to no avail; they were sturdy padded leather with steel buckles. She turned her head slightly to one side and, in the corner of her eye, she could see her swords. "When I get out of here I'm going to cut your fucking head off, Joseph."

"You have some fight in you, Livingston." He traced a finger down her cheek. "Please, struggle and scream all you want; it only makes this more enjoyable for me."

"I thought Charity was bad but you're all kinds of fucked up, aren't you? Well, I'm not going to give you the satisfaction, you creep." Ivy took a deep breath and closed her eyes.

Find your mountaintop, Ivy.

"What are you doing?" he asked angrily.

The flapping sound of the windblown tent drifted in like a half-remembered dream. She couldn't cup her hands, but she could smell the piping hot tea, freshly poured from the chipped ceramic teapot.

Just shut it all out. Protect yourself from the world. She smiled as she walked herself deeper and deeper. *I can stay here forever.*

"You think you can just ignore me?" Evans growled.

Ivy did ignore him; he sounded distant and faded. A part of her still hoped to see her friends again, but she had made her peace with death the moment Joseph had started hunting her.

They'll kill him for me, and then they'll stop the Master.

"Wake up, Livingston!" he yelled, but his voice was a mere whisper to Ivy.

When all is said and done, they'll raise a glass and

remember my name. That will be enough.

A sharp shrill whistle cut through her trance and dragged her back to the waking world with a cry of pain. Her ears rang as the dreamlike state fell away and she was left with the cold hard reality of her situation.

"You do not get to opt out of this, Ivy!" Evans said as he stroked her hair. "You think you know all about pain and suffering, but you haven't any idea what it's like!"

"Charity mentioned the Lamplight experiments, Joseph, and if I'm being honest I really don't care how nasty your childhood was; plenty of people had a tough time as children and most don't end up as psychopathic murderers.

"So save the sob story and get on with whatever you have in store for me."

"Don't you pretend to know me, Livingston." Joseph dragged a chair from behind her and sat in it a short distance from Ivy. His eyes were ringed with dark circles and his lips were cracked and raw. The surgical gloves had torn open, revealing that his fingernails had fallen out completely and the black chitin claws were slowly destroying his hands.

He looks worse than Mallory, she thought. *At least we have a hope of curing him.*

"What are you staring at?"

"Just observing the progression of your condition, Joseph." She raised an eyebrow in mockery. "You're *clearly* taking the transformation well."

"No worse than any other." He smiled, revealing his horrible chitinous fangs. "Soon Mallory Marsh will look just as bad."

"I doubt it," she said with a smirk.

"And why is that?"

"Oh, Mallory's been cured," she half-lied. He frowned for a moment, suddenly confused. "Didn't your Master tell you about the cure?"

"You're lying. There is no way to stop the transformation." He sounded doubtful.

"If you say so, but you could always ask Irving himself." She paused for a moment before continuing. "Or should I say Edwin Finnster? Which name do you use, or do you just call him 'Master' like some spineless lapdog?"

"How did you learn the Master's true name?" Joseph leant in closer.

"Mallory showed us his face, but someone else recognised him from his religious work." *Time for the killing blow,* she thought. "We have his personal copy of a book he wrote, along with his notes. It's an interesting read, especially the part where your Master outlines the cure for your condition."

"The Master told me there was no alternative." His voice was soft. "He said there was no way back from this."

"But there is, Joseph." She looked at him, trying her best to empathise with the murderer before her. "If you let me go I can take you back to the others; we can cure you."

"No," he growled as he got to his feet. "I'm not letting you go, and when I am done here I am going to find and destroy that book, along with all your friends.

"I don't want to go back, and no one can make me!"

"The Master finds you most intriguing, Ivy Livingston."

"I'll tell him that I'm flattered," she said, "just before

I cut his head off."

"Such anger, such fire!" He smiled and pulled his seat closer. "We're a lot alike, you know?"

"You mean us?"

"I do. We don't play well with others, even though our work requires us to. We have to be in charge, even if that isn't always the best thing for those under our command." He traced a finger gently down her cheek. "We're loners, Ivy."

"I'm nothing like you," she said as she tried to turn her face away from his touch. "You're a monster!"

"I wasn't always this way; I went through living hell and it left its mark on me." He moved his finger from her face to the burn on her left arm. "You carry the same scars, Ivy, both inside and out. You live alone, lose yourself in your job, and have no real relationships outside of the professional acquaintances you're forced to socialise with at the occasional work party."

Ivy blinked back a tear and tried not to look at Joseph Evans. She bit her lip to stop it trembling.

"Have I touched a nerve? I am sorry about that."

"Spare me your false pity."

"I mean it, Ivy. What they've done to us is irreversible, indelible; we're doomed to forever be on the outside looking in." He took her hand in his. "I used to be married. I had a wife and a child, a nice house in a small village, and a decent, if ordinary job; I thought I'd escaped the shadows behind the world, Ivy."

"And the Ministry killed them to force you to come back?"

"No. I did." He smiled sadly at her. "We're forever branded, monsters to the bone."

"You murdered your family!?"

"It was an accident. My time in the Lamplight Project was so horrific that I still have nightmares about it. One night the dream was especially horrifying and I started screaming in my sleep. When I finally woke up I found that my wife and infant daughter were dead; I'd burst the blood vessels in their brains with my voice. One of the neighbours perished too.

"That was why I returned, Ivy. The world has no place for monsters like us."

"I am not a monster, Joseph. I haven't killed anybody!"

"Do you really believe that, Ivy?" He dragged his claws back upwards, lingering on her wrist as if feeling her pulse. "Would you bet your life on it?"

He turned to look at her, a sympathetic smile on his lips. Ivy spat in his face.

"You bitch!" Joseph stood angrily, his chair clattering backwards. "I open up to you, I explain your importance, and I was going to offer you the choice of joining us willingly, but you've thrown it all away now."

He walked behind her for a moment before returning with a small cart. Atop it was a blue surgical cloth and several shining metal implements. It took Ivy a moment to recognise them, but when she did she started screaming and struggling with all her might.

"Will you shut up!" Evans roared, rattling the shelves with his voice and causing the door to swing open. He slapped her and she fell silent. He shook his head, clearly in pain. "You know what these are, I take it?"

"Yes."

"Tell me, Dr Livingston," he said with a cruel smile. "Tell me what I'm going to do to you."

"That," she said slowly as she desperately played for just a little more time, "is an orbitoclast."

"This?" he asked playfully as he held up a long sharp spike with a flat striking surface at the blunt end.

"Yes. What you're going to do is place it against the skull of my eye socket and hammer it into my brain; this is called a transorbital lobotomy." She took a deep, shuddering breath as she tried not to be sick. "It's a form of psychosurgery that is no longer used because it is absolutely barbaric. Why would the Master allow you to do such a thing if he is so fascinated by me?"

"There's something in your brain that lets you slip free of the Master's spell." He twirled the gleaming steel spike as he spoke. The glint of the tip flashed in the light almost rhythmically. "He doesn't know what it is, but he wants it gone; one loose agent has done far too much damage already."

"There must be some other way, Joseph."

"There isn't, Ivy." He placed the metal tip gently in the corner of her eye. "If it's any consolation, I'll be sad to see you go; we could've been great friends."

"Don't beat yourself up too much," she growled.

"Oh, I won't. In fact, I've always wanted to perform this particular procedure on someone." He beamed at her. "I plan to really enjoy myself."

She closed her eyes, screwing them up tightly. *I'm out of time,* she thought.

Go down, Ivy, Michaela said. *Go as fast as you can!*

Tent, tea, bells, chill, hair, ashram. Ivy counted through her steps as they flashed by at lightning speed. In a fraction of a second she was under and everything came flooding back to her, as clear as day.

She pictured Joseph Evans standing in front of her and held that image in one hand. In the other she held the orbitoclast. She took a deep breath of frigid mountain air as her fingers tightened, white knuckled, around the spike. She opened her mind's eye as she drove the spike through her eye and into her brain.

In the surgical room her eyes snapped open as Joseph drew back the hammer. His pupils centred on hers, now huge and dark; he wavered for a moment as if he was drawn into them. His hand shook violently as he pulled the orbitoclast away from her eye and turned it towards his own.

"How-" he started to say, but his words were cut short as he drove the spike into his brain. Ivy let out a huge sigh as the Shriek twitched out the last few seconds of his life. *You were right about me, Evans,* she thought, *so you should've been more careful.*

Ivy turned as the sound of footsteps echoed in from the corridor. Her heart began to race at the thought of Nightwalkers ripping her apart as she remained strapped to the chair. She strained and wriggled against the restraints, but they held her firm.

I'm going to die here.

She was about to sob with despair when she heard a familiar voice.

"Ivy, where are you?" Charity called.

"I'm in here!" she yelled as her tears of desperation became ones of relief. "I'm tied to a chair, please let me out!"

"Ivy, I'm-" Charity stopped suddenly as she entered the room and saw Evans dead on the floor. She looked at her former partner and her fingers trembled. She turned towards Ivy, her face a storm of emotions.

She's going to kill me, Ivy thought as Charity crossed the room and drew a blade. She closed her eyes and flinched as the blade swished through the air. Instead of the searing pain of a cut, she felt the strap holding her head fall slack. A few more strokes freed her completely.

"Ivy Livingston," Charity said as she pulled Ivy into her arms, "I'm so glad you're alive."

Chapter Thirty Seven – The Prodigal Son

Thaddeus

"Why would she go to the Warneford?" Thaddeus asked angrily as the bus groaned its way up Morrell Avenue. "What the hell was she thinking?"

"We had a bit of a tiff this morning, and I might've been less than kind to her." Charity looked at Thaddeus as he shook his head at her. "What?"

"You are fucking unbelievable, Charity."

"She gave as good as she got."

"I don't care!" Thad sat back in his seat and tried to calm down, but to no avail. "Your constant bickering is, at best, a distraction to everyone else. Why can't you just be nice to her?"

"So I'm supposed to rise above all her little snips and snipes, is that it?" She shook her head as she pressed the bell.

"Yes, and this stop is too early; we want the one afterwards."

"I want to approach the Warneford on foot, carefully. Maybe Ivy is cornered somewhere nearby and we can do this without having to go into the hospital itself."

"Good idea," Thaddeus said as the bus came to a halt. They both disembarked on to the otherwise empty street and drew their weapons as the bus moved out of sight.

"My main issue with Ivy," Charity continued, "is that she's dishonest."

"I don't see that at all. She's never been anything but upfront with us."

"Really?" Charity asked, incredulous. "Where did

she get all of her military training? Hell, I'll go one better; where is she from? Where is her family?"

"Why don't you just ask her, then?"

"I've tried, and she just obfuscates."

"Maybe she just doesn't want to tell you because you're mean to her?"

"No, Thaddeus. I can read people pretty well, and I'm telling you that she blusters about her past because she has no fucking idea who she is." Charity looked at him. "You can't tell me that you don't feel that there's something strange about her, right? She's dealing with this far too well for someone that has never seen this world before."

"Now you mention it, that is quite odd." Thaddeus stopped as the Warneford came into view. "What's your theory then, if you have one?"

"The weapons training, the situational awareness, the adaptability and sheer breadth of her skill base; if I didn't know any better, I'd say she was a Ministry operative."

"Like you and Mallory?"

"No. The Ministry has a arm that deals more in deniable operations and missions of questionable morality; they only take the very best and Ivy would definitely pass the necessary threshold. They're called Ravenblades, and Ivy has all the hallmarks of one."

"But you don't think she is?"

"No," Charity said softly as she looked through a small pair of tinted binoculars. "I think something far stranger is afoot. Regardless, it puts me on edge around her. Anyway, this conversation isn't for now; take a look at this."

He took the binoculars from her and peered up at the darkened building. Lights were only burning in a few of the windows and it seemed deserted. Just as he was about to look away, Thaddeus saw the familiar twitchy form of a Nightwalker appear in the light. He adjusted the focus and the creature's features snapped into focus.

"Oh my god," he whispered as he lowered the lenses.

"What did you see?" Charity said as she took the binoculars from him.

"The Nightwalker in the window," he said sadly, "it's my mum."

Thaddeus kept a lookout whilst Charity used her various tools to quietly unlock a window. He raised his kukri at every rustling leaf and swaying branch. *Calm down, Thaddeus,* he thought. *You're no good to anyone as a nervous wreck.*

"Gotcha!" Charity whispered as the window latch clicked. She turned to face Thaddeus and gestured for him to look at her. Her voice was so low that he had to strain to hear it over the rising wind. "Right, when we're inside we need to be as near to silent as possible. We're unlikely to get the drop on Evans, but we want to be in and out without bringing the entire nest down on us."

"Okay. I understand."

"Here," she said as she handed him one of her knives. "This will suit you better for the kind of close contact work we're after in here. Can you throw with any accuracy yet?"

"I think so," he said after a moment of hesitation. She shook her head.

"It needs to be a firm yes, or else you're just going to make noise."

"Sorry." He hung his head slightly.

"Hey, no need for that, Thad." She tilted his head back up. "You've been doing this for a few days, I've been at it for decades; just follow my lead and cover me, okay?"

"Got it." She handed him a syringe with a plastic cover over the needle. "What's this for?"

"If it all goes to hell in there and you can't get out, book it down into the catacombs and sting the Master with this. I'm not sure how well it will work, but Ivy said that it was poisonous to the Nightwalkers; it might end this."

"Then why not-"

"No." Her voice was sharp and her face hard. "We are here to rescue Ivy, and that is it. We are outnumbered and outgunned; I gave you that in case an extremely unlikely window is open to us. Live today, fight tomorrow. Understand?"

"Yes, Charity."

"You're a good kid, Thaddeus. I'm sorry that you got caught up in all this." She drew a knife and reminded him of what she'd taught him. "Remember, brainstem if you can get it, but if not go in between the ribs or up and under the jaw. Blade comes out of the top of your hand, by your thumb, to give you more control.

"Always stab, never slash; you will move faster and hit harder whilst being almost impossible to block. If you aren't confident you can bring them down quickly enough, just let me do it."

"Thank you. I'm good to go." Thaddeus went to climb through the window, but Charity pulled him back. "What?"

"One last thing," she said as she put a hand on his shoulder. "If we come face to face with your mum and dad, *I* will deal with them. I guarantee you will be too conflicted to strike decisively, so I will handle it."

"Okay. We're gonna get her out alive, aren't we?"

"We're going to do our best, Thad." She palmed another blade and deftly entered the window, helping Thaddeus through after her. The hallway was dark; the only illumination came from the street lights outside.

Charity still wore her glasses, but lowered them slightly so she could peer over the top of them. Thaddeus dropped into an awkward crouch to move more quietly, but Charity remained upright; she moved slowly and carefully, making her steps almost silent.

Thaddeus tried to take a long step forwards and overbalanced. He fell against the wall with a muted thump and Charity turned her head sharply, her face like thunder. She reached down and helped him back to his feet, pulling his face close to hers.

"Just walk like a normal person!" Charity hissed barely loud enough for Thaddeus to hear. "Go slowly and watch where you walk. This isn't a fucking video game!"

Thaddeus went to apologise, but she put a finger to her lips and continued her slow way down the corridor. There was the soft clatter of footsteps and she leant back into the shadows as she brought one arm up to put him behind her.

Two Nightwalkers rounded the corner, their eyes glinting in the light. They stopped at the end of the corridor and one of them seemed to be looking right at them. *Can they see us?* Thaddeus wondered, his heart suddenly in his throat.

Charity was as still as a statue. Thaddeus couldn't even see her breathing, and he felt his body begin to shake with the stress of the situation. He tried to control his breathing but focussing on it only made keeping calm that much harder.

The Nightwalkers started to slowly make their way down the corridor, twitching and chirping as they did so. Thaddeus felt like his chest was about to explode and his legs were in real danger of giving way.

Just when he thought he could hold on no more, a piercing scream filled the hallway and the Nightwalkers turned their heads to face the sound. It was no longer than a moment, but Charity Walpole did not need any longer than that. She drove her knives into the skulls of the Nightwalkers, killing them instantly.

A short distance away the screaming continued and Charity grabbed Thaddeus by the shoulder.

"New plan," she said, "we run and gun the gauntlet until we reach Ivy."

Without waiting for an answer she took off sprinting towards the source of the noise, and Thaddeus followed her. *Even when she's running, she's freakishly quiet,* Thaddeus thought as Charity barrelled down the corridor like a whirlwind of death.

There were several Nightwalkers in their path, but Charity mowed them down with all the force of a tidal wave. She was getting ahead of him and she disappeared round a corner as two Nightwalkers leapt at him, swinging with their jagged claws.

Thaddeus acted on instinct, drawing both the knife Charity had given him and Arabella's kukri. He ducked under one creature's clumsy swing, and drove the knife upwards through its jaw, just as Charity had taught him. The other creature lunged as he stepped back, bringing the kukri round in a wide arc that caught the Nightwalker in the neck, taking its head clean off.

"Whoa," he said as he got his breath back, "I'm starting to get good at this whole-"

The words faltered as he looked down at the two Nightwalkers that he had slain; the lifeless eyes of Charlotte and Barnabus Thane stared back at him. He felt the tears welling up inside him, but he took a deep shuddering breath and got himself under control.

Live today, Thaddeus, mourn tomorrow.

He was about to follow in the direction Charity had headed in when she came running back around the corner with Ivy in tow; the latter had her shorter samurai sword out. Charity slowed to a trot as she looked down at the bodies on the floor.

"Shit," she said softly, "I'm sorry Thaddeus. For what it's worth, you did them a favour. They'll be at peace now."

"Thank you." There was a terrible howling sound from deep within the hospital. "We better run, I've got a feeling that the Master isn't going to take what happened here lying down."

The three of them ran back up the corridor and exited the hospital through the broken window. The shrieking of the pursuing Nightwalkers drove them out into the night, running for their lives as the Master and Congregation realised what had happened.

The Master is aware that we know about their nest now, Thaddeus thought as they bolted into the night. *Our plan to stop this just got a lot harder.*

Chapter Thirty Eight – Do No Harm

Mallory

Thaddeus and Charity made it home just before dawn after their attempt to rescue Ivy. Mallory and Jessica were all packed up and ready to leave, when they heard their allies tramping up the stairs to the garret.

"How did it go?" Mallory asked as Charity and Thaddeus entered. His question was answered both by Charity's thumbs up and Ivy's appearance not three seconds later.

"I'm so glad you're back!" Jess said as she swept up Ivy in a big hug.

"Evans?" Mallory asked.

"Dead." Charity answered.

"Did you or Thaddeus get him?" he asked. *I hope you got the chance to set the score straight,* he thought, *but for the sake of your sanity I hope it was Thaddeus.*

"Charity killed him just as he was about to kill me," Ivy said. "I'd be dead if it wasn't for her."

"Don't count your chickens too soon, Ivy," Charity said. "In twenty four hours we go back into that nightmare."

"That's plenty of time to adequately prepare." She walked over to Mallory. "How are you feeling? Is the suppressant working alright?"

"It's working great, thank you. I can only hope the cure will be as effective." He placed a hand on her shoulder. "How are you holding up?"

"I'll be better for some sleep and a nice cup of tea,"

she said. "You should all get some sleep; we'll administer the cure at sundown, and it is not going to be easy. Steel yourselves and take the rest of the day to rest and recuperate.

"Tomorrow we take the fight back to the Master for the last time."

Thaddeus took off his shirt and trousers and collapsed into the bed with a blissful groan, and Mallory and Jessica were quick to join him. Ivy and Charity once again took the spare bed. Mallory chuckled as he heard them bickering about who would sleep where.

"You're up against the wall this time, Walpole. And no knives in bed!"

"I'll take the wall but I'm keeping the blades. Just don't shove me and we'll get along famously."

"I can't wait to have my own bed again."

Mallory took comfort in the comparative luxury of his own sleeping arrangements and the quality of his bedmates. He slipped off his clothes and snuggled up with Jessica and Thaddeus, happy in the knowledge that his final day as a Nightwalker had finally come.

Not a moment too soon, he thought blissfully as he drifted off into a dreamless sleep.

"Mallory!"

His eyes snapped open at the sound of Charity's voice. He groaned and sat up.

"What do you want?" he asked angrily. "What part of 'get some rest' did you not follow?"

"It's nine in the evening, Mallory," said Jessica who was already up and dressed.

"Why didn't any of you wake me?" he said grumpily. "I would like to be privy to the plans that are made in my absence!"

"I told them to let you sleep," Ivy said. "You looked exhausted and this is going to be hard enough on your body anyway, so we let you rest. The more strength you have, the more likely you'll survive the procedure."

"Procedure?" *Maybe I'm not quite ready to be cured just yet,* he thought.

"Do you know what a Guinea Worm is?" Ivy asked in an off-hand matter.

"Is it relevant to what the procedure entails?" he asked carefully. He did not want to get sucked into another one of Ivy's tangents only to find out that the procedure was a gunshot to the head.

"The process of treatment is similar, although it should be far quicker in your case, albeit much more painful."

"Why do you sound so upbeat about that?" Charity asked.

"The treatment for Guinea Worm Disease only occurs after the worm has reproduced and it takes almost a week; I'm hoping to cure Mallory before he fully fruits and in a span of about twelve hours or so."

"How is this going to work?" Mallory asked.

"There's going to be two phases. First, we will flood your system with Amphotericin B, an antifungal medication. We'll give it intravenously and it will kill the fungus where it meets your system. We'll continue this regimen for a week or so, just to ensure that we've got it all."

"Sounds simple enough. Why didn't we do this earlier?"

"Because we didn't know it was a fungal infection and the amount of Amphotericin B needed to kill the fungus outright would likely kill you."

"Oh." Mallory's heart sank. "You mentioned a second phase?"

"Yes. The parasite, which is a completely new kind of fungus, I might add, has some interesting macrostructures; the claws, teeth, and the like. Hopefully the antifungal medication will cause the mycelium through your body to retreat into areas with less blood flow and therefore less antifungal.

"This will be your skin. Once the medicine is sufficiently diffused throughout your body, we'll put you in a bath of cold water to cool the fungus down. As it is adapted to both a tropical climate and can colonise the human body, we can safely assume that it will not have much resistance to the cold."

"Will the ice bath kill it?" Mallory asked, shivering at the thought.

"Perhaps. More likely it will enter a dormant state and the retreated mycelium will stay where they are. Then comes the unpleasant part; we need to extract the fungus from your body. I'm hoping that we can pull the majority of it out of you through the fangs and claws, although we might need to do some cutting. We'll need to do this as quickly as possible to stop it fighting against us, so it'll be all hands on deck."

"Lastly, we'll bathe you in ultraviolet light to kill any remaining spores or mycelium that we couldn't cut out." She gave Mallory a sympathetic smile. "This is going to hurt a lot and leave you with some gnarly scars, but I hope it will be worth it to be fully human again."

"Sounds worth it to me. When do we start?"

"Right now."

"I-I-I d-d-don't f-feel s-s-so g-g-good," Mallory said

through chattering teeth. He had not expected the ice bath to be so cold and to be placed in it so suddenly. His insides roiled and he tried to cover his nudity with his trembling hands.

"Try not to talk, Mallory," Jessica said. "I'm sorry about this."

He stifled a gasp as icy water was poured over his head once again, plastering the hair that escaped the messy bun all over his face. Ivy was knelt beside the bath, watching in earnest as the fungus's movement beneath his skin slowed to a crawl.

"Almost there, Mallory, almost there." She looked at Thaddeus and Charity. "As soon as it's been dormant for thirty seconds we get him out and on to the table. I'm worried that if we let him get too cold the fungus will head further in again, and I am not a surgeon."

Charity smiled at him and squeezed his shoulder. She looked at the drip Mallory was hooked up to and then at Ivy.

"Do we have enough medicine, Ivy?" she asked.

"Plenty, yes."

"Could we use some of it on the Master? Would that work?"

"Not quickly enough. If we're going to use chemicals, I can make up something with the remaining allyl isothiocyanate, although copper salts would be best; they're highly toxic to fungi and people alike, however."

Copper salts? Mallory thought as the cold slowed his brain to a crawl.

"Can we get some?" Charity asked.

"No," Ivy said as she continued to stare unblinkingly at Mallory. "We don't have enough time before the eclipse. That's it, lift him!"

Mallory was suddenly swept up and to the table by four pairs of strong arms. They put him on the cleared table a little roughly, and then Ivy quickly strapped him down.

"Why are you restraining him like that?" Jess asked, her voice full of concern.

"This is going to hurt a lot, Mallory, but please try to keep as still as you can."

Mallory tried to respond but he was still too cold and the medicine in his veins made his head swim. He felt a small sting in the centre of his chest as Charity pricked him with one of her knives.

"This is coated in a muscle relaxant," she told Ivy, " but it only lasts a short while, so we'll need to hurry."

"Right. Thaddeus, are you ready with the bag?"

"Yes."

You're putting it in a bin bag? Mallory thought incredulously. *It's an evil vampire fungus, not a mouldy loaf of bread!* He went to say something, but found that he was completely paralysed. He tried to look at the bag to raise his objections, but he saw Thaddeus emptying jar after jar of mustard into it and finally understood their plan.

"I'm so sorry for this, Mallory," Ivy said as she brandished a pair of pliers as she loomed above him. She turned to Jessica and Charity who also had implements of their own. "Everyone know what their goal is?"

They nodded and Mallory's heart filled with dread. *This is going to hurt.*

Through the creeping chill he felt tugging at his hands, and then in his mouth as Charity held his jaw open. It was a strange sensation, all pressure and no pain as they wiggled and loosened the fungal macrostructures from their seating in his flesh. He felt some of the softer tissues in his gums give way as the entire fang ridge came away in one huge piece.

He sighed with relief and then was immediately hit with a wave of agony as the mycelia in his face, neck, and throat were dragged out of him, inch by inch and then metre by metre as the gloved Charity pulled and bundled the writhing fibres.

"This is the most fucked up thing I have ever done in my life," she muttered, and given what Mallory knew about her, that was saying something. The pain spread to his arms as well as the claws and their accompanying tendrils were dragged from his body and tossed, still squirming into the black bag that Thaddeus held open and at the ready.

"Finally!" Charity cried in triumph as the upper row of fangs was finally free and the uncomfortably large mass of wormy mycelia was deposited in the bag for disposal. She immediately turned and latched on to the ridge of toothy protrusions in his lower jaw and pulled with all her might, much faster than before.

The pain was almost unbearable this time as the web was pulled from his chest and abdomen, up his neck, and out through his lower gums. His skin rippled with nauseating movement as Charity hauled with all the speed and precision that she could muster.

If he had been able to vocalise at all, Mallory would've screamed himself hoarse already.

"Aha!" She yelled as the last of it came away. "Ivy, are we done?"

Yes, we are, thought Mallory with relief.

"No," Ivy said gravely. "Now is the hardest part; flip him over."

Jess and Ivy flipped Mallory over as Charity drew

one of her more delicate blades. She traced it gently down Mallory's back, splitting the skin but not damaging the fungus underneath. He felt his skin being pulled back slightly, and in his mind's eye he saw the rootlike structure of the fungus spreading up his spinal column and into his brain.

"Everybody take their positions," Ivy said. There was a flurry of movement as people took their places. "On three; one, two, three!"

There was a wet tearing sound as they pulled the entire entwined mass at once. Mallory's vision flashed white as he felt something tugging inside his skull before it gave way with a slurp and was dragged from his brain and eyes.

The room suddenly darkened as whatever part of the fungus caused the eyeshine was yanked out of him. Ivy, Charity, and Jess carried the trunk of the parasite and dropped it into the bag with the rest. It thrashed and twisted for a moment before it succumbed to the fatal potency of the mustard.

It's gone, Mallory realised. That crackling static and throbbing pressure that he had felt was no more; all that was left was a blissful heaven of agony.

Ivy swiftly changed her gloves and stitched him up. She shone a UV light over his body and let out a huge sigh when Mallory didn't respond or flinch away from it.

"I think we got it all," she said with a nervous laugh. "We actually did it!"

Good show, Ivy, he thought just before he passed out.

Chapter Thirty Nine – Amid Gloaming Spires

Ivy

I hope Mallory survives the treatment, Ivy thought as she walked through the early morning light.

All four of them were as armed and armoured as they would ever be. Charity carried her usual array of knives strapped to her chest and also carried a long case that made her look like a very strange billiards enthusiast. Inside was a shotgun, loaded with copper pellets and a dozen spare shells.

"Even you can't miss with this," Ivy had said gleefully.

She carried one of the Taylor & Bullock Mark Three .357 Giantslayers and had given the other Ministry issue sidearm to Thaddeus Thane. He'd shown promise when they'd talked about firearms the previous day, so she trusted him not to kill one of his comrades using the powerful weapon.

Along with his kukri, he also carried one of the UV batons that Trip had designed, as they all agreed that he was their best hope for getting close to the Master. Ivy carried a UV flare as well as her swords.

"So," Charity had asked carefully as Ivy had packed her swords into their bag, "those are some extremely fancy blades; where did you get them?"

"They're Michaela's." Ivy had looked at Charity in confusion. "I told you that already."

"That's not an answer, Ivy." Charity had said darkly, but she had not pushed the question any further.

She knew I killed Evans, she thought, *and yet she let me tell everyone that she did.*

Stolen valour, Michaela insisted.

It didn't feel like that to me, Ivy responded quietly. *Was she covering for us somehow?*

Don't think about it now, Michaela said sharply. *Focus on defeating the Master.*

"Ivy, are you alright?" Jess asked. "You've been really quiet for a while."

"Just preparing myself to go back into the Warneford once again," she said with a grim smile. "Never setting foot in that place again would be far too soon, and yet that's where we're headed right now.

"A part of me thinks I've only got enough luck to survive one visit."

"We've got your back, Ivy, and we're going in on our terms; no luck needed." Jess gave her a reassuring wink as she hefted the shoulder bag she carried.

"Thank you," Ivy said. Jess was the only one of them who had eschewed a firearm. Instead she carried a copper-nickel short sword, the other UV flare, and a bag full of improvised explosives; small packets of powdered copper and allyl isothiocyanate all packed tightly around little bombs that Ivy had cooked up. The force of the blast wouldn't do much to harm the Nightwalkers, but she hoped that they would disperse the toxic chemicals and harm any of the creatures that were nearby.

Jess and Charity also each had a set of earphones and would be listening to loud music throughout the assault; they weren't sure if it was enough to drown out the Master at full power, however.

"If you feel yourself starting to get mind muddled by the Master," Jessica said as they made their way across a strangely deserted Magdalen Bridge, "remember to get rid of your weapons before he gets complete control."

"Duly noted," Ivy said, whilst Charity simply looked down at her vast array of knives and laughed.

"I'll do my best, but there's a lot of blades here. Also, I'm pretty nifty without them, which the good doctor can attest to."

Ivy chuckled, more amused than irritated by Charity's jibe. Charity gave her a grin and nudged her slightly.

"What was that for?" Ivy asked.

"Just good natured ribbing; typical behaviour inflicted on new recruits, you know?"

"New recruits?" Jess asked. "What exactly are we being signed up for?"

"Well, if we make it out of this alive, I'm going to recommend you all for commendations at the Ministry, along with some cushy operative jobs."

"Are you serious?" Ivy asked. Charity nodded. "Why?"

"You three are some of the most capable people I've ever had the honour to fight alongside, and I know Mallory would say the same too." She turned to face them, lowering her glasses enough to look each of them in the eye as she spoke. "I've served with a lot of monsters in my time, Joseph Evans included, and I've done a lot of awful shit that will stay with me forever.

"But here and now, I can gladly say that I am proud to fight alongside you, and I would be honoured to have you by my side in a more permanent way."

Ivy, Jess, and Thaddeus all stood still, speechless.

"Just think about it, okay? It's a serious offer." Charity paused for a moment before pushing her glasses back up and resuming her usual cavalier attitude. "Of course, we do need to survive the next six hours, so don't get too distracted by the potential glory."

"Oh, we won't," Ivy said, "and for what it's worth, I'm proud to fight alongside you, too."

Charity nodded and they continued on their way. In the sky the moon and the sun made their slow inevitable arcs toward each other and people were already in the streets, observing the early stages of the celestial phenomenon.

We are running out of time.

Ivy's hands began to tremble as they approached the main entrance of the Warneford. Her palms were clammy with cold sweat and her heartbeat thundered in her ears. *Even in daylight this place is evil,* she thought.

"Oh," she said gently as she realised the awful truth. "I'll never be able to work here again, not after what happened."

"I'm sorry, Ivy." Jessica drew her sword. "We might as well arm ourselves before we head inside."

"Agreed," Thaddeus said. "It looks like this place is absolutely deserted."

"Only where humans are concerned," said Charity darkly. "Who knows how many Nightwalkers are lurking in here?"

"I wish we had more time," Jess said, "then we could bomb the building or burn it to the ground."

"You're a right little ghoul, aren't you, Holloway?" Charity said with an approving grin. "Are you going to be alright, Ivy?"

"Of course, I'll be fine," she said shakily, not believing a single word of it. She unpacked her swords from the bag and tried to tie them to her belt but her fingers were trembling too badly. "Fucking hell!"

"Shhh," Charity said gently as she took the weapons from Ivy. "I remember when I was first learning to fight; I would get these tremendous shakes before any kind of engagement. I wasn't afraid of dying, per se, but more so failing those who I looked up to."

"Is this supposed to help?" Ivy asked as Charity attached the weapons to the sash with practised ease.

"One of the trainers spoke to me about it and told me that if I died fighting, then I would have done my best for those I respected and loved; I would have died a noble death." She smiled at Ivy. "A warrior's death. Just do your best, Ivy, and stand your ground; bravery is worthless when you fight in the sun and everything when you war in the shadows."

"Death before dishonour," Ivy said, suddenly tranquil. "Thank you."

"I had a wise teacher," Charity said enigmatically. "You'd have liked her a lot; she had swords a lot like yours."

"Why do I get the feeling that I'm only really hearing half of this conversation?" Thaddeus asked.

"It's not for now," Charity said as she drew a knife into each hand. "No distractions going forwards; keep your eyes on the prize and we'll get out of here alive."

Ivy nodded as she pulled out the maps that Charity had found. She consulted them for a minute or two, to be certain of her route. Her legs felt like jelly as she took a few hesitant steps towards the main doors.

Courage, Ivy, she thought as she turned to face the others.

"Follow me."

"Well that certainly puts a spanner in the works, doesn't it?" Thaddeus said as they rounded a corner to find two out of the three potential ways forward blocked with tangles of furniture that were piled high to the roof. "I'm assuming that one of the blocked routes is our way to the Master's lair?"

"No," Ivy said after double checking her map. "It's actually straight ahead; the only clear path."

"This is a trap." Charity had taken her glasses off to see better in the gloom. The Nightwalkers had boarded up every window that they'd come across so far.

"Thank you for stating the obvious, Charity," Ivy said. "Why don't you go first; you have the shotgun, after all."

"Fine by me." Charity sheathed her blades and slipped the shotgun from her shoulder. Her coat pockets were full of the bulky shells. "Thane, cover me, will you?"

Thaddeus nodded and followed Charity forwards, his revolver in hand. Ivy held Jess back a few metres and then they followed, making sure to stay spread out. The musty smell of mould and decay filled the air as they went deeper and deeper into the maze of corridors, many of which had been blockaded to funnel them onwards.

"We must be nearly there," Charity said softly as they approached a wide open space at the end of the hallway. "Ivy?"

"Yes, straight through that hall and down a short corridor is the entrance to the subterranean passages." Ivy went to join Charity and Thaddeus, but the pale woman waved them back. "We should stay together!"

"Let Thad and me clear the way. If we get separated, you find another route to the Master and we'll draw as many of the Nightwalkers to us as we can."

"That won't happen-"

"This *is* a trap, Ivy." She said in exasperation. "When it springs, and it definitely will, we'll use it to our advantage. You stay back, stay quiet, and use only edged weapons for as long as you can. Thad and I will draw their attention and make some noise.

"Only one of us needs to stop the Master before the eclipse, Ivy." She smiled at her. "We'll see you down there."

Before Ivy could respond Charity sprinted forwards into the hall with Thaddeus hot on her heels. As if on cue, one of the tangled barricades came tumbling down, separating Ivy and Jess from their allies. Jessica went to follow Thaddeus, but Ivy yanked her backwards and into the shadows.

Three Nightwalkers emerged in the corridor and began to stalk their way towards where the two women were hiding. Just as they were on top of them, there was an almighty cacophony as gunfire filled the hall and echoed down the corridor.

The Nightwalkers turned in surprise and Ivy struck. She drew her katana, her earlier worries evaporating as the metallic ringing sound of her blade filled her ears. She dispatched the creatures in three swift slashes and quietly moved into the corridor that they had come from.

Jessica followed, her own blade drawn. Two more Nightwalkers bore down on them, their mad howling drowned out by the dull roar of Charity's shotgun blasts. Ivy brought her blade down on one of the beasts as Jess cleanly decapitated another.

They paused as the sound of gunfire faded. Ivy looked at Jessica, whose eyes were wide with fear.

"Are they dead?" she asked shakily, on the verge of tears.

"I don't know," Ivy said truthfully, "but it's up to us to get to the Master now. If they're alive, we'll meet them there."

"If you say so."

"Find your courage Jess." Ivy smiled at her. "We can do this. Are you ready?"

Jessica tightened her grip on her sword and nodded.

"Let's end this."

<u>Chapter Forty</u> – <u>Beneath the House of Madness</u>

Thaddeus

Thaddeus heard the blockade collapse behind him as he followed Charity into the hall; it was a wide open space that could be used for recreation or as a meeting room. The windows were boarded up and all the furniture had been cleared out, most likely incorporated into the barricades that littered the corridors of the Warneford.

It took his eyes a second or two to adjust to the dim light. As his vision clarified he saw dozens of Nightwalkers streaming into the room from the doorway across from them. He raised his revolver and took aim.

Fourteen shots, Thaddeus, he thought. *Make them count!*

He fired into the charging mass of Nightwalkers at the same time as Charity did. His revolver, deafening in its own right, was a mere popgun compared to the roar of the shotgun as it sent a hail of deadly copper at the attacking creatures.

"You like that!?" Charity yelled as she pumped another shell into the chamber. The Nightwalkers went sprawling as she fired again. Thaddeus continued to fire into the crowd, scoring a head shot here and torso wound there, but it was nowhere near enough to stop the tide.

We're going to die in here, he thought frantically. He looked around the room as the shotgun fired again, keeping the horde at bay; it was working for now, but Charity only had three more shots in the weapon before she would be completely vulnerable.

"Aha!" Thaddeus yelled as he saw the faint glow of sunlight around one of the boarded up windows. He dropped to one knee, and took aim at the three nails holding it in place. He took his time, breathing out with every squeeze of the trigger, just as Ivy had taught him.

The shotgun roared a fourth time, but the Nightwalkers kept coming. Charity's nerve was wavering and the violent kick of the weapon was taking a toll on her thin frame. Thaddeus hit the nails, one after another, and the board came crashing down from the window, taking others with it.

The golden morning sun flooded the centre of the room in a shaft of brilliant light that immolated any Nightwalkers caught in it. It formed a barrier that held back the tide of creatures far better than any fence or barricade ever could.

There were shrieks and howls as individual Nightwalkers were thrown into the light from behind by more reinforcements coming up from the catacombs. Charity lowered her weapon and let out a sigh of relief as Thaddeus smiled at her.

"Not bad, kid!" She yelled over the ringing in her ears. "Not fucking bad at all!"

"Thank you, but there's still all of them between us and the Master." He picked the spent bullet casings from his weapon and let them plink softly to the ground. He fished out reloads and slotted them into place. Across the hall Charity did the same. "Do you think Ivy and Jess are alright?"

"The Doc will keep them safe enough."

"Are you sure?"

"Oh, I'm sure." She turned to look at him. "She killed Evans, Thaddeus. She was tied up when I found her and he was on the floor with a medical implement stuck through his eye."

"Holy shit," Thaddeus said, stunned. "How on earth did she manage that?"

"I can't say for sure; maybe she's telekinetic or she just brainjacked him into killing himself. Either way, Ivy and Jess are gonna be fine." She gestured to the Nightwalkers on the other side of the light. "Besides, we've got bigger problems.

"Soon enough they'll find a way to block out the light and attack us again. We need to get through that lot."

"How?" Thaddeus asked. Charity grinned and handed him the shotgun.

"Way I see it, we've only got one option; the old fashioned way," she said as she drew her knives. "Remember when I told you that Exceptions are a little bit faster and stronger than ordinary humans?"

"Yes."

"I might've undersold my own abilities a bit." She doffed her coat and stood in the sunlight, her leather armoured catsuit bristling with gleaming blades. She pushed the earbuds into her ears and started the music; it was loud enough for Thaddeus to make it out.

"10cc," he muttered as she walked towards the waiting Nightwalkers, "not what I expected at all."

He looked on in awe as she ducked and weaved her way through the throng of creatures, her blades whirling through the air, taking neck after neck and driving into hearts and brains. Two of the Nightwalkers leapt at her in unison, but she sprang backwards into the light and threw her knives at them. They fell dead on the ground and Charity was already moving again.

Thaddeus gasped as he saw her break a Nightwalker's neck with one hand while forcing another to the ground. She drew another pair of blades as she crushed the skull of the prone creature beneath her boot.

The Nightwalkers kept coming but Charity was more than a match for them, occasionally darting back into the sunlight to force the rhythm of the battle in her favour. Thaddeus could see her smiling and hear her singing happily as she tore through the horde like some kind of living meat grinder.

He had no idea how long she fought the Nightwalkers, but their ranks were thinning. The floor was slick with blood and slime, and Charity slipped. She hit the ground hard as one of the creatures loomed above her.

Her eyes looked past the creature as it lunged at her. There was a brief flash of folded steel, and her attacker's head was taken from its shoulders. Charity smiled as Ivy continued to attack the creatures, allowing her to get to her feet and rejoin the fray.

"Everybody back!" Jess yelled as she came barrelling through the Nightwalkers, swinging her sword to clear a path. She dashed past Ivy and Charity, who turned tail and followed her. The three of them crossed into the sunlight and Thaddeus noticed that Jess's satchel was missing. She knocked him to the ground as the bombs went off, spreading copper and isothiocyanate in a cloud through the remaining Nightwalkers.

They screamed and howled as they died, falling to

the ground in a writhing mass of limbs and parasitic fungus. Charity clapped Ivy on the back as they all waited for the last of the creatures to die.

"Is that it?" Charity asked as she pulled out her earbuds.

"I didn't see the Master here," Ivy said as she cleaned her blade, "so he's likely down in the crypt vaults waiting for us."

"We can take him." Charity said as she donned her coat. "Remember, we have to protect Thaddeus; he's likely the only one who can get close enough to Finnster to kill him. Good luck."

"I'm ready," Thaddeus said as he drew his kukri. He thought about Poppy, his parents, Trip, Ray, Jade, Mallory, and even Evans; everyone whose life the Master had damaged. "It's payback time."

The air grew chilly as they descended the stairs into the catacombs and crypts beneath the Warneford Hospital. Thaddeus shivered, both with the cold and the anticipation of finally killing the Master, once and for all.

"This place is fucking creepy," he said as they reached the bottom of the staircase. "Ivy, did you know this place existed?"

"No. I've never been down here before. Perhaps the Master had the entrance hidden when he went into hibernation with his Congregation after Halley's Comet passed." She looked around at the walls, and ran the tip of her blade along the damp stone. It came away covered in slime and she grimaced and wiped it off.

"This is disgusting," Charity said.

"I'm not really enjoying it either," Ivy hissed back as

loudly as she dared.

"Not just the crypt, but this whole fucking affair. Rank fungal monsters with rancid slime spewing out of them and now we're in a dismal crypt trying to find the King Mushroom so we can shoot him with copper bullets.

"My life used to be so easy."

Thaddeus had to stifle a laugh at Charity's discomfort, and remembered her face as they pulled the fungus out of Mallory. *I'm amazed that she didn't pass out.*

Up ahead there was a dim light that seemed to be coming from some kind of chamber. Thaddeus looked at Ivy, who nodded; this was it. Thaddeus took a deep breath and held his kukri in one hand and the revolver in the other.

"Remember," he said in a whisper, "whatever you do, don't talk to him."

The others nodded. Jess and Charity put their music on. Thaddeus counted them down on his fingers and when he pointed forwards they moved as one into the Master's lair.

It was a wide open space, filled with piles of old furniture and bizarre fungal growths. The crypt was of a size comparable to the meeting hall that they'd fought their last engagement in. The dim light came from a makeshift altar that held a wealth of religious paraphernalia and was covered in candles and kerosene lamps.

Almost thirty Nightwalkers crowded around the Master, their heads bowed as if in prayer. Thaddeus knew what the Master should have looked like from Mallory's drawing and the portrait of Edwin Finnster, but what he saw was a monster.

He was a decrepit crippled creature, reclining in a crumpled position in a wicker bath chair. His skin and face were ripped and distorted as large fruiting bodies and fungal growths had forced their way through his skin and skull. His arms and chest were in a similar state and Thaddeus wondered if Finnster could still move under his own power.

He stood on the edge of the Master's lair and aimed his revolver at the parasitic Preacher's chest. *Goodbye, Edwin Finnster,* he thought as he squeezed the trigger. He fired five shots, all of which found their mark. The Master twitched and bucked with each impact before he fell back in his bath chair, still.

"Now for the rest of them," Thaddeus said. He moved forward into the crypt with the others and was nearing the closest Nightwalker when the Master's eyes snapped open. He began to laugh as his congregation got to their feet.

"You're still alive?" Ivy yelled in frustration.

"Ivy, no!" Thaddeus tried to stop her, but the Master's voice, deep and sonorous cut him off.

"Welcome, my children. You can lay down your arms."

Thaddeus spun around as Ivy, Charity, and Jess all let their weapons clatter to the floor. Their expressions were glassy and blank. Thaddeus raised his pistol at them, half heartedly.

"Seize him."

The three women grabbed Thaddeus, who did not resist, and held him tight. They were careful not to touch his bare skin, lest the spell be broken. Charity brought one of her knives up to his neck, unblinking and unwavering in her devotion to the Master.

"Good. Very good." He raised his arms up slightly,

gesturing at Thaddeus. "Why fight, Thaddeus Thane? My Congregation, my Night People, have prepared to spread the word of God from this very room to the city that lies beyond these walls.

"My new disciples will spread the message through the halls of power in every nation on earth. War, strife, and famine will all come to an end when we achieve what the Lord promised us; life eternal and paradise on earth.

"Why struggle against the inevitable? Why fight for the devil, for the losing side? Join me, Thaddeus Thane. You alone must come to me willingly, and then the world will be ours."

"Fuck you," spat Thaddeus, "you cowardly hypocritical bastard! I'll never join you."

"Very well." The Master gestured for Charity to kill him. She drew the blade back to strike him, but was stopped by another voice that filled the chamber.

"My Master!" Mallory yelled, his satchel in one hand and a sawn-off shotgun in the other. "I have come to serve you in your hour of glory!"

Mallory, no! Thaddeus thought. *Please, not you too!*

"Welcome, my son. It is good to finally have you at my side."

"My Master, I humbly ask one thing of you."
"Oh?"
"I wish to slay the heretic, Thaddeus Thane. He must die by my own hand for attempting to rob me of your gift." Mallory walked into the crypt and placed his satchel on the ground near Thaddeus's feet. "Please grant me this one boon."

"As you wish, Mallory Marsh. He is yours."
"Thank you, my Master."
Thaddeus looked Mallory in the eye as he took aim

with the sawn-off shotgun, silently pleading him to snap out of the Master's control, but he knew it was no use. He took a deep breath and steeled himself for the inevitable bang that would herald his doom. Mallory Marsh pulled back the hammers, their loud click echoing around the crypt.

Goodbye, my loves, he thought. *I guess I've lost you both today.*

Mallory held his gaze for a heartbeat, and then winked.

What!?

There was a deafening roar as he pulled the trigger.

Chapter Forty One – In the Name of the Father

Mallory

"Copper salts!"

Mallory's voice was hoarse as he sat bolt upright in bed, suddenly wide awake. The injuries to his back, gums, and hands were already healing at a prodigious rate. Being a Cep changed everyone in slightly different ways; where Charity was unnaturally strong and fast, the Marsh brothers both had freakish vitality.

He groaned and got out of bed. He staggered over to the laundry hamper in the corner of the room, desperately hoping that Thaddeus had been too preoccupied to do any washing.

Mallory's face lit up in a tired smile as he saw the soiled sheets nestled beneath a few pairs of Thad's pants. He pulled the bundle out and carried it through to the kitchen.

He put the plug into the sink and dropped the sheets into the basin. He rummaged through the cupboards until he found what he was after.

Mallory took the bottles of cola and filled the sink until the sheets were covered. He grabbed a wooden spoon from the utensil rack and agitated the mixture until the bloodstains started to dissolve.

Perfect, he thought. He left the sheets to soak and got dressed. As he buttoned his shirt and selected a tie from the clothes Charity had collected for him, he thought back to the memories he'd shown the Master.

"Did you know?" Mallory asked the empty air. "Did you realise that I was showing you that I knew just how to stop you?"

Preachers were a rare breed, even amongst Ceps, and it was rumoured that they were nigh unkillable; an untruth that the Ministry had been all too keen to spread.

But I know the truth, Mallory thought with a smile. *I know how to slay a Preacher.*

Given their extraordinary skills, they were almost always recruited into the Ministry and they were some of its most elite operatives. Their rarity meant that the last Preacher that had worked for them had died almost twenty years prior.

Aubrey Marsh had left behind a wife and two children when he was slain in the line of duty, dying when Mallory was just a child. Although his father had passed so long ago, he still remembered his brother telling him how it had happened.

"Preachers carry the weaknesses of Christ," Francis had said softly as the rain finally stopped after the funeral. "Cold iron for nails used in the crucifixion..."

"And hawthorn for the crown he wore," Mallory said as he looked down at his paintbrushes. He glanced over at the black plastic bag that contained the fungus. "As for you, I think I have exactly what I need."

He tightened his tie and reached into his satchel, pulling out a bottle of verdigris; a beautiful green paint comprised mostly of highly toxic copper salts. He walked over to Ivy's makeshift laboratory and opened the jar that contained the fungal specimen.

He let a single drop of the brilliant colour fall on to the parasite. It immediately blackened and corroded the surface, and the whole severed claw writhed and twitched. Across the room, what little surviving fungus that was left in the bag quivered and died.

"Yeah," Mallory said with a vengeful grin, "that'll work nicely."

He winked at Thaddeus. He saw his lover's eyes widen in surprise as he pulled the trigger on the shotgun, and a deafening bang filled the crypt. The shells contained no shot. Instead they burst packets of blood-infused cola that he'd crammed into the barrels; the same mixture that he'd drunk before entering the Master's lair.

The sticky amber liquid coated Ivy, Charity, Jess, and Thaddeus, getting into their eyes and mouths. *Please let this work,* he thought. Ivy was the first to react, breaking free of the Master's spell, with the others hot on her heels.

"What is happening!?" Finnster roared from across the crypt. "Kill him!"

The remaining Nightwalkers began to rush towards them, shrieking and baying for blood. Mallory dropped the shotgun to the ground and snatched up his satchel.

"Cover me," he said to Charity, who nodded. "The Master is mine."

She picked up her own weapon and fired two quick blasts as Mallory ducked down. Several Nightwalkers went sprawling as he rose up again. Three more sharp shots echoed through the chamber as Ivy fired her revolver.

Mallory closed on the Master, hawthorn brush held in his teeth as one hand rummaged in the satchel for the verdigris. There was a blood curdling shriek from his left as a Nightwalker bore down on him, claws and fangs extended and ready to kill.

Fuck.

A blade flashed through the air as he tried to turn away, striking the creature in the throat. It fell in a crumpled heap and Mallory only had a heartbeat to register that the knife was thrown by Thaddeus, not Charity.

The Master rose up from the womb-like wicker seat of the bath chair, groaning and straining like a beached whale under the weight of his fungal protrusions.

"Stop!" he commanded, but his words had no effect. Mallory's hand closed on the paint and he dropped the satchel. The Master saw the paintbrush and recognised the colour of the wood. "No!"

Mallory snatched the brush from his teeth and coated the handle in the rich verdant colour. It dripped thickly from the point as he drew it to his chest and broke into one final sprint.

"To Hell with you, Mallory Marsh!" Finnster screamed. Mallory hit him at full speed, driving the paint-covered handle of the brush straight through the Master's heart.

"After you," he said as the Master screeched in pain. The dying Preacher threw his head back in an unearthly howl and Mallory poured the remaining paint down his throat.

As the Master thrashed and kicked, his pain flooded the mycelial network and the remaining Nightwalkers fell to the ground, twitching and writhing.

Mallory looked Edwin Finnster in the eye as the last of his life faded away. He shoved the body back into the bath chair as the last Nightwalker perished.

"Nobody lives forever," Mallory said, "not even you."

They stepped out of the Warneford Hospital just as the total eclipse ended and light crept back into the sky. Charity let out a long low whistle as she peered at the celestial spectacle through her dark glasses.

"I think we managed that in the nick of time, don't you?" Thaddeus said to Mallory.

"Definitely."

"What was that you sprayed us with? Some sort of Holy Water?" Ivy asked.

"It was cola, with some of Thaddeus's blood dissolved in it. It was a bit of a gamble, but it worked."

"Where did you get my blood?"

"The dirty sheets. I soaked them in cola for a couple of hours to get it all out."

"Wow, Mallory," Charity said, "that is absolutely disgusting. I already wanted a shower but now I think I need some new skin."

"Are you still craving blood, Mallory?" Jess asked with a sly smile.

"Not exclusively," he said with a laugh. He took Thaddeus's hand in his left and Jessica's in his right. "There were promises made about what we would do after all this."

"I do believe you're correct, Mallory." Thaddeus smiled as he kissed the painter on one cheek.

"Mallory," Ivy said rather sharply, "how did you know how to kill the Master? We shot him with copper bullets but it didn't take."

"Preachers are particularly hard to kill," he said with a sad smile. "My father was one and I was old enough to remember how he died. Not all Exceptions are so durable, but Preachers and Ghosts are notorious for it."

Ivy looked at Charity with a raised eyebrow. The pale woman simply shrugged in return.

"Now I know why you talk as much shit as you do, Walpole." Ivy grinned at her. "It's useful to have someone so durable around."

"So, what do we do now?" Jess asked. "Do we go our separate ways and only see each other at Christmas?"

"Good grief, you have a short memory!" Charity chided playfully. "Did I not explicitly offer you all jobs earlier this morning?"

"Don't we have to pass some kind of entrance exam?" Jess said. "Not to mention that Ivy and I don't have any special powers."

"Being a Cep isn't a prerequisite," she replied, "and some of the best agents we've ever had have been ordinary humans; nobody expects that, so it gives you an edge. Regarding qualifications, I think defeating Finnster and his army is proof enough that you're up to the task."

"I don't want to leave the city," Ivy said.

"You won't have to." Charity smiled sheepishly at her. "I might've jumped the gun a little bit this morning by sending an email to the Director of the Ministry outlining what we were facing today as well as suggesting that we set up a permanent base of operations in Oxford."

"He replied with a decision that early?" Mallory said.

"He doesn't sleep and he's always at work; of course he replied!" Charity turned on her heel to beam at them. "He also provisionally agreed to employ you all, provided that we didn't die fighting the Master. It won't take more than a few days to get everything confirmed and official."

"What's the pay like?" Ivy said. "I do have to buy a new house, after all."

"They'll recompense you for the loss of property, and the offered salary is very generous; that includes a raise for us too, Marsh. What we do is skilled work and they acknowledge that."

"We'll need a base of operations," Thaddeus said, "as the garret is a bit cramped for all of us."

"Taken care of." Charity smiled at him as they strolled through South Park, looking out over the city. She pointed to a tall building on the horizon. "There is our new home!"

"The Jericho Folly?" Thaddeus asked, shocked.

"Yup. The rest of it was owned by the City Council, so they bought them out for three times the asking price." She grinned. "The Ministry has deep pockets. So what do you think?"

"I'm in," said Ivy, "as are Michaela and Edgar."

"Me too," said Thaddeus, and Jess nodded her head.

"What about you, Marsh? Are you ready to put down roots in Oxford?"

"Of course," he said with a laugh, "as long as they're roots, not mycelia; I've had enough of that to last a fucking lifetime."

"Brilliant!"

"All we need now is a name," Thaddeus said.

"Do we?" Charity said with a tired expression.

"Yes, Charity," Ivy said, "something that we can use to differentiate us, to set us apart from the rest."

"Fine," Charity said, "but it absolutely positively

can't mention vampires, because-"

"They aren't real!" Mallory said with a laugh. "Yes, yes, you've mentioned. Are you amenable to an informal name, at least?"

"Yes, I am. Any suggestions?"

The five of them walked on in silence for a few minutes, lost in thought as the sky lightened. Finally, as they neared the western exit of the park, Jessica spoke.

"Given how we've operated recently and who we've just defeated, I know exactly what we should call ourselves!"

"Oh?" Mallory asked inquisitively. She told them and they all nodded in approval.

"Henceforth," Charity said in a semi-official tone, "the Oxford Contingent of the Ministry of Supernatural Affairs shall be known as the Night People."

Epilogue – Regression to the Mean

Ivy walked around the drawing room of the Folly in a state of speechless shock. She traced her fingers over the eerily familiar chairs as her shoes clacked on the pink and black tiles. The room had not been touched in almost a hundred years, evidenced by the thick layer of dust on everything. Still, it was exactly as she had dreamed. She looked down at her hands and then back up at her reflection in the dusty mirror.
What am I?

Charity Walpole moved around the kitchen, almost as large as Thaddeus's entire garret, gently bouncing a knife in her hand. She wore a pretty floral apron and casual clothes; not a first for her, but it had been a long time since she'd last looked so ordinary. She looked at the stove as it bubbled away; Maruti Lamb, Ivy's favourite. She allowed herself a small smile; even though she was still grieving the loss of Joseph Evans, she felt strangely hopeful.
Maybe I finally have a home.

Mallory, Thaddeus, and Jessica were bundled up on the sofa in Jess's section of the Folly, all watching an old Ealing Comedy, The Ladykillers. Thaddeus had insisted upon watching it, as it was one of his favourite films. Mallory had sheepishly admitted to not watching many films as he found the faces difficult to follow. Thaddeus held his hand, allowing him to see, and Jess had her head on his shoulder, gently stroking his hair. In that one blissful moment,

each of them had exactly the same thought.
I love these two so very much.

In the Jericho Folly the five of them fell into an easy rhythm of study, training, relaxation, and companionship. Though they had led separate lives only weeks before, the fight against the Master had forged a bond between them that would never be broken. Emerging from the darkness of the Warneford Crypts into the light of the waning eclipse, the Night People had become family.

Summer wore on into autumn, which came to Oxford suddenly with a chill in the air and the arrival of dark rain clouds. Leaves turned golden brown before falling to the ground in crisp cascades. Flocks of new students arrived and the city, once scarred by murder and bloodshed, began the next stage of its life.

There is beauty in change, but there is horror also. So easily do people forget being hunted in the night, at least on the surface. The memory lingers; a light left on here, a nervous glance there. Even the Warneford, the sight of so much carnage, soon resumed its usual business. As the months wore on and autumn waned into winter, the brief reign of the Nightwalkers faded into the realm of urban legends and pub table folklore.

In the countryside just outside Oxford, however, a new evil was growing. Something strange and deadly lurked in the shadows of the fields and trees, moving ever closer to the city. Soon, it would have power enough to make its malevolent will known.

Soon, it would strike.

The Night People of Oxford will return in...

THE BLACK CARNATION

Acknowledgements

The Ministry of Supernatural Affairs has been a concept that has been rattling around in my head for almost a decade now. The seed of this series was the aftermath of Project Lamplight, which will be explored in later works.

It has taken a long time to finally get around to writing this, and I only started this book on May 17th 2023, as I travelled back to Oxford after my father's funeral. I finished the main draft of this book in a little over two months, but I absolutely could not have done this alone.

Firstly and most importantly, I would like to thank my partner, Syd, for the love, support, and final proofreading of this story. She has listened to me talk about this for months, and has given me both inspiration and encouragement in spades. I love you, darling, and I am so lucky to have you in my life.

Likewise, I would like to thank my metamor, Ben Wright. Thank you for all the support and discussion that has helped this book become the beast that it finally grew into.

I would like to thank you both for inviting me into your life and your home; I feel loved, wanted, and cared for, which I am grateful for beyond measure.

I would also like to thank Syd and Ben's guinea pigs, both for their reassuring presence and constant source of amusement. There will continue to be references to you scattered throughout my writing.

A big thank you goes out to my best friend, Dr

Georgia Lynott. You are a source of light in my life and always a joy to spend time with. I hope you will enjoy this book.

I cannot write a horror novel without thanking my parents, Steve and Samantha Farrell, my grandparents, Frank and Lorraine Keeley, and other members of my family; you have all played a crucial part developing my absolute love of horror. From late night films to tatty paperbacks read in the car on long journeys; it all has culminated in this book, and all those that follow it. Thank you.

I'd also like to show my appreciation for Colum Taylor and James Bullock; two of my oldest friends and the source of much laughter and amusement since my early teenage years.

Once again, I would like to thank my therapist, Zayna Brookhouse, for her help in turning my fear and grief into something constructive that I could share with you all.

I'd like to thank all the musicians, artists, writers, and cinematographers that have contributed to the horror genre and vampire fiction in particular. I write to music, so your help was invaluable in the creation of this work.

I'd like to explicitly mention the writers Guy N Smith and James Herbert; I read your work and realised that I wanted to join your ranks one day, and I hope I have earned the right to say that.

I would also like to thank Blue Öyster Cult for their music, especially Death Valley Nights, which has been a favourite of mine for over a decade.

Of course, I'm sure that I have missed people off of this list; it is not exhaustive, after all! So, to all the other Parrots out there who helped to make this work a reality, I thank you.

And, last but not least, you, dear reader, for choosing to read this book.

Thank you.

About the Author

Eleanor Fitzgerald is a polyamorous non-binary trans woman living in Oxford. Eleanor uses any and all pronouns, and is neurodivergent and disabled. Eleanor is hard of hearing, and completely deaf on one side.

They have a fascination for all things weird and wonderful, and have thoroughly enjoyed writing this work for you. Rest assured, it will not be the last!

Eleanor also paints, and created the base artwork that this book's cover illustration was based around. Their particular style is impressionism, which they love immensely.

If you have any questions or comments, they can be reached at the following email address:

eleanorfitzgeraldwriting@gmail.com

Printed in Great Britain
by Amazon